THE BONES OF AVALON

THE BONES OF AVALON

*Being edited from the most private documents
of Dr John Dee, astrologer and consultant
to Queen Elizabeth*

PHIL RICKMAN

CORVUS

First published in the UK in 2010 by Corvus, an imprint of Grove Atlantic Ltd.

This is a work of fiction. All characters, organisations and events portrayed in this novel are either products of the author's imagination or are used fictitiously.

9 8 7 6 5 4 3 2 1

A CIP catalogue record for this book is available from the British Library.

ISBN: 978-1-84887-270-7 (hardback)
ISBN: 978-1-84887- 271- 4 (trade paperback)

Printed in Great Britain by the MPG Books Group.

Corvus
An imprint of Grove Atlantic Ltd
Ormond House
26-27 Boswell Street
London WC1N 3JZ

www.corvus-books.co.uk

Oh my God, how profound are these mysteries …

John Dee,
Monas Hieroglyphica.

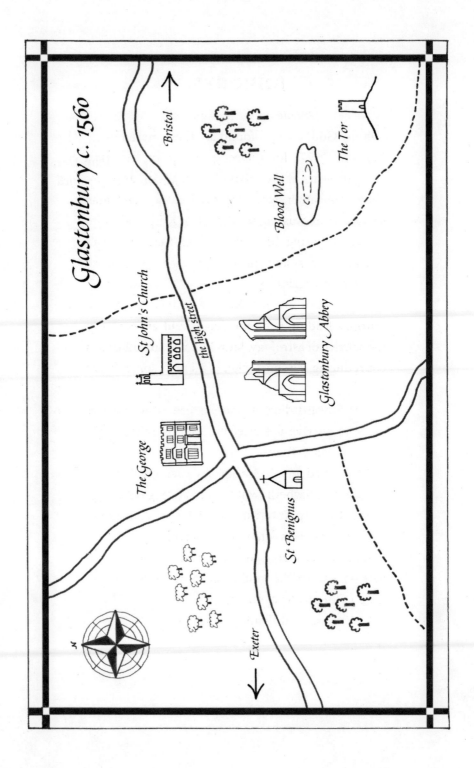

Glastonbury c. 1560

Bristol

The Tor

Blood Well

St John's Church

the high street

Glastonbury Abbey

The George

St Benignus

Exeter

N

JOHN DEE

A note on the background.

Born in 1527, John Dee grew up in the most volcanic years of the reign of Henry VIII, at whose court his father was employed as a 'gentleman server.' John was eight when the King split with Rome, declaring himself head of the Church of England and systematically plundering the wealth of the monasteries.

Recognised by his early twenties as one of Europe's leading mathematicians and an expert in the science of astrology, John Dee was introduced at court during the short reign of Henry's son, Edward VI.

But Edward died at only sixteen, and Dee was lucky to survive the brief but bloody reign of the Catholic Mary Tudor.

Mary died in 1558 and was succeeded by the Protestant Elizabeth, who would always encourage John's lifelong interest in what he considered science but others often saw as sorcery.

Caught between Catholic plots and the rise of a new puritanism, he would feel no more secure than would Queen Elizabeth herself.

1560 was... a difficult year.

Matters of the Hidden

A foreboding.

I MUST HAVE been the only man that morning to touch it. They'd gathered around me in the alley, but when I put a hand into the coffin they all drew back.

A drab day, not long after the year's beginning. Sky like a soiled rag, sooted snow still clinging to the cobbles. I'd walked down, for maybe the last time, from my lodgings behind New Fish Street, through air already fugged with smoke from the morning fires. A stink of sour ale and vomit in the alley, and a hanging dread.

'Dr Dee...'

The man pushing through the ring of onlookers wore a long black coat over a black doublet, expensive but unslashed. Mole-sleek hair was cut close to his skull.

'You may not remember me, Doctor.'

His voice soft, making him younger than his appearance suggested.

'Um...'

'Arrived in Cambridge not long before you left.'

I was edging a cautious thumbnail over the yellowing face within the coffin. All the people you're supposed to recognise these days. Why? They're something then nothing, here then gone. Waste of study-time.

'Quite a big college,' I said.

'I think you were a reader in Greek at the time?'

Which would have made it 1547 or '48. I hadn't been back to Cambridge since, having – to my mother's fierce consternation – turned down a couple of proffered posts there. I looked up at him, shaking my head and begging mercy, for in truth I knew him not.

'Walsingham,' he said.

Heard of him. An MP now, about five years younger than me, so still in his twenties. Ambitious, they said, and courting Cecil for position. His messenger had been banging on my door before eight, when it was yet dark. I hadn't liked this; it put me on edge. It always does, now.

'Lucky to catch me, Master Walsingham. I was about to leave London for my mother's house in Mortlake.'

'Not permanently, I trust?'

I looked up, suspicious. A week earlier, the tight-arse who owned the house where I was lodging had finally raised the rent beyond my means – maybe under the impression, as many now seemed to be, that I was a man of wealth. It was as if this Walsingham knew the truth of my situation. How was that possible? There was also an assumed authority here which I doubted that he, as a mere MP, had any right to exercise.

Still, this matter intrigued me, so I was prepared to indulge him for a while.

'Wax?' he said.

Squatting down in the mud on the other side of the coffin, which was laid across a stone horse-trough. Putting out a forefinger to the face, but then drawing it back.

'Let's see,' I said.

And then, impatient with all this superstition, placed both hands inside the coffin and lifted out the bundle, prompting a gasp from someone as I bent my head and sniffed.

'Beeswax.'

'Stolen from a church, then?'

'I'd guess. Shaped over a flame. See the fingermark?'

What had lain in the box was naked upon a cloth of dark red, edged in gold. It was a foot in length, three inches in thickness. The eyes were jagged holes, the mouth a knife-slit smeared red. The smudged print was on one over-plump breast and another small glob of red made a dark berry in the cleft between the legs.

'An altar candle?' Walsingham said.

'Could be. It was you who found it?'

'My clerk. I live not far away, along the river. He thought at first it must be some nun's still-born babe. When he—'

'Don't they usually just get dropped in the river wrapped in rags?'

'—when he finally found the balls to take off the lid, he returned at once. Had me roused.'

I looked around: two constables, a man of the Watch, a couple of whores and a vagrant near the entrance to the alley. A dying pitch-torch smouldered by the door of a mean tavern on the corner, but the buildings either side were all tight-shuttered, no smoke from the chimneys. Warehouses, most likely.

'Found exactly as . . . ?'

'No, no. The foul thing was in a most conspicuous position out on the quayside, where anyone might chance upon it. I had it moved here, then sent the Watch to knock on doors. A man walking the streets with a coffin in his arms can't have gone entirely unseen.'

I nodded. Probably some drunkard out there still fearing for his sanity. I laid the waxen effigy back in the box and hefted the whole thing. It was quite light – pine maybe, 'neath the tarry black.

'And then you summoned *me*,' I said. 'Can I, um, ask why?'

The question was left on the air; he tossed another at me.

'Dr Dee, given that we both know who it represents, how is it supposed to work?'

I eased what I now saw to be a wooden crown from the hair of plaited straw. I picked it up. Not well carved, but from a distance . . .

'And if it *is* fashioned from an altar candle,' Walsingham said, 'would that be considered to enhance its, ah, efficacy?'

'Master Walsingham, before we take this further—'

Walsingham raised a hand, stood up, waved to the constables and retainers to move further away and then made motion toward a doorway opposite the trough. I scrambled up and followed him. He leaned back into a door frame which was flaking and starting to rot. A man drawn to damp and shadows.

Who evidently thought the same of me.

'My understanding, Dr Dee, is that you're our foremost authority on what we might call *matters of the hidden*.'

A sudden skreeting of seagulls over the river. Walsingham waited, bony face solemn, eyes sunk into hollows. I was wary now. How I'd served the new Queen was no secret, but it carried more risk than profit; anyone given leave to part dark curtains inevitably drew the suspicions of the vulgar.

But what could I say? I shrugged and acknowledged an academic interest. Reticent, though, because he still hadn't given reason why a wax doll in a babe's coffin should be an MP's affair.

'Seems to me, Dr Dee, that in seeking the provenance of this artefact we have two directions.'

We?

'The first… some kind of papist pretence, to spread alarm. Hence its public display.' He nodded toward the two constables. 'See their faces. They fear for their very souls through being in its proximity.'

'Which you do not?'

Fairly sure in my mind, now, that the Walsinghams were a strong reformist family, with a link to the Boleyns and, presumably, a hatred of idolatry in any form. Hence his disdainful use of *nun* for a street-woman.

'And the second direction,' he said, 'would, of course, be toward Satan himself.'

☩

These midnight questions, I approach them daily. Yet with care.

Know this: a few of us are endowed with abilities like to the angels. Some can see the dead or pluck thoughts from the minds of others. And to some are gifted the means to bring about change in the natural order of things.

All this I know, and yet, if you thought to detect there an element of self-reference, then you must needs forget it. Mine's the scholar's way. A commitment to finding and charting pathways towards lights both beyond us and within us. Which, let me tell you, is never easy, for the paths are all overgrown with barbs and briars, and we are ever led by *false* lights.

I've oft-times followed them, too, those false lights, but I'm more cautious now.

☩

'What we both know,' I said, 'is that London's full of cunning villainy.'

Walsingham sniffed tightly.

'Quite. But does this thing have satanic power, or not?'

'It evidently has the power to arouse fear and anxiety.'

I looked at the constables, murmuring one to another now. Muted laughter to disguise a primitive terror. I wished I could take the effigy and its box for further examination but decided it was inadvisable to demonstrate too much interest.

'It's clear someone's gone to some considerable effort,' I said. 'The coffin's passably well made. The doll itself… hardly a work of high art. And yet…'

'What?'

'The one odd thing is that, apart from the fingermark, there's no… I mean, normally an image like this might be pricked with pins. The clear intention being to arouse pain, whether in mind or body, in the person it represents. There's nothing like that here that I can see.'

'It's laid out as a corpse in a coffin! How clear do you—?'

'Death, yes, sure, but what *kind* of death?'

'A prediction, then? An omen?'

'The quality of the cloth and the general workmanship suggest… well, a certain wealth and a serious intent. The crudeness of the eyes and mouth conveying, rather than a lack of artistic skill, a simple contempt for the subject. Which is further emphasised by that smirched finger-mark upon the, um, breast.'

No accident, that.

'It'll get back, of course,' Walsingham said.

'To court?'

'Too many people know already. I can swear every one of those men to secrecy – and I shall – but it'll still get back. Could be pamphlets on the street before the week's end.'

'I can be available,' I said, 'to offer some reassurance to the, um… should it be required.'

'I'm sure you can, Dr Dee. Meanwhile, what's to be done with it? Melt it on the fire?'

'Um… no.' I took a step back. 'I wouldn't do that. Not in the first instance. I'd have its… its inherent darkness… dispersed. By a bishop, if possible. Do you know any bishops, Master Walsingham?'

'I will by tonight, if necessary.'

'Good. He'll know what to do.'

I nodded and was about to walk away, when Walsingham said, 'Suppose there's another.'

'Like this?'

'They could be all over London. A spreading rash of evil. Where can we find you?'

I couldn't see it; a multiplicity of effigies would somehow reduce the insidious effect.

'I'll be leaving today, as I said, for my mother's house. If you get word to Lord Dudley, he'll have a messenger sent to me.'

Taking care to throw in that mention of Dudley. Even though his odour was not good in certain circles, his was yet a potent name. Walsingham nodded and bent over to the coffin and this time he put a finger very close to the wax, as if he *might* be touching it, though I thought not.

'Is that blood?'

The smear of red across the knife-slit mouth. I'd wondered about that. And, more significantly, the glob of red between the legs – preferring to say nothing about this lest my supposition of its intent as regards future childbearing be wrong.

'If it's the blood of whoever made this,' I said, 'it might be thought to carry the essence of that person's hatred to… she who's represented here. Blood was also seen by the ancients as an agent for the, um, materialising of spirits.'

'For conjuring?'

Never my favourite word.

'It's a matter of will. The harnessing of the human will to something from another… level of existence.'

'Something demonic?'

'If the Queen's appointed by God…'

'*If?* You *doubt* that?'

The question lightly posed, his eyes half lidded.

Jesu.

'No, no,' I said. 'Obviously not. What I'm saying is that the corruption of an altar candle could, as I think you've already suggested, be an attempt to subvert the power of God in this respect.'

'Breaking the sacred thread within the line of monarchy?'

'Which might itself be considered already weakened by—'

'The *sex* of the monarch?'

This man thought too fast for my liking.

'This is only my own—'

'Of *course*,' Walsingham hissed. 'That's why you're here.'

I looked at him closely.

'Who *are* you?' I said. '*What* are you?'

'What do I look like?'

'You look,' I said, 'like walking darkness.'

And he smiled and nodded, quite clearly pleased at this.

✛

When I'm asked how it all began, this is the incident I recall: the first example, in my own witness, of a malevolence – an *intelligent* malevolence – directed at the Queen.

You must needs be aware of its effect on me. In my way, I've loved this woman for whom I'll part any dark curtains, seek answers to the most forbidding of midnight questions. For if this is the time for an uncovering of universal mysteries, then I'd like to think *she* has made that possible by displaying a manner of tolerance which many of us had feared we might never see again.

After all is said, should it not be man's most ardent desire to see into the very mind of God? Does not God himself challenge us to interpret His art?

A silence.

Heresy, you whisper.

Burn him.

As they nearly did. A few years ago, in another reign – you may know something of this – I was close to being left as cinders upon a hearth of baked earth. Thoughts of it still sear my dreams, lie smouldering in my lower mind. The charges were manifestly unjust, but when did that ever matter?

Yet I survived, and now the wildfire of another dawn is kindled over the river, and I sit here in my mother's parlour and throw up my hands – for what else is the charge of heresy but a brutal blindfold for the far-sighted?

And I must needs set down what happened. Recount the whole bitter episode before it's murked by memory and rendered impenetrable to the common man by my own exhaustive analysis – oft-times it being said that few can comprehend my writings, full weighted as they are with scientific terms, befuddled by diagrams and arcane symbols. The very tradecraft, some will say, of the devil.

So I'll relate this story as simply and directly as it comes to memory. I shall not, as is my usual custom, carefully dissect and prod over each sentence or avoid what it tells of my inner nature... about what I was and what I am become.

But, before I begin, know this...

...there *is* a shape and pattern to it all. A universal geometry, the changing angles and rhythms of which, through mathematics and the study of the stars, we're learning to calcule again, as men did in ancient times. Twin journeys: above and below, without and within. I try to chart them daily, whilst knowing that I am, in divers ways, no more than an onlooker.

And helpless.

For although some may have abilities like to the angels, yet they are *not* angels.

I've learned this, and in the cruellest of ways.

PART ONE

Yet some men say in many parts of Inglonde that kynge Arthure ys nat dede but had by the wyll of our Lord Jesu into another place, and men say that he shall com agayne and he shall wynne the holy crosse.

Sir Thomas Malory,
Le Morte d'Arthur.

I

Lest Graves Be Open

Mortlake, February, 1560.

MY MOTHER'S ONLY servant disappeared on the night we needed it least. The eve of the Queen's visit. And of Candlemas.

Catherine Meadows had been a quiet maid. Efficient, demure and, more important, discreet. The first servant I'd let dust, or even enter, my library. Given the afternoon for herself, she'd left the house shortly before noon.

Less than an hour, this was, before the Queen's messenger had come to alert us of her arrival here on the morrow. *The Queen!* God, my poor mother had gone wild: so much to *do*, and no servant to do it!

No more peace for me this day, then. By six, the moon was over the river, cold-haloed, and then came the first wash of stars, and still no sign of Catherine Meadows. Although I work best at night, when all is quiet, by half past eight I was obliged to close my books, douse my candles, unhook my long brown coat and venture into the bone-raw February night to inquire after her.

Maybe, in some inner vessel of my being, I had the inkling of an approaching menace. Who can truly say? I've oft-times wished such occult portents were more clear and direct, but – nature's bitter irony – it's rarely been that way for me.

✠

A well-lit night – on the edge of a thaw, I felt, yet still hard as crystal. Hoar frost swelling the twigs and branches of our orchard as I walked out, without a lantern. Out towards the edge of the village and London town, calling first at a smoky old tavern, where I knew the man I sought spent an hour or so most evenings. But he was not amongst the drinkers this night, and hard-faced men were staring at me, so I slipped away and went further along the road to his cottage and found him there.

'Ah, now, as it happened, Dr John, she come to me mid-afternoon. About her gran, Goodwife Carter – took bad.'

Jack Simm, once an apothecary, now my mother's occasional gardener. His cottage, on the edge of a copse of oak and thorn, was strong-built and snug and far warmer than our house – unwise, therefore, to go in, lest I end up passing the whole night before his fire.

'Bad how?'

We always fear the worst. Smallpox, usually.

'Back trouble,' Jack Simm said. 'Bits of her spine took a walk, I reckon. Not my field, really. I left some wintergreen balm and give Cath a message to take to Gerald. The bone-twister?'

'Who's that, Jack?' A woman's voice from the firelit, herb-smelling interior. 'Who's out there?'

'Dr John, Sarah. No problem.' White-bearded Jack stepping out of the doorway, stained sacking belted around his waist, no boots. 'You want me to ride out to their farm for you, Dr John? Won't take—'

'No, no. Too many robbers about. She'll be back at first light, I'm sure. Go to your fire, Jack, and your wife. I'm sorry to have bothered you.'

But Jack Simm was pulling the door shut behind him and shambling out to join me at the roadside. Rubbing his hands together and wincing as he shifted from one unshod foot to the other on the frozen mud.

'God's bones, I'll be bleedin' glad to see some sign of a warming.'

'Candlemas tomorrow,' I said. 'The first gleaming of spring in the olden days.'

'Yeah, well, the sun was kinder in the olden days. Dr John—' Clearing rough phlegm from his throat, lowering his voice. 'There's things I wouldn't say in front of Sarah, a good woman but she gossips. Don't mean to but she does. Here's the truth of it. The Meadowses... A religious family, now. If you understand me.'

For the past two years, at summer's close, Jack Simm had harvested herbs for me, including the small mushrooms which, when brewed, can bring on visions. We understood one another well.

'The father,' he said. 'Always the bleedin' father, innit?'

'Hot gospel?'

'Of an extreme kind.'

'Is there another kind?'

Used to be only priests; now any man might think himself chosen by God as a device. Jack talked, in some dismay, of Abel Meadows – built like a chimney stack, Bible brandished as a weapon.

'You mean he's finally realised who his daughter's working for,' I said. 'That's what this is about?'

'Comes here day 'fore yesterday, blethering about the end of time, like we got maybe weeks. Then he's asking about the habits of Mistress Dee.'

'*Mistress* Dee? The bastard!'

'I says, Master Meadows, I says, you'll find that woman in church four times on Sundays and a good hour every weekday.'

'True. Thank you. And, um… the *son* of Mistress Dee?'

Both of us knowing with what pious delight a religious extremist would delve amongst ill-informed rumour.

'He never spoke your name,' Jack Simm said.

It felt very cold now, the woods all acrackle with the movement of some night creature. I opened my hands to the freezing air.

'All right. What are they saying?'

'They're just ignorant folk, Dr John.' Jack Simm took a step back, blew out a steam of breath. 'Spells?'

'And divination?'

'Yea, yea. And conjuring of spirits from out the darkness – the nights, naturally, being a whole lot darker around your ma's house when you're there. 'Tis said that no man who fears for his immortal soul oughta go past your place beyond sunset, nor walk in Mortlake churchyard lest graves be open. Tell me when you've heard enough.'

God. Slowly shaking my head. You come home at Christmas, applause from the lecture halls of Europe still resounding in your ears, to find you've become a figure of fear and opprobrium in your own neighbourhood.

'You know what didn't help?' Jack said. 'The owl.'

'It's a toy.'

'Go to! Twice the size of a real owl and its eyes all lit up? And it's making... *wooh... wooh...?*' Jack flapping his arms as the owl would with his wings.

'The village children liked him.'

'Yeah, whilst their parents thought demons lived in him.'

'All that's *in* him –' I sighed '– is a cunning system of small pulleys and hidden hinges, and the eyes are an arrangement of shards of mirror-glass and—'

'*That* don't bleedin' matter! It's what they see, innit? Sometimes you don't help yourself is all I'm saying. Rumour and gossip, Dr John, rumour and gossip.'

The real demons. Jack Simm had given up his shop in the city because of fears of persecution during Mary's reign by Bishop Bonner who was now – God help us all – my friend.

'Oh, and Meadows... he says he's heard as how you're building a temple to worship the moon?'

'Observatory.'

'*Temple.*'

'To watch the paths of the stars.' I sighed. 'Or at least... one day. When I raise the money.'

Both of us standing there, dismayed. Much shaking of heads. Star temple, worship of the moon. *Jesu.* At length, Jack Simm clapped me reassuringly upon the shoulder.

'Nah, listen, she'll be back.'

'Catherine?'

'The goodwife finks of the money. Meadows buggered that up, he'd get some real stick. What you reckon: wrath of God or a vengeful wife?'

I nodded. A close call, even for a Bible man.

'Anyhow, what I told him.… I said you was working on secret navigation devices for the navy. Reminding him how highly you was rated by the—'

'*Jack...*'

'What?'

An icicle cracked above the doorway.

'She comes here tomorrow.'

'Who?'

I said nothing. Jack let go a thin whistle. Might've been admiration but pity seemed more likely.

'Again? It was me, I tell you, I'd be spending the rest of the night shivering in me privy. But I suppose when you've known her since she was young...'

'Young still, Jack.'

'Nah, they grows up fast under a crown. All fresh and dewy on the outside; underneath, skin like a lizard. What's the occasion?'

It was over a month now since the incident of the effigy and not a word, so it seemed unlikely to be that.

'I don't truly know,' I said. 'She has an interest in my work...'

'The navigation, this would be?' He may have winked. 'Well, best be going in. Can't seem to feel me toes no more. Good luck to you, Dr John.'

For some reason, Jack Simm found me amusing.

✝

Walking away, my left boot slid across a frozen wheel-rut, and I stumbled. An old man had broken his leg not far from here just a fortnight ago and was not found until morning. Dead by then of the cold.

No use hurrying, anyway; there'd be time for no more work this night. I'd need to help my mother prepare our house for the visit of the Queen... even though I knew the Queen would not enter it.

Hobbled into Mortlake High Street, past the school run by nuns for poor children – well intentioned, but a poor child with a little education would often simply be sold by its parents at the first opportunity. Candles still aglow far back in the school chapel, but the nearby Church of St Mary was black. A big modern church only slightly more interesting amid night shadow than it was by daylight. I should have liked to see a proper steeple – some symbol of a soaring spiritual ambition.

Not that anyone in recent years has dared soar. Not since I was a child. Nowadays, only a fool kneels before God without first glancing over his shoulder, or prays too long with eyes closed. All is confusion. Vision and spirit are fled. How quickly *can* rational thought progress now in England, with zealots like Abel Meadows on the march, warning of a fast-approaching apocalypse? For which, of course, there's no scientific evidence whatsoever.

Candlemas tomorrow. Feast of the Purification of the Blessed Virgin Mary, when the candles were blessed. And no-one knows what to do about it any more. In some churches the blessing of candles is a secret ritual.

Pausing now, by the coffin gate. In the icy night, the stars – the *energy* of stars – felt real and close. Bright orbs, each one familiar, dancing in a formal complexity as satisfying to me as a well-wrought knot garden in the heavens. *My* garden.

A familiar wild excitement arose in me, like to a moon-drawn tide. Closing my eyes, holding out my hands into the palpitating air, open to the nudging, flittering interplay of invisible vibrations, sensing sacred splinters of ice-white light in flow through my body – rendered, in my imagination, transparent in the cold blue night.

Thus, failing to see my mother until she was upon me.

'Head in the stars, as ever, when it's not in a book. Well? Did you find her?'

Jane, the widow Dee. A tallish woman, still straight, although nearing sixty years. She held up her lantern to my face as if to be full sure that it actually was me.

'No.' I relieved her of the lamp as we walked. *Not* the time to tell her about the madness of Abel Meadows. 'But I did find out that she has troubles at home. Illness in the family.'

'Plague?'

My mother taking a rapid step back. The rushing of breath into her throat.

'*No*, Mother… no suggestion of that. She went to get help for her grandmother – to the bone-twister. Probably didn't get back home before it was too dark to return here safely.'

'Well then, she ought to have sent word.'

How? I was about to ask her, but the night was too advanced for argument.

'Yes,' I conceded. 'It's not like her not to send word.'

'Now I shall have no sleep.' My mother expelled a martyr's sigh. 'We should have two servants. Always used to.'

I said nothing. There was nothing to be said. I was a scholar, and the monetary rewards for learning were yet meagre.

'Someone older.' My mother was winding her winter cloak tight around her. 'With such a young woman on the throne, lesser young women seem to think they have some new freedom to behave as they like.'

I had to smile. By *young woman* she meant *flighty, irresponsible.* A queen who was laughing openly in the teeming streets on her coronation day and waving in glee to the crowd. Acknowledging the common horde – what *was* our society coming to?

My own heart, I should assure you, had been alight that coronation day, relishing the rush of such spontaneous goodwill as I'd never known in a public place, even at Christmas. Sunday, the fifteenth of January, Fifteen Hundred and Fifty Nine. Just over a year ago. The choice of this auspicious date having been made by the heavens and interpreted through my charts, and I'd been weak with relief, for if the day had gone badly…

'What's more –' Jane Dee refusing to let it go – 'it was market day today. Now we have no fresh fare. On this, of all days.'

'We'll get by.'

'*Get by?*' My mother, horrorstruck, let the hem of her heavy cloak fall to the road. 'Oh yes – as if the body can be sustained by lofty intellect and little else. Your poor, blessed father, if he could hear you now—'

Exasperated, she stalked across the frost-furred street to enter through our open gate. In truth, my poor blessed tad would have understood too well – all the stories he'd told us of the titanic quantities of waste scraped from the late King Harry's boards. Like stoking a particularly temperamental furnace, he'd remarked once, memorably, after too much wine.

I stood for a moment in the middle of the lane. No movement in the shining night, not even a slinking fox. Few candles still burning behind our neighbours' frozen windows. The richer houses here are set back further from the river. Our own, not the most graceful of dwellings, is built partly on stilts because of the threat of flooding. I called out, across the roadway.

'Mother, you know she won't come in. *She never comes in.*'

When I was last here, in the autumn, Elizabeth had arrived at this gate with her company, and I'd gone out to her, and that was where we'd remained. When I'd wanted her to see my books, she wouldn't. Didn't have time. Had to be off. Queenly things to do.

Still, given the size of her train, if we'd had to feed them all we'd've been on stale bread and small beer for a month.

'John... are you *part* of this world?' My mother spinning at the gateway, her cloak a billowing of shadow. 'Just because she hasn't passed our threshold *thus far*, who's to say that on such a cold winter's morn she won't find herself in sore need of sustenance and a hot drink? Who's to *say?*' She sniffed. 'Probably not you, who sees only the need to feed his learning.'

Always in two minds about my career, Mistress Jane Dee.

And who truly could blame her?

✛

For an hour or more beyond midnight, I lay open-eyed in my bedchamber, one of the house cats curled up at my feet, and thought about the nature of time, how we might make more of it. One lifetime was never going to be enough. A flimsy thing, a stuttering from a candle, then gone. If not extinguished prematurely by some... miscalculation.

In Paris, in the week I was preparing to leave, all the talk had been of an elixir of life. I didn't believe it. If there's a method of prolonging existence, it will never come in a stoppered flask but will be part of some inner process. When I was sent up to Cambridge, at fifteen, I decided one simple step towards an extension of time was to minimise the hours of sleep.

I knew I was lucky to be at the college, for Tad was not as rich as he liked everyone to think. Also knew, too well, that we lived in dangerous times and that the King he served, like to a huge bellows, blew hot and then deathly cold. I was certainly under no illusion that I'd be allowed to remain long at Cambridge, and so I'd hurled myself into study, reducing sleep to little more than three hours a night, all fatigue flattened under the urgency of learning.

Thus, I can still work long hours without sleep, when it's called for. But now I'll accept that this is partly because... well, because I'm a little afraid of it. Afraid of sleep, which is death's bedfellow. And of dreams, which give form to the deepest of fears.

BANG...

And did, by means of sorcery, attempt to kill or grievously harm Her Majesty...

BANG...

Take him.

Lurching up in bed, breathing hard.

For God's sake, it's *a different queen.*

✟

No such accusations against my tad, but his Protestant's fall, under Queen Mary's purge, had been total. They took everything he owned, except for this house. By that time, I was almost famous in Europe, for my learning. In Paris, they'd stood on boards and crowded outside open windows to hear me lecture on Euclid. Famous men had come to consult me at Louvain. Whilst in England...

In England, even living once again in my mother's house, I couldn't afford to build an observatory, nor pay more than a single servant full-time.

This is yet a backward country.

Next summer, in July, I would be thirty-three years old. My God, the journey perchance more than half over, and so much left to do, so much yet to *know.*

The cold moon lit my wall betwixt the timbers. The cat purred. The scent of pastry still lay upon the air – my mother having laboured until close to midnight in the kitchen, baking and making what preparations she could in case the only surviving child of the late Harry should deign to cross our threshold with half an army in attendance. Me trying to help her but being sent away, in the end... for how could I welcome the Queen to Mortlake all wrinkle-eyed and slow from lack of rest?

So, I slept and fell into the worst of my recurring dreams.

My hands are tied behind me, my back is hard against the wood, my eyes are closed and I'm wondering when they'll do it.

Listening for the crackle, waiting for the heat.

There's a silence. I'm thinking, *they've gone. They're not going to do it after all. I've been pardoned. I'm to be freed.*

And open my eyes to a fine blue sky over London, with all its spires.

Thinking to float away into it. Thinking of some way to free my hands and looking down…

…to find my thighs turned black and crisp, incinerated into flaking husks which, like Jack Simm and his frosted toes, I can no longer feel. My legs gone to blackened bone. The remains of my feet lying some distance away in the smouldering ash.

This is when I awake, down on the floorboards, having rolled away in a blind terror from the sudden roaring, guzzling heat and a ghastly sense of hell's halo around my head.

II

Hares

WELL, SHE CAME.

Not long after eleven, the gilded company appeared on the river in a fleet of bright barges and wherries. Banners aloft, sunlight flashing on helms and blades, the air aquiver with frost.

Frost… and anticipation, a vibration never far removed, in my experience, from anxiety. Certainly not this day. By the time she was being assisted from her barge, up the steps to the bank, all the neighbours were at their windows and I, in a fresh doublet, was waiting by the gate.

My stomach grown taut for, unless engaged in intellectual exchange, the dissection of ideas, I was never good with people of *any* station.

My mother, unless summoned, would remain inside the house amidst her pastries and mulled wine. Neither of us had slept, although that was nothing to do with she who now peeled off a glove.

A wafting of rose-petal perfume, as I bent to kiss her hand.

Those long fingers, pale as pearl, pale as ice. An unnecessary number of pikemen behind her, gazing down, unmoving.

'Well met, John. And how's your health now?'

A voice still light and girlish. And yet almost, you might think, still a little unsure. Something I recognised in myself. Too much time spent with books, my tad would say – himself all Welsh and voluble.

'I'm very well, Your Highness,' I said. 'And, um, I trust you also—?'

Looking up in time to perceive movement in her face, a small twist of a small, strawberry mouth. Nothing that could be construed as a smile.

'So,' she said, 'your cold is *better* then?'

The high nose, the wide-spaced eyes. The hand had fallen away. Above her, the weak sun was trembling like the yolk of a fresh-cracked egg.

'Um… cold?'

'The ailment' – her voice firmer now, the mouth suddenly resembling her father's fleshy bud, but all I could think of was a knife-slash in wax – 'which prevented you joining us last weekend.'

'Ah,' I said. 'Better, yes, thank you, madam. Yes… much better.'

'So worrying, a cold.' The Queen wore a fur cloak over riding apparel, and a fur hat. 'Especially when we perceive the long winter grinding to its end.'

'Certainly best kept within one's own walls,' I said carefully. 'That is… rather than taken out and, um, given to other people.'

'Or bears,' said the Queen.

Her dark grey eyes half-lidded. Shuttered rooms, and I thought, *Oh dear God.*

☩

My friend, Robert Dudley, mocks me for it.

Merely what happens in the wild, John. Bears, dogs, they're all killers, and so are we. Part of us. What we are. We're a fighting race, everything we have we've fought for and killed for. Sometimes we're the bear and sometimes the dogs, depending upon whether we're fighting to keep what we have or to grab more.

I point out to him that successful warfare is, and always has been, about cunning, intelligence and invention rather than blind savagery. Reminding him of the machinery I've fashioned to this end, the navigational aids to speed our supremacy on the seas. I insist, with a passion, that we have nothing to gain from observing the conflict of bears and dogs and only our humanity to lose. In war, I say, we fight to get it over, not to prolong agony in the cause of amusement.

Dudley shrugs.

Admit the truth, John. You're a man of books, you simply have no stomach for it.

Well, yes: the anguished roaring and the frenzied yelps, those pitiful echoes from the ante-chambers of Hades… such barbarity I can live without.

But then, with a benign, faintly sorrowful smile, my friend and former student chooses his spot and inserts his blade.

You should see the Queen, John. Clapping her little hands and bobbing in her chair at each snap of the bloodied jaws. Oh my, the Queen has ever loved a bear-baiting…

Let no-one forget, in other words, whose daughter this was. The feelings of pity and distaste, I can cope with those, suppress them when necessary. But some involuntary disclosure of contempt… who dares risk that?

Thus, when invited to a banquet, to be attended by Her Majesty and followed by bear-baiting, I'd swiftly developed a cold.

✝

Her perfume coloured the air. Always roses, as if the wave of a royal hand could alter the seasons. I saw my older cousin, Blanche Parry, the Queen's First Gentlewoman, staying well back amongst the company of guards and courtiers and smirking hangers-on. Watching us, like to a white owl in a tree. Blanche had ever mistrusted me.

'I'm afraid that, with a cold, I wasn't a pretty sight,' I said lamely. 'My nose—'

'—was in a book, as usual, I expect,' the Queen said.

'Yes,' I said, humbled. 'I expect it was.'

A hanging moment.

And then the Queen tilted her head back and laughed, and it was like to a flock of skylarks upon the air. After a breath, the whole company erupted, as if everyone's throat had been released from some social ligature. Only Blanche Parry kept on watching me, unsmiling, as the Queen laid a gloved hand on my arm and steered me meaningfully away from her train.

'I shouldn't tease you, John.'

'Oh,' I said. 'That's what it was.'

'Sometimes,' she said, as we passed into the orchard, 'I think you know me – through your art, no doubt – better than anyone.'

My art? Dear God.

'Though also,' she said quickly, 'through experiences of adversity which are common to us.'

I nodded, grateful for that. Her father's daughter and her sister's sister, and yet, unlike either of them, Elizabeth had heard the key turning from the other side. All too aware, at the time, of the black cards dealt to the Lady Jane Grey, at just sixteen. Awakening to the swish of the phantom axe, just as I would roll from the flames' roar. How secure was she feeling, even now? *Did she even know about the wax doll?*

'John, you invited me once, as I recall, to see your library.'

'Um… yes, I believe I did… yes.'

Thinking at the time that she'd taken it the wrong way, or at least feigned as much. At twenty-six, she was only a few years younger than I.

'The truth of it is,' she murmured, 'I had been most strongly advised to *avoid* your library.'

'Avoid my… books?

Because of their heretical content?

'Advised by someone who was recalling your efforts to persuade my late sister of the benefits of a national library.'

'Oh…'

Breathing again. So that was it. The cost. It hadn't worked on Mary, and I could certainly think of members of the present Privy Council for whom the provision and maintenance of a Library of England would be regarded as good money down the jakes.

'It just seemed to me a tragedy,' I said, 'how many valuable works have disappeared in the years since the Reform. Many of them secretly sold by unscrupulous abbots and the like. But there's no doubt that the, um, the *founder* of a national library would forever be remembered as the greatest patron of learning that this country had ever—'

'*Tush*, John—' The Queen punched me on the upper arm. Her eyes dancing with merriment, a modest cluster of red-gold curls escaping from the fur hat. 'It will *happen*. When we have sufficient funds to spare to do it properly. Meanwhile, we applaud your private efforts… *how* many books is it now?'

'Nine hundred… and twelve.'

'And *twelve*,' the Queen said solemnly. 'A goodly collection.'

I may have blushed. It seemed ridiculous that I could remember the exact number. Most of them were scattered all over my mother's house and my aim, when I could raise the money, was to build an extension to accommodate thousands more essential volumes.

'John –' the Queen, her moods ever mercurial, was looking into my eyes now with a sudden concern – 'you seem tired.'

'Working long hours, Your Highness, that's all.'

'To what end? May I ask?'

The Queen had long been fascinated by matters of the hidden, and we were well out of the hearing of her company. She and I alone in my mother's high-walled orchard, not more than twenty yards from the riverbank, the sun making pin-lights among the ice-pearled apple-tree boughs.

Idyllic, except for the pikemen guarding its entrance. You could never lose the bloody pikemen.

'John, last year we spoke of the Cabala. You gave me to think that the old mysticism of the Jews… that this would help us penetrate the inner-most chambers of the heavens.'

I hesitated. My present work did, in part, have its origins in that rich and complex Hebrew mechanism for communion with higher realms. And, yes, my aim – never a secret – was to discover the levels to which the essence of earthly things, the composition and structure of all terres-trial matter, is ordered by the heavens. I was now in search of a code, maybe a single symbol which would explain and define this relationship. But many a score of candles would burn through the night before I was ready to publish my findings and formally inscribe the mystical glyph upon the frontispiece.

'Your Highness—'

'Are you yet equipped to call upon the angels, John?'

After the religious turbulence of the past two decades, it would be of prime importance to the Queen that any intercourse with a spiritual hierarchy should be firmly under *her* control. I played this one care-fully.

'Any of us can *call* upon them. I think, however, for the Cabala to work for us, it will be necessary to interpret it in such a way that it will be seen as part of the Christian tradition.'

'Oh yes, that's a *very* good point, but –' the Queen had clasped her long fingers together and now shook them as if attempting to dislodge some essential thought – 'is there not an *English* tradition, John?'

'For communion with angels?'

'Well –' a quick, impatient shake of the head, a parting of the hands – 'yes.'

An interesting question from an educated woman, but the answer would not be a safe one.

'Christianity, as Your Highness is obviously aware… is not of English origin, and so—'

'Well, then, should I say *British*, rather than English, you and I being both of Welsh stock?'

Born and bred in England, I'd never, to be honest, thought of myself as particularly Welsh, although my father would forever prate at me – and anyone else who'd listen – about our great linguistic and cultural heritage. Which, having learned some Welsh to please him, I had planned to spend some time investigating, in case he should be right. However…

'All the evidence suggests, Your Highness, that the Welsh religious tradition – which is to say the bardic or Druidic tradition – was not, in its essence, a Christian one.'

'But did it not change when the Christian message was brought to these shores? Or when, as it is said, Our Saviour himself came to England?'

'Um… mercy?'

'With Joseph the Arimathean. His uncle.'

'Oh.'

'You do *know* of this—'

'Of course. That is, I've read of it.'

'So you have books dealing with it… in your library?'

'Um… it's possible. That is… Yes, I do.'

'And Arthur? What of him?'

'Arth—?'

'*King* Arthur?' A smile. 'Our royal ancestor?'

'Oh him, certainly. Several.'

'I should like to see these books,' the Queen said.

'Of course. It would be my—'

There was a sudden, sharp movement in her body, as if in response to a twinge of pain. I thought she was staring at me, but no, it was at something beyond me, her eyes grown still. I didn't like to turn, and so waited for her to speak again. She didn't.

I coughed lightly.

'Your Highness…?'

The Queen blinked.

'Do you have hares,' she said, 'in your orchard?'

'I… no. At least…' Dear God, who had she been talking to? 'Your Highness has seen a hare?'

'I don't… *know*,' the Queen said.

I grew tense, for I had not seen a hare here. Not this year, nor last. And where she was looking… there was nothing.

The Queen smiled – and yet it was a smile like a wafer moon in a cold and smoky dawn. And the hare…

The hare, as you know, because of its curious behaviour, the way it sometimes stands on hind legs to fight with another, as men use their fists, the way it seems to respond to the moon… the hare might be seen as ominous.

The Queen shook her head lightly, swallowed.

'The books,' she said briskly. 'You must—'

Breaking off again, for Mistress Blanche Parry was upon us, her nose wrinkled in distaste at the pervading stench of fermenting hops from the building where ale is brewed, not a hundred long paces from my mother's house. Blanche, who must have been lurking closer than either the Queen or I had known.

'Not now, John,' the Queen said quickly. 'You must bring the books to me.'

'Of course.'

'We'll sup together. Soon.' She found a brittle laugh. '*If* your health permits it.'

'Madam…' Blanche Parry at her elbow. '*If* I may remind you, you have an appointment for discussion with Sir William Cecil at three.' Blanche nodding curtly at me. 'Dr Dee.'

'Good morning,' I said, 'cousin.'

Blanche frowned. The Queen tutted. I said nothing, recognising the interruption for what it was.

'What a shame.' The Queen smiled. 'I was only just saying to Dr Dee that I'd hoped to visit the *school* before we left.'

On her previous visit, she'd spoken of inspecting the nuns' school for poor children, later expressing regret that there would be insufficient time. She glanced at me with half-closed eyes, tacitly confirming that I'd be sent for, and then turning sharply away. Blanche Parry, however, remained for a moment longer, a spindle of a woman, past fifty now, grey-haired and severe.

'Dr Dee, Sir William also wishes to speak with *you*.' Not even looking at me. 'Tomorrow at ten in the morning, at his town house on the Strand. If that is convenient.'

As if there was the remotest possibility, despite my workload, that it would not be. I nodded, wondering if this could be linked to the discovery of the encoffined effigy of the Queen. Of which, never a mention since. Maybe they'd managed, after all, to keep it from her. I'd made discreet inquiries about Walsingham, but nobody knew if he was in Cecil's employ.

Hoar frost was glittering upon the spidery winter branches of the apple trees, and I felt the movement of hidden tides.

✠

Made no move until the last wherry in the royal fleet had rounded the bend in the Thames, and then I went into the house. A fire of fragrant applewood was ablaze in the entrance hall. I'd built the fire myself, my mother adding more logs, in case we should be honoured. I passed by the pastries, all untouched, and found her sitting forlorn in the small parlour, watching the Thames through the poor, milky glass which in summer would protect us from the river's stink.

'I'm sorry,' I said.

Throwing my coat over a chair, tired and more than a little cast down.

'There was a time when Mistress Blanche Parry would have made time for me.' My mother turned away from the grey-brown water, arose and patted her skirts. 'Not any more, apparently.'

'Blanche is jealous of her position at court. It's not your fault. It's me she doesn't trust.'

'Being protective of the Queen's interests and welfare,' my mother said, 'is how she would see it.'

'Also more than a little apprehensive of the advance of the sciences.'

My mother, Jane Dee, looked as if she'd bitten into a onion.

'What?' I said.

'Would Mistress Blanche call it *science*, do you think?'

'Maybe not.'

Avoiding my mother's eyes, I noticed that the panelling on the walls was flaking for want of varnish, while the red-brocaded fabric of my mother's chair looked all tired and worn. I noticed also that a sleeve of her dark brown dress had been patched in two places.

She had asked nothing about what the Queen had said or the reason for the visit. I could have told her that Elizabeth, already renowned as a demanding and expensive guest at the finest homes, would be unlikely to enter one that was conspicuously more lowly. In this case, I was sure, mindful and considerate of our poverty.

And thus I felt ashamed. Inadequate. I should have done better; I was my mother's only child. My father had determined that I should receive the best education their money could buy. I might have become a bishop or even a lawyer, for which I had qualification, instead of... whatever I am become.

The river shone dully, full of animal and doubtless many human carcasses embedded in a city's shit. The sun was pale and hard-looking, like marble.

Conjurer, I was called by some, when my back was turned, and by others even when it was not.

III

His Second Coming

RATHER THAN A crude summoner of spirits, a conjurer may, as you know, be seen in these more enlightened times as one who deals in illusion. And I've done that and found much delight there. Once, at college, for a piece of theatre, I fabricated a gigantic beetle which, through a system of pulleys and the employment of light and shadow, was seen to fly through the air. Spent many days in the making of it and many hours basking in the awe and mystification it inspired.

Nothing wrong with that. I was only a boy, and the beetle did *not* fly. Not as a bird flies, or an angel.

But now I am a man and more exercised by the true nature of angels. Fully accepting, however, that men like Sir William Cecil feel happier with what they know to be illusion, even if they know not how it's done.

✝

No frost today, only a sour sporadic rain as I boarded a wherry by Mortlake pier for my appointment. Low cloud stained with smoke and pricked by a hundred spires, the highest of them St Paul's in the west.

We entered the city past the steaming midden of Southwark with its low-life amusements: bear-pits, cock-pits, whorehouses, gambling and theatre. I no longer noticed the impaled heads of criminals and traitors on London bridge; now that executions of the higher orders had become less commonplace, these crow-picked noddles were more of a grotesque attraction for visitors than a dread warning for the inhabitants.

As for Cecil's new town house… all I understood was that it was on the Strand, where high-powered clergy once lived. But a wherrymen is a floating gazetteer, and mine knew precisely when to steer us to the bank, pulling in his oars by the footings of a new-built stone stairway.

'Ain't the biggest house inner row,' he said. 'But he got plans.'

'The Secretary's a personal friend of yours that you know of his plans?'

Hating at once, the way this must have sounded. Although I'd travelled with this same man seven times or more, I ever find difficulty in the exchange of common pleasantries.

The wherryman only grinned. At least I thought it was a grin, all his top teeth being gone – a fight, perchance, or he'd sold them to a maker of false sets, and I should have liked to ask, but…

'One of his builder's men's marrying my youngest girl,' the wherryman said. 'They gets detailed orders, how he wants it done. Inspects every sodding brick.'

Cecil's pastime, fashioning houses. I knew that. The tide had been with us, and when I found the house, three storeys high, behind a cage of builders' wooden scaffolding, I was more than an hour early. Going in now would convey either over-eagerness or anxiety.

So I walked away from the Strand, arriving some minutes later in a street of brightly painted new shops selling fine furniture, tapestries and good lamps. You could tell how fashionable this quarter had now become by the apparel of the shoppers and the scarcity of children and beggars. Even the street stench here was less putrid, women carrying pomanders more as a declaration of status than to sweeten the air.

It had started to rain. I stepped into a covered shop doorway, from where the street-sellers' cries were muted. Not that there were many of those around – with men as prominent as Sir William Cecil residing hereby, the security services would have seen to all that. If it hadn't been for the rain, I might have wandered away into some other street and never heard—

'—the future! Learn what is to come! Learn how the world will end with darkness and disease before… *His Second Coming!*'

Purple proclamations of apocalypse. Some pamphleteer. Ever cheaper now, the pamphlets. More ubiquitous and more lurid, spewing out their grossly illustrated accounts of murder, executions and devil worship. And end-of-time warnings now, from the puritans.

'—for yourselves the terrifying new predictions of Her Majesty's stargazer! Read the forecasts of Dr Dee!'

Jesu! Now I was out of the doorway and backing clumsily around an unattended cart, finding myself in a cramped alley, the man's bellow seeming to pursue me into the piss-stinking shadows.

'Know the future now... *what's left of it.*'

Beginning to sweat as I peered out to observe quite a crowd gathering around the pamphlet man. Respectable-looking people, women in fur-trim, men in the new-fashion Venetian breeches. All hot for revelations of turmoil in the heavens, discovery of unknown lands full of strange winged creatures, some new war in Europe.

All invention, of course, but too many people were ready to believe anything committed to print and...

...did they not know *I did not do this?*

Second coming? My role was to scribe charts indicating planetary influences on world affairs, the balance of the humours. Possible directions, opportunities, auspices. But never a claim to full-fledged prophecy. That way, until we know more, lies madness.

But why had no-one told me about this shit?

Rumour and gossip, Dr John, rumour and gossip.

Jack Simm's voice in my head, as I moved out towards the crowd. Had Jack known of this? Were there more such publications, about spells and divination and the conjuring of spirits in a house at Mortlake? Did everybody know about it, except for me?

Head in the stars, as ever, when it's not in a book. My mother. *Too much time with books, boy, isn't it?* Even my tad, once, in exasperation – the man who'd been so determined I should have the best education his money could secure.

'Know the time of the End and the evil which comes before it!' the pamphlet-seller bawled, lips plump and wet. 'Prepare yourselves!'

Turning, as if he knew I was there, cowering in the shadows. A lumpen fellow in a leather hat with two peacock feathers, his wares in a crate at his feet.

The rain had ceased. I hung back, not knowing what to do. I could take the rogue to law, but a court case would only invite more of the kind of notoriety I could live without. For I would be questioned in public about the nature of my work and be compelled to answer, and I'd been there – oh God, yes – once before.

Face it: more likely, the man would simply disappear, leaving his pamphlets to blow in the gutters.

Steadied myself on the side of the cart. It was as if part of me had been snatched away to fulfil some presumed role on the public stage. As if, while the mind of John Dee was absorbed in the contents of his library, the *conjurer* strode the streets, dispensing darkness.

'How do we know these are Dr Dee's predictions?' A woman, sounding scared. 'How came you by them?'

'How do we *know*, mistress?' the pamphlet man screamed. 'How do we *know?*'

Evidently playing for time.

'Indeed,' another said, a man in a long gaberdine. 'What proof have you that the renowned Dee is the author of these prophecies?'

A moment's silence as the pamphlet-seller clawed the air for inspiration, and then he sniffed loudly, puffed up his chest like a cock bird on a bough.

'Dr Dee, sir, is a man who must needs guard his privacy. Myself, however, as his secretary and publisher, am given leave to make public those of his words what he considers might help men and women prepare for their fate. These being not *his* words, you understand, for he is a humble man, but the very utterings of messengers of God who communicate with him through his *intelligent devices.*'

'I'll take two,' a man said.

'That'll be four pence.'

I could stand it no more and stepped out of the alleyway.

'So you're –' a sickness in my gut, for I've ever hated confrontation – 'you're Dr Dee's publisher.'

No reaction. My words lost in the chittering. I called out louder.

'You work for Dr Dee?'

'For many years, *friend.*'

Speaking from out of the side of his mouth. He wasn't looking at me, handing over a pamplet with one hand, taking the money with the other. The pamphlet was displaying a smudged engraving of a dark-robed man with a beard to his chest, his hands raised to the planets aswirl about his wide-brimmed hat. I ask you!

'What sort of man is he?'

'What?'

'This Dr Dee.'

'A man of deepest learning and erudition.'

'Does he resemble this picture?'

'It's a fair likeness. I'd—'

The pamphlet-seller broke off, turning to observe me. His skin was oily-sallow and he had a stubbly black mole on one unbarbered cheek. He clearly did not know me and seemed quickly to lose interest in a man in plain clothing and no hat.

'So,' I ran a hand across my fresh-shaven jaw, 'he'd be an old man, would he, with that long beard?'

'If you don't have the money to buy, my friend, then pray clear the way for those who do. Life – as you may read within – is too short for wasters of time.'

'You haven't yet answered the question. How do we know that these... stories are come from Dee?'

'And how do you know that they are *not?*'

'Because I didn't—'

It just happened that no-one else spoke, a random hush.

'—write them,' I said.

Speaking quietly, but in that moment I might as well have bawled it from the rooftops.

'Who *are* you, cocker?' the pamphlet-seller said.

I would have walked away but was tight-pressed now, on all sides. I'd seen this before. Warnings of the end of time could produce a near-riot in the street, fear filling the air like a choking smoke.

'Who are you?'

'Says he is Dr Dee,' someone said.

It had begun to rain again, and the high buildings echoed the clitter-clatter of horses' hooves. The only space was in front of me, and the pamphlet-seller was leaning into it, a fat forefinger levelled at my chest.

'Harken to the scoundrel! *"I am John Dee!"'*

Some laughter, but it was flittery and uncertain. I said nothing, looking quickly among the circle of faces. There seemed to be nobody here I knew. I brought out a handful of small coins.

'I'll take a pamphlet, then.'

The seller leaned towards me, holding out a pamphlet but then, as I reached for it, pulled it sharply back, his eyes alight with an energy of malice and glee.

'If you're Dr Dee,' he said, 'you'll already know what's in here.'

Someone laughed. I held fast to the sneery gaze.

'Dee's a common conjurer, anyway,' a man said to my left.

'Give us a prophecy.' The pamphlet man smiling crookedly. 'Go on then. *Make us a prediction.*'

I saw then that he was not alone. Two boys of fourteen or fifteen were each carrying a stack of his publication. They'd been moving among the audience and now stopped, a hand of one moving to his belt.

'Beware the criminal element!' The pamphlet man whirling himself in triumph to the crowd. 'A beardless youth what dares posture as the Queen's seer. Go on! Tell us the future, boy!'

The mood of the crowd had begun to turn like a great mill-wheel. Someone began slowly to clap, the pamphlet man joining in with his flabby butter-pat hands. And then came another man's loud voice, cold as cracking stonework.

'Prophecy is blasphemy!'

Something wet hit me on the cheek and I flinched. Saw that both of the boy assistants had put down their pamphlets and were glancing towards me and then at their master, as if awaiting instructions to stab me and run.

'Dr Dee trades with demons!' a woman shrilled.

'I've heard that.' Another woman, older. 'He spits upon the Holy Bible.'

Someone pressed against me and, as ever in a tangle, my body tensed, anticipating the fleet fingers of pickpockets, a glint of daggers. Some gentlemen, I noticed, were guiding their ladies away. I glanced behind me, looking for a way out of here.

Staring into a bearded face all too close. The beard splitting into a gap-toothed grin. Now the press of hard bodies, the stench of ale-breath. Before me, the pamphlet man was bloating into a near-frenzy, and the eyes of his peacock feathers were vibrating either side of his head.

'Go on!' he screamed. 'Prophesy! Tell us of the coming of your dark master!'

I froze, watching the feathers wave.

A wild fury shook me.

'All right...' Barely aware of my words coming out. 'I prophesy that before the week's out you'll be banged up in the lowest dungeon in the Fleet, you—'

A forearm was wrapped across my throat. My head jerked back, both arms seized, wrenched stiff behind me. Hard rain slashing my face.

Then a leathered hand across my mouth, and I was spun around to behold a man with a black velvet hat pulled down over his eyes. His dark cape failing to conceal the golden glow of a doublet that was like to a treasure chest split open.

'Take this fucking impostor away,' he said.

IV

Stability of the Realm

EVEN ON SUCH a day as this, the light was everywhere in the room. Windows you could ride a horse through.

He had his back to them. He was sitting behind a trestle of wide oaken boards, which faced a modest coal fire.

'This is merely a humble cottage, I tell everyone that. Plea for privacy.' He poured wine for me, a little less of it for himself. 'And, of course, they all fail to understand. Especially the Queen.'

There was a hanging smell of linseed and beeswax around the empty shelves. It seemed the house, at present, had room only for himself, his wife, two daughters and a mere fourteen servants. But he was already acquiring substantial properties on either side and, by the spring, it would be more than twice its size. In the meantime, I could see it would have its limitations for a man of the eminence of Sir William Cecil.

Who now turned limpid, mournful eyes upon me.

'I do greatly love that young woman, Dee. And shall serve her, God willing, for the rest of my working days. But she does, dear Lord, require constant diversion. *Oh, I shall come to sup with you, William. Soon! Everything must be soon.*'

'It's only the newness of it,' I said. 'The limitless power of monarchy is an intoxication. And she, more than most, knows how short life is. That is, um… some lives.'

'She came through.' Cecil's eyes hardening fractionally, but he didn't move. 'And now she's protected. For ever.'

He wore a black robe over a cloud-grey doublet. Hard to believe he was not yet forty; it was as if a certain tiredness had become part of his nature. Illusion, I knew. The weariness and the drabness of his attire was theatre. He loved what he did and was unfailingly good at it. So good, so

37

efficient and so blessed by fortune that he was now serving his *third* monarch. How many could say that?

'And you had a good meeting with Her Majesty yesterday?'

'For as long as it lasted, Sir William.'

I sank back, still aquiver from the incident in the street. I'd been given a comfortably padded chair facing the great windows. The glass in them was very fine, with large panes. We were on the first upper floor, with a view of river and spires in the blue-grey haze.

'We were interrupted,' I said. 'By my cousin.'

Which he'd know, of course, having – I was sure – personally instructed her to ensure that my discourse with the Queen should not get below surface pleasantries. I was guessing there was something Cecil wanted me to hear from *him* rather than the Queen. Presumably because their respective versions would differ a good deal.

'You have a cousin' – raising of a Cecil eyebrow – 'who would interrupt the Queen?'

'Blanche Parry,' I said with patience. 'Her family and mine are related. As are most families from the borderland of Wales.'

Including, for heaven's sake, his own, the Cecils of Allt-yr-ynys – all of us down from those same hills.

'So I've heard.' He nodded. 'Yes, of course. A formidable woman, Mistress Blanche.'

His eyes were half closed. He'd been Secretary of State in the time of the plot to make poor Jane Grey Queen of England in Mary's stead, and yet somehow avoided entanglement. Thus surviving to serve under Mary, to enter Parliament, become knighted. Protestant to Catholic and back to Protestant – how many could say *that*?

He picked up his wineglass and appeared to do no more than moisten his lips before putting it down again and leaning back into fingers interlacing behind his head.

'You're busy, John?'

'Day and night,' I said. 'When permitted.'

'A man ever driven by an endless flow of illumination.' Cecil peered down at his board on which several letters had been spread, then looked up. 'Glastonbury.'

'Mercy?'

'A small town in the west. Once upon the Isle of Avalon. And once famous for its abbey. You know it?'

'I know *of* it,' I said.

Already making connections.

'*What* do you know of it?'

'I know that it was the burial place of King Arthur.'

Arthur... What of him? the Queen had asked.

Cecil sniffed.

✝

Last night, I'd shut myself in the library to locate the books I'd be obliged to deliver to the Queen.

My shelves were yet rudimentary structures supported by bricks. On them, I'd found the works of Giraldus Cambrensis and Geoffrey of Monmouth, from which Malory had derived his pot-boiling twaddle, *Morte d'Arthur.*

Not that Geoffrey himself was much more reliable. When he ran out of history he'd make it up and, on the subject of Arthur, history was scant. But there must at least be seeds of truth therein, and it hadn't been long before I'd been guided to the town of Glastonbury, Arthur's burial place on the so-called Isle of Avalon. An island town no longer, it seemed, the sea having long ago retreated, leaving a community built among small hills swelling from waterlogged flatlands bordered with orchard.

Orchard.

Odd that the Queen and I should have been discussing this matter in my mother's orchard. The very word Avalon was surely derived from *Afal*, the Welsh for apple. This area of Somersetshire was both rich in apple orchards and close to Wales and therefore seemed as likely as anywhere to be the mystical island to which, in legend, the dying King Arthur had been borne by barge.

Either to be healed of his wounds or to die and to be buried within the precincts of what would become a famous abbey. Depending which version of the story it was in your interests to believe.

A pretty tale, whichever you accepted. An inspiring tale. A tale to strengthen our tradition. The ideal of monarchy, with his round table of knights and his magical sword Excalibur, King Arthur had ever been central to us.

Us? Us the English? Us the British? Us... the Welsh?

You and I being both of Welsh stock, the Queen had said.

When I was a boy, my tad would tell me that we, the Dees – the name is rendered English from the Welsh *Ddu*, meaning black – were descended from Arthur himself. And I believed it, for who would choose not to? I believe it now, but not in the same way. Now I'm more interested in an Arthurian *tradition*, a mystical strand, from which we can draw an ancient energy.

Besides, a far more illustrious family than mine also claims descent from the great British hero.

Our royal ancestor, the Queen had said. With a smile.

✠

'...had it not been for that regrettable business twenty years ago,' Cecil was saying.

'Beg mercy?'

'Over the Abbot of Glastonbury. It's all most of us know of the ghastly place.'

'Mmm. Yes.'

At the time of the Dissolution, the last Abbot of Glastonbury had been dragged through the town on a hurdle and then hanged, drawn and quartered. Tortured first, it was said, slowly and extensively.

This on the orders of Thomas Cromwell, acting for King Henry VIII. The Abbot having been treacherous and uncooperative.

'All rather unnecessary,' Cecil said, 'given hindsight.'

I said nothing. The Dissolution of the monasteries still pained me, whenever I thought of it. Although I understood full well the need to be free of an oft-corrupt papacy, the destruction of such beauty and the loss of the centuries of knowledge it represented was near unbearable to me. All those books torn up and burned. Many of the rescued volumes in my library had, so to speak, scorched pages.

'They say the place has never recovered,' Cecil said.

'As with other abbey towns. Was not this one the oldest religious house in England, in its foundation?'

It seemed more than likely that Cecil had been to Glastonbury himself, on one of his visits to his late friend Edward Seymour, Duke of Somerset. But he said nothing.

'Obviously an important place of pilgrimage, in its day,' I said. 'Given the legend of its foundation…'

As the Queen had reminded me, it was said that the wealthy merchant who had provided a tomb for his Saviour, had travelled to these islands, to trade, landing in the extreme west of England. And that Jesus, said by some sources to be his nephew, had journeyed with him as a boy, and had thus set foot both in Cornwall and Somersetshire.

Indeed, it was further said that Jesus had returned as a man, to train in the spiritual disciplines under the Druids. A thrilling legend which seemed unlikely ever to be proved. However, it was more widely believed that, after the crucifixion, Joseph had also returned, bringing with him the holy cup of the Last Supper which had later caught drops of the holy blood from the cross, and that this cup, the Holy Grail, remained, hidden somewhere.

The most precious, powerful and inspirational vessel in Christendom. The purest of King Arthur's knights were said to have gone in quest of the Grail, thus bringing together the two great legends of Glastonbury. A holy legacy indeed, and out of all this had grown a huge and wealthy monastic establishment, said to have been founded by Joseph of Arimathea himself.

And then King Henry, the Great Furnace, had ordered its destruction.

'Never been there yourself?' Cecil said.

'No.'

'Odd. I mean… given your noted fascination with the great spiritual mysteries.'

I grew cautious.

'It's a question of time, Sir William.'

'Time.' He smiled. 'We can always make time. And you could be there… oh, well within a week, I'm assured.'

He looked at me, placidly. There was never any reading of his eyes.

'Why?' I said.

'For the stability of the realm of course.' Parting his fingers, Cecil sat up in his chair and stretched his spine. 'Why else do I exist?'

I'd wondered why he'd summoned me here, to his *private* home, his *cottage*. Had to be for reasons of secrecy.

Something sensitive. Something unofficial.

Therefore something heavy with risk.

I looked out of the window and now beheld the collected spires as something like to a bed of nails. With the twisted briars of religion and the gathering threats from abroad – the Queen of Scots fresh-married to the boy king of France – did Cecil not have enough tough meat on his plate without concerning himself with *spiritual mysteries?*

'Are you quite sure I'm the man for this?' I said.

V

Bones

OUTSIDE, THE RAIN had ceased and the winter sun hung in the central window, looking heavy as a new coin. It lit the spines of the books on Cecil's few finished shelves. Books dealing with politics, law and property, but nothing, I'd guess, on the spiritual mysteries.

I told Cecil about the pamphlet-seller, but not about my incautious attempt to take him on, nor how I'd been saved from what might have been a severe beating, or worse.

All the time was wondering if he knew full well what had occurred. This man had eyes all over the city, and beyond.

He lifted an eyebrow, reached for his wineglass then abruptly pushed it away.

'There are scum out there who've been putting it around London that I maintain four mistresses and consume a gallon of wine nightly, before horsewhipping my children. Face it, you're a public figure, now. Or at least, a public *name.*'

'But my mother's not. And she'd be alone at Mortlake, where it seems I'm hated and feared by all the new puritans lest I raid their family's graves.'

'Then we'll *protect* her.' His hands emerging from his robe like puppets. 'I'll have armed guards put into Mortlake for as long as you're away. I'll even have a guard mounted on your blessed *library*. How does that sound?'

'Well, I don't think there's need for—'

'Good. Settled, then.'

'There's also the matter of my work. I'm already seriously behind in my work.'

Cecil was gathering up the letters. He did not even look at me.

'*This*,' he said, 'is your work.'

✛

The stories of the four mistresses and the horsewhipping of children had obviously been plucked from the air to make a point. But there was gossip about Sir William Cecil, most of it related to his ancestry. The son of an innkeeper, it was oft-times said, in the same way that it was oft said of me that I was the son of a meat-slicer.

But is it such a bad thing that we are now living in an age where ability may, on occasion, be recognised above breeding?

I think not, and yet I believe ancestry to be important in ways that we have not yet fathomed. For my father, it was simple: he was a Welshman and, now that the Tudors of Wales had secured the English crown, this Welshness was an asset of no small proportion. *I am Rowland Dee and I am a man of Wales!* my tad would declare, with one hand on his heart, the other extended before him, and a comical deepening of his accent.

Sometimes he'd even repeat it in Welsh. Which, I would imagine, cut no ice at all with the Great Furnace, who gave not a shit for Wales, most of the time. It had been different, however, for his own father, the first Tudor king, who'd landed from France in the west of Wales and rode from there with a gathering army and a weight of tradition.

This tradition being King Arthur. According to the legends, Arthur had not died but was only sleeping and would return when his nation had need of him.

And so, within Henry Tudor, was Arthur risen again, and the sense of an older and more united Britain. Henry had married Elizabeth of York, thus meeting the red rose with the white. To seal the family's royal destiny, he'd even given their first-born son, his heir, the name of Arthur and had him born at Winchester, which Malory claimed had once been Camelot.

A masterstroke. I knew the new Queen was much taken with this story of her family's tradition and doubtless recognised its emotive power. *King Arthur. Our royal ancestor*, she'd said to me. And would have said more had not Blanche Parry appeared, the watchful owl amid the

44

winter apple trees. Blanche having been given brief, I'd guessed, by this man, William Cecil, who at all times protected the Queen.

Sometimes, it seemed, from herself.

'She's a young woman,' he said now. 'She's clever, well read, and already carries a weight of experience. And, given the parlous state of the exchequer, she is commendably cautious. But, as a young woman, she's ever prey to the allure of a great romance. And the problems it might pose. For her.'

'Believing she must, in some way, make the mantle of Arthur… fit a woman?'

I could still see no obvious problem. In Arthurian terms, the Queen was not merely Guinevere, nor even Morgan le Fay, the enchantress of Arthurian myth, but, potentially, someone greater, more powerful and more glamorous than either. I understood this entirely and did not think it foolish or wayward, for these were strange and awesome times.

And so I waited, the room awash now with winter sunlight, two unicorns coming to luminous life upon a new tapestry, as Cecil drank the rest of his wine with no apparent appreciation. I doubted he believed in unicorns.

'It all depends,' he said, 'on how dead you believe Arthur to be.'

✝

It was clear that we were now talking of the grave found in the abbey at Glastonbury during the reign of an earlier Henry, the Plantagenet, Henry II. I'd read of it last night in the writings of my father's countryman, Giraldus Cambrensis.

In the year 1191, an excavation at Glastonbury Abbey had uncovered a stone and a cross of lead proclaiming the burial there of the renowned King Arthur. Nine feet further down into the earth, in an oaken coffin, had lain the bones of an inordinately large man and the smaller skeleton of what was taken to be a woman. And a lock of yellow hair which crumbled into dust when picked up by one of the monks.

Guinevere.

And, oh yes, the *monks* had found this grave. Arthur was risen just when the monks had need of him most.

'They needed money,' Cecil reminded me. 'Lots of it. The abbey having recently been ravaged by a very destructive fire. In the twelfth century, the tales of Arthur and his knights were widely read and told to children. Nothing could have brought more fame and pilgrimage to Glastonbury than the bones of Arthur.'

Naturally, it was said by many that the grave was a fake and the so-called discovery of the royal remains nothing more than a deception by the monks. A deception which was also of considerable value to the King in subduing the hopes of the rebellious Welsh.

'Nothing better than bones,' I said to Cecil, 'as evidence that Arthur was very conspicuously beyond revival.'

'Indeed. Almost a century later, the bones were placed in a black marble tomb before the high altar of the rebuilt abbey church. Having first been inspected by King Edward I who, after crushing the Welsh once again, at great expense, would also have been delighted to confirm that Arthur was dead.'

'What king of England would neglect such an opportunity?'

'Ah.' Cecil arose and walked over to the vast windows. 'There you have it.'

'A *Tudor* king of England?'

The sky over the river was clear of cloud; the air would freeze again tonight. I began to see a loose pattern. Highly useful for a Norman king, this evidence that Arthur was truly dead and the Welsh could no longer count on him. But for a king *of Welsh descent*, who had landed from France in the west of Wales and ridden into England under the numinous banner of an *undying* Arthur...

I was intrigued. My books had none of this.

'So what happened,' I asked Cecil, 'to the black marble tomb when the abbey was despoiled?'

'A good question.'

'It's gone, though?'

'Every last stone. It was marble. The abbey's little more than a quarry now.'

A bonus, then, for the son of the first Tudor king? In the early years of his reign, King Harry had also been keen to maintain the connection with an undying Arthur. Had not his own face been imposed upon the likeness of the round table in the cathedral at Winchester where his dead brother, Arthur, had, conveniently, been born?

'You're saying Thomas Cromwell took the bones?'

It was said that Cromwell, perversely, had acquired a personal collection of holy relics looted from the monasteries.

'If he did,' Cecil said, 'he doesn't seem to have bequeathed them to the nation when it was his turn to visit the axeman.'

'What's being said?'

'My intelligence is that by the time the marble tomb was dismantled, the bones had simply disappeared.'

'The monks having removed them, knowing what was to happen? Perhaps burying them in another grave, unmarked?'

'That's one possibility, yes.'

'So all evidence of the death of the Queen's spiritual forebear…?'

'Gone.'

'Do we know where they might be hidden?'

Cecil made no reply, returning to his board.

'Is there a suggestion,' I said, 'that someone has them? And, if so… who?'

'I don't know. The Queen's court's as full of twitterings as a woodland at dawn. It's all rumour.'

For the first time, he looked angry. He was a pragmatist, a practical man, a survivor. Modern politics, certainly at Cecil's level, did not lie easily with superstition.

'John, all I know is this. At my last but one meeting with the Queen, she asked two questions. The first… if there was a great house at Glastonbury to which she might… invite herself.'

Cecil was known to approve of the Queen's extended visits to the homes of her supporters, thus relieving the beleaguered exchequer of considerable domestic expense, sometimes for weeks at a time. Usually, however, the chosen houses were within easy travelling distance of London. Glastonbury would be a journey of several days.

'She seems to have been made aware, maybe through her reading, of the mystical qualities of the place. Talk of visions – your area of expertise, not mine, but *something*'s put it into her mind. And she talks of Arthur, increasingly. As if she's suddenly discovered his importance.'

The coal fire had burned low. Cecil might have summoned a servant by now to stoke it, but he only stared into the whitening embers.

'And what was the Queen's second question?' I said.

His face was dark. He wiped a hand across his jaw.

'She asked me what it might cost to restore the Abbey of Glastonbury to its former golden glory.'

'Costly,' I said.

'*Costly?*' Cecil smacked his board. 'Jesu *Christ,* this was the most extensive, gorgeous, religious fucking edifice in the entire country!'

'Ah.'

I stood up, still not fully understanding. If the Queen's father had been happy enough to destroy the evidence, however discredited, of Arthur's mortality, why was Elizabeth now interested in getting it back?

'All right,' Cecil said. 'Let's hasten to the chase. If these bones exist, we need to have them. Even though they've caused nothing but trouble for more than four centuries.'

My doublet was cheap and I was cold.

'Sir William, I don't know this place. I don't know anyone there.'

'Sit down, John. Not asking you to go out with a spade and a muffled lantern.'

I sat down. Cecil made a steeple of his fingers.

'We've known each other for a good many years. Have our differences, I accept this, but I think we're at least united in our desire to preserve this queen. In body and in… spirit. And it seems her spirit, at present, is troubled.'

'She's talked to you of this?'

'Doesn't talk to *me* of such things. She'll doubtless, in due course, talk of them to you, as her adviser on matters less earthly. Her… Merlin, shall we say?'

I didn't like the direction this was going. Cecil looked down at his board.

'We both of us know her strengths and her… weaknesses.'

Meaning her indecisiveness. Agonising over some issue, going one way then another. An example of this being the inability to reconcile her conflicting attitudes to religion – unable, as was I, to renounce the mysticism of the Mass.

'Restoration's out of the question,' Cecil said, 'even if the money were there. Glastonbury Abbey's too big and already hardly more than a ruin. Its stonework apparently supports new houses for miles around. Hopeless. However… if we had the bones, then we might satisfy the Queen by fashioning a suitably elaborate shrine for Arthur…'

'Where?'

'Here in London.'

'You want me to go to Glastonbury… locate the bones of Arthur… and fetch them back here?'

His nod was almost imperceptible. He *was* asking me to go out with a spade and muffled lantern.

'Alone?'

'You'll be accompanied by someone both of us can trust.'

'Who?'

Sounding as if this had already been organised. I had a dismaying thought.

'Not Walsingham?'

Cecil's gaze hardened.

'I met him when—'

'I *know* when you met him.'

'Does he work for you, Sir William?'

'Francis?' He leaned back. 'Not officially. Let's say I'm trying him out. As he's not the man who'll go with you to Glastonbury, he needn't worry you.'

Could not quite explain my relief. There'd been a close-hung darkness around Walsingham, and not only in his dress. Whatever he'd done after we'd parted that morning in the alley near the river, not a word about the effigy seemed to have leaked out. No pamphlet had published even a hint of it.

But within the relief, there was still trepidation.

'What if they're not to be found? The bones.'

'Oh, they'll be *found*,' Cecil said. 'Not necessarily the full set. A leg bone may suffice, and a ribcage. And of course a skull, suitably shattered.'

'And you think the Queen will be convinced that these are indeed the remains of her... ancestor?'

'That would depend.... on who assures her of their authenticity.'

The thin, grey light of Cecil's gaze settling upon me.

Here would be the bones of Arthur, formally presented to Her Majesty the Queen by her Merlin. And oh, dear God, as you can imagine, I liked this not at all.

VI

The Holy Heart

THE OARSMEN HAD been bidden to take it slowly, and our progress downriver was smooth. Fireshined by the unexpected afternoon sun, the Thames looked near-serene. Legend has this as a holy river, and I've seen it written that the Romans considered it sacred to their solar deity, Apollo.

River of the Sun. I liked that and could believe it, even though today's sun, being yet a winter sun, was shamed by my companion's gold and burgundy slashed doublet. The kind of doublet which, on a summer's day, must needs be viewed through smoked glass.

'Where are your thoughts gone now, John?'

Sprawled in the stern of his low barge, regarding me with that old amusement.

'I was seeing the river as a lake,' I said bitterly. 'Imagining a woman's hand emerging holding a magical sword. The sun's rays spraying from its blade.'

The eyes of Robert Dudley were theatrically wide.

'God's bollocks, John... any woman's arm protruding from the Thames would, for a start, be brown to the elbow with shite!'

My former student's reputation as a great romantic figure is, in my view, ill-founded. Doubtless the Queen sees a different side of her Master of the Horse. But then, how much of Dudley the Queen sees is something I try not to think too hard about.

'Perchance we might *all* go to Glastonbury.' He sank into the cushions, lifting a soft-booted foot to the seat opposite. 'Good idea, do you think?'

'All?'

'You... me... the Queen?'

When he'd told me he'd be lying with her at Richmond this night, I'd taken him to mean simply that he would be accommodated, as Master of the Horse, in his apartment at the palace. They'd been friends since children. But who knew? Who really *knew*?

'You really don't understand, do you, Robbie?'

'Of course I understand. I'm merely thinking how best to loosen Cecil's bowels.' Dudley smoothed his moustache over a malicious smile. 'Apart from the rest of it, the very last thing Uncle Willie wants is for Bess to descend upon some God-forsaken Somerset ruin and set up a round table with a… what did they call that fucking chair at the round table where you planted your arse if it was your lot to pursue the holy cup?'

'The Siege Perilous?'

'That's the one. And the thing is – ' he sat up – 'she'd do it, you know. She'd have a board made and assemble her knights all about her, in splendour. *So* loves her heroes – men of adventure, soldiers, seamen. And you, of course, John, you above all.'

'Go to!'

'I'll admit it foxed me for quite a while, why the Queen should go so often out of her way to visit a pale scholar in a hovel on stilts in dreary Mortlake. And then it came to me – is not John Dee the greatest adventurer of them all? A man prepared… to venture beyond this world. *Woohee!*'

Dudley's laughter ringing like cathedral bells across the water.

✝

With his trusted chief groom, Martin Lythgoe, he'd been awaiting me downstairs in Cecil's yet unfurnished entrance hall, jesting there with the guards. His own appointment with the Secretary had been two hours earlier than mine, which explained why he and his attendants had been on hand to witness the incident of the pamphlet-seller. And make their move.

His barge had been ready at the riverbank, with a hamper of midday meat. *I shall see you home, John, lest the pamphlet-man and his uglies are awaiting you in some back alley.* Shaking his head, incredulous. *However you survived in the cesspits of Paris and Antwerp without me around to save your sorry arse, I shall never know.*

Insisting on taking me all the way back to Mortlake. After which he was to return to the Queen at Richmond. His wife, meanwhile, being sequestered in the country.

'When do we leave?' he said now.

'I've not yet decided… whether to do it.'

'Oh, you'll do it, John, you know you will.'

'And deceive the Queen?'

The word *deceive* hissing like a new-forged blade slid into cold water. Me thinking I was out of that world at last. And to deceive the Queen, who'd saved my reputation, and who was, after all… the Queen.

'That may not be necessary,' Dudley said. 'We may find the bones. That's certainly *my* intention. I should love to see the relics of Ar—'

Me glaring at him, glancing at the oarsmen and his attendants at the front of the barge. He lowered his voice.

'Has anybody ever *really* attempted to find them? I think not. We should easily get to the truth within a few days. Beat the shit out of some duplicitous ex-monk.'

'This is just another small diversion for you, isn't it, Robbie?'

Someone both of us can trust, Cecil had said. Well, this was true, to a degree. I'd known Dudley since, as a very young man, I'd been employed as tutor to him and his siblings, by his late father, John Dudley, Duke of Northumberland. Robbie had fast developed an interest in maths and astronomy, but other subjects that interested him had been beyond me at the time and were, I suppose, beyond me still.

'I was in thrall, as a boy, to Malory's histories,' he mused. 'The sword in the stone… the gathering of the knights – Gawaine, Galahad, Bedivere, Bors. And of course Lancelot, who made off with Arthur's wife… I could well admire *his* nerve.'

Dudley grinned. His beard was close-trimmed, his hair styled like he was ready to pose for a new portrait. He, too, had been close to a public death, feeling the wind of the axe that dispatched his father after the Jane Grey affair. But what had made me wary seemed, in some way, to have liberated his spirit.

'As I tried to explain to you more than ten years ago,' I said, 'Thomas Malory… never trust the bastard and his ridiculous modernisation. Arthur was some tribal warlord.'

'Matters not. Within those tales lies the very essence of knightly chivalry.' Dudley leaned forward. 'Whatever you say about the origins of Arthur, I revere what I *perceive* of him, and I'll be honoured to bring back his bones. To London – the new Camelot.'

'Streets full of thieves and whores and beggars, and a river full of shit?'

'John, he *belongs* here – at Westminster, or St Paul's. The Queen will be delighted beyond words.'

'How will she? The Tudor line is he's not dead.'

'Ah, the body may be dead, but the spirit lives. His tomb shall once again be a monument to the golden age to which we aspire. For Bess, in particular. *She'll* be the one to bring Arthur home in glory. John, we have to *give* her this.'

Downriver, I could already see the tower of Mortlake Church. I didn't have much time.

'This big boys' adventure,' I said. 'Neither of us has the time for that. And there has to be something more to it.'

'Like what?'

'Cecil said he thought the Queen was spiritually troubled.'

'Did he say how?'

Dudley's eyes narrowing; I saw caution there.

'He said she didn't often speak to him of such matters.'

'But you think,' Dudley said, 'that she might've spoken of them… to me?'

'Has she?'

Dudley caught the eye of the thatch-haired Martin Lythgoe and moved a hand up and down to convey that he wished the oarsman to further slow our progress towards Mortlake.

'All right,' he said. 'Look into history. Beginning, if you like, with the death of Arthur – not the king, the Queen's uncle, Prince Arthur, who would've been King Arthur the Second. Born in Winchester, which Malory had identified as Camelot. His early death meant some salvage was required, lest it be thought a sign that God did not, after all, wish Arthur to be reborn as a Tudor. And then comes Harry…'

'Yes.'

How different life might have been, for all of us, had Arthur not died so young, bequeathing his crown and – most fateful of all – his bride, Catherine of Aragon, to his brother, Henry.

Dudley gazed out over the river.

'The Queen, as we know, admires her father. And indeed may be said to possess some of his… resolve. But she's also aware of his very conspicuous failures. Failure, despite six marriages and the resulting division of the churches, to produce a surviving male heir. Bess considers the short life of Edward and the longer but hardly happy reign of her half-sister. Fears a resumption of the decline.'

'Inevitably.'

'And she's superstitious.'

Well, no-one knew that more than I. The Queen, needing to believe she's chosen by God to rule this land, looking always for signs and portents to reinforce her confidence.

One of my own roles being to point them out to her. And Cecil had said she might speak to *me* of her inner problem – while ensuring there was no chance of this happening in the near future by making himself the intermediary in the matter of Arthur's bones.

'Here's the point,' Dudley said, 'Arthur's linked by Malory and others to the Pope and the Holy Roman Empire – forget that he might have been no more than a heathen, go with the lore. What does Harry do? Breaks with Rome and fills his coffers with the treasures of the Church. Finally sacking Glastonbury Abbey… where lie Arthur's bones.'

'Someone's suggesting Harry dishonoured King Arthur?'

Dudley shrugged.

'Thus bringing down a curse upon his line?'

'If the curse was not already there. A few years ago, an appeal was made to Mary to put Glastonbury Abbey back together. Much as she'd have wanted it, there was little money to spare then. Even for God.'

'So now something – or someone' – I began to see it – 'has put it into Queen Elizabeth's mind that she has much to redeem if her reign's to be fruitful.'

'Or even avoid disaster. Glastonbury, John – it all comes together in Glastonbury. Arthur and Jesus Christ, all bound together. The holy heart of it all.'

'Who put this into her mind, Robbie?'

'I don't know. Not me.'

'Cecil speaks of visions. What's that about?'

Dudley shook his head. A shadow fell betwixt us. Martin Lythgoe stood there, a stocky, amiable man, and patient.

'Mortlake, my lord.'

Dudley sighed.

'Get them to row in circles, would you, Martin?'

✠

William Cecil had a certain genius for putting together the right men for a particular task. Here were two fellows of contrasting skills, committed to the same woman, if not for the same reasons. Dudley it was who had introduced me at court, Dudley who had commanded me to select a date for the coronation.

Two men committed, by bitter history, to the watching of each other's backs.

'So when *do* we leave?' he said.

'After I look into the history of this. For instance, if an approach was made to Mary for the restoration of Glastonbury Abbey, was mention made of the bones then?'

'Does Cecil not know?'

I shook my head.

'Bonner might,' Dudley said. 'You still a friend?'

'Needs all the friends he can get at this moment. It's a wonder he still lives.'

'A tribute to Bess, who refuses, bless her, to resort either to the axe or the taper.'

'Thus far.'

Dudley snorted.

'Bloody Bonner. Be a queue of people a mile long ready to set light to *his* pile.' He regarded me for a moment, tongue probing a cheek. 'Thinking about it, you must be the only man he ever spared. Fellow you shared a cell with... *he* was burned. *Are* you still Bonner's friend?'

'For my sins. And his.'

'Have to admire the old bastard's nerve. Still refusing to recognise the Queen as head of the church, even when she offers a compromise.'

'That mean prison?'

'Marshalsea. For good this time, unless he changes his song. If you feel it worth visiting him, I wouldn't waste any time.'

'Yes,' I said. 'That might be worthwhile.' I watched a gull wheeling over the remains of our midday meal, which seemed still to be following in our wake. 'How is Amy?'

'Amy's well.' Dudley's expression unchanging. 'She ever prefers the country life.'

'There's fortunate,' I said.

For a moment, he almost frowned. He swung his feet to the deck and stood up.

'And what of you? Still dipping it in the mercury?'

'Dudley, if a man can barely afford to support *himself*...'

'That excuse, John, wears thin.'

'So we ride out,' I said, 'with banners held high—'

'That's not how a great quest is undertaken. We fast for several days, perform three nightly vigils until dawn and then ride out silently, and with humility. We take few men with us, if any, and each church we chance upon, we stop and pray.'

'Unlikely to get there before midsummer, then.'

Dudley stretched his arms.

'Taking few men – that's certainly part of it. I rather like the idea, to be honest – a rare freedom to move around as a common man, unencumbered by the trappings of high office.'

I may have blinked. Robert Dudley shorn of the trappings of high office was like Hampton Court with no glass in the windows and a flock of sheep in the gardens.

'Cecil intends that we travel as lowly servants of the Crown,' he said. 'Undertaking a survey of historical remains. We're to be accompanied by someone with knowledge of the country. Cecil's organising that, too. Leaves nothing to chance.'

'No.'

'Thinks to remove me from court for a while,' Dudley said.

'Surely not.'

'Doesn't realise that a man who brings to his Queen such an irrefutable symbol of her royal heritage… something which bestows upon her monarchy's most mystical aura. That man… he may expect his reward.'

He was not smiling.

'It isn't a quest for the Holy Grail,' I said.

'Maybe not for you. But for me… possibly.'

Dudley was gazing out, in noble profile, across the broad water, then up at the sky where a buttermilk moon bided its time.

VII

Awe and Stupor

ALTHOUGH I DON'T consider myself sensitive to such intrusions, that night it was as if I were not alone in my library.

It happens. Oft-times I'll hear a scraping of paper, as if the books are conversing amongst themselves. The sound of knowledge being shared and expanding in the air. Or a faint clarion of bells – distant, yet somehow within the room itself, as if proclaiming the nativity of an idea. Oh, I'm fanciful, you might think. But what *I* think is that science must never become dull and roped to rigid formulae, but must always be alive to the omnipresent *otherness* of things.

This night, sitting at my work board under two candles, a cup of small beer at my elbow, I'd thought to work on my creation theory, an attempt to explain precisely, concisely and *mathematically* the origins and composition of our universe… and how we might have commerce with the hidden influences which govern it.

But then caught myself thinking of our lost housekeeper, Catherine Meadows, and the times I'd wished I lay with her, that we might find warmth and consolation in one another, for Catherine looked a gentle girl who would not…

Oh dear God, what am I become?

Dr Dee trades with demons!

'John.'

I almost cried out, in my shame. My mother was standing in the doorway, holding a candle in a tin tray, her face turned to vellum in its light. She wore an old grey robe over her nightgown.

'Sometimes,' she said, 'I like not the way our neighbours look at us.'

Candlelight shadows bounded over the walls of books and manuscripts and the globe made for me by my friend and tutor, Gerard Mercator. Logs shifted on the fire. I sat up.

'Which neighbours? Not Goodwife Faldo?'

'No, they're... not people I know by name. Do you not notice the looks we get?'

I thought of the men who'd stared at me in the tavern where I'd been in search of Jack Simm. And of what he'd said. I wanted to say something reassuring and could only think of Cecil's offer to have my mother guarded – knowing what her reaction would be.

'I don't want it. I have to live here. I don't want us to be seen as... strange.' My mother came into the room and shut the door behind her. 'I thought it would all be different, when you were given the rectorate of Upton-upon-Severn.'

'That was a long time ago.'

'Not so very long.'

'Mother, it was another era. The boy Edward was king, Seymour was protector, the Act against witchery was withdrawn, I was—'

'Untainted,' my mother said, 'by rumour.'

'Unknown,' I said. 'I was unknown then, there's the difference.'

There's ever been a thin line 'twixt fame and notoriety.

Couldn't deny that the eighty pounds a year for Upton had been useful, but I was never going to be a minister of the church. The cure of souls – the very idea of such responsibility was terrifying to me.

'I don't know what you do,' my mother said, in a kind of desperation. 'I no longer understand what you do.'

'I study. Collect knowledge. Calcule.'

Couldn't see her expression, but I could feel it. Must needs do better.

'Studying mathematics' – I closed my book – 'I've become aware of universal patterns. Ordered patterns, which I feel could enjoin with something within us. Allowing us to... change things. I hope eventually to understand something of why we are here. To know, in some small way, God's purpose—'

'How does that change *my* life? Who *pays* you to know of these things?'

I closed my eyes. She was right. The Queen had oft-times spoken of making my situation more formal, but nothing ever happened. No income, no title, not even the offer of a new rectorate. Men had been awarded knighthoods or peerages and estates for smaller services than my work on navigation, while I was yet a commoner.

But, then, who honours a conjurer?

I should not feel bitter. What was a title worth? It made you known to the world in ways I care nought for, only wanting to be left alone to get on with my work. Although, yes, I agree that it would have been pleasant not to have to worry about money.

'Please thank the Secretary for his concern for me,' my mother said, 'but assure him that I shall be quite secure here.'

'You don't think that. You said—'

'I've never lived *entirely* without servants. Indeed, I'd thought you'd be married by now, and there'd be another woman here to—'

'Mother—'

'Still… perchance the very fact that you are *not* here… will make the difference.'

'Yes,' I said softly. 'Maybe it will.'

The candlelight flickered like soft lightning on my coloured charts of the planets, glimmed in my hourglass, brought the eyes of the owl to life. I felt like a man hanging onto a stunted tree bent over an abyss. No firm situation, no wife, no siblings. No family but my poor mother, who only wished for me to be a normal man, and respected as such.

'Don't stay up too late,' my mother said. 'You're not *so* young any more.'

+

The cats. Maybe the rustling in the shelves had been the cats, who liked to prowl the library when I was working here.

Or maybe it was the matter of Arthur, calling to me. I sighed, put away my cosmology and reopened the collected manuscripts of Giraldus Cambrensis.

Gerald of Wales, a respectable chronicler who had travelled widely in these islands and attempted accurate descriptions of what he found there. You might almost have thought that Gerald was present himself when the discovery was made of the bones of Arthur at Glastonbury in 1191, such was the detail.

The thigh bone, when put next to the tallest man present,
as the abbot shewed us, and placed on the ground by
his foot, reached three inches above his knee. And the
skull was of a great, indeed prodigious capacity, to the
extent that the space betwixt the brows and betwixt
the eyes was a palm's breadth. But in the skull there
were ten or more wounds which had all healed into
scars, with the exception of one which had made a great
cleft and seemed to have been the sole cause of death.

Gerald probably was not there when the bones were uncovered, but it seemed unlikely that he could have invented any of this. It was a report. The bones had been shown to him. The bones were real. But whose?

If, perchance, I was able to bring some of them back here, to examine them closely, it would be possible to determine something of their antiquity.

I read of the inscription upon the cross which had been found above the remains.

Hic iacet sepultus inclitus Rex Arturius in Insula Avalonia.
Here lies buried the renowned King Arthur in the Isle of Avalon.

Succinct enough, but a little too perfect. I had seen it suggested that the description 'King' Arthur had not been in use at the time of the burial. It was also in Latin, when it would surely have been more convincing in old Welsh.

The cross might, however, have been put into the earth long after the burial, to mark the place rather than as a memorial. It was possible. Anything was possible.

For, truly, I did not want this to have been a deception. Knowing, all the same, that I could not turn away from any evidence of fabrication.

Unless commanded to?

Dear God, what a wasps' nest this was. I turned to *The History of Kings of Britain* by the less-reliable Geoffrey of Monmouth and the account of Arthur's final battle with his treacherous nephew, Mordred.

Geoffrey claims this happened in Cornwall, with much mortality on both sides.

After which, Arthur is conveyed to the Isle of Avalon, for his wounds to be *cured*.

Geoffrey's tales are powerfully inspiring, yet anyone with a knowledge of the histories can see that he can't be trusted. We recognise, elsewhere in his text, stories from other sources – Nennius, for instance, and the old ballads of Wales. Tales previously unrelated to Arthur. As if Arthur is an all-purpose hero who may be borrowed to fight the Saxon or the Romans or whoever would most please the writer's patron. Malory, as I recall, chose the Spaniards.

I moved on to some manuscripts in French, early translations of Geoffrey, and then to Maistre Wace's account, *Roman de Brut*, which follows Geoffrey's tales but mentions – probably for the first time – the round table, at which all knights sat as equals. Seeds here of the chivalry, so beloved of Dudley.

Then came upon what seemed to be the first English account, by Layamon, a priest of Worcester – a telling of Arthur's passing, as from the King himself.

> *And I will travel to Avalon, to the fairest of all maidens…*
> *the most beautiful of the spirit-folk and she shall make*
> *all my wounds sound and make me whole with healing*
> *medicines, and then I will come to my kingdom and dwell*
> *with the Britons with great joy…*

And then came this:

> *The Britons still believe that he is alive, living in*
> *Avalon with the fairest of the spirit-folk and they*
> *will continue to expect Arthur to come back.*
> *There is no man born… who can say for certain*
> *anything else about Arthur. But there was once a*
> *wise man whose name was Merlin. He said in these*
> *words – and his words were true – that an Arthur*
> *should yet come to help the English.*

Note that phrase: *an* Arthur. As if Arthur was a guise to be donned like some magical armour.

As if Arthur *was* Britain. It was clear where the Queen's grandfather, Henry Tudor, had found his inspiration.

I heard again the mild tones of Sir William Cecil: *You are her... her Merlin, shall we say?*

A status which I could hardly yet aspire to live up to. If any man had ever achieved commune with angelical spheres it surely had been Merlin. So had this been absurd flattery from Cecil, or a touch of subtle irony? For had not the Italian, Polydore Vergil, some twenty-five years ago, made ridicule of Geoffrey of Monmouth, as good as accusing him of inventing the Arthurian tales?

I let it lie and turned finally to a modern work. John Leland, the travelling antiquarian, had spent time in Glastonbury during Harry's reign, having been charged by Thomas Cromwell with cataloguing England's ancient wealth but, in the end, more taken with charting. I'd read all of Leland's *Itinerary* years earlier but, having no pressing interest in this remote town at the time, must have missed what now came up at me like a piercing ray of light.

> *I was a few years ago at Glastonbury in Somerset,*
> *where the most ancient and at the same time most*
> *famous monastery in our whole island is located.*
> *I had intended, by the favour of Richard Whiting,*
> *abbot of that place, to refresh my mind, wearied*
> *with long study, when a burning desire to read*
> *and learn aflamed me afresh...*

A dampness in my palms like to the alchemical dew, for I knew that desire.

> *I straightway went to the library, which is not open*
> *to all, in order to examine most diligently all the*
> *relics of most sacred antiquity...*

Leland. Dear God, how could I have forgotten this?

Scarcely had I crossed the threshold when the mere
sight of the most ancient books took my mind with
an awe and stupor of some kind, and for that reason
I stopped in my tracks...

And it was all there. Geoffrey of Monmouth's Life of Merlin. Records of St Patrick who was fabled to have spent time in Glastonbury. Had not Leland been dead these seven years or more, I should have sought him out, for I knew of his fascination with Arthurian matters and my own twin callings of astrology and alchemy. And yes, it made sense that this oldest and wealthiest of abbeys should possess unrivalled accounts of the wisdom of the ages.

Awe and stupor. Christ, I knew this feeling so well, and the tingle it aroused in me felt near to sinful. What if elements of this library yet survived in the town?

Another reason, beyond the bones of Arthur, to venture there.

I stilled my heart through a steadying of breath and laid my head upon an arm on the boardtop, all thoughts calmed now by a quiet joy, choosing not to dwell on the fact that, for several years before his death, John Leland had been mad.

✠

A barn owl shrilled close to the window, and I lifted my head into air that seemed scented, for a moment, with summer roses.

A candle guttering.

Must have fallen asleep across the board.

And dreamed. For some time now, I've kept diaries of my dreams to look back on, years hence, to see what they might have foretold, what patterns they revealed.

I would set down no record, however, of this one, having dreamed of fair-haired Catherine Meadows, all naked in my arms in her pallet; who, when I gently brushed aside her hair, had become...

I stared, wide-eyed, into the frail flame, horrified at the pressure within my hose. Dear God... in my arms in all her majesty? Two hours in the dangerous company of Robert Dudley, and what am I become?

Shook myself, tried to smile. Deciding that my phantasy woman had only turned into the Queen because the Queen, more than any woman, was so far beyond the likes of me. As far beyond as Guinevere was to Merlin. And therefore, in my sorry state, safe to entertain in dream.

One of the cats was brushing my ankles and in my head the Queen still laughed, punching my arm, ginger curls on white forehead.

Are you yet equipped to call upon the angels, John?

Only in my imagination, shaped by the reading of a thousand books and manuscripts, the absorption of others' thoughts, others' ideas, others' divine inspiration. Equipped, in truth, for little. I wished that Dudley had bothered to snatch a copy of the peacock man's pamphlet so that I might at least know what visions I was supposed to be having.

The last log had died in the fireplace, and the room was as cold as a dungeon. Was a sudden cold not an indication of the impending appearance of an unquiet spirit?

Only in my dreams. Some were endowed with abilities like to the angels and some could see the dead. But not me.

I brought the base of my left fist down on the board to scare away the numbness in the arm on which I'd lain my head and to fragment the dangerous pictures lodged therein.

Dudley was right.

If the bones of Arthur were to be found upon the Isle of Avalon, then *we* must find them.

VIII

Without the Walls

ONCE YOU'VE SMELLED roasting flesh – human meat – you never forget it.

Oh, I've seen men burn. Held there by the frenzy of the crowd when all I wanted was to be far away. Seen the hideous moment of hell's halo, when the hair catches frizzling fire and the mob's fever explodes with a great bull-roar and a score of pickpockets make their move.

But even the sight of that horror has faded in the mind's eye before the smell departs the nostrils... a smell of throat-searing sweetness which seemed to find me again this day, as I was shown in by one of the canons.

Shown not, this time, to the bishop's sumptuous receiving room, but to a small, stone-walled chamber down amongst the servants' quarters at his East London palace.

'Welcome,' Bonner said, 'to my cell.'

He'd always laughed a lot, this roly-poly priest, who'd sent so many to the stake in the darkest of Mary's days. Once a lawyer, a clever man, a worldly man, now... what?

There was a single high, barred window, a low and narrow bed – little more than a pallet. A chest with a ewer and looking glass. A bookshelf high on the wall bearing maybe twenty volumes. A chair and board, a jug and a stoneware cup, and the sweetness I could smell... was probably wine.

He gestured me to the only chair, lowering himself to a corner of his bed. Clad this day like to a friar in humble brown habit, and yet the girdle of his robe had cloth-of-gold strands within it which drew the light betwixt the iron bars.

'What's this place, Ned?'

'Purgatory!' A great fart of laughter exploding out of him. 'Preparation, my boy. Getting into practice.'

'But you—'

'Marshalsea, I gather. I've been before. Could be worse. Could be the Fleet.'

'Why don't you just swear the oath? You're no enthusiast for Rome.'

'No, indeed,' Bonner said.

'And the Queen… you don't dislike her, do you?'

'Admire her enormously, John.'

'And she's made her concession. She's not *head* of the Church of England, merely its supreme governor. There's no persecution, Catholics can still worship, there are private masses in country houses and nobody's been executed for it since she's been Qu—'

'Get thee behind me Satan!'

Bonner bouncing to his feet, pudgy forefinger outstretched. Then he plopped down again, dissolving into giggles and looking around his simulation of a cell with something approximating to a perverse delight. I wondered, for a moment, if perchance he was dying of some malady and knew it, yet he appeared in his usual rude health.

'So…' He beamed. 'Your message says you're come to speak with me about Queen Mary and King Arthur.'

'I am.'

Told him about my mission to Glastonbury. Told him nearly the whole of it, more than I'd told my own mother.

How could I confide in him thus, you ask? This man who, as the Catholic Bishop of London, had threatened and bullied and brow-beaten and choked the city's air with the greasy smoke of religion gone bad, leaving what once had been men in small piles of twitching, blackened limbs. How could I trust this monster? God help me, I don't *know*. Yet trust him I did.

When I'd finished, Bonner sat there nodding slowly, hands placidly enfolded across his not-inconsiderable gut.

'Tell me,' he said at last. 'Young Dudley. Is it true he's dicking the Queen?'

'I've never asked,' I said.

'No.' Bonner smiled, with affection. 'You are the only man in the realm who, yet being close to the boy, would not ask.'

He observed me for a few moments, then threw up his hands.

'All right, yes, there *was* a petition to Mary. Not calling for the restoration of Glastonbury Abbey, as such, merely asking for the site and what remained of the buildings to be handed over to a group of monks. Therefore it *might* have been done at almost no expense... and I believe it had the support of more than one bishop, as well as many of the gentlefolk of Somersetshire, if only because it would have planted the seeds of a recovery.'

'So why didn't Mary—?'

'Hard to say, John. Maybe the Privy Council was against it. Or maybe if Mary had lived longer it might've happened. After all, the place was a treasure house of saintly remains, not all lifted by Cromwell, and that's not something which someone as devout as Mary could easily overlook.'

'Was mention made of the bones of Arthur?'

Bonner's eyes widened.

'If it was, then someone was not thinking.'

'I don't understand.'

'The bones of even a Celtic saint would be holy relics. Was Arthur a saint?'

'Better than that,' I said, 'in the eyes of some.'

'No, no, *no.*' His head shaking. 'What does Arthur represent but... magic... enchantment? The king who does not die but waits in some misty spiritual realm until he shall be summoned? Ferried in a barge to Avalon by beautiful black-clad totties? A fine legend for Henry Tudor, when he needed to involve the Welsh, but can you not see poor little Mary shuddering?' Bonner leaning forward, hissing. 'The S-word, John, the S-word.'

Sorcery. I thought about Mary – a kindly woman at heart, everyone said that, but her religious stronghold had been kept high and firm around her, patrolled by guard-dogs like Bonner. However, it had become clear quite early in our relationship that Bonner, who had publicly professed a hatred of all sorcery, in fact found wizards far less noxious than Lutherans. For did not magic lie at the heart of the Roman Church?

'But what about the abbey's place in the very foundation of Christianity in these islands. Joseph of Arimathea, the boy Jesu… the Holy Grail.'

'God forbid, John! Nobody of *any* church cares for that one. Even the Lutherans will demand where it may be found in the Bible.'

'You happen to know any significant names from the monks' petition to Mary?'

'I never saw it.'

'Nobody you can think of in Somersetshire?'

'There are men I can *think* of, but they may not be the main proponents. I'm sorry, John, this was never a big issue for Mary. It went quiet very quickly and was never raised again. I rather suspect this has been a wasted journey for you, though a great pleasure for me. I'm *so* glad I didn't have you roasted.'

'You just wanted to know about alchemy, you old bastard. You thought I had the secrets.'

☩

My own position had still been fraught in the extreme that memorable day when Bishop Bonner had bustled into my cell.

Casting horoscopes for Mary and her husband, who would be King of Spain, had not, with hindsight, been the wisest of undertakings, but she'd not long been enthroned at the time, and none of us could have known how bad it would all become and how swiftly.

Nearly five years now, since I'd been arrested to appear on charges of *the lewd and vain practices of calculating and conjuring*. A fine May morning. My quarters sealed off and searched, my books taken away as evidence of a dangerous interest in the techniques of sorcery and witchcraft.

Don't know why I'd thought that this would never happen to me. Many of my associates had already fled the country in fear of an indictment for heresy or treason. Anyone, at this time, might be seen as a threat to the reintroduction of the Roman Church to England and I, as a known conjuror, was an obvious target for all those at court who would win some favour with Mary.

Therefore, on the evidence of the horoscopes – which included one for Elizabeth, whose very existence was a threat to Mary's rule – I'd been taken away and thrown into prison. It seemed like madness. Apart from anything, my forecast had been a good one for Mary and Philip of Spain, with Libra rising on the day of the marriage, promising well for their union. And no, before you ask, I *don't* know what went wrong.

The practice of astrology, even then, was not the strongest of evidence for devilry. The charge was enough to hold me for a time, but they knew they'd need more to take me to the stake.

There had followed some loose accusations that I'd tried to kill the Queen by sorcery. But there had been no real evidence that I'd ever used spells, black or white.

Then came a down-at-heel lawyer called George Ferrers, whose finest moment had come during his period as the Lord of Misrule, planning London's Christmas festivities, introducing his company of jesters and 'magicians', who specialised in illusion and festive fakery. Somehow, the merry custom had survived even into the drab and humourless years of Mary's reign.

So Ferrers, of a sudden, steps up and accuses me of blinding one of his children and trying to kill another, some kind of magical assassin for hire. It might have been out of jealousy. He would have heard of my flying beetle, my owls. Either that or someone had paid him to have me stitched up.

The point of defence being that I didn't know the man – or his children.

'Even though you conducted your own defence with some aplomb,' Bonner recalled, 'the judges would not have wanted to be seen to extend leniency to someone who might well be in league with the devil.'

'Thanks.'

Although the charges against me had been ridiculous and ill-founded, breaking them down, in public, into shards of malice had not been easy, and I'd been in a sweat at the end, awaiting a verdict.

And when it came at the end of August of the year 1555, it had not been good. I was to be bound over to keep the peace until Christmas of the following year, stripped of the rectorate of Upton-upon-Severn and – the most sinister aspect – to be sent for *religious investigation* to Bishop Bonner himself.

A burning matter.

✝

He'd come in person to my cell, with a question. Signalling the guard to leave us alone.

'Tell me, Dr Dee… do you believe that the soul is divine?'

Friendly, even then. It wasn't until much later that I discovered he'd been interested in me and what I did for quite some while.

I'd given his question serious thought before replying. It was obviously a trap. If I agreed that the soul was divine I would put myself in God's stead. If I said no, I was challenging His Majesty, so would needs be in league with the devil. Either answer could lead to the stake.

'The soul is… not itself divine,' I said after tense and endless seconds, 'but it can *acquire* divinity.'

His eyes had connected with mine and in them, at this moment, I thought I could see the flicker of an unexpected delight.

And then it had vanished.

'Tell me, then, Doctor, how can the soul acquire divinity?'

I held the gaze. Surmising by now that he had been briefed to look for any theological indications of a Protestant allegiance. That surely was what it had all been about. Mary's people were looking for a plot, with Elizabeth at its centre.

'By prayer,' I said. 'And suffering. And perchance… through learning.'

'And what learning would you suggest?'

'The Bible…' I could see that he wanted more and I'd taken a chance. 'And the sacred knowledge of the Jews.'

He'd been unable, then, to conceal his interest, drawing in a sharp breath.

'And how could one become privy to such secrets?'

In the months that followed, many a long candle had been melted into a pool of wax over this question. I'd expected a butcher and found a man with a genuine sense of inquiry into the condition of the human soul.

Saved from the stake by Bonner's interest in the hidden, and an unexpected friendship had developed. Even made me his chaplain, for a time, and many nights had been spent in discussion of alchemy and the Cabala.

✝

I stood and walked over to the chest and picked up the looking glass. Saw a pale man with mid-length dark brown hair and, in the eyes, what some had seen as kindness, others as sorrow and I, now, as… *lost.*

'Tell me, Ned… as a man who hears things…'

'I'm growing increasingly and wilfully deaf, John.'

'Have you become aware of any rumours of sorcery… against the Queen?'

'What, like yours against Mary?'

Bonner's laughter was like collapsing masonry.

'In the shape of a wax effigy in a coffin. Done with some attention to detail. Do you know of anyone, or any group, which might seek to…?'

'What are you getting at, sorcery or popery? The French don't fear sorcery as we do. If they think it'll get Bess out and Mary Stuart in, they'll use it with abandon.'

'Did I mention the French?'

'It's *always* the fucking French. They hate her with a passion. And with Scotch Mary wed to the boy king… Look, talk to a Frenchman, he'll tell you the English Queen's a witch. Like mother like daughter. Spawn of Satan. England, under Elizabeth, is therefore a cesspit of sorcery.'

'Who believes *that?*'

'You mean you *don't?*' Bonner half rose. 'You're telling me there hasn't been an unimaginable increase in superstition – charms, talismans, fortune-telling, what-have-you, since we stopped burning people? Since little Bess decided to live and let live?'

'Ned, that's simply—'

'No less than the unwaxed truth! Cannot believe a man of your peculiar talents goes around with his eyes shut. It's everywhere, John. That's not, of course, to say that the common folk in England don't live in constant *fear* of it… but that's part of the spell. And therefore anything which links the Queen into *that* world – little effigies, what you like – ain't good. And that's why she shouldn't be meddling with the faerie myths of Arthur. You go and tell her that.'

'I'm not being given the chance.'

'Of course –' Bonner beamed – 'she shouldn't be meddling with the likes of you, *either.*'

'Um…' I'd had enough. 'Doesn't the French court have its *own,* um, interpreter of the hidden?'

'Who? Nostradamus? Good Catholic, and a prophet in the Old Testament tradition. The French are in morbid thrall to his every word – and prophets in general, since their last king's untimely death was forecast in detail.'

I'd never met Nostradamus, a physician by trade, whose sudden, spectacular fame as a prophet seemed largely founded upon his adoption by the French court and the pretentious use of poetry in his predictions. However, although his use of astrology was perfunctory and inaccurate, I'd felt obliged to keep notes on his career and had, in my library, several of his almanacs and a few actual manuscripts I'd bought quite cheaply in Louvain, where the man had been regarded with an academic disdain.

Bonner leaned back. He looked happy.

'You know, John… I intend to enjoy prison. Time and a place to attone, through prayer, for all that I've done which has offended God. Prayer and silence. And self-denial.'

'Self-denial?' I lifted the jug from the board and sniffed. I was not an expert on fine wines.

'Word of advice,' Bonner said. 'Let the bones of Arthur lie. They've ever been trouble.'

'I don't truly think I have a choice.'

'As for Glastonbury, they say that, since the abbey went down, it's like to the Bedlam… only without the walls.'

The mirror rattling on the chest as Bishop Bonner's merriment came crackling back, a firing of dry kindling.

IX

Called into Service

By the end of that day, another warning beacon had been lit. One which was to worry me no small amount.

Mid-afternoon, I'd gone again to Jack Simm, asking if he and Goodwife Faldo might keep an eye on my mother while I was away. Once again, with a finger to his lips and a thumb gestured towards his wife in the house, he led me from his door. Out to the edge of the woodland, tinted pale green now with the first hesitant catkins.

'How long you gonna be away, Dr J?'

'Three weeks? Four? Jack, are we losing our reason? My mother says people around the village give us strange looks, you tell me there are suspicions of necromancy. *Am I—?*'

'Nah, you're just too clever for your own good. We all suffer from the times we live in. Seen too much conspiracy.'

'There are even those who'd profit from my notoriety,' I said. Telling him of the pamphlet-seller with his 'Prophecies of Dr Dee'. 'You heard of this?'

'Nah, but it's bound to happen. There's ever an appetite for prediction, even if it's unlawful now. Even astrology's unlawful, if it's used to make predictions about the Queen, ain't that right?'

'When it may become treason, yes.'

'Unless it's you, of course.'

'So it would seem.'

'Fine line, Dr John.'

'I know it.'

I leaned against an oak tree's rugged bole. The pamphleteer in his peacock hat already merging in my mind with an image of George Ferrers, the Lord of Misrule, as some insane jester with a jingly horned hat and a stick with a dangling pine-cone. When I told Jack Simm there were people in that crowd who'd have bound me to a stake without a second thought, he seemed not at all surprised.

'Look – religion's in disarray. For many ordinary folk the only certainty's bleedin' Satan. You got conjurers everywhere, and they operates a secret trade.'

'But –' was Bonner right about this? – 'not so secret as it was?'

Jack bent and picked up a blackened acorn.

'I let my shop go, when they put it round I was dispensing love potions. Old men'd come in saying they'd heard as how the powdered horn of a ram could harden their cocks. "Then why'n't you go and bleedin' powder one?" I'd say, and they'd look at their boots and mumble about how it needed *somefing else*… You see? That's the fine line *I* wasn't gonna cross.'

He looked around but, apart from rooks and ravens, we were well alone. Came and stood before me in a sodden heap of last year's leaves.

'When you was accused of attempting to murder Queen Mary by dark arts, that was horseshit. But it *can* be done, can't it?'

'Murder by magic? There's precedent.'

I walked a tight circle around a birch sapling, thinking of Henry, Lord Neville, the son of the Earl of Westmorland, who, twelve or so years earlier, had been accused of conspiring to murder his wife and his father by magical means, to obtain his inheritance and pay his gambling debts. Having, it was said, hired an experienced sorcerer, a man well qualified in magic and medicine. And I was thinking, also, of the women who, it was said, could lay down a death-spell, inscribed in blood and sped on its way by days of dark meditation and self-denial – the *black fast*.

'I think…' I hesitated. 'I *believe* the mind is a powerful tool which can unlock doors into the unknown. And thus awaken energies which can be directed, to cause both benefit and… and harm. But if you ask me can *I* do these things…?'

Turning away, feeling, for all my years of study, my knowledge and my practical inventions, worthless and without substance.

'Master.'

I spun round. She was standing on the edge of the path, looking like some woodland sprite.

'*Catherine...*' She was wrapped in one of my mother's shawls. 'You're back?'

'My ma's has been to talk to your... to Mistress Dee. All's quite well now, Doctor.'

Her face was dark, like a bruised apple. I wondered if there'd been a rift with her puritan father over this.

'Please, the mistress says can you come home at once. You've a visitor.'

'Who?'

Becoming tense.

'Someone from court.' Catherine Meadows gave Jack a tentative smile. 'Master Simm.'

'There you go,' Jack whispered to me, as she turned away onto the path. 'You can leave on your mission with no anxiety.'

'Yes,' I said. 'Thank you, Jack.'

No anxiety. Of course not.

✝

Five horses were tethered in our yard, and I saw four armed men standing by the gate, and thought at once of the day my rooms had been searched and sealed and...

Take him.

Almost turning and walking away then, to buy time, before I recognised two of the men from the Queen's company, and one gave me a respectful salute. Me nodding and breathing again.

Only the four of them, so it could not be someone of particular eminence. Other than the Queen herself, there are few people at court I feel safe to trust.

Hurrying inside, past the fire in the hall, I found them in the parlour overlooking the river: two women of similar age, seated by the window, sharing a platter of sweetmeats.

'Cousin?'

'Good afternoon, Dr Dee,' Blanche Parry said. 'I am come to collect the books.'

Remaining seated. Her dark clothing almost nun-like.

'But I thought... that I was to bring them. The books?'

'More discreet, it is, for me to take them from you.'

A small voice, yet oddly pitched, so that it carried like pipes.

I call her cousin, yet am not sure precisely how we're related.

'You've ridden here from Richmond… just for the books?'

'It were best,' Blanche said, 'that you were not seen too often at court.'

'The Queen thinks that?'

'It's best.'

I felt a chill. Looked into her small, shrewd eyes, fine lines around them. It was my tad who, with an uncommon prescience, had advised me years ago that our kinship with Mistress Blanche would one day prove an asset, and it was true that the Queen's most senior gentlewoman had known Elizabeth since she was a babe. Had access, more than anyone, to the innermost sanctum.

I said. '*You* think I should keep a distance.'

My mother frowned at such disrespect, but Blanche's expression remained constant. *Constant* was Blanche's watchword.

'I merely suggest,' she said, 'that it were better for the Queen if your dealings were to remain discreet. You tend to question things too much, Dr Dee.'

'One of my failings.'

'You must excuse my son, Mistress Blanche,' my mother said quickly. 'I sometimes think that John is only ever half in this world and half in some dark place of his own complicated imaginings. Not at all healthy, to my thinking.'

I pulled up a stool, my complicated imaginings telling me that this visit was about more than books.

'As you, more than anyone, would be aware, Mistress Blanche,' I said, 'the Queen's a most intelligent woman, who's been reading manuscripts in Greek since she could barely—'

'And I thought *you* an intelligent *man,* Dr Dee,' Blanche snapped, 'who would realise that it were best that the Queen should not be seen to be inquiring too deeply into certain areas of learning.'

I fell silent. My mother arose.

'Please excuse me, Mistress Blanche. I shall prepare a warm drink before your journey back to Richmond. Also for your men.'

'Thank you.' Blanche looking up, a distant smile like a mist upon her face. 'It has been good to see you again, Jane.'

My mother nodding and slipping away. Me sensing a prearrangement here, as Mistress Blanche gestured me to my mother's chair next to the river window.

'I'm informed, Dr Dee, that you're to perform a service for Sir William Cecil.'

'So it would appear.'

'He's a good man, for whom the Queen's interests are always central.'

'Indeed. His constant concern for the Queen is like to an older brother's.'

'And with you to Somersetshire… also goes Lord Dudley?'

'A man whose support for the Queen –' I watched her eyes – 'is equally beyond question.'

'But whose reputation is, if anything, even worse than yours,' my cousin said. 'If for different reasons.'

'You don't dice your words, do you, Mistress Blanche?'

I pushed my chair back towards the window. A tired sun hung over the river in a cradle of stringy cloud. Obviously, Dudley's relations with Elizabeth, on whatever level, would be a source of anxiety to Blanche, even though it was said she had oft-times passed intimate letters from one to the other.

However, as the women with whom Dudley had been intimate must by now outnumber the wherries on the Thames, his reputation was no more the reason Blanche Parry was here than to collect the books on Arthur.

✝

One thing you should know about men and women of the border – any border – is that they ever use the small and narrow roads, and it can take an endless time before their reasons are manifest. Something embedded in their nature, relating to a need for caution with strangers. Along the border of England and Wales, even quite close relatives can be strangers through many generations, and I was resigned to a lengthy and, for the most part, aimless preamble.

'Even apart from his adventures with women,' Blanche Parry said, 'Dudley is deemed by some to be ungodly.'

'What?'

'For his study of the stars and similar interests. And... for his choice of friends.'

'I see,' I said. 'You mean me. Dear God, Blanche... are we not supposed to live now in enlightened times? My studies follow on directly from the work of Pythagoras and Plato, Hermes Trismegistus... Distinguished scholars, all of them.'

'And heathens.'

'Oh, for—'

'Wait.' Blanche holding up a palm, small fingers spread wide. 'Are there not Catholics who say that the Protestant Church is itself a form of heathenism?'

'Well, yes, there are, but that's only to be—'

'The *Queen*... the Queen, as you know, she seeks, if not a middle road, then at least a calmer situation, where each man may worship in his own way so long as he keeps the details of it betwixt himself and God. And within reason.'

Grey cloud was turning the Thames into the Styx, and I felt my patience ebb.

'Mistress Blanche, you're evidently not just here to sample my mother's famous pastries. What is it you wish to say to me that Cecil hasn't already said?'

'I...' My cousin looking, for the first time, uncertain. '... I'm here to ask that when you report from the West Country to Sir William Cecil, you'll bear in mind the Queen's situation – and our kinship – and report also to me.'

This I had not expected. I was wondering how to proceed without the use of the word *why?* when she came quickly back at me, all the Welshness in her pouring through now apace, words tumbling like mountain water over bedrocks.

'...because Sir William, as you well know, is a pragmatist who will not permit whatever faith he has to interfere with his political judgement. You're aware of that, we all are, but the Queen, she is ever troubled over what may be right or wrong in the eyes of God and feels a weight of responsibility, not only to her father's legacy and what he would wish of her, but to her subjects, all of them, whom she loves, every man and woman, like her children.'

'Yes.'

There was indeed a complexity of responsibilities here, to which no previous monarch would have felt the need to respond. Yes, we *were* moving, if more slowly than I would have wished, towards a new enlightenment, and yes the Queen was determined to be an essential part of that process, and yet…

'Mistress Blanche.' It was time to meet this good woman halfway. 'Let me try to identify your dilemma. The question of the Arthurian succession is potentially a more complicated issue now than it was in the days of the Queen's grandfather—'

'When there was but one Church,' she said.

'The roots of the Arthurian history or legends go beyond all that. May well be pre-Christian. Is this what you're approaching?'

'Your family and mine,' she said, 'have deep roots in Wales, where the old bards sang of Arthur and his deeds in versions of the story which would indeed shock readers of Malory. Furthermore, in the days of the first Henry Tudor, the entrails of religious belief were not laid out and pulled apart for all to interpret, in the way that they are today.'

None of which would matter much to Cecil, unless it should threaten to cause a collapse in the exchequer. This, evidently, was something private. Something unspoken of outside the Queen's immediate chambers. I waited. We were, it seemed, getting there.

'Rumours reach us from abroad,' Blanche said.

'As ever.'

'The Queen has been spending much time with Sir Nicholas Throckmorton, the envoy to Paris.'

'In relation to what?'

Blanche made no reply. I had the suspicion she didn't know. And there wasn't much happening around the Queen that Blanche didn't know.

'In France and Spain,' she said at last, 'the Queen is regarded with suspicion. And also with *superstition*.'

'I know.'

When you spend time in Europe, you have to listen to it. All the support in Catholic-heavy France is for the Queen of Scots, newly wed to the boy king François.

'Relating, principally,' Blanche said, 'to her mother.'

Who'd gone smiling, it was widely said, to her own execution, in anticipation of being soon united with her infernal master. The lips of Anne Boleyn still forming satanic prayers as her head was held up by the swordsman.

The talk of London and a gift to the pamphleteers of Europe, who wondered how long before the result of the unhallowed union 'twixt the Great Furnace and the witch would be called into the service of that same master.

Blanche said, 'In your garden... your orchard... what did the Queen see?'

'I don't understand.'

'I think you do. Before I came to you.' Leaning toward me. 'John, I've seen it before, the way she stiffens, the way her eyes... What did she say to you?'

I was remembering how quickly she'd appeared on the orchard path, wrinkling her nose against the pervading smell of hops as if it were the sulphurs of hell.

'What did she say to you, John?'

'She asked if there were...'

Hares in our orchard. I said nothing.

Blanche waited.

I said, 'I'll take this no further.'

Could almost see my world curling at its corners, like parchment touched with flame. Blanche Parry sat quite still, as if her spirit temporarily had left her body. How long we remained in this awful silence I do not know.

Finally, I said, 'What did you mean you'd seen it before? What happens to her eyes?'

'They see more than they should,' she said. 'Sometimes.'

Blanche's hands seized one another in her lap, as if in a spasm, and I turned away.

'And what, at such times –' so breathless it didn't sound to me like my voice – 'do they see?'

Outside, night's tapestry was already unrolling 'twixt the trees above the river. There was a crocus-bloom of light on the water, the lamp on a wherry.

'I've stayed too long,' Blanche said. 'Send messengers to me, and I'll send them to you, if there's anything...'

'What does she see, Blanche?'

Holding on to the arms of my chair, the darkness at my back, as Blanche whispered it to the wall: how the Queen had said she saw the sanguinous shade of Anne Boleyn at her bedside, that small smile all twisted with spoiled ambition.

PART TWO

It is hardly credible what a harvest, or rather what a wilderness of superstition had sprung up in the darkness of the Marian times. We found in all places votive relics of saints, nails with which the infatuated people dreamed that Christ had been pierced... small fragments of the sacred cross. The number of witches and sorceresses had everywhere become enormous.

John Jewel, Bishop of Salisbury, after a journey
through the west of England, 1559.

X

Relics

ON THE RIM of nightfall, sudden sleet had tossed us, with a stinging contempt, back into the worst of winter. Still some miles to go, and my cloak was a sodden rag.

Dudley, riding ahead, looked out toward middle-distant trees as bare as fishbones and hills still ermine-furred with snow. Then up at the spattering sky and back at me, over his shoulder.

'Can't you *do* anything about this, John? Change the weather? Shift the skies to France?'

He was rearing up from his saddle, and my horse took fright and I leaned forward to calm her. I was better with horses than with women, just about, but Dudley, as usual, made me feel a feeble creature.

Still, I was glad he'd spoken so – a hint of the old Dudley in a man who, since we'd left London, had been uncharacteristically silent, almost reserved. Something on his mind.

There were six of us, including the big northerner Martin Lythgoe. Lythgoe was Dudley's chief groom, a man he'd known all his life, whom he'd taken with him to court.

'Call yourself a magician,' Dudley said.

'I don't.' Bending my head into the blizzard. 'As you know. Can we not find an inn?'

'There isn't an inn. Can *you* see an inn?'

'I can see very little.'

'Is there an inn near here, Carew?' Dudley shouted.

'There *is*.' Sir Peter Carew riding up alongside him. 'But spend the night there and by morning you'd have scratched off your balls. As for this poor fellow...'

Carew glancing back at me, as if unsure whether I possessed balls. He was a stocky and muscular man, older than Dudley by a good twenty years, but his long beard was still as dark and thick as tarred rope.

'Well, perchance we could rest there at least until the sky shows some mercy,' Dudley said. 'Is the food fit to eat?'

'Press on, my advice, you want to reach Glaston tonight. You and I, we've known a fucking site worse than this – *and* with a battle on the morrow.' Carew turned briefly to me, eyes slitted against the sleet. 'I gather you've not served your country as a fighting man, *Doctor*?'

Behind me, Carew's two men were, I suspected, sniggering. I made no response. Could not, in truth, speak, for the cold. As Carew pulled ahead, Martin Lythgoe, the groom, was alongside me, low-voiced.

'Yon bugger's fought for too many countries, you ask me, Dr John.'

Smiled and turned away, urging his horse back on to the whitening road.

✠

My tad had talked of Carew, who'd found favour at Harry's court when little more than a boy. A far-travelled boy, however, who had already seen much action in Europe.

Sent by his father, Sir William, as a page to France after years of truancy and rebellion at his grammar school in Exeter, he'd ended up with the French army and then, after his master was killed, changed sides to join the Prince of Orange. Still only sixteen when he'd returned to England, with letters of introduction from the royalty of Orange to the King. Impressing the Great Furnace with his horsemanship and finding a place, two years later, as a gentleman of the Privy Chamber. *A great individual,* my father had said. *Sir Peter goes his own way.*

Certainly knew his way through the west of England, having risen to become MP for his native Devon and Sheriff of that county. Now he was its senior knight and, as such, wielded power in Somerset, too.

And also – the reason he was with us – Carew was the present owner of Glastonbury Abbey. *Safe pair of hands,* Dudley had assured me. He wasn't sure precisely how the Queen had come to place the holy ruins in Carew's hands, and wasn't sure the Queen knew either. But no one better to keep the papists out.

It was very near dark when we rode at last into the hills above Glastonbury but, by then, the sleet had turned to rain and then ceased, and a fragment of moon was visible, and we soon could see why those pleas for restoration had fallen upon muffled ears.

Carew had told us that, because of its history, a strong Protestant presence at the abbey had been deemed essential. In Seymour's time as Duke of Somerset, it had been given over to a community of Flemish weavers – followers of the insane Protestant John Calvin – who'd set up a flourishing industry within its precincts. Thus had the town's economy been sustained through the years of the boy Edward. But when Mary came to power and the Bishop of Rome was reinstated, through fire and blood, as our spiritual leader, the weavers had fled back to the low countries.

As we rode down the last hillside, the moon's sickle cut through the cloud. In its cold light the abbey was a grey ghost with stony arms raised as if to clutch us to its cracked ribs.

✝

The George Inn, in the well of the town, had been strong-built of stone to accommodate pilgrims of status and must once have blazed with welcoming candlelight. Tonight… well, there must be light in there somewhere, but the ground-floor windows facing the road were as black as hell's privy.

Carew had sent one of his men ahead and, by the time we arrived in the yard at the rear, two boys were on hand to look after the horses we'd ridden from Bristol.

'Cowdray!' Carew bawled out. 'Where the fuck's Cowdray?'

'I'm here, Sir Peter, I'm here.' A man stumbling down from some wooden steps, leaving pale flame hissing from a pitch-torch on a wall-bracket. 'Having fires built for you, sir, the big ovens lit.'

'Why were the bastards not already lit?'

'Sir Peter, we've had no travellers here for a fortnight or more. 'Tis February, man.'

'Told you, didn't I?' Carew turning to Dudley, coughing out a laugh like a pellet of phlegm. 'Arsehole of the west, this town.'

Town? Even though its main street was on the road to Exeter, I'd noticed no more than a dozen buildings of any substance, including a tall-towered church. And the abbey in all its smashed splendour.

'Bring in plenty logs, Cowdray,' Carew said. 'First light tomorrow, I ride to Exeter, but these gentlemen will be staying for several days. This is Master Roberts and Dr John, of the Queen's Commission on Antiquities.'

It had been Cecil's insistence that we should conceal our identities. I was not sorry to obscure mine, but I guessed that Dudley already was feeling naked without his panoply of privilege. At the Bristol inn where we'd spent last night, his mild advances to our chambermaid had been quite scornfully rebuffed. A mere civil servant... small beer.

Carew, however... even in Bristol, Carew had oft-times been recognised. A famous man of the west, it seemed, his legend widely circulated. A favourite tale dated back to his Exeter youth when, escaping school, he'd scaled a turret of the city wall and threatened to jump off if pursued further... his father eventually leading him home, it was said, on a dog-leash.

After we'd dined passably well on broth and mutton, in a small, oak-walled room, Carew summoned the innkeeper.

'Shut the door, Cowdray. Sit the fuck down. We have need of your local knowledge.'

The innkeeper was a bulky man with sparse ginger hair, a good week's uneven growth of beard and the air of one resigned to disappointment. Wiping his hands on his apron, he lowered himself to the end of a settle near the door. Four candles spread a creamy glow over the oak board, and a fragrant wood was burning in the grate – apple logs, I guessed. No shortage of these in the one-time Isle of Avalon.

Carew stood with his arse to the fire, his eyes, under wide black brows, aglitter in the candlelight.

'These good men, Cowdray, are appointed by the Queen to inquire into the disappearance of certain documents and artefacts from the abbey.'

'Bit late now, sir,' Cowdray said, 'if you don't mind me saying.'

'Say what you like to me, but if a word of it gets beyond these walls I'll have this fucking hovel closed down by midweek. We understand each other?'

'We do,' Cowdray said mildly, not appearing too oppressed. 'We always have.'

'Full twenty years since the abbey was removed from the greasy fingers of corrupted monks,' Carew said. 'Now we're in fairly settled days, the Privy Council feels it's time for a reassessment of what remains.'

'Monks are long gone.'

'Good fucking riddance. All of them?'

'Well… mostly gone from the town. They had good pensions, about five pounds a year.'

'What are they now then?'

'One's a farrier. We use him here.'

'A more useful life, certainly,' Carew said.

'And you gets to marry.'

'Everything has its downside.'

Carew glanced at Dudley, who made no response. I'd thought Dudley's marriage was for love, but of course my friend was renowned for having love to spare.

'Might it be worth you speaking with this farrier, Master Roberts?' Carew said.

'Oh, yes.' Dudley shook himself. 'Doubtless we should.'

The points had been lopped from his moustache and his doublet was the colour of a stagnant ditch. As Master Roberts, his clothing must needs be more humble and muted, and it seemed to be constraining his manner. Even at the inn last night his moves toward the chambermaid had been cursory, as if he'd felt no more than obliged to keep topping up the levels of his lust. He sighed, raised himself up and drank some ale.

'This is… not bad.'

'Brewed to a recipe the Flemish weavers brought to us,' Cowdray said. 'Good people, on the whole. Some folk accused 'em of bringing the wool-sorters' disease but, hell, 'twas here before *they* come.'

'Much of that about now?' Carew asked.

'A few deaths. Likely we just notices it more, now all the money's from sheep again. Folk's in fear of the black scabs, but more of starvation.'

'Our understanding, Master Cowdray,' Dudley said, 'is that certain items may have been removed from the abbey by the monks. I'm thinking items that are not necessarily what might be considered treasure. I'm thinking documents – of which Dr D— Dr John has knowledge. Also sacred relics.'

'Many a saint' – Carew was pulling his long black beard into stiffened plaits – 'and many a king has been entombed at that abbey over a thousand years or more. Or so you tell the pilgrims.'

''Tis a fact,' Cowdray told him. 'And many of their relics removed by the King's men.'

'My information,' Dudley said, 'is that some were removed beforehand, in anticipation of the Dissolution of the abbey. It being hardly the first establishment to go. They could see the darkness on the horizon.'

I saw that Cowdray shifted, for the first time uneasy, Carew watching him, head on one side. Carew had been summoned by Cecil and told, in the strictest confidence, what it was that we sought in Glastonbury, but I wondered how much he already knew.

'Look, masters.' The innkeeper slumped back in the settle, head sinking betwixt his shoulders. 'Times are hard for this town. For all of us. A few bad things been done, out of desperation.'

'A town which grew fat on superstition and idolatry in place of honest work can hardly expect much sympathy,' Carew said. 'What bad things were done?'

'Things taken. Stone and lead, mainly. Glass.'

'And?'

'And... that's it. What was *left*. We were given to understand a blind eye...'

Yes. You could see that, once all conspicuous treasures had gone to the Crown, it would be deemed expedient for local people to be permitted, within reason, to help themselves. Thus involving them in the destruction of the abbey. Buying their complicity.

'I'd heard that some fine houses had been built from stone from the abbey,' I said.

'More the case that houses already built were repaired,' Cowdray said.

'Well, that's all over now.' Carew straightened up. 'They've had their pickings. Now it's in my charge, they want stone from there, they'll pay. Or anyone caught stealing masonry might find his knuckles crushed 'twixt two slabs of it on the way out.'

'No-one goes there,' Cowdray said quickly.

'I bet they don't.'

'No,' Cowdray said. 'They don't. Apart from anything, Sir Edmund Fyche hands out a stern sentence to anyone caught taking stone.'

He looked down, one hand rubbing the back of the other. I'd thought of something and was raising myself in my chair, my inner thighs much aching from the ride.

'You said that some of the monks were gone. Where did *they* go?'

'Dispersed. Some to seek sanctuary at those monasteries allowed to continue. And some—'

'Hah.' Dudley smiling at last, if thinly. 'Offering... gifts to these monasteries in return for sanctuary?'

'Relics, you think?' Carew was back at the fireside, easing off his boots. 'A sackful of holy bones? Aye, I suppose that makes a degree of sense.'

'I know naught of that,' Cowdray said. 'And the ones still here, 'part from the farrier, they're all gone to work the land, or teach at the new college.'

A silence.

'College?' Candle flames going horizontal as Carew sprang up. 'What fucking papist shit's this?'

'The college to be started up by the tor,' Cowdray said. 'Nothing papist. Meadwell, Sir Peter. Sir Edmund Fyche's charity?'

'Ah.' Carew subsided, turning to Dudley. 'Fyche was a monk – a bursar – at the abbey. After the Dissolution, an inheritance gave him the wherewithal to establish a farm. Employed a few monks as labour. But a college, now?'

'Where gentlemen's sons may be educated,' Cowdray said. 'The Bishop of Wells gave sanction for it, but nothing—'

'Bourne? He's *gone*. Papist bastard's banged up.'

'He's still in Wells.'

'Not for long,' Carew said. 'He'll be in the Tower by spring.'

And he probably was right. I didn't know Bishop Bourne, but I knew he'd refused, like Ned Bonner, who'd consecrated him, to swear the Oath of Supremacy.

'Nothing papist, though,' Cowdray said. 'Sir Edmund—'

'Is a survivor,' Carew told Dudley. 'Fyche found it expedient to revert to Rome during the last reign, when it looked as if the abbey might live again, but he's a JP now and knows which side of the hearth won't singe his beard. All the same, I'll make a point of inspecting the place when I get back from Exeter.'

And doubtless he would, but I was glad that Carew would be gone from here on the morrow; it would hardly help our inquiries to have him raging around making wild accusations against plans for some entirely legitimate college which just happened to be administered by former monks.

'Need to get some sleep.' He gathered up his boots. 'Cowdray, tell my men we'll leave at seven.'

'I've ordered a brick to be put in your bed, sir.'

'Well, take the fucker out,' Carew said. 'I'm not a woman.'

Cowdray nodded, making for the door, me wondering if Carew would have rejected the hot brick with such alacrity had Dudley and I not been present. I thought not.

✠

'But underneath it all,' Dudley said wearily, 'he's a sound enough man. A solid Protestant.'

He was hunched hard over the fire now. His face looked narrow and starved – this emphasised by the selfless butchery of his moustache.

'From what my father told me of Carew,' I said, 'I'd thought him little more than a mercenary. Perhaps you're right, but it'll still be easier for us to function without him. What's the plan for the morrow?'

'Kicking arses can sometimes cut a few corners. However… I think we'd best begin by surveying what's left of the abbey. Then, if there's a tame ex-monk…?'

'The farrier.'

'Yes. Talk to him.' Dudley shivered. 'I hope the bugger's put bricks in *our* beds. He looked at me. 'What are you thinking, John?'

It was the first time since leaving London that we'd had a chance to talk, and I'd hoped to approach with him the problem of Elizabeth and her mother and the hares. Maybe tomorrow.

'I suppose,' I said, 'I'm thinking, what if this is a wild goose chase? What if the bones are already in London? What if they were taken, on specific instruction, by Cromwell's people, at the time of the Dissolution?'

'We'd know. Or at least Cecil would know.'

'Or if they were simply destroyed?'

'That's more of a possibility. To Fat Harry, they might just have repre-sented some old Plantagenet scheme to demolish the myth of an immortal Welsh hero. Harry might even have seen it as symbolically grinding up any final hopes of a Plantagenet return to the throne. I...' Dudley drew a hand across his forehead, then looked at the sweat on it. 'I don't know, John, I feel... I was seized by the romance of it – the Isle of Avalon, the Grail Quest. But when you see what a shithole the place is...'

'It'll look better in the morning.'

'And now my throat's gone dry and my head aches. All I need's a cold. You were right. We should've stopped at an inn until the storm was over. That *bloody* Carew with his harder-than-thou blether.'

'Get some sleep,' I said.

☩

Because the inn had been empty, we were able to have separate chambers on the upstairs floor, while the attendants were accommodated below. Mine had a ruined four-post bed with one post hanging loose, all acreak, and the drapes so dense with dust that I dragged them down. Close drapery around a bed can be suffocating when you awake in the night from some smoky dream.

I'd brought a few books with me, in my bag, and laid them out on the board before the window – some stained glass in it, I noticed, but it was only a murk in the light from my single candle.

Kneeling before the window, I asked for God's blessing for our mission, then prayed for mother's welfare. Scarce remembered climbing into the bed, dragging the pulled-down drapes across it for more warmth. Hadn't been given a hot brick.

What I next remembered seemed more in the nature of a dream.

Ever responsive to noises in the night, I must have slept no more than an hour when there came the creaking of a door.

Lay for a moment listening, aware of slow footsteps on the stairs, but it was the sliding of bolts that brought me out of bed and across to the window, clutching the drapes around me, for the room had no fire and was shockingly cold now.

The window was next to the inn sign, which bore the red cross of St George, drained to grey by the night. Below me I saw the outline of a man stepping down from the cobbles to the mud. In the thin moonlight, I saw him stand for a moment, leaning back, hands pushing against the bottom of his spine.

Dudley?

On the other side of the street was the abbey wall; beyond it, those great, lonely fingers of stone. After a while, he began to walk along the street, close to the wall until he vanished into shadow. The man of action who, sleeping alone, was restless.

....*a man who brings to his Queen such an irrefutable symbol of her royal heritage... something which bestows upon her monarchy's most mystical aura. That man... he may expect his reward.*

My own reward would be the discovery of any ancient books quietly removed from the abbey and hidden away. Books that Leland had seen, leaving him in a condition of *awe and stupor.* But it was unlikely they'd be secreted within the precincts of the abbey itself.

So I didn't spend long wondering if I should go down and join Dudley. He didn't need me, and I was cold and aching from the ride. John Dee, the conjurer, returned to his musty blankets.

Ever the observer, separated from life by the screen of his own learning.

It was probably fatigue and aching that turned the sudden dread I felt into something as real as another person in my bedchamber.

XI

Delirium

IT WAS LIGHT when I awoke to heavy footsteps and a banging on my door. Before I could speak, it had been thrown wide and Dudley's attendant, Martin Lythgoe, stood there, his wide face creased with anxiety.

'Doctor,' he said. 'Can tha come at once. Me master...'

'What?'

'Took severely ill, sir.'

Me rolling out of bed, forgetting how high it was and stumbling foolishly to my knees. Looking up at the straw-haired Martin Lythgoe from the floorboards.

'Ill?'

'A fever. Sweats and moans and rolls in his bed.'

Should not have been shocked. Had it not been obvious last night that something was coming?

'Have you sent for a doctor?'

'But I thought *thee*...'

He stood looking at me, hands on his hips, like if I was not a healer what was the use of me?

'No.' Groping for my old brown robe. 'I'm not... that is, my doctorate's...'

It was in law, if you must know, another of the pools I'd paddled in. I sighed.

'I'm coming now...'

The door of Dudley's chamber was directly opposite mine across the narrow landing. A bigger room with a bigger window and more stained glass oozing reds and purples.

He was not lying in his bed but sitting hunched on the edge of it, the curtains thrown back. Wrapped in blankets like a sweating horse, hair matted to his forehead.

97

'John.'

Hardly more than a sigh. The piss-pot was on the boards at his feet. A weighty shiver wracked his body, and the eyes turned to me were marbled with fear.

'Lie down,' I said.

'John, get Lythgoe to prepare the horses. If I'm to die, I'm buggered if it's going to happen here.'

'You don't need a horse. You're not going anywhere, Robbie, least of all to the next—'

I stepped back. Of a sudden, he'd bent over the empty piss-pot, hands either side of his head, retched. Looked up betwixt his fingers.

'God's bollocks, John… this task of ours – cursed, or what?'

Rolling back on to his pillow, his back arched, face full-oiled with sweat. Martin Lythgoe throwing mute pleas at me from the doorway. Never, I would guess, having seen his famously elegant master so vulnerable.

And God help me I knew not where to start.

Born under Cancer, Dudley, like me – a water sign and thus ruled by the moon. If I'd had my charts and the necessary hours to spare, I'd no doubt be able to calcule how the planetary aspects might be affecting the organs of his body and the balance of its humours. And if I'd had Jack Simm here, we might, betwixt us, have come up with some remedy. Not for the first time I wished I *was* a doctor of physic.

'When did this begin?'

'Whuh…?'

'I saw you go outside last night.'

'Couldn't sleep.' Dudley was struggling up again, as if he might overcome this malady through strength of will. 'Nose blocked, couldn't breathe. Thought just a head cold. Hadda… gessome air.'

Which would have made it worse, chilled his blood.

'This a plague town, John? Might as well tell me. Has the air of it, no question.'

'Of course it isn't.'

'Just me, then, is it?'

'Lie down.'

'John, that place is… wretched and…'

'What place?'

'...colder than the night. Colder than all the night.'

A shiver coursing through him again, like a bolt of wild lightning, his head nodding, teeth clenched as he hugged himself under the blankets, moisture shining on his flushed cheeks.

Cowdray, the innkeeper, came in with a wooden tray bearing a jug and a cup.

'Cider. Ain't much that good cider don't help.'

Me nodding thanks as Cowdray lowered the tray to a board, next to the ewer of water, backing swiftly away into the doorway – understandable enough: who knew what contagion a Londoner might have brought out of his filthy, overcrowded city?

'Awful dreams, John.' Dudley pulling his hands from the blankets to clutch at his head. '*Awful* bloody dreams.'

'Dreams mean nothing,' I said.

Knowing that to be untrue, although I believe that the meaning of dreams is oft-times obscured.

'If dreams they were,' Dudley said.

'It's the fever.' I turned to Cowdray. 'Is there a doctor here?'

'Used to be,' Cowdray said, 'but he died.'

Dudley laughed sourly into his hands.

'There's a couple of them in Wells, for the cathedral,' Cowdray said. 'Proper doctors. One trained in London. Long cloak, one of them pointy masks and all. I could get one of my boys to ride over. 'Twould... cost you a bit, mind.'

'Cost isn't important.' I looked hard at him. 'But time is. Who do *you* go to?'

'I tries not to get ill, sir.'

'You know what I'm asking.'

His lips tightened. Men from London, he'd be thinking. Who from London could you trust not to have you arrested for the use of alternative healing by witchcraft?

'Sir Peter Carew,' I said. 'Is he...?'

'Gone. Left over an hour ago with his men. Before we knew about Master Roberts.'

'Good. Help me. You wouldn't send all the way to Wells, if someone in your family were sick.'

He made no reply. I poured some of the cider into the cup and gave it a sniff.

'Perhaps you could water this down a little. He's delirious enough already. That's if your water is drinkable.'

Cowdray accepted the jug, stood for a moment looking into the clouded ferment.

'There's a feller we go to. Herbalist and surgeon.'

'Good?'

'We reckon so.'

'How far?'

'Up by St Benignus. Two minutes' walk?'

'What are we waiting for, then?'

+

Well, of course, it would be the local cunning man.

The kind of hedge-healer possessed of an ancestral knowledge of plants and herbs. The kind of practitioner of whom, in London, Jack Simm had been a touch afeared lest he became known as one. Afeared because of the persecution urged upon such people by the beak-nosed piss-sniffers with papers from the Royal College of Physicians.

It would be a safer life, however, for a cunning man out here, where there'd be fewer registered doctors. And also fewer criminals and foreigners to degrade the healing crafts with so-called magical powders ground from stones and animal bones.

I stayed with Dudley, having asked Martin Lythgoe to go with Cowdray to this healer, describe the symptoms and give him whatever money he demanded to come at once. At least I knew enough from my own studies, my astrology and my work with Jack to be able to assess, to some extent, the cunning man's abilities.

'Carew?'

Dudley shifting in his bed, turning hunted eyes to me and trying to rise.

'Gone.' I pushed him gently back. 'Gone to Exeter.'

'Thank Christ for that. He'd think me weak as a woman.'

He began to cough. He'd left most of the watered cider, saying it made him feel sick.

'Women are not all weak, Robbie,' I said. 'I'd expect that you, of all people...'

'I know it.' He rolled onto his side, his face mottled as a cockerel's in the light from the stained glass. 'I *do* know it. Jesu, do I know it. But tell me... you tell me this... how's it possible for someone to rule a country well and keep the ways of a woman?'

'It might help if there's a good man to share the burdens of power.'

I meant Cecil, but Dudley almost cried out.

'Should've been *me*...' His eyes full of hot tears. 'Would've been so *right*. Everything my father died for, John, and if *I* should die this hour...'

'Jesu, you're not—'

He raised a limp hand to forestall me, then closed his eyes and took in a hollow breath. Shut his mouth and tried to swallow, but his throat must have been too dry, and when his eyes flickered open again they were empty, defeated.

'Saw it coming.'

'What?'

'Death coming for me. I'd not expected it so soon, but God knows I deserve no better.'

'So,' I said upon a sigh, 'what does death look like?'

'Old man. A sad old man.'

I said nothing.

'Both feet above the ground, and looking down on me with a terrible pity. And the white moon shining through him. The whiteness aglow in his eyes. And cold, John. So very, very... cold.'

Delirium.

'And he knew, God help me, *he knew what I am.*'

Dudley's hands clutching the blankets, knuckles white as bone. I heard children shouting in the street.

'Fever dream, Robbie.'

'Could see through him.' Dudley gazing, blank-eyed at the beams. 'And he... he *knew.*' Teeth bared now, the breath sucked through them. 'John, I'm no more than a piece of shit.'

'Don't—'

'No! I need to tell you. Make my confession.' His head turning towards me. 'You're an ordained man, are you not, John?'

'No!' I almost leapt back from the bed. 'No, *no...*'

'Bonner's chaplain? Rector of... somewhere.'

'No...' Wiping my hands across the air before me. 'I swore what was necessary to obtain the income from the rectorate of Upton. I do not cure souls, so don't you fucking tell me *anything.*'

'God help me, but she's not been well of late.'

She?

Don't ask, don't ask, don't—

'Who?' I whispered.

For some moments he was silent, lying in the sun-reddened glow of the stained glass like an effigy upon a tomb.

Time passed. And then the words were drifting out of him, as if they were not his words but those of some maleficent spirit that lived within him, poisoning his thoughts.

'Found myself half wishing that she were... gone from my life.'

Raising himself on an elbow, staring past me as though we were not alone in the room.

'No such thing as a half-wish, is there?' Dudley smiling a sick smile conveying private agony. 'I *was wishing...* that she might be gone...'

'Robbie.'

'...in the night. Might quietly succumb, in the deep hours before dawn, to some swift sickness.'

'You don't know what you're saying.'

'With no pain. I could never wish her pain.'

I looked away. Wishing not to be here. Wishing not to know what he meant. Tightening inside, for I knew that he'd wed Amy Robsart, a squire's daughter, at the age of eighteen when he would have thought he had no chance of winning Elizabeth.

But now he was closer than ever to Elizabeth, scandalously close, so close that she'd showered him with gifts and land, and Amy, meanwhile...

Amy lived in the country.

'He knew,' Dudley whispered. 'I could tell the old man knew.'

'Your father? Your father's shade came to you in a dream?'

'Not my father,' Dudley said. 'And not a dream. I may be fevered, but I know what is... not a dream.'

His head sinking to the pillow as if all loaded with lead. I felt that he'd gone to the abbey last night in search of some kind of absolution and found... no comfort. Maybe the reverse.

'Instead, it's me who'll die,' he said. 'And not in the dark hours. Here in the full light, so that all may see.' His breathing had become shallow. 'That all may see.'

'The doctor's on his way,' I said, numbed.

XII

Watchtower

MOMENTS LATER, WITH the strengthening sun now risen over the coloured glass and into the clear, leaded panes, Robert Dudley slipped into a merciful sleep.

Merciful, at least, to me.

I keep telling you, I'm no good with these matters. A quiet man, a scholar. A mathematician and an astronomer, who understands not the geometry of love, nor could think to chart the erratic trajectory of desire. And when that desire is further powered by worldly ambition, then God help us all.

I moved away from the thickening sickbed miasma, walking towards the sun.

Thinking how fever caused confusion and sickness skewed the senses. How a man who could face, with courage, an enemy he could see might become like to a frightened child when the enemy was within himself.

And who had not, in times of anguish, found the foulest of ideas snaking into his thoughts?

But now Dudley's unguarded thoughts were locked into *my* thoughts. And his momentary showing of an inner guilt behind the usual arrogance and the banter would not quickly be erased from my memory. Nor would the implications of what he'd told me.

It was well known that he aspired to the Privy Council, and the word from court was that he would soon be receiving a title well beyond Master of the Horse. Found myself recalling one particular day when I was first awakening in him what would become a real interest in astronomy. *I want to go there, Dr Dee,* he'd said, aged thirteen or so – me about twenty-one. *I want to be among the stars.*

What if he *had* looked into the summoning eyes of death last night?

What if he died?

I gripped the window sill.

And what if he did not die? When he was over this sickness, should I remind him of what he'd said this morning from the dark pool of his delirium?

And, you see, the worst of it, the worst was this: with all those grasping, foreign would-be suitors knocking shoulders with each other for prime position in the queue, there could indeed have been no safer and more capable consort for Queen Elizabeth… than my friend Robert Dudley.

I knew it. William Cecil would, at the heart of him, know it, too.

And of course poor Amy would know it.

✛

Standing, morose, at the upstairs window of this one-time pilgrim inn, I realised I'd been looking down, for the first time, into the daylit town of Glastonbury. Watching it going about its morning business, the familiar circle-dance of laden carts, goodwives with their baskets, children, horses and dogs, the flutter of voices in the air.

Unaware, at first, because of the graveness of my pervading thoughts, of what was so *wrong* here. Just as they seemed unaware, the goodfolk of Glastonbury, of what still was raised above them, in all its empty splendour.

This was not Bristol, nor Bath. Glastonbury itself was hardly bigger than a village, an untidy huddle with few buildings of any age and none at all on the other side of the street. Only the abbey wall and, beyond it, the golden shell of what had been the finest, wealthiest ecclesiastical building in the west of England.

Two decades, now, since its forty monks had been displaced, their abbot tortured, killed and quartered.

What can I say of this? I would not deny the case for reform, or at least throwing off the papal yoke. But the destruction of so many noble build-ings with the consequent dispersal of treasures and books – and the pointless slaughter of men who understood them – was as distressing to me as the sacking of Rome by barbarians. The abbey had been the reason for this town, and now all reason had fled.

Yet the abbey glowed, still. Even with its roofs ripped away, its nave reduced to naked ribs and unrestrained greenery sprouting from its damaged central tower. Even in wan February, the soft glow remained in the golden stone, and you could understand why some people had refused to believe that all here was lost.

Only, where were they today? The spirit had left and the people in the street appeared oblivious of the continued presence of the body. Did one of *them* know the fate of Arthur's bones? With Dudley so sick, it was my task now to find out. Which would be easier were I better at discourse with common people.

Stood there at the window, helplessly shaking my head. A book-man, incapable of preparatory small talk. Where Dudley would have impressed the men and charmed the women, I would arouse only suspicion.

Footsteps on the stairs, then.

I turned quickly away from the window and crept across the boards, for it would be best to appraise the doctor of Dudley's condition outside of his hearing. But no sooner was I through the doorway than this doctor had walked past me into the bedchamber.

And I felt a damp disappointment.

For it seemed this might actually *be* a doctor, not the local cunning man I'd expected. The long black cloak, its hood drawn full over the face to protect against contagion. The bulky Cowdray following, carrying a black cloth bag.

Piss-sniffers. The last men I'd consult if I were sick. They might have papers professing their authority but they know nothing, most of them. Worse, they have no instinct for healing.

Before I could speak, Cowdray had put down the case and withdrawn from the bedchamber, and the door was shut against us. Bolts sliding, and me feeling foolish, knowing that, in my old frayed robe, I'd probably been mistaken for a servant.

'You'll be wanting to break your fast, Dr John,' Cowdray said. 'Worry not, eh? Your colleague's in the best of hands.'

'I'm sure,' I said.

✠

When the serving girl had brought my cheese and bread and a jug of ale, I asked both Cowdray and Martin Lythgoe to stay and share it. Not wanting Cowdray to think I considered my status above his. Not wanting anyone to be afraid to speak to me.

Dr John, the ordinary man.

Something, anyway, encouraged Cowdray to approach the question that must have been troubling him since our arrival with Carew. He pulled off his apron of sackcloth, sat down at the board amid the dusty sunbeams, broke bread.

'Something particular, is it, you're looking for?' he said.

'My field of knowledge is documents,' I said truthfully. 'Manuscripts and books.'

Cowdray stared down at the broken bread on his platter.

'Like Leland?'

Did not look at me. Of course, he would have encountered John Leland, as King Harry's antiquary toured the west, doing much as we now purported to do. Because, for us, the listing of antiquities was merely a cover story, I hadn't considered how we might be perceived... in the wake of Leland.

Oh, dear God.

'Friendly enough feller,' Cowdray said. 'Scholar and a gentleman. Didn't look like anybody's idea of the Angel of Death.'

What could I say? I doubted that Leland, compiling his lists of monastic treasure, could, at the time of his itinerary, have foreseen how the information would be used by Thomas Cromwell after the Reform of the Church. As Harry's wish-list.

'I wouldn't've said this in front of Sir Peter Carew,' Cowdray said, 'but there's folks here who won't forget Leland.'

I sighed.

'Man comes here with his script from the King,' Cowdray said. 'Telling everybody how much the King wants to know about all the great writings held in the furthest reaches of his realm. Ten or more years later, he's back again, and now it's all in ruins, and he hardly seems to notice. Blethering about making charts. All I'm saying... You'd be well advised not to make a show of your mission. Might be misunderstood.'

'I can assure you that the Queen's intentions—'

'Not as there's anything left she could do to this town. Nothing left but wool and apples.'

I knew not what to say. When Leland had returned to Glastonbury, some fifteen years ago, it would have been as part of his aim to list the topography of every county in the realm. A task which had proved too massive for him to deal with and may have driven him into his final madness.

That and his scholar's guilt at the dreadful outcome of his earlier mission. All those books, the first sight of which had raised him into *awe and stupor.*

'What *did* happen to the books in the abbey library?' I said.

Cowdray massaged his red stubble.

'A few got took away by the King's men – the ones with gold bindings, I'd guess. The old black ones… thrown out in a heap. With the monks gone, not many folk left with an interest in books. Well, not in reading them.'

'What happened to them?'

'You can get a good fire going with a book.' Cowdray smiling sadly at my reaction. 'That distresses you, Doctor?'

I did not say that books had value beyond gold, only nodded wearily.

'All right, maybe some were saved,' Cowdray said. 'Maybe the monks took some. Maybe some were taken to Wells, or further. For safe-keeping. Nobody could believe it was all over for ever. Hard for strangers to understand the power the abbey gave out, owning land for miles all around – down in Cornwall, up in Wales. 'Twas like to a great beacon, man, always alight.'

'You'd've supported the appeal to Queen Mary,' I said, 'to restore the abbey?'

'Everybody did. Not for any big religious reasons, most of us. 'Tis just our only hope of returning to any kind of prosperity. Aye, we're still on the Exeter road, we gets regular traffic through here, travellers stay the night, nobody starves to death. But for those of us who remember the foreign pilgrims throwing their money around, drinking all the wine and cider we could provide.' Cowdray smiled. 'Happy times, Doctor. But then… I was a young man then.'

'The pilgrims,' I said, 'came to venerate the bones of the saints. What remains of them?'

'Pilgrims?'

'Bones.'

He eyed me with the kind of suspicion that made me glad we had Carew here to vouch for our status.

'Bones,' he said. 'That's why you're here?'

'In part.'

'I know not where the bones are,' Cowdray said. 'Gone. From the earth, anyway.'

'All of them?'

'Maybe. There's people could tell you better than me.'

'Were they taken by the King's men or were some… removed to places of safety?'

He was blinking, wary now, and I guessed I could not expect an honest answer.

'Listen, I'm a lowly civil servant,' I said. 'I don't want to persecute anybody. I won't be reporting any names. Myself and Master Roberts, our report will simply be a list of what remains and what does not. So tell me… who'd know better than you about bones?'

Cowdray thought for a moment and then shrugged.

'The bone-man?'

I waited. This might be mockery.

'Benlow the bone-man,' Cowdray said. 'He collects bones. People take him bones and he pays for them and then sells them to the pilgrims. At least, he used to. Obviously, his trade's not so good nowadays.'

'He's *known* to conduct this trade? Without getting—'

'Bothered by the law? What crime does he commit? No doubt they could find one if anyone wanted to, but they don't seem to.' Cowdray got up to add a log to the fire in the ingle. 'The more bones, the holier the place looks to pilgrims, and this was the holiest of all.'

I tore off a piece of bread, spread it with white cheese.

'*You* think so?'

'Christ himself walked these hills. We gotter believe that.'

I watched the new flames licking at the apple logs in the hearth, the sun lighting the flags.

'The people here must have been sick at heart when the monks were driven away.' I caught the flicker of alarm in his eyes. 'It's all right. You have my word...'

'Aye.' Cowdray looked up at the window. 'The day they took Abbot Whiting to the tor, 'twas like the end of the world. A good man. Not all abbots are good men, I'd be the first to agree that, but he was a mild old feller, and kind. Never turned his back on the town.'

'You... saw what they did to him?'

'Saw him lashed to a hurdle, dragged through the high street.' Cowdray's grizzled head in a sunbeam, his words coming out of darkness. 'Bumping along like a deer carcass. An old man, beaten, bruised and cut about like a low-born thief? Where's the reason in that?'

I said nothing. I was thinking of an amiable man called Barthlet Green who'd shared my chamber in Bonner's lock-up, before being burned.

'Don't think he knew what was happening,' Cowdray said, 'or else he'd given up caring. His eyes were closed. 'Course, there were cheers and trumpets all around – like to a holiday. That's how stupid some folk are. All following him up the tor, half-pissed. I couldn't take it. Came in and served drinks and kept quiet.'

'The tor...?'

'Yon little pointy hill, doctor,' Martin Lythgoe said. 'Wi' a church on top as were brought down by an earth tremble. Too dark for thee to see last night.'

'Of course.' I nodded. 'That's where the abbot was executed?'

'Some say 'tis the devil's own hill,' Cowdray said. 'Why they built a church on it, and why the church fell down. They say that next to every holy place there's a high ground as the devil takes for his watchtower. And, aye, that's where they hanged the abbot and two good monks. And then they cut him down and hacked his body into four, and the pieces they took...'

'I know what's involved.'

'Is it any wonder he don't rest?'

'Mercy...?'

I looked up at a movement and saw that a woman had come in and sat herself down at the smaller board just inside the door. Evidently not a servant; she wore no apron and had entered uninvited.

''Tis why folk don't go in the abbey after dark,' Cowdray said. 'Why they ain't helping theirselves to stone much n'more. They reckon as first you sees the abbot's candle in the nave. And then, if you got the sense you was born with, you drops your sack of stone and runs like buggery. Or there's the abbot himself in front of you, in his full robes.'

I saw Martin Lythgoe shudder. The woman in the corner by the door sat motionless, and I wondered if this was Cowdray's wife. She had long dark hair pushed back over her shoulders, wore a washed-out blue over-dress with a loose girdle around her waist.

'If you takes a stone from the abbey and puts it into your wall,' Cowdray said, 'you should kneel and do penance every morning for seven weeks. Or 'tis likely your house will not be at peace.'

'As good a means as any,' the woman murmured, 'to deter people from stealing the abbey. Especially if they have stiff knees.'

Cowdray turned on his stool.

'Nel... never heard you come in.'

'Let me know,' she said, 'when you feel your increasing deafness is worth the expense of a consultation.'

'Ha. How's Master Roberts?'

'Sleeping. The more he sleeps now, the better will be his chances.'

The heavy-panelled room seemed to tilt. Even as I was adjusting to the realisation that this young woman must be Dudley's doctor, I was hearing his voice in my head.

'...both feet above the ground, and looking down on me with a terrible pity... the white moon shining through him... Cold.'

XIII

Elixir

GHOSTS. OFT-TIMES I'd be asked about ghosts, and what was I to say, never having seen one?

Would I have *wished* to see one?

Of course. My God, yes.

And yet...

Wait. Let me try to explain this simply, as a scientist but without, I promise, any employment of arcane symbols.

There are, as is well known, three spheres: the natural world, the celestial or astral world, and the supercelestial, wherein are angels. Much evidence exists, in certain forbidden books, that some living men can move, in thought, to the astral realm and, in thought, exist there for a while.

Not me. I've never been there. Let me make my position full clear: my own searching suggests this to be unhealthy and dangerous, not least because of what may be brought back to the natural world. *Our* world.

Therefore my work, as I've oft-times stated, must needs be aimed towards communion with the supercelestial sphere, wherein lies truth and light. Not ghosts, which the reformists anyway seek to banish from our beliefs along with the Catholic purgatory.

What, then, can be said, realistically, about the walking dead? Well... if a living man can exist in thought in a higher realm, then it follows that a dead man can return to the lower or natural world – our own world – and exist *here*. Long enough, it would seem, to enshroud with fear anyone who might glimpse his shade. Fear, because the seer knows that the only reason a man or woman should wish to return, without body, to the lower world is because they left it while in a state of imbalance,

112

preventing them rising into the light of God. That the presence of the shade in this world must needs be *wrong*.

✠

'Let me try to reassure you,' the doctor said. 'There's no taint of imminent death around Master Roberts. I've examined him for signs of the worst things and find nothing obvious.'

'Smallpox?'

''Tis more likely to be wool-sorters' disease in this town, of which fever's sometimes a sign. But you'd be unlikely to find that in a London man. I'm inclined to think this is a less sinister kind of fever. And… he's young and strong.'

I nodded, much relieved.

'Though clearly troubled in his mind,' the doctor said.

We were in the courtyard behind the George, and clouds had killed the sun. The air was warmer than London but still had the knife-edge of February. Yet the doctor carried her cloak over one arm and the other had its sleeve rolled to the elbow, and the arm was speckled like a hen's egg.

'Troubled, mistress?'

'Oh.' She shrugged lightly. 'He mumbles words that are… anguished. But not clear,' she said hastily. 'Not at all clear.'

'Words?'

….wishing… that she might quietly succumb, in the deep hours before dawn, to some swift—

Maybe I'd gone pale.

'Anyway,' the doctor said brightly, 'he's not the only one I've seen with the fever this week. 'Tis sent from France or Spain, I reckon. Where did you lie before arriving here?'

I told her Bristol and she nodded, as if this explained everything. Across the yard, one of Cowdray's boys carried hay into the stables. The doctor saw me looking at her bare arm and, frowning, rolled down her sleeve.

'I'll need to see him again in two days. He must needs lie in his chamber till then.'

'And how would you suggest I make him do that?'

She smiled, her front teeth slightly crooked. She was younger than I'd thought her in the dimness of the inn. Especially for her trade – in London I knew of no women of any age who were qualified doctors, only wise-women working in the shadows, and I'd not imagined it being so different out here.

'Am I to assume,' I said, 'that you've aided his sleep?'

'A harmless potion, that's all.'

'Containing?'

'Mostly valerian and hops.'

I nodded. Jack Simm would approve.

'The other constituents I'll keep to myself,' the doctor said. 'Be assured that sleep will do most to make him well. Meat is not necessary – not that he'll want any – but you should see to it that he has as much fresh water as he can drink. And a bigger pot to piss in may also be required, for he must piss away the fever. Oh… and it would do no harm if some of his drinking water was from the holy well.'

'Oh?' Why some water should be held sacred is something that's long interested me. 'Would prayer not suffice?'

'The well's renowned for giving strength. Its water runs red, like… blood.'

'Or iron?'

'Or iron. The holy well,' she said, with a heavy patience, 'is just its name.'

'And this well is where?'

'Master Cowdray's boy will show your servant.'

'I think,' I said, not quite knowing why I spoke thus, 'that I'd like to see it for myself.'

'Well…' She paused. 'I suppose *I* could take you. It isn't too far from here.'

No doubt the time spent on guiding me to this holy well would be added to her charges. But I was sensing that it might be worth it in other ways, for it was beginning to seem that this young woman was not such an orthodox piss-sniffer after all.

'Thank you. Mistress…?'

'Borrow.' She shook out her cloak, spun it about her shoulders. 'Eleanor Mary Borrow. Do you wish to call your servant to accompany us?'

'He's not my servant.'

Martin Lythgoe had gone up to check on his master, leaving me to pay the doctor. I'd get the money back when Dudley was well enough to undo his purse.

Mistress Borrow bent to pick up her cloth bag, but I'd reached for it first.

'Might I... carry this for you?'

She shrugged.

'If you wish.'

In London it would be considered unseemly for a man to walk in such isolation with a young woman he'd barely met, but it seemed to worry this one not at all. Being a doctor, I supposed.

The bag must have had pouches inside for the potions and the leeches or whatever she carried around, for it didn't rattle when I slung the strap over my shoulder.

'I've nothing in there to hide,' she said. 'if that's what you were thinking.'

'No, no, I didn't...' Even my attempts at crude chivalry were ever misinterpreted. 'Where did you train, mistress?'

'Oh...' She was walking swiftly across the yard towards the rear gate. 'I've studied for many years.'

'You don't look old enough' – catching up with her – 'to have studied for *many* years.'

She stopped at the gate, a hand on the bolt, and looked up at me, her eyes widening.

'I don't *look* sixty years old?' Her head on one side. 'What a marvellous thing is my father's elixir of youth.'

'Little short of miraculous. How old's your father?'

'Oh... he must be near to ninety years, now. Though looks barely fifty.'

Turning quickly away, Mistress Borrow drew back the bolt with a clank which almost, but not quite, obscured what I thought might be laughter.

'You're following your father's trade?' I said.

'And my mother's,' she said. 'Though my poor mother's been dead for …a while.'

The gate had opened on to a patch of greensward, grazed by half a dozen geese, behind the high street. I followed Mistress Borrow onto an earthen path alongside it.

'Both your parents were doctors?'

'My father still is – he's the finest doctor in the west. Would have come with Master Cowdray to your friend but had been summoned to the bedside of an old woman about to quit this world. No, my mother grew herbs. My father uses them.'

'And you grow them still?'

'I borrow them – from the land.'

Oh, these clearly were not physicians as I was used to them in London. This sounded to me like a cunning man married to a wise woman. Which was like a breath of air to me, but Mistress Borrow could not know that.

Ahead of us, pale as ash, rose a high and elegant tower. The church of St John the Baptist, I imagined, having read of it in my research. Leland calls it *fair and lightsome*.

'A proud tower,' I observed.

'Built by Abbot Selwood a century ago.'

'And who cares for it now?'

'Who cares for anything?'

She walked on, head down, dark brown hair flowing behind her, unrestrained by cap or coif. We passed through the churchyard, emerging at last on to the high street, where I saw a baker's shop doing good business and a man having less success selling sheep fleeces from a cart. I followed Mistress Borrow along the street, which wound uphill past a building site backing onto the abbey wall – doubtless the plan was to use this as a supporting wall for new homes, but nobody was working on the site, and I recalled Cowdray:

If you takes a stone from the abbey and puts it into your wall, you should kneel and do penance every morning for seven weeks. Or 'tis likely your house will not be at peace.

116

But back at the inn Mistress Borrow had sounded sceptical. I caught up with her again.

'The ghost of Abbot Whiting… do you not believe he's seen?'

'I didn't say that. I said that such rumours might be employed to deter people from stealing stone.'

'Then *do* you believe that he's seen?'

'It doesn't surprise me. The poor man has little cause for rest. But as I don't go in there it isn't my business.'

'You don't sound afraid.'

'Because I remember the abbot. From… when I was a small child. I remember him walking through the town, not far from here. He stopped to talk to us, my mother and me. His face… I remember his wrinkly smile, and his eyes had a kindness, like…' She looked up at me. 'For a long time, I thought I'd seen the face of God.'

'How old were you?'

'Three or four years.'

People passed us, entering the pale Church of the Baptist. Outside, on the edge of the street, a young man was plucking discordantly upon a patched lute, another slapping at a goatskin drum, chickens pecking in the mud around them. It seemed to me, for a curious moment, as if the people were behaving as though in a play and feigning ordinary life. That the real life here happened on some other level.

'At least, unlike the abbey, the church is in full daily use,' I said. 'Does it have a library?'

'I don't know. Should it?'

'Everywhere should have a library.'

'Why?'

Walking faster, now she was away from the town centre.

'Because –' feeling the pull of my breathing as I kept up with her pace – 'only through learning can we hope to attain…'

The words unaccountably dying on me. I felt suddenly foolish. And inadequate, somehow, as Mistress Borrow stopped at the entrance to a narrow track, tall, bare trees on either side, and turned to look down at me.

'And is learning acquired only from books?'

She turned away again and began ascending the track.

'Well, no,' I said, 'but the *process* of learning is surely much hastened. Is it not remarkable that, by means of a book, one man's whole lifetime of learning can be passed to another in a matter of hours?'

'*All* learning can be passed this way?'

'Most of it. In my experience.'

She stopped at a low wall with a stile. Stepping away from it and waiting while I climbed up and jumped down on the other side. Giving her my hand, to help her down. Her own hand was bare, not like the Queen's rose-petal glove. I experienced a most disturbing reaction and let go of it quickly when she was down from the stile, and turned away, feeling the warm blood suffuse my cheeks.

'The well is that way,' she said

Pointing towards a wood, a well-trodden path leading through it, and I had the sense of a mocking laughter rising within her. A laughter that seemed to be translated into a sudden, raucous cawking of crows, which caused me to look up in a hot displeasure mixed with apprehension and thus, through a gap in the trees, to espy, almost directly above us, a green mound like to a gigantic mole's tump.

A stone tower projecting from its summit, like a stalk from an apple and black against the cloud.

XIV

A Mortifying of the Flesh

THE CLOUDS BEHIND the jutting tower were a strange and blinding white, the hill itself a more vivid green than was common in February. A shock to the senses, and I felt a momentary separation that I liked not.

Division: part of me longing to go rushing to its summit, another part hissing, *turn away.*

'So close to the town,' I said, 'and yet...'

'Not *of* it,' Mistress Borrow said. 'It is its own place.'

We stood on the edge of the wood in full silence. No birdsong. The hill, I saw, was ridged, had terraces approaching the summit, like the mounds of the castles in my family's country burned down in the Glyndwr wars. But no castle mound I'd seen was so imposing, so steep or quite so startlingly conical. It was utterly strange, as if it were planted here, constructed by men – or angels – for some purpose.

And I felt, oddly, as if some inner part of me was already familiar with it.

Most likely from an engraving in a book.

I said, 'So an earthquake brought down the church.'

'Nigh on three hundred years ago. Except for the tower. The church was rebuilt after the quake, but after that it never seemed happy to be more than a tower. After the Reform and what happened to the abbot up there, the church was abandoned, and they took away the bells. Now it is... as some say it began.'

'As what?'

Her eyes sparkled.

'What brought about the earthquake? Was the church cleft to the bone by an act of God, or was it the work of Satan?' She pointed upwards

119

to the tower, shrunken now by our nearness to the hill. 'Is it not become the finger of Satan?'

'Meaning what?'

A faint, serpentine mist was apparent around the tower, the white sky grained as if lightly dusted with soot. As if the tower was a chimney for some fire within the hill.

'Like to a standing stone,' she said. 'A Druid stone? 'Tis well known that in the years before Our Saviour, this was a place of Druid worship. 'Tis said that Merlin's own stronghold was there.'

A throb in my chest.

'Arthur's Merlin?'

''Tis also said that inside the hill was the great gathering hall of the King of the Faerie, who rides the stormy sky with the hellhounds of the wild hunt. So, you see, to the religious, that tower *is* the finger of Satan.' Mistress Borrow let her arm fall, then turned away. 'The holy well's along here.'

✝

Most holy wells I knew had stonework, crude statuary. This one was entirely unadorned. Twisted apple trees had grown around it in a rough circle, their branches curling into a protective nest.

When I leaned to it, I heard the water threshing and tumbling with a rare power. Dark red in my cupped hands. I brought some to my mouth and tasted it: iron, as I'd expected. Iron for strength.

'Many people have been cured by it.' Mistress Borrow knelt in the damp grass. 'Many pilgrims.'

'And local people?'

'Even local people. The most effective medicines come free from rocks and hedgerows. But you can see why this well's best called *holy*.'

I looked into her green eyes and tried not to blink.

'*Is* it called holy?'

'No.' She smiled. 'They call it the Blood Well.'

'Whose blood?'

'Ah...'

A finger to her lips. I felt a pulsing inside me.

'What kind of doctor are you?'

'Oh… some would say, not a doctor at all, compared with my father who trained at good colleges. What do I know of leeches and the balancing of the humours? Not much at all. Only of crude surgery. And herbs. Which are more important, for all plants hold life and the energy of dew. Some more than others. If we know where and how to grow them. And when.'

'And what mean you by that?'

I'd felt a real quickening of interest, now. Mistress Borrow was winding a strand of her brown hair around a forefinger, looking suddenly and startlingly young. Must be a few years over twenty, but seeming no older, at this moment, than my mother's housekeeper, Catherine Meadows.

There was… a certain not-quite symmetry in her features which made me want to study them at length, calcule their proportions.

'How do you know,' I asked softly, 'when it's best for certain herbs to be grown?'

She looked wary for a moment, and then her shoulders went loose and out it came.

'Some 'tis best to sow under a new moon and then to harvest under a full moon. Or the other way around. Or cultivation may be more profitable when certain heavenly bodies are in certain portions of the sky. Also the curative qualities of some planets may be improved under certain planetary… what's the matter?'

'Where did you learn of this?'

'From my mother, but –' her eyes, of a sudden, sharpening with a defiant light – 'I've also read *books*.'

'And where did you obtain such books?'

Thinking: the abbey library, which left Leland in awe.

'Pass me my bag,' she said. 'There's a flask inside which we can fill with water for your friend. You should give it to him sparingly, betwixt larger quantities of ordinary, pure water. Not that much of the water in Glastonbury is truly… ordinary.'

'Why is that?'

In London, water was seldom drunk these days.

'Because… they say that the holy essence, all the sacred life in this place… flows with the water… underground. Even with the abbey going to ruin, the place itself is still hallowed. There are some things you can't destroy. Some things about a place that are *in* that place.'

'They say Our Saviour walked here.' I handed her the bag. 'As a young boy.'

'Yes.'

'And that's why it's holy?'

'Did I say it was holy?'

'I believe you said *hallowed*.'

'I meant it has a power,' she said. 'Maybe something to do with the flow of water beneath it. Maybe the abbey was only put here because of the unusual… that is, it may indeed be that Our Saviour was only brought here *because*…' She must have seen the rapt stillness in me. 'Oh – am I stepping close to heresy?'

Not looking, it must be said, as if she cared. Pulling a small, stoppered jug from her bag, she bent with it to the holy well. Despite the water I'd drunk, my mouth felt dry. Although the sun was still hidden in cloud, the day seemed warmer than any since Christmas. A close and airless warmth. No breeze. Unseasonal. I felt a discomfort. Everything here, in this odd, disfunctioned town, seemed to inflict discomfort.

'What's the power you speak of?'

'I… don't know. The reasons for it may be long into the past. Perchance you'll feel it for yourself, when you've been here a while. It… alters the sense of things.'

'I'm told,' I said, 'that some people here have had visions.'

She took the vessel from the well and put in the stopper.

'Who told you that?'

'I forget,' I said lamely.

She placed the jug carefully in her bag, tucking it in like an infant.

''Tis certain true to say that some men and women here are driven very speedily into madness.'

'Driven by what?'

'Maybe by what they see or hear. Maybe no-one's supposed to be living here. There *are* such places, are there not?'

'Are there?'

'Where people find it hard to live an easy life. And monks... monks would seek out such places, would they not?'

'For a monk –' an excitement like hot coals in my gut – 'a monk must needs be challenged in his soul?'

'Exactly.'

A glowing smile.

'But now all the monks are gone,' I said.

'In which case, it might be thought –' she brought a knuckle to her chin, as if there were something new here that she was considering for the first time – 'that we needed the monks here to keep a balance in the place.'

She fell silent. I felt the weight of the hill behind us, had a feeling of the devil's finger scratching at the clouds, something in me wanting, unaccountably, to cry out.

'Balance?'

'To keep the peace. Daily prayer and chanting creating a balm. Lying soft upon the air.'

'And there's no peace now? Worship at the Church of the Baptist does not have the same effect?'

'Dr John,' she said, 'don't make me say these things.'

I said nothing. She would hardly be the first to suggest that the anglicised services of the reformed church were a poor substitute for the older rituals it had discarded.

'You haven't been here long enough to know this town,' she said.

'Then tell me.'

'Feelings...' She sighed. 'Feelings here run to extreme. When you try to describe it, it sounds like nothing much – bitter quarrels which are not healed...feuds, street fights. Thieving and wife-beating and men killed over very little. *Very* little. But put them all together and sometimes it seems that this place is become like to a wound left open, where there's gangrene and rot. A mortifying of the flesh.'

My eyes must have widened at her eloquence and the force of her argument. I was thinking of what Cowdray had said about the power the abbey had given out. *Like to a great beacon, always alight.* A calming light. And the abbey had been here *before* the town, which had grown up to serve it. And now the light had gone out, leaving the town bereft and prey to...

Next to every holy place there's a high ground as the devil takes for his watchtower.

I'd thought myself well qualified in theology, but this was unfamiliar territory and made me feel as if all my years of learning were of little consequence. I looked down at the holy well, the blood well, the *iron* well, and felt the weight of the strange hill, like the burden of a hunchback.

There are places – I *know* this – where the earth itself speaks to us. In olden times, men were closer to it. *All* men, not only priests. When I think on this, I sometimes feel that even the Bible men might be closer to regaining this lost faculty, yet the rigidity of their beliefs prevent them from the experience of it. I turned to Mistress Borrow.

'And the visions?'

She drew her cloak over her knees.

'Who's to say what are visions and what are signs of an oncoming madness?'

'Or possession?'

'Oh yes, there's much possession in Glastonbury. The demons have a rare freedom here.'

'Could you –' my throat was as dry as parched earth – 'explain this to me?'

'And this is important, Doctor?' Looking up at me, of a sudden suspicious. 'This has an importance for your work in the listing of the Queen's antiquities?'

As if she were awakening from some daydream... as if we both were held in a spell which she must needs break.

'I'm interested,' I said. 'That's all.'

'We should go.' She was looking away, to somewhere beyond the circle of thorn trees, scrambling coltishly to her feet. 'I have visits to make. To the sick.'

Snatching up her bag before I could reach it, she moved away betwixt the apple trees and was almost in collision with the panting bulk of Dudley's groom, Martin Lythgoe.

✠

'Beg mercy, Doctor…'

Red in the face, his thatch of yellow hair standing up in spikes, a ragged scratch scoring one cheek.

'I'm reet glad to've found thee. Me master—'

I leapt up.

'Is he *worse?*'

'No, he's… much the same. He were asleep when I left him. It's just he said – before he become ill, like – as how we should watch out for thee.'

'Me?'

'And what do I do, wi' the master all laid up, but go buggering off checking on th'horses and let yer go wandering off on yer own. Well…' He looked at Mistress Borrow. 'Pardon me, I din't known tha were wi' him, Doctor.'

If he'd been following me, he must have known, but I let it pass.

'Martin, I'm a grown man.'

'Aye, well, I can see that, but me master, he reckons…'

However you survived in the cesspits of Paris and Antwerp without me around to save your sorry arse I shall never know.

'Yes,' I said. 'I think I know what he reckons. Martin… ' Looking into his eyes and speaking with deliberation in the hope he would get the underlying message that I was engaged in picking up useful intelligence. 'Doctor Borrow… has shown me the holy well… to get some iron water. To aid Master Roberts's recovery?'

'Aye, aye.' He nodded. 'Not a problem, sir.' Straightening his leather jerkin, casting a sideways glance at Mistress Borrow. 'Anyroad, I think, under t'circumstances, Master Roberts would understand.'

'Circumstances?'

Martin Lythgoe gave me a discreet… what looked to be a wink.

What?

I felt my cheeks suffused with blood.

'I'll leave thee to it, then, sir.'

He beamed.

'No… Martin…'

'Aye?'

'If you want to help me –' groping wildly for something sounding halfway authoritative – 'there's someone you might talk to. Cowdray spoke last night of a former monk from the abbey who'd become a farrier. I thought that, with your own work with horses, you might find a plausible reason to approach him?'

'I could do that.'

'You know what we're looking for. What information we seek, and to what purpose?'

'Oh, aye.'

'And could inquire with discretion?'

'I reckon yer mare could do wi' some new shoes for t'journey back to Bristol.'

'That would be a very good reason to make an approach.'

'Awreet then, I'll seek out this feller, and I'll sithee back at th' inn, Dr John.'

He patted down his haystack hair, nodded to Mistress Borrow and blundered away amongst the guardian apple trees, leaving me struggling to assemble an apologetic smile.

'My… usual work being with manuscripts and books, my colleagues think me unused to the outside world.'

''Tis a real mystery to me how they could think that.'

Lips unsmiling, but her eyes were dancing, and the discomfort in me burst its dam.

'I'd like to see the church.'

'Church?'

'*That* church. Upon the tor. The devil's hill. Whoever the devil may be, in this instance – the wizard Merlin, the King of the Faerie, the… to a Catholic, the Protestants are devils.'

Flinging out too many words, as usual, when I'm in a turmoil.

'But there's nothing up there,' she said. 'Even the tower's all but hollow now.'

'You call the remains of a church *nothing*? And what's that terracing around the hill? Like to old fortifications.'

She shrugged.

'Antiquities are my business,' I said stiffly. 'I can't very well neglect this one.'

Knowing not, in truth, why I had to go up there, to a place that seemed so forbidding. Maybe *because* it was forbidding. To demonstrate that I was a man unafraid to challenge the devil.

Or even just a man.

'Very well.' The doctor gathered up her cloak. 'This way...'

☩

The path curved, making the ascent less steep than the appearance of the tor suggested. But it still was not a pleasant climb, and all the way I carried a damp and dolorous feeling of what it must have been like for the elderly, aching Abbot Whiting, hauled up on a hurdle to a certain death.

Like to the labouring of Christ, with his cross, up the hill of Calvary, the place of skulls.

Or worse. Close to the summit I stopped and looked back. The path was quite treacherously steep. Imagine pulling an old man all the way up here on a hurdle.

And *three* men?

Why? Why three?

A trinity.

Why here? Why have a public execution on this most inaccessible of hills? If they'd wanted to make an exhibition of it, entertain a crowd, why not the centre of the town?

The tower began to rise before us, as if it were thrust out of the hill, and the wrongness of everything became blindingly evident. For who in his right mind would build a church upon such an isolated, sharpened point of land? A castle or a fort, but not a place of worship.

As we came closer, the tower was revealed to be of grey-brown stone, and cracked open down one side, a fissure in it like a broken tooth, and the body around it was little more than foundations.

When I clambered to the top of the hill a few yards behind Mistress Borrow, it was like arriving upon a cloud in the sky. And when I stood close to the tower...

'Do you not feel it relates more to the air than to the earth?' she said.

'Yes. Maybe.'

A needle to pierce the heavens and draw down lightning. Illumination.

I looked down, dizzied. Despite a thin mist, the views on offer were unexpected. Not only a vista of the town and the abbey like to a close-sewn crop betwixt the other hills, but of the flatlands to the west, all the way to the grey sea – the level country veined with narrow channels of water, swollen here and there into pools and lakes, and you could feel that it still belonged to the sea and might yet be reclaimed, becoming a true island again. For this, I realised now, was surely the very heart of what remained of the Isle of Avalon.

Merlin's lair and known to Arthur. An excitement trickled into my spine, like a spring through rocks, and my head was as light as down-feathers. There was a momentary kindling of illumination and then – *dear Christ* – all my senses were crowding together, dropping as one into the bottom of my gut, where lies the lower mind, the arousal becoming a slow-swelling alarm as all the land fell into a tilt, a vast platter of greens and greys and browns and…

…I found me on my back on the turf, with the tower racing away from me towards a bright hole in the clouds.

'God!'

Rising up on my elbows, all leaden-headed, dazed and ashamed that such a short climb should have so sapped my strength that I should fall into a womanly faint.

The lightness of her feet over the springy turf as she came to stand above me, arms folded. That cross-toothed smile and a barely veiled merriment in the green eyes.

'Be not alarmed, Dr John, you're hardly the first to lose his balance up here.'

Holding out a slender hand to me, but I wouldn't take it and struggled unaided to my feet and still felt unsteady, cold sweat on my forehead. On the top of a high mountain, it becomes harder to breathe, but this was a mere tump. I was shaken and more than a little afeared that I might be coming down with Dudley's fever.

'It's my fault,' she said. 'I should have warned you. As I said, this some-times—'

'Not to you,' I said. 'Evidently.'

'No indeed,' a man's voice said. 'How swiftly the devil's claws reach out to his children...'

I turned.

He had his back to the tower.

His tone was soft and unhurried and weighted with a drawling *ennui* that spoke more of parts of London or Cambridge than this wild place.

'Throw a witch into a pond and she's said to float,' he observed mildly. 'Expose a witch to the seething air around Satan's altar and she'll gather all the floating imps to her rancid tits.'

XV

Maggots

THE MIST... I hadn't noticed how much it had thickened, enclouding the tower and writhing like a living thing around three figures, as if they had arisen with the mist or were formed out of it. Two of them in monks' habit, hands hidden in conjoined sleeves.

Mistress Borrow addressed the third, a secular man, as tall as me, strong-built and limber as a larch tree, his witch taunt still smeared across the chilled air.

'And since when' – facing him, pale-cheeked but not, I thought, with fear – 'since when has this land been yours, Sir Edmund? Some desperate deal with the Bishop of Wells?'

No response. His hair and beard were as one, close-barbered from the top of his skull to the edge of his full jawline. He wore a dark green doublet and black hose above boots of good leather. Wide belt, a sheathed sword hanging from it.

'The Bishop of Wells,' I observed, 'would seem to be in no position to make deals.'

'And who would you be, fellow?'

I'd expected a deep, roughened voice, but his was high and clipped. I held my ground. While my dark attire was hardly at the height of fashion, it must be evident that I was not of the peasantry.

'Dr John,' I said. 'Of the Queen's Commission on Antiquities.'

This intelligence was received, I'd concede, with no conspicuous awe.

'Here on instruction of the Privy Council,' I said mildly, as if by rote. 'If you wish to inspect my papers of authority, I have them at the George Inn.'

Well, as you know, I was never good at this. Moving closer to these men to signify that I was not intimidated, I was still unsteady. Aware of the turf lifting with each step and praying that I should not be cast down again by some unaccountable slippage of the air.

'And *your* name?' I said.

'Fyche. Sir Edmund. Of Meadwell. Owner of this ground.' A vague gesture toward his monkish companions. 'Brother Michael, Brother Stephen.'

A greybeard and a thin-faced youth. Connections forming: last night Sir Peter Carew had spoken of a former monk from the abbey using an inheritance to develop a farm and then establishing there a college for the education of the sons of gentlemen.

'Dr John, if you' – Mistress Borrow was pointing down the hill towards a wind-bent fence – 'if you care to consult the records, you'll find that the estate owned by Sir Edmund stops *there.*'

'However,' Fyche said politely, 'the way you came, you *would* have to cross my land to get here.'

'*Fie!*' Her back arching like a cat's. ''Tis a right of way!'

'I'll have its ownership ascertained when I return to London,' I said briskly. 'However, as an officer of the Queen's Commission I can take, with impunity, whichever route be most expedient for the furtherance of my business, which—'

'Yes,' Fyche said. 'Tell us, please, about your particular business.'

His accent was of the west, yet educated. A survivor, Carew had said. Close up, I could see white specks in his beard. His skin was weathered but still taut. He was maybe five and forty years.

I explained that I was charged with a new listing of ancient structures and notation of their surviving contents and prevailing condition.

Fyche's head tilted.

'Like Leland?'

A loaded question.

'Somewhat like Leland,' I said. 'But not, of course, with the same masters. What I mean is… no-one here need fear treachery.'

Fyche smiled. The curious mist wove yellowy wreaths around his boots.

'And how would you know, Doctor? Did *Leland* realise his purpose when he took his list to London?'

'I don't know. Leland died.'

'Having first gone mad, I'm told. However –' Fyche raised a thumb to the broken tower – 'as you can see, this church, despite its dominant situation and its dedication to the Archangel Michael, is ruined beyond easy repair. Does the Queen's Commission have an answer to that?'

If it did, I couldn't think of one.

'Obviously,' I said, 'the continued need for a church up here would have to be weighed against other causes. For example… with the Church of the Baptist in the town, would there be much call now for continued worship up here?'

The mist stung my eyes. Fyche's smile was looking worn.

'Well,' he said, 'it certainly goes on.'

'What does?'

'Worship,' Fyche said.

I looked up at the tower, mist oozing from the crack in its side, a jagged tear as if it had been knifed.

'The witch can tell you,' Fyche said. 'If she's a mind to.'

Instinctively, I turned my head to Mistress Borrow.

Only to see her moving away towards the path winding down, her black cloak pulled around her, its hood up. She didn't look back, and I felt an uncertainty within me and an unaccountable sense of coldness, longing… and loss.

I spun angrily back at Sir Edmund Fyche, but he'd already turned away.

'Come with me, Dr John,' he said, 'if you have the time.'

☩

Up to the very apex of the Glastonbury Tor. Through an archway into the tower itself. Which was, as it had seemed from afar, as Mistress Borrow had said, all but hollow, a vast chimney. Cracked flags and broken stones around our boots, Fyche kicking at one.

'Defiled,' he said.

Far above us, the white sky was stretched like a soiled bedsheet beyond a rotting cross of old timbers.

'I'm told an earthquake did this,' I said.

Fyche bent and picked up a dead rook by a black wing.

'When a church is abandoned,' he said, 'it festers like a corpse. And attracts maggots.'

I said nothing, but recalled Mistress Borrow: *Sometimes it seems that this place is become like to a wound left open, where there's gangrene and rot. A mortifying of the flesh.*

'A mess of them,' Fyche said. 'Squirming and roiling. A sickness. Can you not smell it?'

In truth, all I could smell was a Bible man's soapy odour. Fyche tossed the wretched bird back into the rubble.

'As a Justice of the Peace, I'm tasked with breaking up all ungodly assemblies. Whether dealing with the instigators myself or handing them over to the Church courts.'

I nodded, wary now. Although the extent of their powers seemed to vary from town to town, a local JP was never someone to be lightly dismissed. He would have firm connections in this county while, with Dudley ill and Carew gone to Devonshire, I had none.

Yet it would not be good to be seen to back down before this man or to appear less than confident in my own authority.

'This talk of witchcraft... Sir Edmund, Mistress Borrow is simply the physician summoned to treat my colleague – abed with a fever. Nothing she's done so far suggests devilry.'

He made no response to this, strode back to the archway. I followed him out of the tower, across the springy turf until he stopped on the eastern flank of the tor where the air was clearer. Woodland lay below us dark-haloed by a curling of smoke from tall chimneys.

'Foul rites,' Fyche said. 'Lewd practices.'

'I see.'

And thought that I did, as he spun at me.

'No. You do *not* see. You don't see the fires in the midnight, you don't look up and see the maggot-people chattering and squealing to the moon. Nor walk up here the next day to find new-born babes in the grass with their throats cut in sacrifice.'

'You're serious?'

I didn't believe it, of course, thought it a Bible-man's bullshit. But a Bible man who was also a JP... you did not just walk away.

'Why was a church built here?' Fyche said. 'Hardly an obvious spot. No community here.'

'Just a hill.'

'A hill. Exactly. And before the church, right where we're standing… were stones. High stones. Raised by low men.'

'You mean Druid stones?'

'Heathen stones.'

I nodded, feeling the trickle of an old spring in my spine.

'Paganism,' Fyche said. 'Witchery.'

Looking down at the turf, as if something black and noxious might be seen oozing to its surface.

'Fools say the King of the Faerie, Gwyn ap Nudd, has his chambers here, under our feet. Hence the church's dedication to St Michael, the warrior angel, to drive out old superstition.'

'Sadly, no defence against an earthquake,' Dr John said in his prosaic, list-maker's way.

While Dr Dee thought, *What does this truly mean?* Dr Dee, who knew too much to dismiss heathenism as primitivism, aware that these men, these Druids, in their ways, knew more then than we do now about the forces within the land. Or at least *experienced* more through natural magic, natural science. For these *low men*, whether they knew it or not, lived in the days when Pythagoras heard the music of the planets.

'Earthquake?' Fyche smiled sourly. 'That was Gwyn ap Nudd shaking the hill in his rage. That's what the peasants'll tell you. And in their fear, they'll make obeisance to him, lest their hovels collapse around them. Encouraged, always, by the witches, who yet come creeping to the tor in the belief that something here empowers them.'

I looked down the hillside with its veil of mist. No sign now of Mistress Borrow. Something tugged in my breast. I wrapped my arms around myself, wanting to be away from here, from this man, to ponder on how this place might yet empower *me*.

And to find her.

'It would seem to me,' I said, 'that if this hill is become infested with heathen practices since the collapse of its church, then the surest way to keep the evil at bay would be to… rebuild the church?'

Fyche shook his head.

'Maybe. In good time. Not yet. Before any restoration is even attempted – yet *again* – the area around and beneath the stones, the very earth, must needs be cleansed.'

'How?' I said. 'By blessing?'

'And prayers, thrice daily. I'm also seeking leave, through the Church courts, to have all access to the tor prohibited… for laymen… until such times as we learn how best to re-sanctify it.'

'This is why you surround yourself with religious men?'

I considered the two monks, only one of whom remained: the elder seated on the grass some yards away, reading from a small book, the title of which I could not make out.

'Dr John,' Fyche said. 'Let there be no doubt. *I* am a religious man. The law of the land and the law of God are, at last, as one, and I'm called to uphold them both.'

I had answers to this, but Dr John had none.

'When I was a young monk,' Fyche said, 'at the abbey, in its latter days, my older brothers would look over here – to the tor – and they'd shudder and say, *Who'll keep back the darkness when we're gone?*'

'Knowing what was to come to the abbey?'

'We all knew it *would* come.' Fyche breathed in slowly. 'I thought myself, at the time, to be more fortunate than most of my brothers, having inherited this land from an uncle. Not realising, at first, that this came with a terrible burden of responsibility. God… places us in the roles where we can most effectively do his work.'

The mist had thickened and with it came confusion. I'd begun to see Fyche as a man reborn into puritanism's narrow passageway, but nothing here was simple.

'This is the most sacred place in England,' he said. 'Blessed by Our Lord Himself, and thus invested with a rare spiritual power. Which others seek to corrupt to gratify their earthly lusts and base desires. In the absence of the abbey, there must needs be a bastion against this, or the town will become a pit of filth.'

'Yes.'

No-one could deny the *sense* of this, but…

'I met with some of my former brothers, and we prayed together. And then, in answer to those prayers, other men of God travelled to join us. It was interpreted to us that God wanted us to collect all the knowledge that might have been lost.'

An aim, I'd admit, not far removed from my own in establishing a national library.

'Were you among the monks who petitioned Queen Mary for a restoration of the abbey?'

'Not the answer,' Fyche said. 'Times change. God shows us new ways.'

'A school?'

While monasteries fell, schools and colleges survived and prospered. As a graduate of Cambridge and Louvain, I knew how influential a cluster of powerful minds could be. And, on occasion, how disruptive.

'Sons of the nobility were sent from all Europe to study at the abbey. We plan to restore that tradition... from a different viewpoint, obviously. While it's true that we began with the blessing of the Bishop of Wells – who, as you noted, Dr John, is now in disfavour – I can assure you that every man here has put papacy well behind him and is ready to swear allegiance to the Queen as his spiritual—'

'Not my business, Sir Edmund.'

If there were cause to suspect his loyalty, he'd hardly have remained a JP. And it would hardly be the role of Dr John, the antiquary, to question his religious allegiance.

'As regards your own assignment,' Fyche said, 'I'd suggest that what was important about the monasteries was not so much the buildings nor the treasures they held, which are now scattered to the winds. It was the depth of knowledge and wisdom retained by the monks themselves. Which should and will be passed on.'

Dr Dee would agree with fervour; Dr John said nothing. The older monk was standing now, peering over his book, smiling gently. He wore a soft black hat and his beard was like to a pointed spade.

'He can't hear us,' Fyche said. 'Brother Michael is deaf and mute. The story is that he awoke from a beatific dream one morning, with neither hearing nor speech. Since then, with no men's talk to distract him, he hears only the voices of angels. Thus, as you may imagine, his moral and spiritual judgement is… much valued.'

'So he's one of the men whose vision…?'

'No-one,' Fyche said, 'should ignore the words of angels.'

At once, I wanted to know more of this. Wondered if the day would come when I would be willing to sacrifice my own speech and my ears for an inner communion with the higher spheres. Recalling nights when I'd been in such frustration and despair that I might happily have made the deal before dawn.

'So…' Fyche had come closer. 'Would you care to search my buildings, Dr John?'

'Sir Edmund—'

'My farm? The school? Are you thinking that some of the monks here came with treasures from the abbey? Could we, perchance, be serving small beer from the Holy Grail?'

'Thus turning it into the finest wine?'

He didn't laugh.

'There's no gold here, Dr John. Only a treasury of learning. And the desire to contain what must be contained.'

I stepped back from him, thinking hard. There might never be a better opportunity to approach the matter of the bones of Arthur. Of a sudden, I felt tinglingly close to an elusive mystery. Yes, the real treasure here, in a landscape where spheres of being might merge one with another, would indeed be more elusive than gold. But what, in the material sense, might be inside this too-perfect conical mound?

However, Dr Dee must needs conceal his esoteric interests. While Dr John would be yet wary of this one-time monk turned lawman. As for the other person within me…

Oh yes, there was another, now. A third person.

One who, looking down towards the path, wanted nothing so much as to be on it, and running. For inside this third person something was fluttering like to a trapped bird.

The mist had thinned again, as if some old enchantment had been broken, or a new one formed. And it was the third man who spread his hands to prevent them shaking and prepared to lie.

'Sir Edmund... even if there were cause to suspect you or your establishment of concealing treasure—'

Fyche watching me steadily, like to a hawk upon a bough.

'Then what could I do,' I said, 'but take my suspicions to a... Justice of the Peace?'

His eyes widened momentarily, then dulled, and he smiled. Knowing now what he was dealing with: a jobbing servant of the Crown who'd muddy no pools and was, like most of his kind, corruptible. There was even a kind of contempt in that smile. I was glad to observe it and made a small bow.

'And now, if you'll excuse me, I think I should go and inquire about the health of my colleague.'

Fyche nodded.

'If I were you, Dr John, I'd set about finding him a qualified physician. If the witch has dosed him with nightshade, you'll never prove it once he's dead.'

'We needed a doctor,' Dr John said humbly. 'And were told that, apart from Mistress Borrow, there was no-one.'

'Then, trust me, Dr John,' Fyche said. 'No-one would have been the safer choice. Good day to you.'

He nodded a stern farewell, his face quiet, then turned and walked away, and I headed for the footpath. I would not give way to the third man and go looking for Mistress Borrow, I would continue with my mission and seek out the bone-seller mentioned by Cowdray.

But then, at the footpath's edge, I stopped, of a sudden, as if both my legs were seized, and looked back at Fyche over my shoulder, calling to him.

'Would it be permissible, Sir Edmund, to ask what evidence there is against Mistress Borrow?'

He stopped.

'In the matter of witchcraft?' I said.

Fyche turned, remaining a good twenty yards away, fingering his jaw, considering. Then he approached slowly, until he stood before me again.

'Dr John, you might think me a harsh man. But our roles in life alter, according to the will of God. Until the Dissolution of the abbey, I was a monk. Now I'm the father of two sons. A landowner. A Justice of the Peace. The words *justice* and *peace* being at the very heart of God's teaching.' He paused for a moment. 'The main evidence against Eleanor Borrow would be of birth and circumstance.'

I waited. The ruin of the church tower shimmered in the lightening mist, spectral. As if it were *of* the mist. Or made of glass.

'I was obliged,' Fyche said, 'to hang her mother.'

✢

Yes, I *could* have taken this further, but that would have meant pursuing him, maybe revealing too much. I'm not good at this.

I walked away, slowly.

At first.

Until I was out of sight of Fyche and the monks, and then there was a green-grey blurring of turf and sky as I went stumbling in a frenzy down the devil's hill, eyes flicking this way, that way, ignoring the path, tripping twice before ground level, then tumbling over the stile to the holy well, wood-splinters piercing the soft, white flesh of my bookman's hands.

Calling out for her, an owl-screech in my head yet still deafening in its intensity.

Eleanor!

And even once…

Nel…

No-one there. Only the powerful hiss of the blood water racing through the veins of the sacred earth.

'Tis certain true to say that some men and women here are driven very speedily into madness.

How speedily? Two hours? Three hours? Or had whole weeks and months gone by since I first walked with her – as with men and women captured and taken into the faerie world?

Now I was falling, near-sobbing, to the ground, splashing the blood-water on my face, into my eyes.

Jesu, what am I become?

XVI

Love the Dead

No bones were visible within the shop, only raw skin, and I began to wonder if I were tricked.

The premises were in a mean and stinking alley off what was called Magdalene Street, opposite the abbey gatehouse. The sky was darkening now, and swollen like a vast bladder, with unshed rain.

Inside the shop, however, all was pale and soft: everywhere, the skins and fleeces of sheep, some made into rough garments and bulky hats.

And could this truly be Benlow the bone-man?

I'd imagined him old and shrivelled, clad in rags, but this man was no more than my own age. Tall, fair-haired and fresh-faced, and his apparel was of a quality far finer than mine and almost certainly above his station – the silver brooch in his hat, that fashionable slash in his doublet, red as a fresh wound.

He bowed and made gesture toward an array of garments hanging from hooks along one wall.

'Fleece cloak, my lord?'

'Fleece—?'

'You don't want to be took in by this fine weather. 'Twill turn biting cold by the week's end, that's what all the shepherds say, and nobody knows the weather better than a shepherd.'

'I already, um, have a cloak,' I said.

'Fleeced?'

'Well—'

'Thought not!' He bounced upon his toes, his tone light and soft as down-feathers. 'I'm guessing, my lord, that you ain't from these parts. London, am I right? Not been here long?'

'Not yet one day.'

Jesu, it felt like a month.

'Thought I knew not your face! Well, let me tell you, my lord, the winters in London they don't compare – they *do not compare* – with what it's like out here when the snow comes. And it *will* come again, before spring, sure as I'm standing here. Don't mean to put fear into you, but this is God's absolute truth – without a fleece about your shoulders, my lord, you may die. Ask anybody.'

Eyeing me, now, from head to boots, as if estimating what size coffin I'd require. His accent was more London than the west, which maybe explained why Cowdray had been so quick to finger him to me.

I was silent for a moment, and then looked him in the eyes.

'No man need fear the cold, ' I said calmly, 'if he has the love of God in his heart.'

'Ah.' His face turned at once solemn. 'How true. How very true that is, my lord.'

'You're Master Benlow?'

'So my mother tells me.'

'Well, I'm here with a friend.'

'A *friend*.. I *see*.'

'We've ridden for many days. My friend –' my voice falling away – 'is ill.'

'Oh.'

'*Sorely* ill.'

'That saddens me, my lord, it truly does.'

'And, since his arrival, is become worse.'

'Oh, that *is* bad news.' He folded his arms. 'Because, you know, they say that however strong a man's faith be...'

'Sometimes prayer alone is not sufficient.'

'I've heard that, too.'

I was, as you know, not much good at this, but kept step with him.

'We came here,' I said, 'having been told of... miracles?'

He leaned back at last, arms folded, lips pursed at an angle.

'Been many of those, true enough. Glaston be famous the world over for its miracles. The mark of the Saviour's been upon this town since He walked these hills as a boy and his uncle, old Joe Mathea, laid down the first stones for the abbey, but I expect you know that.'

I nodded. 'Once, a true pilgrim might have gone to the abbey and prayed over the relics of saints. All the hundreds of saints buried there.'

'All gone now.'

I took breath, met his slanting gaze.

'*All* gone?'

'Gone from the *abbey*,' he said.

'But not necessarily from...' I'd run out of byways and subtlety. 'Master Benlow, my friend is a man of considerable wealth.'

'Where's he lie, my lord?'

'At the George.'

'Aye,' he said. 'There *is* a man lying at the George, I've heard that. They thought it was the plague.'

'We don't believe it to be the plague,' I said. 'But he's very weak, all the same.'

'Do you know,' he said, 'two women were *cured* of the plague after a visit to St Joe's shrine. Sure as I stand before you. You knew of that?'

'Where *is*... the shrine?'

To my knowledge, there was no evidence at all that Joseph of Arimathea had ever set foot in Glastonbury, never mind been buried here... only lustrous legend.

'*Ah!*' Benlow tapped his lips. 'Not many know that, and those that do keeps silent.'

'And are you one of them, Master Benlow?'

'The Vicar of Wells, now,' Benlow said. '*He* couldn't walk proper and he comes limping over here one day and he was cured in no time at all! And a *boy* - no word of a lie - was carried in stone dead and was, there and then, *raised*. Oh, your friend, he's come to the right place.'

'Yes.'

'It just ain't so easy no more... to find a bone to kiss.'

This was the first mention of bone. I told him we'd thought to take something home with us, some small, blessed relic that might be kept in our own church... secretly, of course.

'Oh, *must* be secret, my lord. Must!' He peered beyond me toward the door. 'What did you have in mind? A splinter from the true cross? Bottle of water poured from the Holy Grail itself? Or… a *fragment*…'

'A fragment?'

'A piece' – he leaned close, his voice a wisp upon the air – '*a shard of sainted skeleton.*'

I waited a moment, lest I be thought too eager.

'How much?'

'Well now, that would depend upon the *size* of it… and the eminence of the saint.'

'Who was the *most* eminent here?'

His eyes went still. I sensed his greed.

'I am,' I said, 'a man of discretion.'

'Follow me then,' he said, 'my lord.'

☩

In the windowless storehouse behind the shop, a single candle burned from a ledge, and the smell of new fleece was overlaid by the almost suffocating scent of incense around the foot of a ladder to the loft.

'Lambs of God,' Benlow said. 'Poor beasts.'

He giggled. Picking up a broom, he brushed wool and rushes away from the centre of the boarded floor, exposing there a shallow well. He paused, peering at me through the gloom.

'And you were sent here, were you?'

I nodded.

'See, I don't usually do no business in town. Some folk feels strongly about certain items being taken away, if you get my flow. When the weather's better, I usually goes on the road – with a big, hairy friend, naturally, for holy theft's still a problem in some parts. Though *I* do reckon a relic stole is a relic cursed and he who steals it won't last long in this life.'

Bending to the well in the floor, he pulled out a short board and then a second.

'Pass me the candle, my lord.'

I saw a wooden ladder, leading into blackness.

'You may go first.' Benlow held up the candle. 'Mind your head.'

I held tight to the ladder, not knowing how deep this well might be, but after three or four rungs my feet were both on the ground. It was no deeper than…

…a grave. And as cold.

And smelled like one. An acrid richness, full of earth and damp, and I began to wonder if I'd descended into some kind of cemetery vault.

Benlow handed down the candle, and I saw that the ground was earthen, with rough stone flags set into it, and the wooden ceiling was too low for me to stand upright.

'There's a bench to your left,' Benlow said. 'Best to sit, or you may emerge unable to hold up your head again. I always sit myself. Or lie.' He giggled. 'Not always alone…'

He arrived at the foot of the ladder. Dusted down his doublet, then gestured me to a bench against a wall of what looked to be rubble stone and took the candle to fire two rush-lights on brackets.

Sinking down uncomfortably on the bench, I perceived that the smell of damp and earth was overlaid now with a strange sweetness. Turning my head as light flared, I saw another smile and shuddered: a human skull sat on an arm of the bench, jawless, as if the teeth were sunk into the wood. Hitting my elbow on something hard, turning to see another on the opposite arm, this one with a hole in its cranium.

And then, as my eyes grew accustomed to the faint light, I saw that the wall was not of rubble but of hundreds of tight-packed bones – skulls and pelvises and skeletal hands, all jammed in, some with numbers painted on them in black and red. Benlow looked over them, waggling his fingers, then darted and plucked something from the wall, and I saw that the fat for the nearest rush-light was held in what was, unmistakably – *dear God* – an upturned human brain-pan.

Benlow saw me taking all this in and grinned, a diadem of small, pointed teeth.

'Out of death comes light. I do so love the dead. Do you not? And where in the world would I find such company as here? Tell me that, my lord.'

He came and sat down next to me, and I saw he was holding a slim, curved bone, brown as a willow-twig.

'See this? A rib of St Patrick. One of the very bones that caged his noble heart. Did you know St Patrick was here, and all the Irish monks that followed him? And look...'

Opened out his other hand. The specks in his palm looked like birdshit.

'Teeth of St Benignus, after whom the new church is named. He was Patrick's heir, did you know that?'

'Why aren't they in the church? Where did you get all—?'

'Relics? In a church? Where have you *been,* my lord?' He sniffed. 'Bloody old cold coming on. I don't think you have yet introduced yourself.'

'My name is Dr John.'

'A *doctor.*'

'Not of physic. Tell me... what of other relics?'

'My lord, how many do you *want?*'

I said nothing, unsure how to approach this. He leaned close, and I realised then that the sweet smell came from Benlow himself. Either his clothes or his body was copiously scented. A kind of incense mingled with sweat. Feeling, of a sudden, alarmed, I edged toward the end of the bench. Smiling faintly beside me, Benlow stretched out his long legs, hands behind his head, St Patrick's rib lying in his lap.

'I do have –' he whispered it, not looking at me – '*apostles.*'

'In Glastonbury?'

'Many famous people came here to die, in a state of grace. And because death comes easy, here, where the fabric between the spheres is finer than muslin.'

I did not hesitate.

'Like King Arthur?'

Maybe it was my own apprehension, or maybe not. But I felt something. A change. A troubling of the air. Benlow sat up, apparently unhurried, but I knew it was not so.

'A hundred saints in the wall,' he said sourly, 'and all the bastards want is Arthur.'

'All who want?'

I saw his full lips compressing.

145

'Who sent you here, my lord?'

'The innkeeper at the George, that's all.'

He turned to look at me.

'And what use would Arthur be to your *sick friend?*'

'Arthur stands for strength and valour. My friend's been a soldier.'

'Well, *I* don't think you have a sick friend.'

'Actually, I do. *And* you know of him. Because you keep your eyes open, Master Benlow. As anyone would, in your particular trade.'

He sniffed. Wiped his nose with the back of a hand.

'And there was me,' he said, 'thinking that such a nice-looking young man might be not averse to some boy-play.'

'*What?*'

'You're a much-travelled man, I can tell that. And you came down here without a word. Always a good test. Most men tell me what they want and wait in the light. Whereas a man drawn towards darkness and death… I can tell you that down here among the dead, you get a rare—'

'Master Benlow!'

Oh my God, a buck-hunter. Louvain had been full of them. I backed up against the skull.

'Master Benlow, who else has been here in search of the remains of Arthur?'

'And who are you to ask?'

'I'm an officer with the Queen's Commission on Antiquities.'

'Oh, blind me!' Benlow laughed shrilly. 'There's a bloody ole mouthful for you.'

'And the only mouthful, I'm afraid, that you're likely to get from me. Now, who—?'

'Ho fucking ho!'

The light flickering wildly in his eyes.

I said, 'Listen to me… I'm not Leland. I'm not here to take away your livelihood. Or any of your bones. Bones, as you say, are not much in favour any more.'

'Except for Arthur's, it'd seem.'

'Someone's been here in search of the bones of Arthur?'

He said nothing. His face was sulked in the yellowy light.

'Did you have them?'

'No.'

'Do you know where they are? Do you know who took them when the shrine was toppled at the Dissolution?'

'I can't help you. Not with bones.'

'Meaning what?'

He half rose. He was panting.

'If I give you what I have of Arthur, will you go away?'

'That depends.'

'*Wait.*'

He sprang up and was gone into the shadows. I tensed, keeping my eyes on the ladder in case he should double back and leave me down here, boarded up with the dead, but I could hear him scuffling about, the clacking of bones pulled out and flung aside. All the saintly bones that never were.

I saw then that the underground chamber was longer than I'd supposed, and in the dimness beyond the light I made out a wooden door. A door? Where could it go? We were already, I guessed, beyond the walls of Benlow's shop.

I'm not a complete fool and was about to make for the ladder when Benlow emerged at last from the shadows bearing a wooden box, clearly modern and hardly big enough for Arthur's foot-bones. He knelt at my feet and lifted its lid.

'Look...'

On a bed of fleece lay a fragment, not of bone, but of splintered wood.

'There,' he said.

'What is it?'

'Touch it.'

I placed a finger inside the box. The wood was hard, probably oak, blackened with age.

'Picture it, my lord,' Benlow said, but his voice was strained now and desperately wheedling. 'See a great hall hung with banners and lit by a thousand torches. Hear the walls echoing tales of valour.'

'Don't piss with me, Benlow.'

He slammed the lid down on the box and thrust it at me.

'Take it.' His jaw trembling. 'Take it back to London with you. Please. Don't come back! How many other men alive today can say they've laid hand on the round table?'

XVII

Crazed Bitch

IT WOULD HAVE been about half an hour past midnight when I dragged on my old brown robe and went to sit with Dudley in his room.

A small candle was burning on the water stand. He lay asleep and unmoving, his breathing even. Earlier, I'd watched him swallow half the jugful of holy water, enough returned to his everyday mind to wince at its metallic taste.

Discreetly, I'd unstoppered the bottle of his potion and sniffed it. As if that would tell me anything, for who could identify the scent of deadly nightshade? Nonsense, anyway. I'd had little hesitation in giving him more, and he'd slept.

I sat upon a stumpy wooden stool by the night-muddied window, staring into the candle flame, wide awake. A mathematician and an astronomer, who understood not the geometry of love, nor could hope to chart the trajectory of desire.

Least of all his own.

I'd awoken thrice before midnight in the hollow, stony silence of the George Inn, rolling in my bed and thinking at first that I'd caught Dudley's fever.

Becoming all too aware there was more than one kind of fever. It was as if all the suppressed bodily demands of my bookish youth had broken their chains at once. In the minutes when I was not awake, I was dreaming of the emeralds in the eyes, the abandon of the dark hair and the foxy crossing of those front teeth. The witch's daughter.

And I will travel to Avalon, to the fairest of all maidens…

…and she shall make all my wounds sound and make me whole with healing medicines…

Witchcraft… sorcery… conjuring. Despite its air of abandonment,

149

apathy and decay, I could well believe now that some element beyond our known science lived in this watery place, and the bones of Arthur were the least of its secrets.

'Meant to tell you…'

I spun round. Dudley was turned upon his side, his eyes open, bulbous in the candlelight.

'How are you now, Robbie?'

'Throat feels like I've swallowed a dagger.'

'It'll pass.'

'That's what your doctor says?'

A warm pulse inside me. I sat up.

'She came to me again,' Dudley murmured.

'When?'

'Dunno.' Raising his head on an arm. 'God's bollocks, John, she's a beauty. If I'd the strength to lift the sheets, I'd have had her in here with me before you could say…' Unable to come up with a suitably distasteful word, he let his head fall back. 'At least I'm beginning to feel I might not have to bargain with the evil one… in the short-term.'

'Pity,' I said. 'Dying was good for you. You spoke more truth than I've heard from you in years.'

'What did I say?'

'It'll save. What was it you meant to tell me?'

'What?'

'You said you meant to tell me something.'

'God knows.' Dudley rolled onto his back, making the candle flame bend. 'Oh… bears? Was it bears?'

'I don't know.'

'I'll tell you 'bout that anyway. The Queen's fondness for the bear-baiting, the way it distresses you so. This is from when we were children – eleven or twelve. There was to be a bear-baiting one day—'

'*We?*'

'Bess and me. We'd overheard my father discussing it with my uncle – the evening's sport. We were in the gardens, behind some holly bushes and my father's going, "How shall the women be entertained, meanwhile, and the maids?" Making it clear that the bear-baiting was strictly for the men and women and maids might faint at the… flying blood and flesh. Thus spoiling the enjoyment of the men.'

I got up and poured out more water for him. He glanced at me and scowled.

'Though some men – *half* men – remain oblivious of its… Anyway, I remember watching Bess, as we're crouching behind that bush. She's but eleven years old, don't forget. Never seen a mouth set so tight. Stamping her little foot till they let her in. So they did. She came to the bear-baiting… and though at times her eyes strained with tears she never once looked away and, at the end, she's clapping longer and harder than any man round the pit.'

'I see,' I said.

'I thought you'd be interested to know that,' Dudley said.

'Would explain a lot.'

Dudley said softly, 'I think that what I saw in her eyes that day was a sensing of her destiny in a world of men. For a little maid, you had to admire her balls.'

I wondered why he'd never told me this before. Maybe he thought he owed me something for his avoidance, once more, of an early death. Although, in truth, all thanks were due to Eleanor Borrow. The witch.

'God, why do I feel so weak, John. Barely drag my arse to the damn piss-pot.'

'Well, don't think I'm going to hold it up for you.'

An image of Benlow came into my head, and I shuddered.

'No, fair enough.' Dudley summoned the shade of a smile. 'So who is she really?'

'The doctor?'

'Doctors don't come with good tits. Doctors are white-faced, humour-less bastards, who… is she still in the inn?'

'I don't know where she is. I… tried to find her earlier.'

I'd asked Cowdray where she lived, and he'd sent one of his boys for her, but the boy came back saying the house was empty. I'd looked also for Martin Lythgoe, to find out if he'd spoken to the farrier, but he wasn't around either, and I'd eaten alone and sparsely in the ale-house, surrounded by cider-swilling farmers.

Dudley said, 'What the hell are we doing in this shithole, John? Remind me.'

'We've come to search for the bones of Arthur.'

'Have we found them?'

'Not yet. I... went, on Cowdray's advice—'

'You told Cowdray why—?

'No. Not exactly.'

'*Jesu*, John!'

'I went to see a dealer in relics. He had a load of old bones... any old bones...'

'From where?'

'I don't know. Stolen from church crypts, dug out of graves. People bring them to him, I'd guess, for pennies. He sells them to gullible pilgrims as saintly relics.'

'He'd be a source, I suppose,' Dudley mused, 'if we don't find the real bones. Though we'd probably need to get him killed afterwards.'

I stared at him. It might be the fever speaking or he might be serious. Either way, no time to tell him of my suspicion that Benlow might indeed know where the actual remains were to be found. What had been very clear to me was that something pertaining to the matter of Arthur had left that man sorely afraid.

'*I'd* find them,' Dudley said, 'if I could get out of this pit.'

'Give it another day. Get up too soon and it'll come back, only worse. Robbie...'

'Get me a new nightshirt, would you, tomorrow? This one stinks to heaven.'

I pulled the stool away from the wall and sat down just outside the circle of candlelight.

'He offered me an obvious fake.'

'Who did?'

'The relic man. He had a lump of wood which he said was from Arthur's round table.'

'Have you heard of the round table still preserved?'

'Not here. Only the one in Winchester Cathedral. And we all know the truth of that.'

Everyone accepted that this huge artefact was Plantaganet fakery, maybe from the time of Edward III, who was crazy for Camelot, or even Edward I who had travelled to see the bones entombed at Glastonbury Abbey. The Winchester board had been further tampered with by the Great Furnace who, at a time of his own enthusiasm for all things Arthurian, had caused his own features to be imposed upon it.

'This Benlow… he would've told me it was a piece of the true cross if he'd thought that was what I was looking for. Glastonbury seems to be a place where it's ever difficult to make out the real from the false. If you're an outsider, anyway. Look, your own vis—'

I broke off. Without thinking, I'd found myself giving voice to another matter which was denying me sleep. Too late, now.

'Robbie, when you walked out to the abbey, last night, you said you'd seen—'

'Don't recall going to any abbey.'

'I saw you from my window. You walked across the street.'

'You were dreaming.'

'You said you'd seen an old man. You said the old man was looking down on you, as if he was in the air, and you could see the moon—'

'I was full of *fever*!' Dudley pulled the blankets tighter around him. 'Don't you go throwing my sickbed fancies back at me!'

'What about the Queen?'

He stared at me.

'Does the Queen have delusions?'

'How dangerously do you want to live, John?'

'It's said the Queen… sees her mother.'

'Who says that?' He tried to rise, slid back down. 'What shit are they spreading around court now?'

'I wouldn't say that it's being spread around. My source is… a discreet source.'

Dudley closed his eyes.

'Anne Boleyn. God…'

'Is it true?'

'Crazed bitch.'

'Anne Boleyn?'

'Could've stopped all the talk. My father always said that. But maybe she liked it.'

'The talk of witchcraft?'

'Also, probably thought Harry liked it. Added to her allure. Her having a extra finger and all. And moles. They say she had a furry mole shaped like a...' He closed his eyes. 'And maybe he *did* like it. Maybe it oiled his lance. For a while. Until she was his wife – would all have to stop then. But, by God, if anyone thinks that Bess...' Dudley's eyes came open and he looked hard at me across the shadows. 'You know, unless you really think you can help, you'd do best to forget this, John.'

'Help?'

'But then you don't go in for the cure of souls, do you? Didn't you once tell me that?'

I said, 'Queen Mary—'

'I always thought you'd prefer to forget Queen Mary, too.'

'Do you remember telling me, some years ago, how Mary had oft-times warned the Princess Elizabeth to be seen to reject her mother and the Boleyn nest of Lutherans. Pleading with her to embrace the old faith while she yet could?'

'I need to sleep,' Dudley said. 'Did you not tell me that?'

✝

Back in my bedchamber, I stood by the window and gazed down into Glastonbury's moonlit high street. Beyond it, the abbey's arches, a company of the mournful dead.

I was remembering the townsfolk yesterday and my sense that they went about their business as if in a play. As if all of them knew that the town possessed a life *beneath*, which must needs be concealed for its own protection... except when reference to it might be used to secure the future, the way the monks of the twelfth century had used the bones of Arthur.

The monks. Guardians of this sacred ground for more than a thousand years.

What did that mean? What did it mean *now*? All abbeys and monasteries were repositories of ancient and esoteric knowledge, and if this had been the oldest of them all – the very foundation stone of Christianity in England – then, yes, it would have been heavy with sacred secrets.

As for the conservation of physical items of value, the gold and the bones… well, plans would have been made well in advance, individuals selected for the task of secreting them away when the abbey fell into the Great Furnace.

It could be that some of these items had been smuggled across to France or hidden in the wildest parts of Wales.

Yet…

…a hallowed place. Even with the abbey going to ruin. There are some things you can't destroy. Some things about a place that are in *that place.*

I thought of Brother Michael, the mute who'd been with Fyche, and what jewels might be enclosed in his silent world. And I thought of Abbot Whiting, the benign old man who'd held on to his secrets, held out under torture, before a slow and savage death on the devil's hill.

It seemed to me that I'd done the right thing in not asking Fyche about the bones. The man to ask would have been the abbot himself.

A shuddering breath came into me. Across the street, under a bloating moon, the corpse of the abbey lay restless and violated.

It was past three in the morning. I felt a pang of anxiety about my mother and Catherine Meadows at the house in Mortlake and knelt and prayed for their safety.

And then, knowing that if I went back to bed, my thoughts and dreams would once more go searching for the witch's daughter, I shed my old brown robe and reached for my day apparel.

XVIII

The First Age of Light

THREE SPHERES.

The natural world, the celestial or astral world, and the supercelestial, wherein are angels.

Though she's never spoken of it to me, I've reason to believe that my mother once went with our neighbour, Goodwife Faldo, to visit a woman who kept a skrying crystal through which she professed to see the faces of the dead.

This would have been not long after my father's death, so I could understand why my mother had done it. But I knew, even then, that my ambition must needs be loftier, aiming for communion with the supercelestial, wherein lies truth and light and not deception.

Therefore *not ghosts*. A ghost in the natural world is *un*natural. To call down a spirit of the departed into *this* world is necromancy. Even if it be the spirit of my poor tad.

Or the shade of what once was a man of God?

I heard again the voice of Bishop Bonner, the day he came into my prison cell, asking the question which would determine whether I lived or burned.

Tell me, Dr Dee… do you believe that the soul is divine?

Me telling him what I believed to be the truth:

The soul is… not itself divine, but it can acquire *divinity.*

And Bonner going, *Tell me, then, Doctor, how can the soul acquire divinity?*

Extending my string, his little eyes tindered like the glowing tips of tapers.

By prayer, I'd said. *And learning. The Bible… and the sacred knowledge of the Jews.*

Getting it right, guessing what Bonner was after.

But I'd omitted *martyrdom.*

As in tortured, hanged, drawn and quartered.

✢

The night was cold and still but not quite freezing. Cloaked and shadowy, I entered the abbey grounds through the open gateway, finding the gates closed but unlocked. Never thinking it would be quite so easy to gain admission. But then, what was to steal now but the stones themselves?

I'd read what I could find about the history and layout of the abbey. Enough to recognise the plundered remains of the abbot's grand house and his distinctive kitchen, with its ornate pinnacle, pale as ice in the moonlight, and the Lady Chapel above where the bones of Arthur had been found.

But I was shocked at the condition of the place. What once must have been well-scythed lawn was now a wilderness of bushes and black brambles whipping and ripping at my boots. Broken walls were rearing around me like an old carcass left to the weather and the crows, and I could even smell its decay, all moist and foetid.

I stopped and looked around in the silvered pool of moonlight. An apartment had been built near here for the one and only visit of the Queen's grandfather, Henry VII. When, of course, he would have seen the black marble tomb. What had he been told about it, this man who'd ridden into England through Wales, trailing the legend of the undying British king? Would he have seen this evidence of the great Arthur's death as a threat to the credibility of the next Arthur, his son?

But there'd been no indication of a future religious division then, and King Henry would never have thought to lay a finger on this or any other tomb. And, anyway, the new King Arthur... this was not to be. The prince had died before his father who had himself departed soon afterwards. Heavy with melancholy, it was said, and sick with the fear that his Tudor line might, through hubris, have brought down upon itself not dynastic glory but some old curse.

As if *he* should have worried about hubris. If this comparatively frugal, cautious man had reason to think his line accursed, what could be said about the son who'd succeeded him in Arthur's stead? Starting wars, building palace after palace – temples to himself – and then, to help pay for it all, directing the wreck and plunder of religious houses. Little wonder that the Queen feared the worst and thought herself haunted by evil.

Haunted.

I looked up in search of my far-off friends, the stars, finding Orion's belt and then, prominent tonight, the seven-starred body of Ursa Major, the Great Bear, my hands instinctively reaching out to cup it like a cluster of jewels. While *I* was embraced by the skeletal frame of the abbey whose walls, honeyed by daylight, now came in weathered-bone shades of white and grey.

It was not a welcoming embrace. I heard a movement and turned and saw small, moonlit orbs.

Jesu...

Ewes. Sheep grazed in here, now.

I sat down on a low wall until my breath was regular again, imagining these walls aglow in the light of a thousand candles which would flicker in rhythm with the ethereal rise and fall of the Roman chant. It was this incandescence which I held in my head as I stood and, with right arm extended, inscribed, in the air and then on the ground before me, the sign of the pentagram.

The old protection, but it needed more. Kneeling in the centre of the imagined pentagram, amongst broken stones at the entrance to the nave, I began to pray in a whisper, invoking the ancient shield of St Patrick's Breastplate, which would almost certainly have been known to Arthur.

'Christ be with me, Christ within me
Christ behind me, Christ before me
Christ beside me...'

Breaking off, aghast, remembering how I'd held a bone purported to be part of Patrick's actual breastplate.

What was I *doing?*

But the words went on inside my head, as if creating their own momentum.

Natural magic.

'I bind unto myself the Name
The Strong Name of the Trinity
By invocation of the same
The Three in One and One in Three...'

When I'd finished, keeping my eyes tight closed, I called back the words of those who'd known the abbot in life, in good times and then the worst of times.

Cowdray: *saw him lashed to a hurdle, dragged through the high street. Bumping along like a deer carcass. An old man, beaten, bruised and cut about like a low-born thief...*

Mistress Borrow: *remember his wrinkly smile, and his eyes had a kindness. For a long time, I thought I'd seen the face of God.*

Better, yes. But more important...

The poor man has little cause for rest.

If he was still here and rested not, then this surely would not be the crime against God and State which was called necromancy.

Which, I swear to you, I had never attempted. Not my direction. Smelled too much of grave-dirt and divination by the examination of entrails. Necromancy: the very word whispered *death*. As if the dead had no purpose but to serve the desires of the living.

Afraid, then?

I came to my feet. After all my years of study, I hadn't expected to be afraid. Our grandparents crouched over their fires, the slits in their walls shuttered against the storms. Even in Tad's day there were still those who believed a ghost was a walking corpse, an earthen being rising putrid from the grave.

But now we live in the first age of light. Now we stand behind walls of glass like great lanterns and watch the bending of the trees and the bursting of the skies. We stand, protected, and study, in warmth, the force and the violence of nature. And thus old shadows fall away, and the spirits of the dead are become flitting, half-seen moonbeams.

I gripped cold stone, slick with slugtrails.

Perchance I can help.

Listen to me.

Perchance we might help one another, you and I, Abbot, two men of learning divided only by the thin skein of mortality.

Here, within my protective pentagram, upon the cold hearth of our faith, intoning words and phrases borrowed from the grimoires, rendered safe and wholesome, or so I must needs believe, by Christian prayer.

Not conjuring. I won't command, in the manner of the old sorcerers. I only request....

'...humbly, in the name of the Father, Son and Holy Spirit, if the Trinity doth so consent. Dear God, if it be your will that I might help your servant Abbot Whiting find peace... that I may bear a portion of his burden, in return for some small enlightenment, then let him appear to me now in... in a not unpleasant form.'

A not unpleasant form. Essential, that. Always important in the grimoires to imagine how you would wish to view the spirit.

State it firmly. *A not unpleasant form.* Say it strongly, then let it go. Imagination, when bound to our human will, can be a powerful tool for altering the course of events but, when left to its own devices, can cause havoc in the mind.

So, do I feel, or do I *imagine,* the air growing cold around me? Should I, as a scientist, try to still such feelings, separating myself from them to stand aside, become an observer? Or allow these fancies to form around me, creating a numinous cloud into which a spirit, some watery essence of a man, might gradually become manifest?

The conjurer at work.

Dear God.

✠

You think me reckless?

You who watch from behind your window glass. You who were not there that night, cold in the belly of the abbey.

Slowly lifting my face, I placed him there, imprinting him upon my closed eyelids, marking that look of helpless sorrow on his face and his hands raised in formal, weary benediction.

Who's to say what are visions and what are signs of an oncoming madness?

I must have been close to the edge of a kind of madness when, in a instant of heart-lurch, I knew that I was not alone.

Knew? How did I know? *How?* Did I hear then movement, a footfall among the riffling of last winter's crispen leaves, the slow beat of owl wings?

It was none of that. None of anything. Only an absence, a flatness, a deadness, a *not-hearing*. A void which spoke of the dreadful.

I'm trying, God help me, to explain this. Without diagrams or arcane symbols. To evoke the crawling fear it awoke in me as, with a last, slack-lipped prayer, wildly slashing another pentagram in the air before me, I began moving, open-eyed now, along the moon-washed, rubbled nave towards the chancel.

Towards what was there.

XIX

Beyond Normal

COWDRAY CAME BACK with me to the abbey.

I'd battered every door in the George Inn until I'd found the chamber where he lay – with one of the kitchen maids, I believe. Now he stood on the edge of the chancel and shivered and looked again at what was there and shivered again. Crossing himself, I noticed, before turning away, almost in anger.

'I'll send a boy for Sir Edmund Fyche. And constables. There should be a hue and cry.'

'No... wait.'

A little light. A single lantern, burning in the vastness.

Dear God, dear God, dear God...

'Doctor, this is...' Moonlight deepening the furrows in Cowdray's face, turning them black. ''Tis beyond normal, man.'

'What's normal?' I was barely in control. 'How are men *usually* killed here?'

'In hot blood. And strong drink.' His voice flat. 'Never like this.'

The man who lay dead had arms spread wide, like to Our Saviour on his cross. Shadows flucting like the wings of angels on the walls above and to the sides.

'I must needs consult my colleague,' I said. 'Master Roberts.'

'He's ill.'

'Yes, and needs sleep, however—'

'He doesn't need *this*,' Cowdray said. 'God's word...'

'No.'

I've lived through violent times, seen men executed in divers gruesome ways but nothing, since the burning of Barthlet Green, so heartsick close.

I turned again to face it, swallowing bile and self-loathing, the lantern held high.

Like something sanctified, the dead man lay pointing east, towards where the high altar would have stood and the tomb of black marble.

The remains of a candle were wedged in his mouth, his tallowed lips obscenely around its stem. Throwing a hand to my mouth and nose, for now I could smell it: cold fat and shit. The candle must have been lit, its melting making a ruined deathmask of the face. And, on the rim of its fading rays, was also displayed what had been done, dear God, to the chest.

The body raided, organs laid out glistening in a sludge of black blood like a breakfast of sweetmeats among the stones. I bent over and vomited again, and saw, for the first time, what lay in the left hand.

'Oh Christ, Cowdray...'

Dudley used to say that Martin Lythgoe had been a part of his household since his boyhood. I did not know him well but thought him a fine man. A good man.

'This town's starting to stink to hell,' Cowdray said with venom. 'Come away, Doctor.'

But I was making myself look again, to confirm that in poor Martin's left hand lay what even I – no anatomist, a doctor only by title – knew to be his unbeating heart.

Then following Cowdray back to the gatehouse, the abbey rearing around us, like nothing so much, in this sour dawn, as the open-ribbed skeleton of a great ox.

'You're right.' I said. 'You'd better send for him.'

✝

Lanterns aplenty now. The last of the night alight and the abbey looking, perversely, as if it were made active again. I felt confused and dislocated, the weariness of a sleepless night descending damply around me as I watched Fyche marking the scene from his horse and then dismounting and strolling over, unhurried.

'This is the corpse of your servant, Dr John?'

He'd ridden in with three constables and the first lines of dawn in the sky. Leather jerkin and riding boots. He picked up a lantern to light my face, as if he might see guilt written upon it. And maybe he would.

'Interesting that you should be the one to find him, Dr John. Why exactly *were* you in the abbey, on the wrong side of midnight?'

'I...' Christ, I hadn't even thought to invent a reason. 'I couldn't sleep. Seemed like a good, quiet time to inspect the ruins. When there was no-one about.'

'Except the dead. You're not yourself afeared of the walking dead, then, Doctor?'

'I have a job to do.'

How unlikely all of this was now sounding.

'For were you not a servant of the Crown,' Fyche said, 'I might have assumed you'd gone there to steal.'

'Steal what?'

'Or even to kill,' Fyche said. '*If* you were not supposed to be in the Queen's employ.'

I said nothing. Two constables patrolled the extent of the nave with their swinging lanterns.

'I regret this, Dr John, but I think it's time for me to inspect your documents of authority. Don't you?'

'I'll fetch them.'

My letter of authority was not from Cecil himself, which might have caused unnecessary alert, but it carried the necessary seal. I made to walk away, but Fyche put out an arm.

'Not now – I've more questions. When did you last see this man alive?'

'I... last afternoon. Not long before you and I met upon the tor.'

'You and the witch? He was with you and the witch?'

'I'd sent him back to attend to his master.'

'I thought you told me *you* were his master.'

'I spoke loosely. In strictest truth, he's in the employ of my... of Master Roberts.'

'The man who lies sick. But, despite his doctor – not yet dead.'

'Improving,' I said.

'Unlike this wretched man.' Fyche turned to look down at Martin Lythgoe. 'The manner of whose death— how would *you* describe it?'

'Foul and unjust.'

The rising stench was worse, but Fyche made no attempt to move away. He removed his hat, bent to Martin's plundered body.

'Yet efficiently accomplished. Split from throat to groin. A butcher's tools, would you say?'

'I'm a clerk, not a coroner.'

'Or an axe to split the ribs. Look...'

Didn't want to look. Looked up instead, to where one of the nave's own ribs had collapsed in upon itself, another smashed corpse.

'Both lungs most *carefully* detached,' Fyche said. 'And the long entrails of the guts – do you see? – wound tightly around one arm, like to a coiled serpent.'

Through the hole in the roof, the cold sky was lit by bright Venus, the daybreak planet.

'And the heart placed, like a sceptre, in the left hand. Reasonable, therefore, to assume that the killer would be plentifully daubed with gore. So, what *did* happen to this man?'

'Sir Edmund, we can fully see what happened to him, I just can't tell you why. He was a groom. He talked more to horses than men. A gentle man, a harmless man...'

'But the manner of his killing...?'

'It has... an element of ritual.'

Fyche nodded, pricks of white in his half-grown beard. He'd wanted me to say it.

'And an element of sacrilege, also,' I said. 'If you accept that the abbey remains sacred.'

'Oh, it's still *sacred*,' Fyche said. 'The question is, to whom?'

'You see the hand of Satan everywhere, don't you, Fyche?' I maybe should not have spoken thus, but I was tired. 'Yes, yes,' I mumbled wearily, 'cry mercy. If this isn't satanic evil, I know not what is.'

Feeling the heat of his lantern, now, as he leaned close.

'Hands,' he said. 'Show me your hands.'

'I...' Looked into his grizzled face. 'What?'

'Hands. Both of them.'

Two of his constables had appeared either side of him. I held out my hands, humiliated, while he examined them at leisure under a lantern.

'Thank you. A necessary formality.'

I could only nod.

'For what it's worth,' Fyche said, 'the last time I was summoned here it was a cockerel on a makeshift altar of fallen stones. The element of sacrilege noted… but not pursued.'

'A blood sacrifice?'

'Wasn't the remains of a chicken supper, Dr John.'

'Who are the people who commit such crimes against God?'

'The same as those who dig up graves and remove bones.'

Given our surroundings I thought he must mean Arthur and couldn't make the link. But I was wrong.

'No more than a week ago,' Fyche said, 'the grave of a man laid to rest some years ago was dug up from the graveyard of St Benignus across the street. Necromancy, Dr John. I told you, there's filth in this town. Ask the Borrow woman.'

'She's a *doctor*…'

'You're naive, Dr John. And I'll give you another thought. Was this poor man, perchance, asking questions, on your behalf, about what treasures might be acquired by the Crown? Thus awakening bitter memories of another list gathered more than twenty years ago?'

'Leland?'

'Was this man's visit to the abbey tonight made for the same reason as your own? To look for relics? Had you sent him?'

'No, I… I don't know why he was here.'

'It's an odd coincidence, is it not?'

'I suppose.'

'Well,' Fyche said. 'I have no choice but to send a messenger to Sir Peter Carew in Exeter. With the abbey in his charge, he'd thank neither of us for concealing from him a killing of this nature. And, ah… was he not your travelling companion?'

I nodded, hardly relishing the thought of Carew rampaging through the town like some beached pirate.

'He'll be here within a day or so,' Fyche said. 'Even less likely than I to allow the scum who did this to remain free for long.'

I looked for Cowdray's reaction to this, but he'd wandered away. I wondered how extreme had been Fyche's latent conversion to the reformed church. There was ever a certain kind of man who would find personal fulfilment, even a bloody pleasure, in the persecution of a particular species, be it Catholics or Protestants, Jews or Saracens. They said Bonner was one such, but Bonner had never changed sides, even to stay out of prison.

'I'll have more constables brought in from Wells,' he said, 'and then we'll be obliged to set to and take this town apart. The innocent will be inconvenienced, doubtless. But the murder of a servant of the Queen – no matter how menial – is no occasion for a soft tread.'

An excuse to flatten the maggots. The air was full of the stench of tallow, blood and shit. I swallowed my nausea.

Fyche took a long, slow inbreath against the stink and turned to bend over the corpse, and I...

What I saw next... you must understand that I was tired. I'd had no sleep this night and insufficient the night before. My head ached and my vision was blurred and imagination, left to its own devices, can, as I may have said, cause havoc in the mind, and who was to say what were visions and what were signs of an oncoming madness?

The candle wedged into Martin Lythgoe's mouth had formed itself into a cone of yellow wax spread beyond his lips across his chin and cheeks. My first impression – of a piss-sniffer's mask – was swiftly replaced as I took in blackened wick standing erect from the steep, yellow cone, slicked with rivulets of melted fat.

'John... what the hell...'

No!

'...goes on?'

I twisted around, to find Robert Dudley, half dressed, steadying himself against a collapsed wall, his face sweat-oiled and eyes dark smudges. I wanted to scream at him to get back, but could not speak, for inside my head was bobbing the image of the melted candle which, I swear, had resembled nothing so much as a grotesque waxen likeness of the Glastonbury Tor.

And that... that was when I became aware – one of the strangest, most creepingly invasive feelings of my life thus far – that this place, in some unholy way, was beginning to live inside me.

PART THREE

Although the semicircle of the Moon is placed above the circle of the Sun and would appear to be superior, nevertheless we know that the Sun is ruler and King. We see that the Moon in her shape and her proximity rivals the Sun with her grandeur, which is apparent to ordinary men, yet the face, or a semi-sphere of the Moon, always reflects the light of the Sun. It desires so much to be impregnated with solar rays and to be transformed into Sun that at times it disappears completely from the skies and some days after reappears, and we have represented her by the figure of the Horns.

John Dee,
Monas Hieroglyphica.

XX

Our Sister

'Wife,' Dudley said. 'Seven children.'

The window glass was full of pinky light, the unwintry dawn creaming the sky like some sickly syllabub.

'Five boys,' Dudley said. 'Two girls.'

This was a side of him I'd rarely seen. He sat, shivering in the cold and his anguish, on the side of his bed, still too weak to be out of it.

'My father's stable boy when I was young. Would, I swear, have died for my father – gone to the block in his stead. Loyalty, John. An immovable loyalty.' He sucked in a hissing breath which must have pained his swollen throat. 'The hell with Carew, if I find these bastards first, I'll cut them down where they stand, piece by fucking—'

Then began to weep, knowing that, in truth, he couldn't cut down a bed of reeds. His sword lay on the floorboards, half unsheathed as if he'd not the strength to draw it.

I stood up at the window, looking down into the high street, where the goodwives huddled watching men dismounting by the abbey gates: Fyche's constables from Wells. They'd put Martin's body, his insides on his lap, in an outbuilding at the abbey for Carew to inspect as soon as he arrived from Exeter.

I turned back to the pink-washed chamber.

Confession.

'I sent him away,' I said. 'Yesterday. He'd followed me.'

'Aye. Like a good hound.'

Dudley was sobbing, his shoulders aquake, and I sensed the murder of Martin Lythgoe all bound up, in the dark of his sickness, with the execution of his father and all the other dread memories of unjust killings he'd known in his score and six years.

At last, he looked up at me, without shame, through his tears.

'With Lythgoe, there always had to be someone to watch over. After my father was gone, it was me. With me sick in bed, the poor bugger was looking out for you.'

'And I sent him away.'

Fingernails piercing my palms.

'Chrissake, John, how could you have known?'

Well, I couldn't, but it didn't matter. It was the circumstance. The fact that I'd dispatched this man to the most sickening and degrading of deaths because…

….because of some half-formed fascination with Eleanor Borrow. And you know the worst of it? The worst of it was that Dudley, being Dudley, would have understood.

'Where did you send him, John?'

'Back here. To… make sure you were drinking enough water.'

I know. I *know*. But if I'd told him about bidding Martin Lythgoe to find the farrier, he'd go dragging himself through the streets like a leper until he'd located the man himself.

'I don't remember.' Squeezing his head. 'Don't remember him coming back. It was the last time I saw him and I *don't remember*.'

'You'd be sleeping. As you should be now.'

'Can't even…' Head sinking into his hands. 'Can't even think. What… I mean, for God's sake, what was Lythgoe *doing* there in the middle of the night? In the abbey?'

'May not have happened in the middle of the night. He may have lain there some hours.'

How long for a candle to burn out? How long had the candle been? Or had someone else come along afterwards and stuffed it in his mouth? But only a madman would do that… and not possible, anyway, if the rigor had set in, jaws and teeth clenched tight.

'And what were *you* doing there, John? What in God's name took you to the abbey?'

'Couldn't sleep.'

'You went out there alone… because you couldn't *sleep?*'

As if he hadn't done the same the previous night. Yet I was growing tired of lies and half-truths. I'd tell him, spell it out, the whole folly of it.

'The abbot,' I said. 'They say the abbot doesn't rest.'

'Who says that?'

'Cowdray. And if such a thing was there to be seen... I wanted to see it.'

Dudley stared at me. Reluctantly, I met his gaze.

'For Christ's sake, suddenly, everyone sees them. The Queen, you... everyone but me. There. A sorrowful admission from a half-man.'

From the street came the merry honk of a hunting horn, then a billowing of laughter. The blood was up, the chase was on.

'Let me get this fully clear,' Dudley said. 'You went into the ruins intending to conjure the spirit of the last abbot?'

'*No!* I don't conjure. Don't *do* that. I just wanted...'

Courage dying on me. Dudley slid back on to his pillow, staring up at the ceiling beams.

'Do you know something? I think if I were a ghost, the very last man on earth I'd want to appear before would be John Dee. Walking all around me, peering and prodding and unrolling his measuring device and exhausting me with his endless questions about the condition of the afterlife and have I seen God yet and what does—'

'*All right.*'

'Or perchance you thought the spirit might conveniently point you in the direction of the bones of Arthur?'

Too close. I sat down on the stool under the window, said that I could only wish I'd gone there earlier, when Martin Lythgoe was yet alive.

'What? So they could slay you, too? Where would that leave us?'

'I might –' wiped a hand across my unshaved jaw – 'might've been able to—'

'Display your mastery of the fighting arts? Throw a couple of heavy books at them?'

I said nothing. Dudley weakly raised his hands.

'Forgive me, John, who am I to talk, weak as an infant born before time? God help me if I didn't awake this morn with the sure knowledge that this whole adventure was no more than a scheme of Cecil's to keep me out of Bess's bedchamber long enough for him to talk sense into her.'

'He's alarmed by the gossip from France,' I said. 'That's all.'

'And who are the fucking French to lecture *us* on morals?' Dudley's head rolled back. 'What's this JP fellow say?'

'Talks of devil-worship. But then, he's a man who sees witchcraft and sorcery everywhere. He's also thinking there are those with bitter memories of Leland's list and its consequences for Glastonbury. Lives and livings brought to ruin by the destruction of the abbey. Maybe fears of another crackdown.'

'And disembowel a man for that?'

'I don't—'

'And are *we* next? Should we get out while we can? Am I the kind of man who'd run from some small-town malcontent with a butcher's knife?'

He fell back, coughing like a sheep. I went to the bedside.

'Things have changed. Death changes everything. Maybe it's time for you to remember who you are. You only need lift a finger, send out a letter, and you'll have two hundred men here by—'

'No. We finish this.'

'God damn it, Robbie, you're *Lord Dudley*, the heir to—'

'A pile of hatred. All England hates me for an arrogant cock.' He turned his face to me, all smirched with dirt and sweat. 'They should see me now, eh, John?'

I recalled him on the river, his talk of humility, of fasting for three days, vigils until dawn, riding out silently and stopping at each church to pray. I'd thought this jesting – only now remembering at how many churches we *had* stopped on the way here, how often he'd wandered off alone.

That a man who brings to his Queen such an irrefutable symbol of her royal heritage... something which bestows upon her monarchy's most mystical aura. That man... he may expect his reward.

A quest for some manner of redemption? Could not think on this. Not now.

'You're a sick man,' I said. 'Get some sleep.'

'It's *day*.'

He ripped a hand irritably across his forehead, as if wiping off the dust of some battle he was being denied. I stood up.

'Even you can't fight sickness. Let it run its course. I'll pull the curtains.'

'Leave them.'

I was at the door when he called me back.

'John.' He rolled onto his side to face me. 'Martin's body…'

'Yes, I… Should I find a carpenter to make a coffin? Will we take him back to London?'

Dudley's eyes had closed.

'His heart,' he said. 'We'll take his heart home.'

☨

At the foot of the stairs, I found Cowdray with a young man of about eighteen years who, he said, had ridden from Bristol, with a letter.

'From London, sir,' the young man said.

I recognised the seal at once, told Cowdray to give him a good break-fast and ale and charge it to Master Roberts.

'I've also found Joe Monger for you,' Cowdray said.

'Forgive me… who?'

'The farrier. You asked me last night?'

Last night: another age.

'He's out back now, Dr John. Summoned to trim the hooves of my old ass.'

'Thank you. I should pay for that, too, then. Please… add it to our bill.' I nodded to the messenger. 'Thank you, also.'

'No letter for return, Master?'

'It's possible. Go and eat. Take your time.'

My head was aching. Found my way through the ale-smelling passage to the rear door, a small cobwebbed window above it. Leaned my back against the door and broke the seal on the letter.

Blanche Parry. She must've written this not long after we'd left London, to get it here so soon. I unfolded the paper, held it up to the glass.

Odd. Written not with Blanche's customary distant formality. Had an immediacy not of her usual character, and it addressed me in a familiar way I'd not known before from this severe and cautious woman.

Cousin,
All is not well with our good sister.
Her nights are tormented, and
daytimes fraught.
This is what I have learned: our sister
hath been informed of dire prophecies
and is told she will have no peace from
Morgan le Fay until such time
as her heroic forefather be entombed in
glory. I therefore pray you speed to a
resolution in this matter and send early
word to me of your progress.

For obvious reasons of security, it was unsigned, but the references were clear.

... *she will have no peace...*

Mistress Blanche. Born not far from my own family in countryside ravaged by the Glyndwr wars, Wales against England, castles burning. And then the great war Lancaster against York, local families changing their allegiance one to the other, neighbour against neighbour.

Cautious like no others, these Border people, and would never show their hand until the direst peril loomed. But Blanche's devotion to Elizabeth would smash all barriers before it.

I *therefore pray you speed...*

I read it twice more. The use of the word *prophecies* put me at once in mind of a man with peacock feathers in his hat shrieking, *Know how the world will end.*

Prophecy. Most of it is based upon empty air. It preys on the night-terrors of the subject and the desires of the prophet himself. Never, never confuse it with the ancient discipline of astrology, which charts the movements of the cosmos, from which *estimates of probability* may be drawn.

How wrong my neighbour, Jack Simm, had been when he suggested that all monarchs would grow skin like to a lizard's. Royal skin, in truth, was pale and petal-thin and bruised if you blew on it, and the wind of a prophecy blew colder than blizzard snow.

Fear not prophecy, *I* would say, fear only prophets. Not least the ones who speak in such specifics as: *until such time as her heroic forefather be entombed in glory.*

The forefather: *Arthur.*

And *Morgan le Fay?*

The witch queen of Arthurian lore, leader of that dolorous sisterhood which, in legend, had conveyed Arthur by barge to the Isle of Avalon. There seemed little doubt that Blanche was here making reference to the Queen's own mother. And my feeling was that this was not Blanche's own coded reference – she had little imagination – but came from the orginal wording of the prophecy.

Anne Boleyn. Poor bloody Anne Boleyn, no more a witch than Mistress Borrow. Whose mother…

Oh God, what did *I* know? What did any of us know? Witchcraft – *white* witchcraft, at least – oft-times would be no more than a condition of belief, an approach to more or less the same spiritual ends we sought as Christians. And, to a Catholic, Anne Boleyn's notorious Lutherism had been the worst kind of witchery. And not considered white.

So was this how it had begun, our quest for what remained of Arthur? Some 'prophecy' the Queen had read? She has a rare appetite for learning, but also a thirst for trivia and gossip and, as I've said, is ever prey to night fears and uncertainties, moving this way and that way and watching always for signs.

And under the new freedom, London teems as never before with false prophets and tricksters, men and women intent on weaving whole mystical tapestries to achieve ends far removed from the expansion of human knowledge.

Why had she not consulted me?

I stood with my back to the yard door, shadowed by a sense of isolation like the onset of night. Was there something I was missing, something so blindingly clear that everyone else had been laughing over it for years? Was I, in truth, trusted by no-one, respected by no-one? A man lauded abroad but in his own land either feared as a conjurer or scorned as a mere book-learner in this age of adventurers in golden doublets which shone like the sun. A poor clerk who charted starry patterns and made cautious *estimates of probability.* Not good enough. Little wonder that this man had been rewarded with neither land nor title.

Are you yet equipped to call upon the angels, John?

Says she who sometimes visits me at my mother's house but never comes in.

I felt watery in my spine. Did the Queen, in fact, have some other secret and more potent adviser in matters of the hidden? Why had she told me nothing either of the prophecies or the perceived omnipresence of her mother's shade?

And what was the provenance of the predictions she was taking so seriously? Who was doing this? Who in England had such access to the royal chambers? I wondered about Sir Nicholas Throckmorton, ambassador to France, with whom Blanche had said the Queen was spending discussion time.

How dangerously do you want to live, John?

Unlike Robert Dudley, I had no love of danger – seldom compatible with study. However, with Carew likely to return before nightfall, time was against us.

I went up to my chamber for paper and sat down at the board there and wrote a note to be delivered to Blanche Parry. Nothing cryptic, nothing hidden. I asked if she could supply me with a full script of this and any other recent prophecies seen by the Queen and any ideas she might have as to their origins.

Then I stowed Blanche's letter inside my doublet, next to the dagger.

XXI

What Constitutes Sorcery

FYCHE, IT SEEMED, would not be waiting for Carew. Stepping outside the yard door, under a low and foaming sky, I could at once hear the criers from the street.

It was all we needed…

The town of Glaston was being informed that the Justice of the Peace had formally proclaimed the hue and cry and every man was now to make himself available to hunt the unholiest of bloody murderers who, this night just past, *in the service of Satan himself,* had mutilated and slain a pious officer of the Queen.

A silence now. The air would be fouled with fear – not so much, I was guessing, at the thought of a killer in the town as of what penalty might be imposed upon the townsfolk if he were not caught.

'Not the most useful exercise,' the farrier observed. 'No man's obliged to inquire into a crime where there's no known felon.'

This was true in London also. The hue and cry, whilst effective on occasion, was a blunt instrument and limited and would oft-times create the kind of mass panic and confusion which would only make it easier for an unidentified offender to escape.

'It's a black day for you and I'm sorry,' the farrier said.

A sad-eyed, willowy man with thin grey hair at shoulder length. His working apparel, the colour of dark earth, was evidently made from his old monk's habit cut off at the knees. He resumed his trimming of the ass's hoof, like peeling an apple. Like he had no curiosity about me or why I should want to speak with him.

'Master Farrier,' I said, 'if I may ask… our servant who's murdered, did he come to you yesterday?'

'Maybe. What did he look like?'

'Big man. Yellow hair, thick on top. A northerner's accent.'

He considered, examining the hoof then picking out a small pebble.

'No, sir. Never recently crossed paths with anyone possessed of all of those good qualities. Also, I was out towards Somerton the whole day, shoeing plough-horses. Not back till nightfall.'

The grey ass farted gently as Master Monger put down the hoof. He stood up, easing his knee-pads.

'Why would you think I'd had dealings with this tragic man?'

I was tired and couldn't quickly respond. Monger put away the last of his tools in a leather satchel. Patted the ass's rump, with affection, and the ass lumbered off into the stable.

'I only ask, Dr John, because there are armed men on the street, and if *you* had reason to think I was the last to speak with the victim of a most savage murder, then so might they.'

His eyes were calm, accepting. He had a stillness I've oft-times observed both in priests – though not Bonner, obviously – and men who work closely with animals. Seldom in men like myself who roam the world in search of learning the way other men pursue women and strong drink.

'The full savagery of what was done,' I said. 'Is that widely known in the town?'

'Known to all. Except, possibly, to Simeon Flavius, who's said to be ninety-five years old, deaf and no longer in his mind.'

The farrier waited in silence, perfectly still. From inside the stable, we heard the ass's jaws at work on the straw. I sighed.

'We're sent here by the Queen's Commission on Antiquities, as you doubtless know. Instructed to find out what has been removed from the abbey and what remains in the town. We were told some monks from the abbey were still in the area... including you. I'd asked Martin Lythgoe to go and find you. That's all.'

Monger raised a grey eyebrow.

'You sent your *servant* to speak with me? Rather than come to me yourself?'

I might take this as a statement, and so made no reply. Monger was reopening his toolbag.

'I was at the abbey until the end. Until there was nothing left there that was holy. And you were no doubt wondering if perchance your servant came to me in search of valuables I'd stolen from the abbey, and I killed him?' His hand sliding into the bag. 'Split his ribs with this—?'

'*No.*' Backing off, groping for the line of the dagger in my doublet, as his hand emerged...

...empty.

'I *could* do it,' he said softly. 'I've tools here that could do it. And I'm stronger than I look.'

'And a monk.'

'*Formerly* a monk.'

I nodded.

'As indeed,' Monger said, 'was our esteemed Justice of the Peace. And *he* now has men hanged.'

'And women.'

'Oh, indeed.' He closed the bag, lowered it to the ground 'twixt his feet. 'They'll catch someone for this, of course. This very grievous crime involving London men. They'll want a lid on *that.*'

'What are you saying? Even if they have to force a confession out of someone who may not be guilty?'

Monger shrugged.

'Look, I'd merely wondered,' I said, 'if perchance you'd pointed our man in the direction of someone else. Maybe someone you thought might have knowledge of items removed from the abbey. Someone who—'

'Killed him for fear of exposure? We keep returning to this motive. But, beg mercy, isn't Sir Edmund Fyche, in light of the mutilation of the body, proclaiming it an act of *devilry*?'

'He is, yet...'

This would be a gamble; Fyche and Monger had both come out of the abbey and the JP might well be an important source of income for a farrier, but I'd grown tired of verbal swordplay.

'...might it not be possible,' I said, 'that when Fyche insists this town has a multitude of witches and sorcerers... he exaggerates?'

The farrier let slip the kind of smile which, along with the earthen colours of his apparel, suggested the dominance of the melancholic Saturn in his birth-chart.

'Fyche exaggerates,' he said, 'only by his own perception of what constitutes sorcery.'

'Ah.'

'Do you wish to know about this?'

'Know?'

'Where his problems lie.'

I sought his eyes but he turned away, shouldering his toolbag.

'It's market day. If you walk with me into the town, it may all become apparent.'

He walked away and I could only follow him, a thin wind whistling through my head. Not for the first time since arriving here, I had the feeling of events being in some way beyond my powers. As if I were a chess-piece and there were only certain directions in which I might proceed.

The main problem being that I knew not which piece I was, nor who – or what – was moving me.

✠

MARKET DAY IN Glastonbury was not the event it might once have been – certainly not this day – but still colourful enough. Cart-top stalls hung with rabbits, sheepskins and fresh fish. Barrels of cider and ale. A pieman and a blacksmith selling spades and mattocks. Mainly essentials in these, for Glastonbury, worn-down times.

Yet there was also a board offering lurid-hued foreign sweetmeats for those who could afford them, as well as local preserves. And a band with battered lutes and skin drums played some country dance tune outside the Church of the Baptist.

No-one danced, though. Small groups stood in wary silence under a sky of roiling cloud. Shouts of arousal could be heard in the distance, the criers and constables summoning a rabble.

Monger nodded toward a thin little woman in a doorway. She wore an eyepatch and was purveying jams from a tray.

'Joan Tyrre,' he said. 'Moved here about three years ago from Taunton. Used to do the market there until she was taken in for questioning about her relations with the fair folk.'

'The *fair...*'

I looked at him. A soured gash of watery sunlight leaked between the clouds like pus from a poisoned wound.

'Met a strange man at the market one day who sought her friendship,' Monger said. 'And she followed him to his… dwelling place. When they found her, she'd lost the sight of both eyes.'

I blinked. Memories. A legend I'd heard in my childhood: if you saw what men and women of this world were not supposed to see, you might be robbed of your sight. *Don't you go wandering away*, my mother would say, *or you might go where you're not wanted and come back blinded.*

Must needs admit I'd never before encountered one on whom this punishment had been inflicted.

'By the time she was brought before the church court,' Monger said. 'She had some sight back in one eye.'

'Accused of…?'

'I don't know the *exact* nature of the charges. Discourse with the faerie? *Is* that a charge, or does it all come under the gross heading of witchery? Someone probably reported her to the local vicar. I imagine she was lucky to escape prison at the very least. And knew it, which was why she moved herself over here.'

'I don't follow you. Why here?'

'I guess she thought it best to leave Taunton for a place where such peculiar talents might be not wholly condemned. 'Tis said that if she takes off the eyepatch what she sees through that blinded eye is not of this… Ah… now… observe that woman over there.'

A gentlewoman in a grey cape was bending to speak with a younger woman with a faded red shawl over her hair and shoulders, sitting on a step with a basket of pink ribbons in her lap. As I watched, she stood up with her basket and the gentlewoman followed her into an alleyway.

'In the bottom of the basket,' Monger said, 'under the ribbons, lies a much-prized skrying crystal.'

I said nothing. Back in Mortlake I had five of them. From a stall, I bought two winter-withered apples and gave one to Monger, and we moved towards the top of the town, where he pointed out a woman who, he said, read the mystic cards from France which foretold destiny. Then he nodded to a man with two terrier dogs.

The man grinned.

'Just off home for my ole stick, Joe. Case I runs into a feller with horns and claws drippin' blood.'

He was short, with a cloud of hair and a beard white as a napkin to his chest and eyes that glinted like chips of quartz. Monger smiled thinly at him.

'A touch more discretion may be called for this day, Woolly. Even for you.'

'Oh ar? I'm supposed to join the hue and cry in pursuit of whoever they decides cut up this Lunnon feller? Well, you know what I says to that, Joe, man? I says they can *piss off*.'

He nodded, patting his thigh, and the terriers followed him into the throng.

'Like so many of them,' Monger said, 'that fellow gets away with it because he's useful. Hired by Fyche to find the original well at Meadwell, and he found two.'

'Found?'

'By use of the forked twig that jumps in the hand.'

'A water diviner.'

'A water *witcher*, some called it.'

They did. Once outlawed as witchcraft, but always far too useful to be banned for long, and I only wished I could do it myself. I shook my head.

'It's science, Master Farrier. Science we don't yet understand. There's a man named Agricola, who is said to be able to find metal ore in the ground by similar means. You'd think it were not possible.'

'Most things are possible,' Monger said. 'And some things which are not possible are *said* to be possible... here. Especially those involving water, for we're yet an island. Avalon, in spirit.'

He continued to stroll placidly, almost gliding, through the market, walking like a monk. As if he still were a monk and protected.

'All gone!' An old man in an apron stood in the doorway of a baker's shop, waving his arms at the queue outside. 'Bloody constables took a whole batch, look, nothing I could do.'

'Pies,' Monger said. 'Master Worthy makes the finest mutton pies in Somersetshire.'

As the queue dispersed, muttering, Monger led me into the shop.

'All gone, Joe,' the baker said. 'I just—'

'Yes, we heard. Master Worthy, I'd like you meet Dr John, from the Queen's Commission on Antiquities, here to make account of what remains from the abbey.'

The old baker, plump and bald, I'd guess, beneath his cap, went conspicuously stiff.

'Dr John seeks only assurance,' Monger said, 'that such items that were not destroyed are… in good hands. You have nothing to fear.'

I looked at Monger. How could *he* be sure that this man had nothing to fear from me? He knew me not.

Something here was not right.

☩

When we emerged, the tip of the tower upon the tor had appeared 'twixt two market stalls, lit by a sudden angel-fan of creamy light.

'And this is it?' I said. 'These are Fyche's sorcerers?'

In a hole in the wall, concealed behind a disused oven, several old books had been hidden, the finest of them being the first volume of *Steganographia*, the masterwork on magic and cypher by Johannes Trithemius, the late Abbot of Sponheim. It could only have come from the abbey, and you could have locked me in that bakery with it for a week.

'Emmanuel Worthy fancies himself as an alchemist,' Monger said. 'For no reason other than the possession of those books with their arcane diagrams that he'll never understand. But I could point you to others more potent. A healer who cures through the toes in the old Egyptian way. A seventh child of a seventh child who foresees the future. At least five people who insist they can commune with the dead. Oh, and a maker of charms from the wood of the cross – though I might take issue with that.'

185

'But all known to—'

'All known to one another, yes. Even scattered over the town and various of the outlying villages, they're a community. Some of them will gather together later, when the market's spent. At least –' Monger glanced over his shoulder – 'they would usually gather. Tonight, things may be different.'

'Were they here when you were a monk at the abbey? Did you know then who and what they were?'

'Some were here. Not so many as now. Or maybe it was just that we didn't notice them the same because we, the pious brethren, were in the majority then.'

I learned that many of these seekers – Monger could only call them that – had journeyed here from the ends of the country, and some from abroad. When the abbey flourished, this had gone, if not unnoticed, at least uncommented on. The town was growing and always full of pilgrims. It was only after the fall of the abbey and the exodus of the wealthy and the pious that people began to notice the nature of the incomers who did not leave... who, in fact, began to increase their numbers, some arriving like poor travellers, living in camps and abandoned houses. Attending church only as much as was necessary to avoid prosecution, for their own religious obediences clearly belonged... elsewhere.

A whole immigrant community spurning the bigger pickings of Bristol and London to scratch a living here. Why?

'Not so simple,' Monger said.

I heard Fyche again in my head with his talk of the fires in the midnight and the maggot-people chattering and squealing to the moon.

Feeling again the most acute strangeness. Why was Monger telling all this to me, a clerk from London who was almost certainly of the reformed church? It was beginning to make me anxious, but my interest had been trapped, and all caution had long been dismissed by the scholar in me.

Like the woman in the eyepatch, I seemed to have gained entry to an unknown realm.

'How came you to know these people, Master Farrier?'

'My trade.' Monger glided on, not looking at me. 'The abbey was where I learned my trade. Attending to the horses of visitors and pilgrims – remarkable how little regard the pious may have for their animals. Eventually I was given a forge in the abbey grounds, and now I have one on the other side of the walls. While still keeping a monk's hours… and – more quietly – a monk's religious observances.'

'Without harassment?'

'A farrier's an essential man in any community. A *good* farrier is nigh-on untouchable. And this is still a Catholic town, whichever church its goodfolk attend. The abbey… cast a spiritual light over the place, and there was healing. People who'd limped in on sticks walking out and tossing the sticks over the hedge.'

'But that's gone…'

'No, no… you're not getting this, are you?'

We'd reached the edge of the market, and the houses were becoming poorer and crumbling into fields and heath, and when the farrier turned to me at last there was a kind of intense serenity in his grey gaze.

'It's not *gone,* Dr John. It was here before the abbey and it's *still* here. Do you see? It was always *here.*'

I stopped walking, feeling something like a gathering of stars in my abdomen. Oft-times I'd fancied that places where great churches and abbeys were built had some quality, some atmosphere related more to the balance of hills and fields and water than their orientation toward Jerusalem. An eagerness had seized me, but I said nothing.

'With the abbey itself just a shell,' Monger said, 'there's a need to provide channels for… energies which might otherwise overflow, perchance causing harm.'

Hadn't Eleanor Borrow said something similar, about the monks being needed to keep a balance? For all my learning, I felt like a child again who saw before him adult human knowledge like an outline of distant mountains.

'Most of us had little understanding of it at the time,' Monger said, 'but if you consider the *real* function of the abbey was to transform the energy that was there into a Godly substance, and spread it afar. Lay it soft on the land… a spiritual irrigation…'

'Yes.'

I could see it and hear it. The river of a Gregorian chant, in all its glorious mathematical symmetry.

Ice in my spine.

'How was this known?'

'Tradition,' he said.

'Not written down?'

'Some traditions –' he smiled – 'are *never* written down.'

'Then how...?'

But he'd moved away, holding up both his long hands as if in benediction over the townsfolk clustered below us around the myriad market stalls.

'Still they come. People in search of something. People who think that just by being here, on this holy soil, their lives will be transformed.'

'Holy?'

'A big, bad word,' Monger said. 'But everything has its darker side. There are some who would... speed the process.'

'By sorcery?'

I thought of what Fyche had said about the cockerel in the abbey. And earlier about finding new-born babes in the grass *with their throats cut in sacrifice.*

'By the use of ritual magic?' I said.

'When the new religion is in disarray, some may turn again to the older ones.'

Monger the farrier gazed placidly down across the huddle of the town. Like the player over the chesstable, and I was the knight, which is moved in such a fashion that he cannot easily see the way ahead.

The farrier turned his grey gaze upon me.

'Where stand *you*, Dr Dee?' he murmured. 'For this surely is the town in England closest to your own heart.'

XXII

Black as Pitch

SOMETIMES I'D THINK that, for all my learning, I was still like to an infant, milky-eyed and unknowing. That, being sent early to college and raising my eyes but rarely from printed pages, a whole part of my being was yet undeveloped, leaving me with little understanding of a world so carelessly traversed by the less-educated.

A child of two and thirty. Dudley knew that. *However you survived in the cesspits of Paris and Antwerp...*

The plain truth being that I'd never been in the cesspits of Paris or Antwerp, only in their lecture halls and libraries.

Now I was walking numbly through the streets, as if naked, following the farrier into a mean, cramped drinking hovel on the upper edge of town.

Huddling in its dark, cider-smelling belly, beside a sooted inglenook with a fire of peat, while the stained ceiling sagged threateningly betwixt beams and my head was swelled with questions I had not the will to ask.

Cowering into the shadows, I watched a wench of about fifteen serving cider from an earthenware jug. Watched Monger waiting in line behind two farmer-looking men, four others sitting around the room on stools. The only talk I could hear was of sheep-prices until Monger returned, setting down two mugs upon the board and himself on the low, three-legged stool opposite me, pushing his thin hair behind his ears.

'It was Nel,' he said.

'What?'

Monger drank some cider with the same restraint that William Cecil had displayed over a glass of fine wine.

'People here follow your career with interest. Through pamphlets and such passed around amongst the seekers.'

Pamphlets. God help me.

'Still,' Monger said, 'as you must have gathered by now, for a good many in this town, the word *conjurer* is far from a term of abuse.'

The fire coughed out weak yellow flames. My mouth was dry but I couldn't drink.

'A man deep into fever,' Monger said, 'is seldom aware of his indiscretions. And is even, in his fuddled state, apt to call out for his friend by name.'

'Oh.'

I drank some of the strong cider.

'A name alone being not, of course sufficient,' Monger said. 'Many men have the same name. Indeed, poor Nel was at first reluctant to believe her own ears.'

'Who else has she told?'

'Only me, after much havering... in the hope that I might be able to confirm it.'

'Which you seem to think you have.'

'At some risk, I may say, if you'd turned out, after all, to be an agent of the Queen.'

'I *am* an agent of the Queen.'

'Yes,' he said. 'It's what we like about you.'

I sensed a smile which it was too dark in here to see.

'And what, after all,' Monger said, 'would a mere clerk know about Agricola the dowser?'

✝

In better circumstance, I might have even been laughing. It was all so clear, to me now, all the traps laid out in my path. The daring talk of Mistress Eleanor Borrow:

'Tis best to sow under a new moon and then to harvest under a full moon... It has a power... Oh, am I stepping close to heresy?

And Monger... would he have revealed Emmanuel Worthy's magical library to someone who might have regarded the books as heretical? Would he have fingered to me every penny-a-poke street-seer in the Glastonbury market, if not sure of his ground?

'While both Nel and I accept,' he murmured, 'that Dr John Dee is a man of science rather than a procurer of spirits, we still find it curious that someone renowned for the breadth of his learning should arrive in a little town much reduced in its fortunes… merely to make account of what miserable antiquities remain there.'

Now here was trouble. If I failed to quench the farrier's curiosity, he could expose me to whoever he liked. Might, indeed, choose to enlighten Sir Edmund Fyche, for whom the distinction 'twixt science and sorcery would be a line not so much fine as imperceptible.

'It's not so far removed from the truth,' I said.

And, in the hope that the fevered Dudley had not announced himself as the Royal Master of the Horse, was about to tell him more of the truth… when the door of poor planks creaked and opened to a slit of light.

A shadow fell across the crack, as if an eye was peering in, and then the door opened just wide enough for a woman to slip inside.

Shutting it rapidly behind her, pushing it tight with her arse, wild grey hair springing from a ragged coif.

'Pour's a big one, Sal! Us could be deep in the shitty yere, girl.'

Eyepatch.

Monger raised himself from his stool.

'Joan. Over here.'

'Zat you, Brother Joe? Be hard enough to zee in this hole with both fuckin' eyes.'

'Mug of strong cider for Mistress Tyrre!' Monger called out, as she came bundling herself towards our board, bony white hands groping the air like it was muslin. 'Something amiss, Joan?'

'Constables. Zo-called. They'ze everywhere. Big bazzards on big 'osses. Weren't good to trade n' more today, Joe, we come outer there damn quick, look.'

I dragged over another stool for her and she peered around the room with her one eye and then lifted her skirts and sat down with her knees shamelessly apart.

'Normal thing, they comes nozyin' around, you offers 'em a readin' for free or a feel o' your tits, and they's sweet as you likes. But not today, not today, boy.'

'Man was murdered, Joan,' Monger said. 'That's probably—'

'Howzat tie up with the likes of us? I never kilt 'im.' She stiffened at the sight of me in the recess. 'Whozis?'

'A friend. Dr John, over from London.'

'Wozze do?'

'Works for the Queen, Joan.'

'*Do* he? Well, that's all well and fine, Joe, but I en't gonner truss no bugger today. There's a funny air, look. Dark as you likes.' Wrapping her twig-thin arms around herself as if all warmth were fled from the room. 'Black as pitch over the tor. Somethin' a' comin'. You zee it a' comin'? You zee— Oh fuck and buggery…'

A flash of brightness as the door shuddered open. At once, a couple of the farmers were putting down their mugs, shambling quietly to their feet, placing themselves flat to the wall.

Two men black against the light.

'Joan Tyrre?'

'Shitty,' Joan breathed. 'Coulder sweared they fuckers en't follered me.'

'Over there.'

One of the men was pointing at our board. Now the other was coming over slowly and Joan Tyrre was rising, putting the legs of her stool out in front of her.

'Now then, you boys, you juss keep away, yer knows I en't done nothin', look—'

'Only led us a merry bloody chase, you old puttock.'

Throwing out his arms as a barrier, Joan skipping from side to side, laughing, jabbing the stool at him until he snatched it away from her.

'Enough! Don't you think to go nowhere, Joannie. You know what we wants.'

'What? Front of all these folks?'

Joan cackling, dodging nimbly as he hurled the stool at her, and it splintered on the wall behind.

'Where's the woman calls herself a doctor?'

I went rigid.

'You was with her earlier, we knows that. *Where is she?*'

'How'ze I gonner know that?' Joan Tyrre said. 'How'ze a poor ole bag like me gonner pay for a doctor?'

'You'll talk fuckin' civil to us or I'll—'

Making a lunge for her, and Joan was leaping back, but not quite quick enough.

'Get yer gurt hands off of me, you— *uh!*'

Her head whipping to one side as the second man struck her with full fist on the side of the face.

Joan's head hanging now like a broken doll's, and I came to my feet, but Monger grabbed my arm, hissing into my ear.

'Don't make this worse…'

XXIII

Lowest Form of Doctoring

THE ONLY SOUND was the dribble of ale over the edge of our board from an overturned mug. Joan Tyrre was down on the flags, squirming away, an arm raised to protect her face. The two constables standing over her, silent now.

'The *doctor-woman*, Mistress Tyrre. If you please.'

The one who spoke now, the one who'd struck her, he was just a boy, with a boy's voice.

'En't seen her.' Joan mumbling into the stone flags, her eyepatch all askew. 'Swearder God.'

'Where'd you see her last?'

'Don't recall.'

'Think harder.' Bringing back his boot. 'This help?'

'All right! Bazzard! Her was off to zeein' to a man in the George.'

'What man?'

'Man who's lyin' there.'

'What's his name?'

'All I knows, swearder God.'

'Better be true.'

''*Tis* true.'

He kicked her hard in the side. A sliver of light from the doorway opened up a cold grin like a gash in his face, and it seemed like a face I'd seen before.

Joan made small moans but didn't move until they'd left, the alehouse door swinging and the farmers coming away from the walls and calmly taking their seats again as if this happened every day. Maybe it did.

'Man with the fever!' Joan screamed from the floor. 'And I hopes by the Lord Gwyn as you both fuckin' gets it off of he an' dies afore the morrow!'

Monger helped her to her feet and she stood feeling at her jaw with the tips of her fingers.

'En't broke, anyways. Do it look broke?'

'You need to see Nel.'

'Sounds like everyfucker needs to see her today.'

'So where is she?'

'Dunno, Joe. Out of town, she got any sense.'

'What do they want with her?'

'They gonner tell me that?'

'*Could* she have gone back to see the man at the George?'

'Dunno. He's from Lunnon, en't he, so they can beat the piss out of him, all I cares.'

'I see.' Monger turned to me. 'She won't have gone home. If she knows they're looking for her, the last thing she'll want is to bring any of this down on her father. Joan, where else might she be?'

Joan Tyrre said, 'Where's my drink?'

✠

She'd swallowed two mugs of ale, not touching her jaw again. A bruise was beginning, green and purple in the firelight like a bad sky.

Joe Monger had made her promise to send for him at any time if she suffered any further ill-effects of the beating. He'd questioned her about the number of constables on the streets; she reckoned there must be over a dozen of them, and more seen riding down from the Mendip Hills.

'Joan might well have counted the same man three times,' Monger said. 'But, all the same, this doesn't look good. If either of us had intervened back there, they'd have summoned others at once. We'd all have been beaten, arrested... the place smashed up.'

He beckoned me to follow him outside, where we stood for a moment blinking in the harsh white light. Market stalls were being hurriedly taken down, carts loaded.

All of it done in near silence. Monger looked around.

'This is Fyche. He's long been looking for an excuse to move against the... the worshippers of the stars and the stones.'

'The maggots,' I said.

'Mercy?'

I shook my head.

'So if the constables have gone to the George…?'

'That's not a problem,' Monger said. 'Cowdray will deal with it. When they find out Nel's patient's the man from London, they'll back off. They won't go far away but they won't seek open confrontation in front of an officer of the Crown.'

I was still sickened by the two constables' treatment of Joan Tyrre and felt responsible, having told Fyche where I'd last seen Martin Lythgoe – Fyche seizing upon the fact that Eleanor Borrow had been with me at the time. I related to Monger what had occurred 'twixt Nel Borrow and Fyche upon the tor.

'And that was the last time you saw her?'

'I searched for her afterwards, but…'

I felt like shit. Yet how, within all reason, could Fyche claim that what had been done last night to Martin Lythgoe had been done by a woman?

'Master Monger,' I said, 'why did Fyche hang Mistress Borrow's mother?'

'He told you that?'

'Without explanation.'

Monger strode away across the street.

'This isn't London,' he said over a shoulder. 'It's easier here.'

Determined to learn the facts of this, I followed him down the hill through the dispersing crowd toward the centre of the town. He kept close to the wall around the abbey grounds, past the gatehouse.

'Where are you going?'

He pointed to the modern church near the bottom of the town, its tower more modest than St John the Baptist's. I drew level with him under a sky now as tight and dark-flecked as a goatskin drum.

'Tell me about Fyche, Master Farrier.'

'I don't know Fyche.'

'Was he not at the abbey the same time as you?'

'That doesn't make me his friend. The abbot was happy for me to work at my forge. Tended to meet the others only at prayer. Monks don't talk much at prayer.'

'He's a Protestant now.'

'Or finds it appropriate to look like one. During the last reign, when there was hope of money to restore the abbey, he'd become a good Catholic again. Such conversions happen in a flash, as you know.'

We'd come to a narrow street behind the church. Its dwellings were mean, but it was surprisingly dry underfoot – in London, the gutters would have been ripe with shit.

'Fyche's proposed college of monks,' I said. 'You weren't invited to join them?'

'They'd want a farrier?' Monger sniffed. 'Anyway, there are few monks from the abbey at Meadwell. Most are come from outside – learned men. Heavyweights. God's army, Fyche'll tell you, against the rise of an evil older than Christianity.'

'Evil? Joan Tyrre and her faerie? The men who find wells with a forked twig? Why should he fear *these* people?'

'What makes you think it's fear?'

'Trust me, Master Monger,' I said. 'It's always fear.'

We'd arrived at the end house, near the church. It was bigger and in better repair than the others, its timber-framing oiled. The man in the doorway wore an apron, faded but clean, and a skullcap the colour of old parchment over stiff white hair.

'They've been, then,' Monger said.

A tightening of the man's lips and a nod so small and cautious that it barely happened.

'How many, Matthew?'

'Three. Including Fyche himself.'

This man's voice was dry as ash, his face taut and unfleshed, his eyes watchful.

Monger said, 'But Nel wasn't with you?'

'Must've left early, Joe. I know not where to.'

'But she *was* here last night?'

'I don't...' The man's shoulders sagged. 'I was out till late. Delivery of twins at a farm towards Butleigh, and I had to cut them out or they'd be dead and the mother with them. I thought Nel to be abed when I got back. And then... out before I was up.'

Monger turned to me.

'This is Nel's father – Dr Borrow. Matthew, this is Dr John, a visitor to the town, for reasons… yet to be established. But who can, I think, be trusted. What did Fyche say?'

'Not much. He just looked everywhere in the house, having his men empty lockers, sweep the content of shelves to the floor.'

I remembered his daughter's jest about the elixir of youth – ninety but looked fifty. Probably *was* fifty, but had a sinewy, capable look.

'And that was it?' Monger said.

'No.'

Monger waited in silence, arms hanging by his side.

'My instruments,' Dr Borrow said. 'Didn't get in until nigh on three of the clock. Went straight to bed, having thrown my bag of instruments… just, you know, in the corner. Which is where one of Fyche's men found them. When they picked up the bag, I never gave a thought to it at first. More concerned that they shouldn't find the wrong… the wrong books.'

I was guessing he meant the books from which his daughter had learned of the science of stars. More books rescued from the abbey, maybe.

Saw Monger's jaw jut and stiffen.

'Your *surgical* instruments?'

''Tis my normal habit, Joe, to clean them soon as I get home. Pulling out a blade in front of a new patient when it's all splattered with the blood of the last one, that's… never helpful. But I was too damn tired to think.'

'Let me get this right,' Monger said. 'Your surgeon's knives. You're saying they found a surgeon's knives with blood—?'

'Yes, yes, yes…' Borrow's eyes squeezing shut. 'I'm afraid that's what they found, yes.'

'They accused you?' Monger said. 'Of butchering this man?'

'I wish they *had* accused me. They asked if Eleanor had ever performed surgery.'

A stone in my gut.

I said, 'Has she?'

'Only when there's been no better way.'

Surgery: the lowest form of doctoring, next to butchery in anyone's book. I turned to Monger, but he wouldn't meet my eyes, and Dr Borrow, evidently in near despair, if reluctant to show it, was looking down at the holes in his boots, while Joan Tyrre cackled in my head about the darkness over the tor.

'I told Fyche why there was blood on the tools. I don't think he even listened.' Dr Borrow said. 'Picks up the bag, thrusts it at a constable to take them all away. Evidence, he says.'

'All the evidence he'd need,' Joe Monger said.

✠

How swiftly everything changes when the heart holds sway, altering the order of need. When people had spoken of the heart torn assunder, I'd known not, until now, what emotion they were trying to illustrate.

Or maybe it was all heightened here in Glastonbury, where the very air seemed to hone the perceptions like a whetstone to a knife, sharpening the colours of thoughts, the tastes in the mouth, the pictures which are seen when the eyes are shut.

Leaning back into the oak settle in the panelled room at the George, I could see the outline of the sun pushing vainly at crowding clouds. And then there she was inside my head, sitting amongst the big stones by the iron well, inside the circle of bare thorn trees: the emerald eyes, the faded blue dress, sleeves pushed up exposing, oh God, those brown speckled arms.

'How can we stop this?' I said.

Monger was silent for a long moment, sitting opposite me in the square, panelled chamber.

'*We?*' he said. 'Are you sure of this?'

Me looking down to hide a coming blush and banishing her, with her green eyes and her haunting, crossed-tooth smile, lest I give away too much.

'I should also ask you about a carpenter. A coffin-maker. A gravedigger. Vicar.'

'All that can be done tomorrow,' Monger said. 'I'll send them to you. Although I gather you may have to wait for the return of Carew before they'll release the cadaver.'

When we'd arrived back at the George, Cowdray had told us that Fyche himself had been here, insisting on questioning Master Roberts in his chamber. But Dudley had been sweating again, his eyes full of heat, his sickness beyond dispute, and Fyche had not ventured beyond the threshold, for fear of contagion.

'Don't expect Carew to take a different stance,' Monger said. 'There's no harder reformer in the west. If Carew's given good evidence, he won't prolong things any more than Fyche would.'

'Carew has real power here? A sheriff's power?'

'As much power as he wants. Senior knight in Devonshire, owns the abbey and its lands. Has more power here, I'd guess, than he would have in a similar role in London, where knights, I'm told, are two a penny.'

'She's a healer,' I said, wanting to scream it to the beams. 'In the real sense. Not like the piss-sniffers in their masks. What about the mother of those twins? The woman whose life was saved, and her babes, she'll surely state before a court that Dr Borrow had to cut into her belly. That it was *her* blood on the knives?'

'If she survives. Wounds like that oft-times turn bad. And, anyway, she'll say what her husband wants her to say. And her husband... The farmers out towards Butleigh they're all tenants and struggling. They'll state, albeit with regret, what suits their lord. I know him, too, shoe the horses for his hunt – with which his neighbour rides now and again. His neighbour, who also happens to be the local JP.'

'Fyche?'

'You never know when you're going to need a JP, do you, Dr John?'

'My colleague,' I said, with care, 'has influence. He'll talk to Carew.'

Monger looked pained.

'You don't understand, do you? The poison's spreading as we speak. A man precisely disbowelled and laid out like a decorated altar? The older townsfolk will already be quaking behind their doors. Who'll be next? And who'll be accused? So Fyche puts out a name... and those will emerge who'll state before a judge that when they couldn't afford to pay Nel's doctor's bill, their cattle died. I tell you in sorrow... it doesn't take much.'

'She's a *doctor*.'

'She's a doctor who's become too much associated with the worshippers of the stars and the old stones.'

I shut my eyes, remembering how swiftly all the apocryphal tales had arisen of Anne Boleyn's dark ways after her husband had first denounced her as a witch.

'What you must needs understand, Dr John, is that these people – the seekers – there's still only a few of them compared with the old families of Glastonbury. The old families who hold tight to a Godly fear of the power of this place... who'll turn their backs upon the tor at certain seasons. Who are afraid of what meddlers like poor mad old Joan might cause, through their meddling, to happen.'

'Another earthquake?'

'You may laugh, in your learned, London way...'

'If you think I laugh at such things—'

'Mercy.' Holding up his hands. 'Yes, I know, of course, where your interests lie. What I'm trying to explain is that most folk here are not men of science and inquiry, all they want is a quiet life and bread on the board. They don't *meddle*. For all the talk of treasure, you won't find hill-diggers on the tor, for 'tis said that when a man once took a hammer to the tower, thinking to obtain stone, the heavens were suddenly aflame with lightning. Out of a cloudless sky. One bolt strikes the hammer, man falls down dead.'

'This is fact, or legend?'

'In Glaston... no division. They say that if you put your hands on a certain buttress on a corner of the tower you'll feel the shock of the thunderbolt.'

'There'll be an explanation.' Recalling my own fall on the tor. 'Through science. If I had the time here—'

'Then you, too, would very swiftly fall foul of the old families. They don't welcome pokers into the unknowable. What you call science.'

'I know.'

'Nel was tempted onto a path which is... unstable.'

'Like her mother?'

Monger smiled his unhappy, priestly smile.

'Cate Borrow dug her own pit. Through kindness, perhaps, but she dug it none the less.'

It was growing dark. From behind the oaken panels, Cowdray and his maids could be heard serving cider to the farmers and maybe a constable or two. But the room was reserved for overnight guests, and we were yet alone.

'Tell me,' I said. 'Tell me about her.'

XXIV

Fungus Dust

SHE WAS A gardener.

Two acres of land reclaimed from the sea, down towards Wells – this was where she was most at peace, passing the lengthening days among its fragrances, harvesting herbs to eat: carrots and onions and leeks, cabbages and beans, to be sold at Glastonbury market.

And also herbs for healing. Behind her husband's surgery, near the Church of St Benignus, she had a little workroom where they were hung and dried and ground into powder. A quiet woman, who preferred her husband to take the credit for balms and ointments, the cure of infected wounds and upset guts.

'I knew her first more than a score of years ago,' Monger said, 'when I was at the abbey. This was when she worked in the abbot's kitchen. Before she took the eye of the new physician and learned the arts of herbs and the growing of them… and then became the abbot's friend.'

After the Dissolution of the abbey, she'd continued her work with curative plants, if less openly, occasionally helped by a woman who'd been a cook at the abbey. And then, in the boy Edward's reign, the years of the protectorate, there was more tolerance, and this was when Cate had found the freedom to experiment in areas where doctors of physic seldom strayed.

'Not all ailments,' Monger said, 'are physical.'

Telling me of a certain man – a wool-merchant, therefore not without money – who, after the death of his wife and daughter in a house fire, had lost his faith in God and was so cast down that he was near to taking his own life.

'Also suffering from blinding pains in the head,' Monger said, '*not* a result of dousing his sorrow in wine, I should say – this was the kind of agony that comes out of nowhere with flashing lights, and no darkened chamber can bring ease.'

'I've heard of it.'

I could hear a clanking of flagons from the alehouse, Cowdray's hoarse laughter.

'Cate had given him a certain kind of fungus dust,' Monger said. 'To be mixed with a large quantity of water, and the results were… frightening. Like an act of God. Powerfully mystical.'

One startling morn, Monger had met the wool-merchant on the fish-shaped hill to the east of the town, and here was a man raising his arms to heaven, extolling all the sublime beauty of creation. Talking of colours he'd never known. Confiding to Monger, later that day, in the George where we sat now, that his spirit had been awakened neither by prayer nor Bible… but by Cate Borrow and her fungus dust.

'Not only eased the pain in his head, but opened his eyes to a brighter world.' Monger's tone was yet drab. 'A vision of heaven on earth.'

I was intent, for this was said also of the mushrooms which Jack Simm had found for me and which I'd dried and brewed in private. Drinking the brew late at night in my library, amongst my books, surrounded by the wisdom of the ages.

Without any effects, in my case, beyond a mild headache. It was ever thus.

'There could be considerable demand for such a potion,' I said cautiously.

'But, regrettably,' Monger said, 'there was – there always is – a hazard. The results were… not predictable. Indeed, rather than a sense of exaltation, there might, oft-times, be visions worse than the blackest nightmare. You see? Heaven or hell. A roll of the dice.'

The *elixir of heaven and hell*. I'd heard some talk of it in the low countries a year or two back, but it was like to the *elixir of life* – you never know how much to believe.

'So random were its effects,' Monger said, 'that Cate Borrow would dispense it only in the most extreme circumstances – that is, for terrible head pains or when she had reason to think someone so deep sunk into misery than he might be about to take a length of rope into the woods.'

'So, apart from this wool-merchant, who—?'

'She tried it on herself. But with restraint, in the merest quantities. Matthew took it once – never again, he'll tell you. When it was used they'd make sure whoever took it was never left alone, lest they might cause harm to themselves.'

'How?'

'I'll come to that.'

'So these...' I recalled Cecil's words. 'These visions...'

'I...' Monger was hesitant. 'I've heard it said that the place where the potion was ingested... might alter the response. And I imagine it would also be affected by the humour of the man ingesting it. Or the woman.'

I waited. So dim was it now that I could barely see his face, let alone read his expression.

'Joan Tyrre,' he said. 'On hearing of the dust of vision, Joan Tyrre... was eager. And thus, in her foolish, innocent way, became the cause of Cate's downfall.'

✠

Joan Tyrre was herself a herbalist, if hardly in Cate's company, and years earlier had been making another precarious living, in Taunton, out of her relations with the faerie. Joan apparently naming people the faerie had told her were bewitched and offering them help.

I'd heard of this unsavoury practice, preying upon the poor and desperate, and knew it couldn't have lasted long before drawing the attention of the Church.

It hadn't. Brought before the church court, Joan had admitted all and sworn herself to the service of God... while thinking to return, more discreetly, to her former trade in another part of the town when all the fuss had died down. But the faerie do not easily forgive such a betrayal and – or so she'd claim later – would no longer confide in her.

Having also left her near-blind. This was when she'd decided to leave Taunton for what she'd heard were the more openly mystical humours of Glastonbury.

'She'd seen the tor,' Monger said. 'In the distance, magical in the evening light. And heard the tales of the King of the Faerie, Gwyn ap Nudd, still in residence in the heart of it.'

Thinking that the great Gwyn might be responsive to her urgent pleas, Joan had walked to Glastonbury, joining a band of travellers for protection. In a wood near the foot of the tor, she'd fashioned for herself a rude shelter out of bent saplings and thatch. It was summer, and she'd slept there for some weeks, praying that she might be taken into the hall of the faerie.

'So Joan's relations with the faerie,' I said, 'were not just...'

'Of her own invention?' Monger said. 'Many people say she's mad as a hare, and yet...'

Weeks had passed. Joan had been chilled to the bone by the winds of autumn, no illumination to warm her nights. Joe Monger himself had found her one day, collapsed in her shelter, half-starved. Bringing her into town and taking her to Matthew Borrow, who gave her a bed in the ante-chamber of his surgery, sometimes used as a hospital. When she was recovered, the Borrows had found her a position as housekeeper to an old woman who shared her fascination with the faerie.

But Joan was still cast down, and her sight was worse. Hearing of the experience of Monger's friend, the wool-merchant, she'd returned, in despair, to Cate Borrow, begging her to disclose the herbal ingredients of the powder which offered entry to the very Garden of Eden, with its skies the colour of green apples and the forests all blue like some distant sea. Or, as *she* would see it...

'The land of faerie?' I said.

'Cate Borrow, of course, refused, deeming Joan to be a woman of unsound temper who might be left sorely damaged. But Joan wouldn't leave her alone. Her proposal was to go one last time to the top of the tor and dose herself with the dust of vision, there before the ruins of the church of St Michael.'

'A bold woman.'

'Moonstruck,' Monger said. 'She'd stopped eating by then. Starved herself for weeks. If you think she's thin now... my God. Clothes hanging off her, hair falling out. Opening her arms to death. In the end... Cate relented. On condition that she and Matthew should accompany Joan to the tor and remain with her while she took the potion. Matthew having resisted it to the end, of course, repelled by thoughts of Joan Tyrre screeching to the sky in helpless ecstasy in possibly the most visible place in all Somerset. Then finally accepting that it should be done on All Hallows Eve.'

I shrank back.

'Quite,' Monger said. 'Matthew, however – you should know that Matthew goes to church just enough to avoid penalty and only too glad to be called away to a case of sickness in the middle of it. His science is, I would say, a narrower science than yours.'

'You mean he has no belief in God or the spiritual?'

'No faith I'm aware of, no fear. Matthew fears only men – unlike most others here, as you can imagine. On All Hallows Eve, the town lights its lamps, bars its doors and firmly turns its back on the tor.'

'The devil's hill.'

'This might be the one night they could be sure to be alone there. Or that anyone else up there' – I sensed a rueful smile from Monger – 'would be too far gone in madness to pay heed to Joan Tyrre.'

'Or, presumably, that Joan would, on the eve itself, be too affeared to go on with the venture and...'

'Exactly that,' Monger said. 'Matthew said that if Joan backed away now, at least that would be an end to it.'

I sat and waited for Monger to tell me what had happened in the end, but he became reticent, saying only that Joan did not back away, with the result that they went, the three of them, on All Hallows Eve, to the tor.

To my own mind, having myself been aware of the strange air upon the tor, Joan Tyrre was either very brave, very mad or very sure of the nearness of another sphere of existence. And of its charity towards her.

'All I know,' Monger said, 'is that Joan claimed that from the following morning her sight – in her best eye at least – had begun to improve by degrees.' He shrugged. 'But we have only her word for that.'

'You didn't talk to the Borrows about it?'

'The Borrows spoke of it to no-one, until much later. Matthew, needless to say, remains convinced that whatever Joan had seen was within her own head. The worst of it, you see, John... the very worst of it is not what they saw, but that *they* were seen. The three of them. Ascending the tor, on the night when the dead are abroad.'

'Who saw them?'

'A tenant farmer, Dick Moulder, looking for some runaway ewes, *stated* that he watched them ascending the tor with lighted candles in the dusk and later saw them clustered near to the church ruins. Dancing and chanting to the moon, he said.'

I'd caught his emphasis.

'You think he didn't see them at all?'

'I think *someone* saw them, or heard of it. But I know Moulder as a Bible man who wouldn't go within a mile of the tor after dark. The truth, more likely, is that they were seen from the Meadwell land. But, this being too close to Fyche, Moulder was ordered – or paid – to say he'd seen them. Put it this way: this came some weeks later, when more evidence was being sought, to support a... a graver charge.'

And so it emerged. The whole bitter tragedy of it.

Whether Joan Tyrre had been loose-tongued in the town about Cate's potion improving her eyes through some inner vision, Monger didn't know. All he knew for certain was that, within the week, a travelling dealer had called on Dr Borrow offering him a substantial sum of money for a quantity of the dust of vision which could offer glimpses of heaven. He'd sent the dealer away but it seemed the man returned when Matthew was with a patient and Cate was out in her herb garden. Two days later, the potion would sold in the market in Somerton, a town some miles away.

Which made no sense to me, for if the thief knew not which was the magic potion...

'He took everything he could cram into his bag and sold it all – people'll buy anything if it's cheap enough and said to be from abroad. And if just one person achieved a vision of heaven, as a result, that would be sufficient to set up a clamour.'

The clamour that resulted, however, was not the kind the thief expected.

'As Cate herself told me more than once, what was most important was the quantity in which the potion – the fungus dust and whatever was mixed with it – was administered. The quantity is—' Monger held a fore-finger and thumb barely apart '—very, very small.'

According to Monger, a small flask of the potion had been bought by the sixteen-year-old son of a prominent landowner. The boy had gone out that night, on the roister with some of his fellows. Never came back.

'His companions had left him, in fear at his behaviour,' Monger said. 'They spoke of the dreadful convulsions of his body… in a kind of dance. He was screaming that devils were pinching him and his arms and legs were afire.'

I must've shuddered; Monger glanced at me.

'They found his body about a week later, entangled in branches under the river bridge. Thrown himself in the river to put out the fire in his limbs.'

Monger said the dealer had fled from Somerton but was caught in the hue and cry. In return, Monger guessed, for his life, he confessed to the theft of herbs mixed by Cate Borrow.

'And *was* this established to be caused by swallowing some of the… the dust of vision?'

Thinking that I'd heard of something similar in France.

'Although no-one else died in this way, the boy was the first of several to complain of burning limbs, visions of angels and monsters made manifest under unearthly skies. All had been sold quantities of Cate Borrow's potion. And then, as she was awaiting trial, word came in of the deaths of infants.'

'What?'

'Babes whose mothers, it emerged, had taken the potion to ease the sorrow which can follow childbirth. The wrath of God visited upon them, people cried.'

Within a day Cate Borrow had been arrested for witchery.

Within a short time she'd be dead.

'Hanged for mixing herbs?'

'For murder.'

'Any half-competent advocate could take such a charge apart.'

'In London, maybe.'

His voice riven with bitterness. The window to the high street was murked with dusk now, the fire low and red in the ingle.

Even in London... I thought back to my own imprisonment. How, through a knowledge of the law, I'd been able to discredit the so-called evidence sworn by the Lord of Misrule.

Even so, it had been perilously close, and I'd still have gone to the flames had it not been for the curiosity of Bishop Bonner.

'Presumably,' I said, 'she couldn't be tried by Fyche at the quarter sessions... or are things different out here?'

'Oh they're *different*. Everything's different here. But the law's the same. A crime warranting a death penalty may be tried only by a circuit judge at the assizes.'

'In Wells?'

'The trial was swift,' Monger said. 'There was an extra witness, whom no-one had seen here before or saw afterwards, but claimed to have watched Mistress Borrow taking pails of wet earth from new graves. To scatter on her herb garden. These were the darkest days of Mary. Everyone in snare to fear and superstition. So when at last they brought Dick Moulder before the court to say how he'd seen two or possibly three of them with their candles on the tor on All Hallows Eve, recognising Mistress Borrow who oft-times came to pick herbs on his land...'

There was a crack in Monger's voice and I sensed his usually placid face becoming knotted with pain at the memory of Cate Borrow standing up in the court and crying out that Moulder must've been mistaken, for she was alone that night on the Tor.

Monger could only guess she'd said this to save her husband. And Joan Tyrre, too, who'd already had one appearance before a church court.

The hollow silence had been smashed by this man Dick Moulder, rearing up and warding Cate Borrow away with his hands in the air and screaming, *If her was alone, then they was spirits!*

'And if I tell you,' Monger said, 'that at that moment, the wind blew open the courtroom door, and then it slammed. A blast of cold air blowing through the court, and a woman screaming and... the way all that happened, it would've been enough to convict the Pope.'

'What about the boy's death?' I said. 'Surely she didn't *admit* any blame there?'

'Neither admitted nor denied it. She simply said nothing more. Refused to answer any further questions in the court, only stood there very pale. Ghostly pale, as if she were already passing into another place. I remember Matthew, in his desperation, trying to catch her eye, and she never looked at him. Would not look at him. Never looked at him again. It was the worst thing.'

'Not wanting him to be implicated?'

'As if she was saying, it's over, nothing to be done. Go back to your work. Forget me.'

'And Eleanor, was she…?'

'Not there. She'd been instructed, in her mother's best interests, to keep Joan Tyrre well away from the hearing.'

The next day, Matthew Borrow had led a group of elders from the town to Fyche, at Meadwell, to plead for his wife's life. Returning encouraged, after Fyche – a former monk, for heaven's sake – had told them he'd do what he could. Borrow restraining his distraught daughter, assuring her they would find evidence to get the verdict reversed, appeal to Queen Mary…

The following day, at dawn, Cate Borrow had, without ceremony, been hanged in Wells. Fyche announcing kindly that at least he'd spared the witch's family a burning. Generously allowing them to collect the body, as long it was not buried in consecrated ground.

This was not much more than a year ago. Little wonder that Eleanor Borrow could not bear to be in this man's presence.

'No-one in this town could quite believe it,' Monger said. 'A woman of quiet charity who lived for her garden and what she might learn from it. The cures that could be found, the sick people she might help.'

'But… Christ, why did he do it? Why did Fyche want this woman dead?'

'My guess… the dust of vision. It was rumoured his son once took it. I don't know what happened, but it must have frightened Fyche. He'd see it as dangerous… uncontrollable. An instant religious experience without the discipline of the Church? If she'd made the dust of vision, what else might she be working on?'

'She had to be made an example of and therefore—'

'I can't say what goes on in the man's head.'

'And Eleanor?'

'She was not long back from college at this time – Matthew had sent her away a couple of years earlier, to be schooled in medicine in Bath. She… always was a gay, laughing child. You always knew what she was thinking. Afterwards… well…' Monger's eyes were cast down. 'You know what's most bitter about all this? Before the Dissolution, the Justice of the Peace here was the abbot himself. Cate's friend.'

I looked to his eyes, but it was as if shutters had been erected.

'Despite its mysteries, despite its air of spirtual rebellion, this is an unhappy town,' he said. 'Why, truly, are you here, Dr Dee?'

XXV

Trade

WHEN MONGER HAD left through the back door, I stood for a while on the edge of the yard, watching the dregs of day soaking into a sad tapestry of cloud around the tower of the Baptist's church. The sky was darker than it should be at this time: a storm coming. I went back inside and stood in the gloom of the rear passageway and my own lightless thoughts.

Of the cold ruthlessness of Fyche and the victims of it. Of the doctor, Matthew Borrow and what he had to live with: awakening each day to the memory of his wife's face in that courtroom, fixed and white. And turned away.

Would not look at him. Never looked at him again.

The agony of a non-believer. No consoling dreams of their eyes meeting some day in heaven. Yet Borrow worked on, staying out half the night to save others' lives, regardless of his own health. Probably not caring if he worked himself into the grave or how soon.

I could still see him in my head, how he'd stood in that backstreet by the church. A stringy, ashen man in the shadow of the final injustice: his daughter meeting the same fate as his wife, at the same man's hands.

The George Inn was silent now around me, the farmers having fled for their homes before the storm, Cowdray likely in his quarters with his kitchenmaid. And *she* was out there. Nel Borrow, somewhere under the massing sky.

✠

I ran up the shadowed stairs, paused for only a moment outside the door of Dudley's bedchamber where, hearing nothing, I went in.

As the door closed behind me, the air moved. An arm drawn back against the green light in the square panes, a silvery skimming on a long, tapering blade. Its point finishing a foot, at most, from my throat.

Time suspended in a moment of glittering terror, smelling the diseased sweat. Watching the blade of the soldier's side-sword quiver once, almost touching my softest skin like a crooked finger under a babe's chin.

And then seeing it fall away, clattering to the boards. The tumble of a body on a bed in a room which was as dark as the floor of a pine-forest.

'Christ, John, you could've knocked.'

I took a breath.

'Thought you were asleep.'

Guessing that he'd been more affeared wafting his blade than I'd been at the point of it. Physical weakness was a condition new to Robert Dudley.

'Can't take any more sleep. Filthy dreams sucking me in soon as I close my damned eyes. Head feels like a cannon ball.'

'You eaten anything?'

'A little broth. Tasted like piss.'

'The throat?'

'Better. A bit. Maybe. I don't know. Hate this cell, reminds me of the Tower. You haven't brought your *doctor* back with you?'

'No, she...'

'What?'

'Doesn't matter.'

But it did, of course. It mattered more than anything.

'We need light,' I said.

My innards felt cramped through lack of food, but too much time had been wasted, through concealment. I stumbled to the window, where I found two candles of good beeswax on their trays and took them down the stairs to the panelled room and lit them with a taper from the fire in the ingle. Back in Dudley's bedchamber, I placed one candle in the window and one on the bedside board.

'I'm not deaf, John.'

He was sitting upright under the high oak headboard, a pillow doubled at his back, his sword, sheathed, across his knees.

'So you heard the hue and cry,' I said.

'A murder in the service of Satan?'

'Robbie, this is a man who sees witches and sorcerers under every—'

'And is he deluded?'

There were no plain answers to this. I sat at the foot of the bed, staring into the white gasses of a candle flame. Telling him about Cate Borrow, what had happened to her. Dudley leaned forward, his face narrow and blotched, his beard ragged. Looking far older than his years, a man stripped of all finery, pretention, status.

'He thinks your doctor's a witch, by heredity? Is there not good reason?'

'He hanged her mother for, in truth, no good reason.'

'And you're saying... what was done to Martin Lythgoe, *that's* no good reason? Does it look like a random attack, a robbery? What's the matter with you? It has all the marks of ritual sacrifice. You've studied all this.'

'Yes, but—'

'Blood sacrifice, John, is a *trade*... to summon a demon to do the bidding of the magician.'

'In theory.'

Oh, I knew all the theory, having dissected in detail the rituals set down in *The Key of Solomon* and the grimoires of Pope Honorius. All the divers conjurations involving the sacrifice of cockerels and farm animals, the belief in the power of spilled blood to invoke... *not* the kind of angels with whom I would ever wish to commune.

Oh, Glastonbury... did I perceive that there were answers here to some of my deepest midnight questions? Maybe. I didn't know. It was all too immense and complex. Too close to see.

But Dudley, coherent at last, would not let it go.

'To bring about a death, could not the sacrifice of a good man to the devil or some demon of destruction, in a once sacred place... a once *very* sacred place... would that not be considered effective?'

I could hardly deny that a ritual sacrifice in the Abbey of Glastonbury might well be thought to invoke a demon of substance. I considered the sorcerer Gregory Wisdom – also a doctor of physic – hired by Lord Neville to commit murder from afar. And that was merely the most

215

celebrated case of recent times. These things, the abuse of magic, occurred all around us. I considered the way the candle had burned down over Martin Lythgoe's lips. Had that been in my own warped perception or *had* it been shaved into a likeness of the tor?

'And the supposed victim is Fyche himself – in revenge for the hanging of her mother? I don't see that it worked.'

Dudley snorted.

'So it didn't work. Or it hasn't worked *yet*. Christ, I don't *want* it to have been the woman who cured me of the fever. I just want this matter of Martin's killing… I want it settled, whether by noose or sword, and us out of this stinking little town.'

'And the bones of Arthur?'

He made no reply. Who could blame him, in his condition, and after all that had happened, for almost forgetting why we were here.

'Give me your opinion of this,' I said.

Pulling from my doublet Blanche Parry's letter and taking it over to the candle in the window, just as there came a blinking of white light and then the first low shuddering of thunder from the east.

XXVI

Le Fay

THESE THINGS I purport to create, with all my astral charts and maps of the Zodiac, my pages of calculating and configuration… have I ever *once* been able to state, *this will happen*?

And those who do – which books have *they* read which are not available to me? Is there some holy grail of revelatory knowledge passed from hand to furtive hand? I don't know. That's the worst of it. I, who despise ignorance, *do not know.*

'Who wrote this prophecy, John?'

Dudley's face aglow with new sweat in the candlelight. I'd taken the letter to his bedside, and he'd bade me read it out again, but I repeated only those key lines.

Her nights are tormented and daytimes fraught. She will have no peace from Morgan le Fay until such time as her heroic forefather be entombed in glory.

'All right then,' Dudley said, 'who *might* have written it?'

'Could be one of ours, could be from abroad. There's a seer on every corner in London. Europe's thick with prophets. Especially after what happened with the King of France.'

Dudley leaned into the light.

'You were there, weren't you? In France, when that happened.'

'No. But I had an account of it sent to me.'

By a student who'd attended one of my lectures in Paris. He'd sent it together with a faithful script of the horoscope said to have been sent from Rome – the one warning King Henri to avoid all single combat in an enclosed field, especially around his forty-first year. The one making reference to a head wound which would cause blindness.

'Rome?' Dudley said. 'I thought it was all down to this fellow Nostradamus, at the French court.'

'No, it was an Italian, Luca Gaurico. Not personally known to me any more than is Nostradamus – *he* was asked by the Queen of France to investigate Gaurico and his prophecy. This was after the King chose to laugh and ignore it. I find the whole thing doubtful in the extreme.'

'Oh, well, of course. We all know, John, that you merely indicate *the moods of the universe*... and would never be so foolhardy as to forecast injury or death.'

'And mistrust those who would.' I let the sarcasm go, folded Blanche's letter. 'I'd understood that was what the Queen found useful in me – an ability to see through the fakery, offer informed advice. Apparently not. It seems she has a secret craving for the sensational.'

'Of course. That's why she's so fond of me. But what would *you* have said about this fellow from Rome... had he heralded *her* demise? Not possible?'

I thought of the wax effigy in its coffin in the alley by the river. Had I been too dismissive of that and its power to do harm to the Queen? Did I continually dismiss what I, with all my scholarship, could not think to accomplish?

'I think... that it *is* possible, but not likely. I believe there are some who see the same stars as I do, draw the same charts and then... either God himself intervenes or some faculty comes into play, some hidden organ of sensing which... doesn't function in me.'

'Your blind arrogance leaves me breathless,' Dudley said.

'Most times, however, it's still trickery, for monetary gain.'

And yet...

I bit down on my lower lip, all too aware of the widespread fear and awe engendered by the prophecy apparently fulfilled at a jousting tournament held to celebrate the marriage of the French King's daughter to Philip II of Spain.

Lest you forget... the King, though indeed in his forty-first year, had been far fitter than our own King Harry at that age and had elected to take a primary role in the jousting on that fateful day – the 30th day of June, 1556.

The reason we had a full account of what happened was the presence at the jousting of Sir Nicholas Throckmorton, the Queen's envoy to Paris. Throckmorton had a good seat. He'd seen the lance hit Henri's helm, watched it break, causing the splinters that would pierce the King's eye and enter his brain. Had seen him helped from his horse and stripped of his armour. Reporting, at first, that the wound was not as severe as had been feared – unaware of the French surgeons frantically dissecting the heads of newly executed criminals to try to work out how the splinters might safely be removed.

All to no avail. By the second week of July the King of France lay dead in his darkened chamber, and soon the whole of Europe knew of the power of prophecy through astrology.

'You don't believe that prophecy was ever made, do you?' Dudley said.

'It's too exact for my liking. But leaving that aside, is this –' tapping Blanche's letter – 'the first you've heard of a prediction linking Arthur with Anne Boleyn?'

'How sure are you that Morgan le Fay's even supposed to represent Anne Boleyn?'

He would, of course, have read only Malory, who likes to play down the role of the enchantress Morgan in Arthur's story.

'I think this is Blanche's own coded reference.'

Le Fay. Though sometimes portrayed as Arthur's half-sister, in the earlier tellings she's at least a partly supernatural being. And certainly a witch.

'An evil influence?' Dudley said. 'I was never sure.'

'Not wholly. It's true she's accused of trying to wreck the marriage of Arthur and Guinevere. She's not trustworthy by human standards, causes mischief.'

'Well, that's Anne, certainly.'

'However, in the story of Arthur – the earlier tales – Morgan's role seems to be to test the faith and courage of the knights of the round table. And, in the end, all is reconciled, for she's one of the ladies who accompanies the King on that last dolorous voyage to Avalon. Which brings us to the essence of *this* prophecy… that if what remains of Arthur is *returned* to Avalon…'

'Then the Queen will have no more trouble from the witch.'

'I thought at first that it might be nonsense, pamphlet trivia. Yet it's being informed by a knowledge of the oldest accounts of Arthur… It could, when you think about it, be the reason we're here. Or a big part of it.'

He was silent for just a moment too long.

Saying, at last, 'How do you know Blanche didn't make it up?'

'Credit me at least with a knowledge of my cousin. Look, even if it were mischievously cobbled together to upset the Queen, it was done by someone who knew what he was about. And so…' I tried to catch Dudley's eye, but he was turned away. 'As a man about court, have you heard of other prophecies of this nature?'

'No.'

His head still turned to the wall as if he found the candle too bright. He knew something. He was not a duplicitous man – not with me, anyway – so I reasoned that his only cause for concealment would be the light it might throw upon his own relations with the Queen.

'Or any other matter which might disturb the Queen's rest?' I said. 'Because if anyone—'

'You know what it's like at court.' Dudley flipped over a hand. 'Rumours coming from all directions. Rumours of new plots to put the Queen of Scots on the English throne. Even the story going round that Mary's reign was founded on a lie because Edward's not dead.'

I nodded. I'd heard that one, too, but it was predictable – either a yearning for the return of a powerfully adult Edward or a hint that it was time Elizabeth found herself a man to rule the country. To the end of her reign she'd have the burden of proving that a woman on the throne of England was actually the will of God.

I kept up the pressure, quoting again from the letter.

'*Her nights tormented…*'

Thunder rattled the panes. Dudley's body pulsed under the sheet. He rolled over to face me.

'What are you trying to say?'

'What are you trying to *avoid* saying?'

'I'm sick,' he said, with a childish pathos. 'What the hell's got into you,

John? You're a mild man, a man of books. Why don't you piss off and read one?'

I stood up and looked down on him, stripped of his finery and his waxed moustache, his hair all matted.

'I have to know this, Robbie. We must needs fathom why we're *really* here.'

He sat up, reached for the pitcher of water and the mug. The jug was too heavy for him and water spilled. I took the jug and poured him some, but he did no more than wet his lips. The thunder was like far-off war drums and, at the same time, Dudley spoke.

'There was a night... three weeks ago... four, maybe. I was summoned to court at Richmond. A message brought to me, in private, by someone we both know.'

Maybe Blanche.

'I was admitted to the Queen's chamber, past midnight and all her ladies had been sent away, and I found her... distressed. In need of comfort.'

'Comfort,' I said.

'And we talked. Long into the night. *Talked.*'

Hmm. I waited, guessing I'd be the first person ever to hear this and probably the last.

'Bess was... much disturbed, you might say, by forecasts of her impending death.'

'How? By whom?'

'God knows. Omens and portents. Hardly the first. Hardly the *thirty-first*, but she demands to be told about all of them. Nothing must be hidden. All manner of letters and writings are put before her every day. This one was from a prophetic pamphlet found on the streets – treasonous drivel. She'd caught two of her ladies whispering about it.'

I felt an unease.

'What did it say?'

'That her death would occur... I know not when exactly... But that she need not worry, for she'd not be alone but would be guided through the veil. That she who'd brought her into the world would watch her out of it.'

'Those words?'

'Something like that. That Anne would watch her out of it. Watch her all the way to...'

'Hell?'

A hush. A fluttering of lightning on the wall.

'Widely known,' Dudley said, 'that the ghost of Anne Boleyn haunts the Tower.'

No thunder came to smash the silence. Dudley swallowed.

'You can imagine what happened. The very next night, she has a dream. A vivid dream. The kind of dream where you dream of being asleep in your own bed and then you awaken and...'

'Anne?'

'Oh God, yes. Wearing that cute little smile from the portrait, and there's a thin circle of dried blood around her neck. As if she's decently popped her head back on, for the visit.'

I nodded. The images of myth full formed: Anne Boleyn smiling with a foxy serenity on the edge of the abyss. The mouth in the severed head, held up, still forming words. It took little imagination to envision the effects of the merest suggestion that the wilful Anne was there, in the shadows of the night, ready to beckon her daughter over death's threshold.

'Wouldn't sleep alone in her chamber for several nights after that,' Dudley said. 'There'd be various ladies in attendance through till dawn, and extra candles alight.'

'It continued?'

'Happened twice more.'

'And did this... did Anne speak?'

Dudley shook his head, drank more water.

'Bess asked me if I thought she should summon John Dee to cast around her bed a protective circle which... which her mother couldn't enter. I said, well, why not?'

'Thank you for your confidence.'

'However, it seems that someone else swiftly advised her against it. The Archbishop of Canterbury was privately summoned instead, to do what he could.'

'*Parker?*'

'Bless her bedchamber, anyway.'

Didn't ask if *that* had worked. I leaned into the candlelight.

'So this prophecy of the Queen's death… were any attempts made to trace its origins?'

'What's the point? You know what these bastards are like. Some small printing shop in a cellar deep into Southwark. There was a name at the bottom, from the Bible. Some prophet – Elijah or Elisha or…'

At least it wasn't Dee. But still this worried me. I'd already been brought within singeing distance of the stake as a result of one royal horoscope.

'Look,' Dudley said, 'her mother… you need to understand this is not something new. When we were in the Tower, as children, she'd oft-times talk of… I mean, what would you expect in the place where your father had your mother's head sliced off? She was growing up into a world heavy with omens and foreboding and the ever-presence of what you might call… sudden death.'

The keening of the axe in the air. Or in Anne's case, thanks to Harry's mercy, a sword wielded by a master.

'All right, let's examine this,' I said. 'Anne… Morgan. Two women said to be witches who've caused havoc. An undying king, whose aura of sacred magic was harnessed to the Tudor cause…'

'Until this holy heritage was taken apart by Harry's *un*holy desire for Anne.'

'By whom he'd insist, when it suited him later, that he'd been bewitched. Just as Arthur and his knights were bedevilled by Morgan le Fay.'

I was chilled at how neatly it fitted together.

'If the Queen fears the curse of her own immediate ancestry, as the child of a witch and a monster… and the suggestion is made that the only way it can be repaired…'

'If we follow this road,' Dudley said, 'then the bones, when we find them, should stay here in Avalon. That is, not go to London, as Cecil prefers. And the Queen *should* come here, as did Edward I, to watch them re-entombed… in glory.'

'In an abbey rebuilt at crippling expense?'

A barrel of worms. The window paled with lightning.

'I tell you, John, I'm out of here tomorrow,' Dudley said.

'The town?'

'Out of this *bed*. I want those fucking bones. And when we find them, we don't immediately send word to Cecil, right?'

'Robbie, he's your friend, he's been a friend of your family for—'

'Be not naive. He has his own script; he wants *the right marriage*. And it won't be an Englishman. Cecil believes that the only worthwhile royal marriage is a political marriage.'

'Who?'

'It varies. I know for a fact he's been tossing around the idea of a union to unite us with Scotland – finally break France's hold through Mary Stuart. And if... *if*, when he finds the right match, the chosen foreigner finds out that his virgin queen is not...'

Dudley fell back, coughing. The thunder rolled closer. The bedside candle went out.

...*not a virgin*. A shiver sped through me.

'I think we've talked too much,' I said. 'Get some sleep, rest your throat.'

✠

I blew out the other candle and closed the door on Dudley, shaken. Pacing the landing, lighting a tallow candle in the sconce there.

So much I hadn't told him. How, for example, would he have reacted to the knowledge that at least two people in this town knew exactly who I was, and that one of them was the woman now sought by Fyche in connection with the murder of Martin Lythgoe?

Who, in this situation, could we trust? How would Dudley feel about the farrier, who seemed to me an honest, well-intentioned man?

But then what did *I* know? What did I know about the life outside of books?

I went into my chamber and sat at the foot of the dusty bed in the darkness and wondered whether I hadn't made a terrible mistake in giving an answer to Monger's simple question.

✠

Madness. Night thoughts.

Why, truly, are you here, Dr Dee?

A smitter of rain on the window, and then it stopped and I thought of what Monger had said when I'd told him what we sought.

The lead went first from the roof and then the glass from the windows. The marble tomb? It just disappeared.

All of it? At once?

I've heard the old cross has been seen – the one from the original grave – but I know not where it is now. I don't think any of us cared one way or the other. They'd cut out our heart. Lesser abbeys were kept on as cathedrals, but we were too close to Wells. Would be better the abbey had never been here than we're left with an open wound.

I'd asked him if it was true that Abbot Whiting had been tortured because it was thought he was concealing the famous eucharistic vessel of the Last Supper, the Holy Grail. I'd asked Monger if he believed it yet existed.

That depends on how you define existence. It may well have existed as a vessel, of metal or pottery or wood. May well have existed here. But it might also have a spiritual life, a holy symbol, experienced only in visions.

Those visions again. Monger had shaken his head in a weary bewilderment.

Some say this is the holiest place in these islands, while to others it's just a tawdry town with a history of fraud and deception and the monks at the rotten core of it.

In the old days, Monger said, there had been whisperings, even amongst the monks, of things hidden, certain wonders pre-dating Christianity. Rumours still passed around by the town's ragbag of half-pagan mystics... although *they* were in thrall to an essentially different Arthur, representing the magical legacy of the old Celtic tribes and Druids.

What had we stumbled into?

I undressed swiftly, because of the cold, threw on my robe over my night shirt, sat on the edge of the bed. Outside, the thunder crawled like a black beast on the hills, and I could not but think of Joan Tyrre and her dreams of Gwyn ap Nudd under his spiked hill.

A rustling now in the chamber. Rats, most likely. There were always rats. I thought, inevitably, of Queen Elizabeth, her bedchamber red-hued from the fire. Afraid to sleep alone lest she awake under the dark glower of Anne Boleyn, the talking head with its blood-rimed neck.

Jesu... *stop this.*

Sliding off the bed, scrabbling on the board for a candle to light from the sconce on the landing. I would bring out my few books and study until the dawn came or sleep overcame me, or...

There was a shadow before the window.

I twisted urgently away from the board, my hand going to my mouth. 'Who's there?'

Could see it seated by the window in the greyness.

XXVII

A Sister of Venus

'I'd thought,' she said, 'to bare my breast.'

A candle fell on to its side.

The storm prowled closer, the beast at the door. All fumble-fingered, I caught the candle before it could roll from the board and hurriedly re-lit it from the flame of another. Three were alight now, including the one from the sconce on the landing, all in a bunch so that their flames mingled in a spiral of fire.

'It having occurred to me,' she said delicately from the chair by the window, 'that you might wish to be sure I was not in possession of such a thing as a third nipple.'

She wore the blue overdress, and her hair was down over her shoulders. In the candleflare, the panes of stained glass in the lower window were the colour of dried mud.

'With which to suckle my familiar?' she said. 'As some say.'

'Yes,' I said. 'I've heard that… I mean… how such an appendage is said to be employed.'

Stepping back from the light, in pursuit of my breath.

And – if you were thinking to ask – only one woman since my infancy had ever bared a breast for me.

Mistress Borrow was smiling distantly, as if across a long room, say a lecture hall, some lofty-ceilinged forum for civilised, cultural debate.

'Oh, of course – from the books.' Musing very softly, as if to herself. 'He'd know it from his books.'

Holding my old brown robe together, my right hand shook. We'd not spoken since she'd walked away from the tower on the tor, after Fyche's naming of her as a witch. It was as if she'd picked up from there: a line drawn, with geometrical precision, betwixt that point in time and this present moment, and…

…*all right*… a Sister of Venus, if you must know. It was in Cambridge, on a rare night I'd drunk too much in an effort to be one with my fellow students, all of them older than me who, proving too young in worldly experience, too overawed and fumbling, had not… Oh God, how she'd laughed, that woman, a cold and brittle laugh, like a chisel chipping stonework from the buildings which enclosed the alley where we'd stood, tight 'twixt walls.

A very sour memory which must surely have retarded my progress into manhood.

I said, 'You know they're looking for you…'

Hoarse words, meagre as the scrapings of a rat. Within an instant, cruel lightning had exposed what I guessed to be my raging blush.

'I try not to let these diversions interfere with my work,' she said, almost briskly. 'Which oft-times, as you know, is also a matter of life and death. I beg mercy if this visit disturbs you, Dr John, but a man's bed-chamber, for me… well, I've been in so many.'

The thunder shook the panes.

'As a doctor,' she said. 'Dear Lord, what a night this is become.'

And placed a calming hand above her breast and, in my head, I was spinning again down the green flank of the tor, sky and hills falling around me like a cascade of playing-cards, crying *Eleanor*.…

…*Nel*…

Oh my God, she seemed so small now, with her narrow shoulders, her eyes half-lidded, demure, hair over her cheeks.

'Well,' she was saying. 'I came really to inquire after your friend. Thinking it best to knock on your door first, but it was hanging open, so…' Looking up at me, skin white-gold in the haze of light. 'How *is* he?'

'Not yet well.'

'Then he has need of me?'

Reaching for the black cloth bag at her feet on top of her folded black cloak.

Need… Dear God…

'He's sleeping,' I said quickly. 'And… and better in body, most certainly, than yesterday, thank you. Though much damaged by the murder of his servant.'

'Yes, that was—'

She broke off. Only seconds after the thunderblast, lightning had flared again, like full day, in the glass. And then, on the sudden, as she flinched at the exploding sky, I saw in her eyes what had been so well hidden by her voice.

Her doctor's voice, which would be well practised at smoothing fears in herself and others. But the green eyes… to me, in this moment, they were the wild eyes of a bewildered animal in a forest of predators. And I felt calmer for seeing them, for they surely were not a witch's eyes.

The chamber had fallen dark again. Could it be that she had nowhere else to go but here that was safe from Fyche's hue and cry?

But, truly, how safe *was* this place?

I said, 'You've seen Joe Monger this night?'

'No,' she said. 'Nor this day at all.'

I nodded, feeling this to be the truth. Time, then, to hasten to the chase. Not that this was any kind of chase, for if I were a predator then she'd walked into my den.

Holding my robe together with my left hand, I stood and held out the right.

'John Dee,' I said.

✛

Thus began the hours of change. The night of a wild transformation.

How can I begin to tell this?

Tell me, then, Doctor, how can the soul…?

Alchemy.

We *talk* of it. We talk of *transmutation*, we, the men of science, the men of books. We say, *there is a formula, there has to be a formula* to turn low metal into solid gold, to make man into something close to God. Some ancient secret, maybe known to Pythagoras and addressed by Plato. A matter of the occult.

Most times, we say glibly, it will involve a painful passage through darkness towards a distant planet of light. But the truth is that almost none of us of us will ever attain that light, seeing only momentary glimpses like flashes from the beaten sky in the black belly of a storm. And then, having watched the flashes and searched deep within ourselves for something more lasting, will only – God help us – dwell forever in a deeper darkness.

✟

Worldly matters must needs be dealt with first, some small mysteries opened out. It seemed she'd left early this morning to see a sick child at a poor farm in the marshes, towards Wells, when a rider carrying letters to that city had spied her and stopped to tell her of the murder. Returning later to Glastonbury she'd had the wit to exercise caution, knowing how some men, under cover of hue and cry, can behave towards women alone.

Slipping back into the town, not by the road but along sheep paths, she'd encountered Joan Tyrre, who'd told to her the worst of news – that she was sought – and she'd hastened away, back into the woods, only returning, well cloaked, after dark.

And had gone, not home, but to Cowdray who, having seen off Fyche and his constables, had given her food and drink and an attic room. Sending word, discreetly, to her father that she was safe. Cowdray, she said, was a good man, if you didn't mind waiting a full half-year for settlement of your bill. Her father had cared for Cowdray's wife before she died, easing her pain a good deal, and he'd not forget that.

I assured her that my friend, Master Roberts, would be swifter to settle. Anxious, naturally, to know if Dudley, as well as giving away my name, had betrayed his own identity. He hadn't, but it seemed he'd come perilously close to it.

'Your friend awoke that morning,' Mistress Borrow said, 'and knew not where he was. Nor who *I* was. Once, he called me Amy.'

'Good,' I whispered.

Meaning, good that he hadn't called her Bess.

'And then, in his delirium, he called out for you twice by name. *Where's John Dee? Send John Dee to me.*'

'Um… there must be others,' I said, 'of that name.'

'Not in my knowledge. And anyway, there was something about your friend's manner. A man used to giving orders and being obeyed, in a snapping of the fingers. But now I was less interested in him than in you. I had to find out. Obviously.'

At last I found a smile, recalling all her educated talk of astrological herbalism as we walked through the town and sat by the holy well. And all the time, she would have been charting the rising excitement in me, as we discussed the inherent power of places.

All that blithe skipping on the rim of heresy.

Heresy! Of a sudden, I wanted to cry it to the beams. Embrace it.

Or her.

'I've tried to follow your work, of course,' she said. 'As best I could, from pamphlets left around the town by travellers. Some of them insist that you're the cleverest man in Europe, while others…'

'I know well what the others say. Anyway, both are distortions of the truth.'

'Ah, but all say the Queen thinks *very* highly of you. That's distortion, too?'

She sat, all serious, prim and decorous, looking down at her small hands in her lap. Why would *my* hands not be still? I sat on them. On the bed. Should not be sitting on the bed with a woman here, but she had the only chair.

The candles, still in a cluster on the board I'd took care to keep betwixt us, made a bright ball of light and shot golden arrows to the beams. Mistress Borrow bent and pushed aside her cloak to delve into her black cloth bag.

'I suppose,' she said, 'that you've seen this one.'

I rose and accepted the crumpled pamphlet, holding it close to the candles.

IMPORTANT FOR ALL
THE SECOND COMING

Know that the Queen hath been served with
clear warning of the ending of the world. That
which was foretold in the Book of the
Revelation of St John will soon come to pass.
Dr Dee, the royal stargazer, hath been

commanded to foretell the date when England,
wherein lies the New Jerusalem, will see the
Second Coming of Our Saviour...

I read no further.

'It's bollocks,' I said. Then blushed. 'Beg mercy, mistress—'

'Jesu, I'm a *doctor.*' She rolled her eyes. 'Men cry out far worse when having a foot cut off.'

This casual mention of surgery tensed me. But I would not think on it now. Handing the pamphlet back, I wondered if this could be the peacock man's paper, or were there more? Was this one mere twig from a huge oak tree of fakery? Or – more disturbing – was there something in the stars I'd missed?

'Where did you get this?'

'Some wool-merchants passing through.'

'Well, you should know that no-one in this world has ever asked me to name the date of the apocalypse or the time of the Second Coming of Christ.'

'No?'

'You sound disappointed.'

'*Tush*, Dr John, you're the Queen's astrologer.'

'So they tell me.'

She fell silent. At some point she would be asking what the Queen's astrologer was doing here in Glastonbury. And in the light of what had happened since we arrived, this no longer seemed like a secret worth preserving.

So I waited for the next thunder to fade, and then told her. Told her, without identifying Robert Dudley, about our hitherto discreet mission to recover the bones which, whoever's flesh had once been upon them, had lain in the tomb of King Arthur.

Something like relief was at once apparent in her eyes, a tightness departing her body. Evidently, she'd feared worse.

'But the bones are gone,' she said.

'Gone from the abbey, yes.'

'Gone from the town.'

I settled back on the side of the bed.

'How do you know that?'

'I...' She hesitated for a moment and then shrugged. 'My mother told me once.'

'Oh?'

'And now you're about to ask how my mother knew.'

I said nothing. Mistress Borrow took breath.

'She was close to the abbey. Always. That is, to the abbot. When I told you I remembered the abbot, that was because he was oft-times at our house. Which my father, though he'd little time for men of God, would tolerate because the abbot had an interest in healing.'

'But it was only your mother who had the abbot's confidence?'

'And whatever he told her always remained in the most *sacred* confidence. She told neither my father nor me, and we learned not to ask. It was just that, one night my father was reading to us from Malory, while scorning his version of the tales...'

'With good reason.'

'It was read for amusement only. And we talked of Arthur in Avalon and his burial, and my father remarked on the tomb being plundered for the marble and my mother said to me later that it was of no import because it was empty by then. The tomb was empty.'

'You think the abbot had the bones removed, knowing what was to come?'

'Someone must have.'

'But your mother said they were not in the town.'

'I think her words were, *it's no use anyone looking for them in Glastonbury.*'

'Thus suggesting that she knew where the bones *were* hidden.'

'I don't know. I truly don't know. She never spoke of it again, though sometimes, when we were alone, I thought she came close.'

Which didn't take us much further but was a start. But Mistress Borrow hadn't finished – hesitating a moment, as if considering how sacred a confidence might be when both parties were dead.

'My mother... knew, I think, where many secret things were to be found. Other remains of Arthur.'

I sat up, recalling what Monger had said about hidden wonders. But her smile was regretful.

'I don't mean the Holy Grail. Anyway, most people say the Grail's not real. That it's only a vision.'

'*Only—*'

'But there *was* once mention of King Arthur's round table.'

'Your mother believed King Arthur's round table remains? Here? In this town?'

'It was just a passing— What's the matter?'

I told her about Benlow, the bone-man and his piece of oak in a wooden box which I might have taken away but, in the end, had bade him keep. She laughed.

'Did he suggest you stow it away inside your codpiece, and then offer to help you?'

'Um...' I sighed. 'I gather that Benlow is not regarded as one of the seekers of Avalon.'

'You gather right.'

'So he'd not be trusted with secrets...'

'Dr John, that man would sell his own mother's bones to flavour a Christmas stew.' Her face sobered. 'When my mother spoke of the round table, I felt it was in a more spiritual sense, in the way that mystics speak of the Grail. She was a rare woman. I think she knew much of what happened under the surface.'

'You mean underground?'

'I truly can't say, Dr John,' Mistress Borrow said. 'But I do believe that's why—'

She broke off at the white spatter of lightning, and we waited for what followed. *Very* soon afterwards, this time, and the whole frame of the window was atremble.

'I do believe that's why she was murdered,' Eleanor Borrow said.

XXVIII

The Great Unspoken

A PALE MOUND of lustrous candlefat had spread upon the boardtop betwixt us. Tallow. Smelled like a butcher's slab.

I leaned back, hands as in prayer, thumbs pressed into my jaw, thinking: *when does execution become murder?*

An answer: when the deed has an expedience beyond justice. When the cords and strands of the law have themselves been stretched and twined to devise a death. Ask yourself: was not King Harry guilty of the murders of Anne Boleyn and Catherine Howard?

This is the great unspoken. The laws of man, held up as the laws of God, are just more tools in the practised hands of the powerful.

'It would not be a good thing, mistress,' I said softly, 'for you to be known to talk like this.'

'I seldom do. Unless in the presence of someone I trust –' she hesitated – 'in some odd way, as I would my own kin.'

I felt a light inside, as small and strange as a glow-worm.

'Mistress Borrow, I'm—'

'Oh, there are divers kinds of kinship. At college in Bath, I read some of your papers. Also met people who'd had dealings with you in Louvain, where they said all talk just ran free. I formed the impression that you were a man for whom knowledge and spirit were as one. And also –' hands entwining in her lap – 'also I know that you were once close to a death which… would've been worse than my mother's.'

'It doesn't compare,' I said gently. 'Because it didn't happen.'

I'd made known to her what Joe Monger had told me about the trial and execution of Cate Borrow, a woman who evidently had shared my own curiosity about the limits of the natural world. Was this what her daughter meant by kinship? I'd have to admit a certain disappointment if it was.

'Tell me about Fyche,' I said. 'Why, after what was done to your mother, he yet seeks to damage *you*.'

'No mystery there. He looks at me and he sees... *her*.'

'You mean it's a reminder of what he did?'

'No, no!' Shaking her head hard, hair swinging across her cheeks. 'That would imply a sorrow over my mother's death, and there *is* none. He sees another woman with the eyes of Cate Borrow and an education.'

'A threat.'

'Dr John, let me tell you about this man who was a monk at the abbey in the last days. Then had this land granted to him. And the money to farm it and build upon it.'

'He inherited the land... from an uncle?'

'An *uncle!*'

'Did he not?'

'It was gifted to him, I'd bet all I own on it.'

'Gifted by whom?'

'Who gifts land?' Her body rocked. '*Who gifts land?*'

'Mistress Borrow—'

'Eleanor.' Tossing back her hair. 'Nel. Call me Nel. It takes up... far less time.'

Nel.

There was a sense of energy in the chamber. Moisture in the palms of my hands. And the thunder was coming so frequent now that it was like to being inside some vast drum of war. But not so loud as my own heart, the pounding of my blood.

'Dr John...'

She was looking into my eyes, and I wanted to whisper to her, *John, just John,* and could not. That toss of her hair... *dear God*. I pulled my robe across my knees.

'....if this makes it any more plain,' she said, 'you should know that much of what is now Fyche's land was once abbey property.'

'You mean land which was taken by Thomas Cromwell on behalf of the King? Which, from then on, was the King's to place in whoever's hands he wished?'

We were upon dangerous ground.

'My father knows more than I do,' she said. 'The house, Meadwell, was on the edge of the abbey grounds and had become derelict. And then… well, all that was known in the town was that, some years after the Dissolution of the abbey, this abandoned farmhouse was suddenly being rebuilt in grand style. And that Edmund Fyche, a former monk, was in residence there. And then he was *Sir* Edmund.'

'Is all this *widely* known in the town?'

'Well, it's known, but makes no odds. Fyche, as well as the voice of the law, is seen as a benefactor. A poor harvest now, no-one starves, as many did after the abbey went. What you have now is more than half the people here thinking him a good presence… or the lesser of several possible evils.'

I nodded, could have named a dozen landowners, here and in Europe, who'd bought themselves popularity with which to turf over past misdemeanours.

But one question stood out here like a robed bishop in a brothel.

'Why would the donor of the land have so favoured a former monk?'

'Why indeed?'

'You think your mother knew something of this? Knew what Fyche did for Cromwell and Fat Harry to earn such a lavish reward?'

A sudden apprehension enfolded me and I looked around. Stood up, went barefoot to the door and opened it and looked out, and then walked to the top of the stairs and looked down. In the well of the stairs, pale lighting flickered from doorway to doorway as if men were signalling to one another with lamps and blankets to cover the light.

But there was no-one about, and I came back and shut the door as the thunder broke, feeling embarrassed in my night-attire, wishing I was full-dressed. I pulled my robe across my bare knees again and sat back on the bed, in deepest shadow.

'All quiet,' I said. 'All… under the sky.'

'Good.'

Falling into an easy intimacy I'd never before felt with a woman. All the more rare, when you considered the hellish nature of what we were approaching.

'So the Abbot of Glastonbury,' I said, 'is taken up to the top of the tor and hanged before the ruined church. And drawn and quartered. And, afterwards, one of his lowly monks becomes a wealthy man.'

'Yes,' she said. 'That's the crux of it.'

✠

There must have been more lightning, more thunder, but for several minutes I was unaware of either.

'You can have no idea what it was like then,' Nel Borrow was saying. 'I was only a child, but some of my earliest memories are of a pervading fear and misery – all these dull-clad, stooping figures, their eyes cast down. The skull still up on the gatehouse. Nobody was asking questions then, lest their own heads be struck off.'

I was thinking on it. Laying it all out. The charges against Abbot Whiting, as I recalled, were that he secreted items away when Cromwell's men came, including a gold chalice. Also, that writings of his were found that were disloyal to the King. *Critical* of the King.

Found by whom? Who could say? But it would be a good deal less easy for an outsider to put his fingers on such items than someone who was resident at the abbey.

'Fyche betrayed his abbot,' I said.

'It was more than betrayal.'

A pivotal role in the stitching-up of Whiting for theft and treason. Had to be, for Fyche to be rewarded with land and money and position, a small slice of the most succulent monastic pie in England.

Unless... unless this rare and lovely woman lied. Or was deluded by grief. Dear God, I didn't want to think on either of these, but you learn that survival in this dark world means that all things, however painful, must needs be considered.

'You might also ask yourself,' she said, 'why it was felt necessary to have the abbot killed.'

'To make an example of him.'

'Oh? For what purpose... at this stage of the game?'

She was right. Glastonbury had been among the last abbeys to be taken by the Crown. It was not as if there was a dangerous army of rebellious priests out there to quell by intimidation. The ceremonial slaughter of the abbot, the division and display of the body… it seemed gratuitous, even for the times.

To silence him, then? And then cover the deed with bloody spectacle?

Again – why? And yet… whilst I couldn't doubt, from what she'd told me, that Fyche had indeed conspired in Whiting's downfall, did it follow that he'd fashioned charges of witchcraft and murder against Cate Borrow merely to gag someone who suspected him of it? It must have been clear she was not alone in her suspicions, but no others had died… had they?

As if she'd seen my thoughts, Nel was half risen from her chair.

'I'm aware that there's more to know…' She sat down again, shaking her head. 'If we but knew where to look.'

I saw that she was shivering freely. She had no real evidence against Fyche and knew it, but the last thing I wanted was to appear to be turning away from her at such a time. Nevertheless, another matter must needs be approached – questions that Robert Dudley would be asking when, on the morrow, I would have to put all this before him.

'When Fyche talks of witchcraft at the tor, sorcery and the sacrifice of new-born babes—'

'He said *that?*'

Her eyes were wide.

'Spoke of people massing like maggots on the hill,' I said, 'chattering and screaming to the moon. Babes with their throats cut.'

'Christ help us all.' She bent to the cloak folded on top of her doctor's bag. 'All right, yes, I know where this comes from. A babe was found there last year. Still-born. One babe. It happens. And yes, obviously there *has* been old worship to the sun and moon, if you can call it worship. Usually no more than superstitious pleas thrown out in poverty and desperation. But not blood rites, Dr John. Not any more. I swear to you.'

'Except,' I said, 'in the abbey?'

The thunder now was like to a blind giant blundering around in the high street. Nel was shivering freely.

'No, look…' She pulled her cloak around her shoulders. 'What happened to your servant… yes, that was terrible almost beyond belief,

239

and more so because he seemed a most decent man. But all this talk of devil magic, sacrifice…'

'It's said that there's no more effective place for the summoning of devils than a holy place in ruins.'

'For Christ's sake, Dr John, we'd know! I tell you, if there were people like that here, we'd *know*.'

'*We?*'

'There are those here' – her eyes were cast away towards the window – 'who would know.'

'But none of them,' I said, 'is Justice of the Peace.'

Now she was tightening her fists.

'Look,' I said. '*I* know it's nothing to do with you. This hounding of you… this is all madness.'

'*Not* madness.' A sudden fury. 'Were you not listening to me? This is contrivance. Fyche spreads these lies – this *smoke* – only to cover something darker. He shows this picture of himself as a Godly man in combat with the forces of Satan, and at the core, I'll swear… that's where you'll find the real evil.'

I didn't understand.

'Nel, we live in enlightened times – relatively. What happened to your mother, that's not going to happen again. Burnings, even hangings, for heresy and witchcraft are to be avoided. That's the policy now. The Queen's ever mindful of the way such retribution gathered pace during the last reign. She won't go down that dark road, and this is being made known throughout the realm.'

Nel Borrow opened her eyes as the thunder resounded, and I saw that her eyes were weeping and my heart strained in my breast.

'We'll get help for you!' Hoarse with desperation. 'I'm schooled in the law…'

She looked at me through the screen of her tears, and it was not scorn, but it was not faith either and who could blame her? I wanted to tell her that my companion was – potentially, at least – one of the most powerful men in the realm. That we were in a position to call down support from the very highest quarter.

Yet were we? I thought of Robert Dudley and his growing suspicions of the motives of Sir William Cecil. *He has his own script.* Thought of the Great Unspoken.

And then, worst of all, I thought of those surgeon's knives all conveniently coated with gore, as if circumstance itself were bending to contrivance. I doubted that Nel Borrow even knew about the bloodied knives, not having seen her father since last night, and I did not think it would help to tell her.

'You said there was a chamber made ready for you here,' I said. 'For the night.'

'If I need it. But if I'm found there, it'll come down on Cowdray. Don't want that.'

She rose. I wanted to cry out to her: *Stay here and let it all come down on me!* But said nothing and dared not even stand, for fear that my basest desires would be insufficiently concealed by the threadbare robe across my knees.

She began to lace her cloak together at the neck.

'Perhaps it were best if I left.'

'Where will you go? They'll be watching your father's house.'

'Joan Tyrre will take me in. It's no more than a hovel, but better than a dungeon.'

'It's late. She'll be abed.'

'Oh, no.' Nel smiled. 'Not tonight, Dr John. Not in a storm. Joan will be in her doorway looking out over the tor... watching for the King of Faerie and his hounds.'

'The Wild Hunt?'

Remembering my tad terrifying me as a child with his tales of the Hounds of Annwn. The faerie king and his white hounds with red ears, reputed to ride the storm in search of lost souls.

Nel said, 'Joan has ever hoped that one stormy night he'll take her to his hall, to be his earthly bride.'

She laughed, the crossing of her teeth disclosed like a confidence as she began to draw up her hood.

'Don't go,' I said.

She raised an eyebrow.

I said, 'Stay here.'

She looked up at the ceiling 'twixt the oaken beams, her half-smile rueful now.

'It was kindly of Cowdray to offer, but I'd rather not. The attic chamber here...'

'Is probably cold and damp. However—'

'And most severely disturbed. Or so they used to say, the pilgrims and the travellers. Doors which go banging in the night when there's no wind. A babe's whimpers. Boards that creak as if someone walks across them, though there's no-one there.'

'Haunted?'

'So 'tis said.'

I must have thought on this for all of a second.

'Then you should stay here in this chamber,' I said, 'and *I* shall see out the night up there.'

XXIX

The Storm

THE WALL WAS lit white again, and new thunder seemed to break before it had faded into shadow, huge and exultant in its violence and loud enough to be directly above us.

Maybe in the attic. Always one floor beyond me, these manifestations of the spiritual. It was ever thus. I felt like a clown, and all of it was apparent, all my folly lit by the unsparing sky.

'And you wouldn't be afraid,' she said, 'to pass the night up there all alone?'

'My life's experience tells me that ghosts tend to avoid me.'

She looked at me, with her hands hidden inside her cloak and her doctor's bag at her feet. The hood had fallen away and her head was tilted to one side, as if inspecting some rarity.

'Perchance, because you try too hard to know them?'

In my head, Dudley's voice: *I think if I were a ghost, the very last man on earth I'd want appear before would be John Dee.*

'It's rather,' I said sadly, 'because I'm a dull and bookish man who has not the sight.'

Standing up at last, for the shame of it had diminished me. I recalled Dudley sprawled in his barge: *is not John Dee the greatest adventurer of them all? A man prepared... to venture beyond this world!*

The unwaxed truth was that I was a sham, a hollow man with a big library, and the only time Dudley had spoken with any real honesty was when, in faking my arrest, he'd hissed, *Take this fucking impostor away!*

'There,' I said, wearied. 'The secret's out. A man oft-times accused of conjuring who can't even see what he's supposed to have conjured. Others might be witness to the seepage 'twixt spheres. Not me.'

I suppose it was the first time I'd disclosed this directly to anyone and, in the silence which followed, I regretted it. Although doubtless mumbled miserably, it had sounded to my ears like strident organ chords swelled with bitterness.

'*Tush*, Dr John.'

Nel Borrow's head was still atilt. She made a small, soft bud of her lips. It might be pity or it might be mockery, neither of these much to be desired. She leaned back against my bed.

'Remember when you first came to the tor and set foot on the top…'

'I fell over.'

'But if I'd said to you, Oh, have a care, for you might fall over due to the strange force of the place… then you might *not* have fallen over.'

I said nothing.

'You think too much. Weighing every new thing against all the volume of knowledge you hold in your head. In fact, it might even be said that you *know* too much.'

'Mistress, most of the time, I think I know not half enough. If you're saying that in order to see and feel what's hidden I must needs forget myself and all that I've learned—?'

'Forget yourself? No. It's probably necessary that you should *remember* yourself.'

'I don't understand.'

And, God help me, I didn't.

Light flared like laughter on the wall.

'Well,' she said, "tis something I find hard to achieve myself for longer than a few moments. To grow quiet inside and become aware of my thoughts and my feelings… but to be no longer one with these earthly things. To become separate. To stand apart from who I think I am. In such a state… things may be received. So they say.'

'Who say? Where did you learn of this?'

'There are still a few people who come here on pilgrimage.'

'What I mean is… this is not Christian, is it?'

A cautious observation, her reply less so, as the thunder cracked. But the air betwixt us was calm. She placed her palms together.

'Did I say *Christian* pilgrimage?'

'Go on.'

'There are those who occasionally travel here from… distant places I've never heard of. Further than France or Spain or the low countries, anyway. Further even than the Arimathean travelled, I suppose.'

'The East?'

'Some.'

'You mean holy men? Magi?'

'On – what is it – camels? All in silk robes?' She laughed. 'Rags, more like, and on foot. Not wealthy, except in spirit. We feed them and we give them shelter, and they take our air. Visit our high places, drink from our wells. And share with us their… ways of being.'

'Does Fyche—?'

'Good *God,* no. Although some of them came to the abbey, in the old days. To meet with the abbot and senior monks.'

'And your mother?'

'It's possible.'

I moistened my dry lips.

'What was she growing, Nel?'

'Collecting, mainly. She collected from the fields and hedgerows more than she grew. In search of cures – smallpox, wool-sorters' disease. Her ambition was quietly boundless.'

'And the dust of vision?'

The first splotter of slow rain came on the window glass.

'Oh,' she said, '*that.*'

'Maybe I've also been sent here to learn.'

She made no reply.

'If I'd been here in your mother's day I suppose I might've gone pleading to her, like Joan Tyrre, for a little flask of…'

Nel unlaced her cloak with a small pull and it slid from her shoulders. My hands shook.

She bent to dip a hand into her cloth bag. When it emerged it was holding a small, stoppered earthenware pot.

'This?'

Now the storm was all around us.

✝

You think me mad to trust this woman with the sovereignty of my senses?

Maybe you're right. Maybe there *was* a madness in me that night, born of years of unsatisfied longing. All I can say is that, as soon as I'd heard of it, I knew that if it were still to be found in Glastonbury, this dust of vision, then I could not leave the town without having tested it upon myself.

Never thinking for one minute, though, that Nel Borrow would carry it around in her bag.

'It's been found to help pregnant women,' she said, 'when the child won't come. And for the relief of those who bleed too much afterwards.'

'Is this the common use?'

'And also for the severe head-pains with bright lights and no cause.'

'Your mother discovered it?'

'Of course not. It's been around, in one form or another, since the most ancient of days. I'm surprised you haven't come across it in your studies.'

'In truth,' I said, 'I think I have.'

It all came back to me now, watching Nel Borrow laying out an array of items from her bag on the candlelit board. I hadn't read of it, merely been told, and what was not put down in a book was always suspect to me, but what else could it be?

Ignis sacer.

A small but severe plague of it had been spoken of when I was in France last year. Many people had died, but from the disease itself rather than its effects on their minds, the survivors speaking of visions both dreadful and exultant.

The holy fire.

The disease was a burning from within: terrible agonies, convulsions, loss of all control over movement. *A dance*, Monger had called it, and this would certainly have described what happened in France, where the talk had been of the wrath of God visited upon a faithless community. I hadn't read of it, so I'd dismissed it as exaggeration to frighten people into some religious conformity.

Nel had spread out a clean white cloth over the board. Brought out a small knife and a wooden spoon. There was also a flask of water which reddened when shaken, leading me to suppose it from the Blood Well.

Then a crystal goblet, a scrap of paper. An apple and a small wooden cup.

She unstoppered the earthenware pot.

I said, 'Tell me what this is.'

'The powder? 'Tis ground from a fungus. It grows on grain. In this case, barley. Hangs from it like a black ear. My mother would pound it in a pestle with… other herbs.'

'She showed you how to make it?'

'No. Never. It took me over a year to get it right – driven, at the time, by the need to relieve the suffering of our neighbour, Alice – aching head. Keeping the whole street awake, with moans all through the night. Some strange cries, indeed, the night Alice took—' She looked up at me. 'Are you sure about this?'

I nodded decisively. There'd be no chance of trying it when Dudley was up and about again.

'Anyway,' I said. 'It will probably have no effect.'

Telling her of the night I'd brewed some powder of the mushrooms gathered in our orchard by Jack Simm. The little mushrooms that come in the autumn.

'This was in London?'

'In my library in Mortlake. Thinking that if I were surrounded by all the wisdom of the ancients, its effects might be… why are you smiling?'

'No reason, Dr John. No reason at all.'

I was able to smile, too. But had not Monger, speaking of the dust of vision, told me: *I've heard it said that the place where the potion was ingested might condition the response?*

'Where's it best to drink this?' I asked her, for I was anxious now for it to be done before I could change my mind. 'Should I take it outside?'

'In the storm? I think not. I heard of a man once for whom the falling rain turned to a hail of arrows.' She looked at me. 'You'll have no control.'

'Is that not the point of it?'

'It's just that you strike me as a man for whom a degree of self-control—'

'May be the cause,' I said, almost breathless, 'of all my deficiences. As you've implied.'

Yet had not the man of science in me already dwelt on the possibilities for further research if I could obtain some of the potion to take back to London? Was I not already wondering how its effects might be conditioned by the movement of seasons or the positioning of stars at the time it was ingested?

Nel Borrow was bent over the board, spooning something from the earthenware pot onto the paper.

'The quantity must be so small as to be almost invisible to the untutored eye, else the consequences… God only knows how much that boy in Somerton swallowed.' She looked up. 'Have you ever heard the affliction called by the name St Anthony's Fire?'

'Have you?'

'Though I don't know why. Did St Anthony have visions?'

'All saints seem to have had visions.'

'Yes,' she said, 'but are visions that come as a result of taking a potion… are *they* still what you would call sacred?'

'I know not,' I said. 'And there may lie more heresy.'

There was a silence, even the rain holding back. Or so it seemed from this golden sanctum.

'Would it not be possible' – Nel Borrow held the flask before the candles, and the liquid turned to amber – 'that the senses, through the action of the herbs, might be *awakened* to the spiritual?'

The liquid was lit red-gold. Her eyes were amber green. The admonishing rain was coming hard now at the window as she lifted the paper betwixt her fingers and funnelled powder into the little wooden cup. Adding a little water and pouring more into the crystal goblet.

Could the pathway to divinity be glimpsed through the bottom of a goblet? Or the road to hellfire…

And what, oh my God, was to be be glimpsed behind those lustrous green eyes?

✝

What followed had a certain sense of the Mass, in which I still strongly, if quietly, believe, for it surely is an ancient, alchemical formula for the highest transformation.

She handed me the goblet.

'This is from the Blood Well. And this… is for you to hold.'

A stone. A pale brown pebble, as if from a riverbed, near the size of a hen's egg. It felt cool in my hand.

'What is it?'

'I found it inside the tower on the tor.' With the knife, she was cutting the apple in half. 'It will ground you.'

I nodded, kept the stone in my hand as I raised the goblet to my lips. She said, 'Wait…'

When I put the vessel down, some of the fluid was spilled across the boardtop.

'You're afraid,' she said. 'Your hand's trembling.'

'It's the cold.'

''Tis not good to do this when you're afraid.' She took my hand; I shuddered at the warmth and energy in her fingers. 'John… I think… I feel that you don't need to do this. You, of all people, must know that there are other ways. Think about it.'

'Am I not the man who thinks too much?'

She said, 'What have you not told me?'

I wanted so much to turn over my hand to grip hers, but her face was so solemn. Instead, I drew a hard, slow breath, bad memories hauled in on a long, frayed rope.

'I have dreams,' I whispered. 'Recurring dreams.'

Didn't go on. Didn't tell her about the dreams of fire, my arms and legs as blackened twigs. I felt apart from myself now, but maybe not in the way she'd spoken of. Recalling how, watching the parade of townsfolk before the Baptist's Church the other day, I'd imagined them in a play, their bodies feigning ordinary life, while their real lives were happening on some other level. Now I felt I was to become part of that play. Was given the means to enter that other reality.

'Listen…' She leaned forward. 'There *are* other ways. We'll work together on the other ways.'

She reached out for the goblet, but I snatched it up and turned away and drank down the liquid, all of it.

The thunder was dying, now, but maybe the storm had only just begun.

XXX

Like to the Sun

I WENT TO sit on the edge of the bed, and we talked. Or she did. I only sat and listened to the soft, sad music of her voice as she spoke of her father and how, after her mother's execution, he'd thrown himself into his work, riding out each night to care for the sick, spending no more waking minutes than he needed in the bed where his wife would lie no more.

The tragedy of it was so extreme and there was such physical pain in my heart that I began to weep into my hands.

'Damn,' Nel Borrow murmured. 'What do you do to lose the cares of the day, Dr John?'

'Cares?' Wiped my eyes on my sleeve, dragging out a smile. 'There *are* no cares if I'm working. Did your mother have cares when she was tending her garden?'

'She had –' a wistful smile – 'two hundred kinds of herbs. They took a lot of care. If life were only work and we were allowed to do it unmolested...'

'Then there'd be no sorrow, for some of us.'

And no joy either, my mother would snap back, she who understood not the heady pleasures of scholarship.

'Felt so safe in her garden,' Nel said. 'Open to the land all the way to the sea, and the tor rising on the other side and the soaring golden pinnacles of the abbey. It was a paradise. Avalon.'

I thought of my own garden in the sky, its constellations laid out like arrangements of flowers in a fine elusive symmetry that awoke in me a yearning deeper than the night.

'You still maintain her garden?'

'Well... best I can. Fewer than half as many herbs now. When the abbey was alive, she'd have help. Even the abbot... the abbot came and

250

went and they'd go for long walks through the fields and along the marshland, by the river, gathering plants…'

As she talked, I could see the shining river as in summer, the strips of water shimmering on the edges of the fields, blue-white mist rising like the ghost of the long-departed sea.

'…and also Master Leland, for a while.'

I looked up.

'*John* Leland? John Leland the antiquarian?'

I began pinching my lower thigh to confirm that I was not yet taken into some other sphere.

'And maker of charts. Recorder of topography.'

'John Leland worked with your mother and the abbot?'

'Not with the abbot. I think the abbot was wary of him. He came sometimes and walked with my mother. Poor Master Leland.'

She sighed, and the sigh became a tapestry of shadows drawn around her. Her body was outlined with quiet light against the umber shades of the woods in the tapestry, and I had to turn my eyes away. Knowing nothing of Leland's interest in herbs. Only old manuscripts and the arrangement of the land.

'So this was not on Leland's first visit to the town.'

'He came back.'

'I know. After the Dissolution.'

Dissolution. The word bubbling out of me, a pelucid stream over pebbles. I bent and let it ripple over my fingers.

'I've a memory of Master Leland coming to our house. Can still see his beardless face, all bony like a Roman statue. I remember him shouting, "You don't understand, I'm my own man now." He kept saying that.'

'What did he mean? Was he in his right mind? Because—'

'How would I know? I was young.'

Still young.

I gazed into the core of the candlefire, where small, tight flames were coalescing into a single body of light like to a full and golden moon, and I felt my heart swelling in my breast like a blood-red poppy close to exploding from its bud.

But stop. Dear God. *Think*.

I looked up, which seemed to take a very long time.

'You know that, in the end, John Leland went mad?' Feeling my body begin to list I put out a hand to the nearest bedpost. 'It was said that his mind was overloaded with the magnitude of his obsession… his task of chronicling the topography of the whole country?'

'All I know is my father mistrusted him. Said his first visit was to collect treasure, and his second was to collect… the place itself.'

The stone moved in my hand.

'My father says that on that last visit he went in search of former monks from the abbey. He went looking for them.'

'Leland?'

I opened my hand and the stone was still.

'But they'd have nothing to do with him. Blaming him, in part, for the killing of Abbot Whiting.'

'What did he *want* from the monks?'

This question seemed at the crux of it. *What did the monks know?* I reached out for an answer, the stock of the apple tree hard against my shoulder.

'I know not. Nor what he wanted from my mother. All the treasure was long gone.'

I looked for her expression, but her face was in complete darkness, for she'd moved deeper into the circle of trees and bushes, away from the probing moon.

The stone in my hand was squirming and pulsing like a toad.

Long gone.

I crooked an arm around the tree at my side and saw the cold majesty of the tor rising before me out of the thick, brown mist with the sky aswirl around its tower. And now it was no longer night but not full day either, a darkness overhead, a dark beating, and I looked up to see the air all full of cawking crows, and a man labouring towards me down the hill, swaying slightly, side to side.

'When did Leland…?'

The words beaten away into the air by the wings of the crows all around me, and I turned away and covered my head with my arms. But the crows swooped and pecked at my hands, ripping the flesh from the backs of them and sought my eyes, and I was crying out and fell on my face on the damp earth and lay there for a long time.

Hours passing, me smeared upon the richness of the soil, born of dead matter, new life out of decay. Thinking on this for many long hours, all the fecund beauty of it, until I felt the silence growing around me, a black pressing that, with time, I could not ignore and, turning, with great apprehension, upon my back, I saw, above me, Martin Lythgoe.

Gazing down upon me, a look of bafflement on his face and his hands linked at his abdomen to receive the shining intestines slithering out of him in a soup of blood.

Tried to turn away and couldn't. Couldn't move.

Knowing now, for sure, that it was me. That I'd killed him. Sending him away to his death. Murdering him just as sure as Cate Borrow had killed the boy in Somerton… twin souls, the witch and the conjuror. In seeking knowledge, we court the night.

Guilt.

And did, by means of sorcery, attempt to kill or grievously harm Her Majesty…

Struggling to breathe.

'Still,' she said. 'Be still, John.'

Take him.

Taking my hands as I'm bound from behind. My back to the post and the rusted iron hoop around my chest and the air's tainted now with the grey smoke of foreboding, and now comes the smell of old dry straw and the excited crackle of bone-dry twigs at first kindling.

Heresy.

A sudden rush of acrid gases to the throat, and I can't breathe, nor hardly cough, for there's only smoke, all about me now, and I try to cry out, but the air is full of choking gas and the crickle-crackle of the twigs and the chitter-chatter of the gathering crowd.

Fine line, Dr John.

A rush and a fizz as the straw catches light. A little sizzling.

The s-word, John, the s-word.

Here's Bishop Bonner in monk's habit with that plump and full-toothed grin. Observing, with a giggle, the ignition of clothing, points of savage heat and piercing agony, now, in the skin, and a slow funnelling of smoke from my sleeves.

Tell me, then, Doctor, how can the soul acquire divinity?

His laughter's a peal of discordant bells, and there's a smell on the air of roasting pork, rich and succulent.

By prayer...

Whispered through the hiss of spitting fat.

...and suffering.

Bonner's beam outshines the fire as I look down at my hands, and one hand's gone charcoal black, the skin all shrivelled and the fingers crisped and flaking away.

And I'm screaming hard against the roaring in my ears, the molten wax, but there's no release for the scream, for my cheeks are full of gas, and there's a core of heat behind the eyes, a boiling in the sockets and then, of a sudden, the sparks have found my hair, making there a small forest fire, and then there's a great *whooooop...*

...the feral ecstacy of the crowd in that glorious moment of hell's halo: a conjuror's head all raging with the madness of fire.

And the head's become a ball of light. Like to the sun.

Like to the sun.

XXXI

Haze

WHEN I WAS dead, it was raining.

Soft, coloured rain, iridescent against the charcoal sky.

A distant singing, all soft and melodious, and the air laden with the vague scent of apples.

I tell you these things, knowing not how many hours had passed, for time was not the same. Nothing was the same and, though I knew I was dead, I knew also that it was not over for me.

Walking through water, now.

Clear, soft water that was flashing over the grass and cascading down the hill. Water like music.

Me walking barefoot, the grass slick between my toes. Led by the hand, feet in the soft flowing land, down towards the nest of apple trees, and I could smell the breeze around them, the scent of apples and the ferment of cider, and all the juices of late summer.

And the tor rising on the other side and the soaring golden pinnacles of the abbey.

Walking through an old orchard, and the twigs of the apple trees were scraping at my bared skin.

And then, with no awareness of a journey, I was in the sky.

Not in my body but as a spirit made of finest air, and I was walking in the garden of the firmament, stars around my hands, whole worlds that I could hold, yet did not wish to hold, wished only to exist with them in peace and a sense of eternal wonder. And for a split instant, I *almost* knew His mind.

Seemed to be here for many hours, but it might have been mere seconds before I was falling back in vague dismay.... back to a place that was close to our world yet not *of* it. Where I saw the land again – the Glastonbury land – veined with clear water.

Then saw through the skin of fields and woods and hills, to the innards of the island, all the inner chambers and vessels linked by the flow of water underground, a low and rumbling power, the engine of the earth, held together by the bones of the hills and all the bones of the saints which lay here, the bones of Avalon...

...and I drew back and all the shapes of the land were moving. I saw creatures there, made of the earth... a lion and a dove... fishes that swam in grass. And the earth went atilt, and the creatures formed a great circle all around me.

'*Where are you?*'

'I'm flying,' I said.

'*Come,*' she said. '*This may be too much too soon.*'

When the vision faded to a pastel blur and the body's weight returned, I felt a stab of sorrow. But then I heard the old soft singing, a flow of molten gold, and saw the abbey from above, laid out below the tor like to a golden body.

A paradise. Avalon.

And I heard these words, soft-spoken but quite clear:

The whole magistery depends upon the Sun and the Moon. The Sun is its father and the Moon is its mother, and we know truly that the red earth is nourished by the rays of the Moon and the Sun.

The sun was in me. My head burned with gasses like to the orb of the sun. And the moon...

...the moon was awaiting the sun.

☩

I was walking towards the summit of the tor.

What can you see?

The sky.

And...?

The tower.

Go to it. Put your hands upon its nearest corner at chest height.

Opening my hands, and the stone which had lain there was gone. A connecting. A shiver through the arms and into the breast, and I sprang away but did not fall this time.

Did not fall.

Knowing that the stone which had been in my hand had been absorbed back into the high standing stone whose spirit lived inside the tower upon the tor. And tower and stone both lived in me, when I walked back down the hill, lured by the the wappling of the water in the Blood Well at its foot. Rolling and sliding down the hill, my apparel left strewn out behind, and she was waiting and wore no cloak, nor over-dress, nor shift, and was but a haze in the soft air.

Soft. The softness of the grass where we lay. The softness of lips and breasts, the yielding of flesh, the rising of the tower, all the energy entering into it as I rolled over and felt the opening of the well-head in the thicket and then the tower sliding deep into the well. And, oh God, a tongue 'twixt criss-cross teeth, greenlit eyes in bright water, a fluid white light, the light of a thousand candles, a river of white light flowing through me.

And then, later, the sunrise in the heart.

And I will travel to Avalon, to the fairest of all maidens…
…and she shall make all my wounds sound and make me
whole.

PART FOUR

Superstition requires credulity, just as true religion requires faith. Deep-rooted credulity is so powerful that it may even, in false beliefs, be thought to perform miracles. For if anyone believes most firmly that his religion is true, even if it is in fact false, he raises his spirit by reason of that very credulity until it becomes like the spirits who are the leaders and princes of that religion and seems to perform things which are not perceived by those in a normal and rational state.

Cornelius Agrippa (1486–1535),
De Occulta Philosophia.

XXXII

The Word

When I awoke before dawn, it was as if I'd slept for whole days. Or rather as if I'd been *away* for days. And I felt…

…felt my body was a strange place. Stretching out in the bed, I could feel all of it at once, from the soles of its feet to the weight of its skull and, betwixt them, the slow pulse of the unbound heart. And I felt…

Whole. I felt whole. Entire. Complete. Felt the heaviness of the sun in me, its holy rays opening me up into an aching, languid release, and I rolled over, reaching out an arm for her.

Nothing. Absence.

When the arm closed on cold air, I was in terror, my eyes falling open like a trapdoor into darkness. I sat up and took in the empty chair, the empty board. The empty bed. I was alone in the half-light.

Gone. Performed her alchemy and gone. I was thrown into panic: had it been a dream, a night excursion of the soul? I fell back, an aching void in me.

Then, as my face slipped between the pillows, the scent of her came to me, her body's wild-animal musk, and my breath caught in my throat.

God. *God, God, God…*

Rolled out of bed and found myself naked, the cold dawn seizing my flesh. Yet, for the first time, welcoming its bite. I stood and pulsed and tingled as if all the stars were lit within me. Had other men felt this? Did *all men* feel this, after…?

After *what,* the condition of the bed and its emanations left little doubt. Thankful, tearful, I went back and laid upon it, burying my face in the scent of her, and when I closed my eyes the dust rose again, a ripple of images of moon and water, earth and…

...fire. Even the fire was good.

Jesu!

I came off the bed again, moved slowly to the window. Touching it. The strangeness of glass. The miracle of seeing out from within.

Of course, there must have been more to it. More than the potion, although that clearly had opened doors between my inner being and something that was *out there*. But, in some way, *she*'d made that happen in the way it had, and there was a word for this.

The lower panes were jewelled with red and blue and orange, a pool of water on the sill reflecting these colours and more, and my eyes were drawn into it and I must have lost several minutes and...

Oh, yes, *the word*.

It had ever been with us, ever misunderstood, feared and rendered demonic by the churchmen – those same churchmen who preach that we should ever be open to higher influence.

I saw the wet roofs shining red. Raised my eyes to the first sunlight running like syrup along the ramparts of an old night cloud. Felt a trembling of my whole being. And uttered the word, breathing it softly into the coppery fire of the nascent day.

The word was *magic*.

I knelt, then, and prayed.

☩

'You all right, Dr John? You look...'

Cowdray in his sackcloth apron at the bottom of the stairs, all grey stubble and troubled eyes.

'Thank you, I'm well,' I said.

Hearing my own voice for, it seemed, the first time. It sounded frail, immature, a boy's voice.

'None of us slept much last night, mind,' Cowdray said. 'Worst storm of the winter, by some way.'

No, I wanted to tell him. *This was the best of storms.* Yet I knew there was much that was wrong. Moving down the stairs still feeling as if I walked in a body of light, yet knowing that even the rich magic of it must needs be contained before it hardened into a kind of madness.

'Have you seen Nel Borrow?'

This name like a sacred name to me now, some angelic invocation.

'No.' Cowdray's face had gone empty. 'Not this past day.'

Of course, he *had* seen her, having offered her his attic room, but his caution was commendable, and I asked him nothing further. She would have slipped away while it was yet dark, without disturbing anyone. It was what she did: slipped away.

But I'd find her again. Needing her with me, more than ever. And the finding of her was a quest beyond all other quests, for she was Circe and Medea and Morgan le Fay and… I saw her in vivid image, looking down on me between two tall trees at the entrance to a track leading to the Blood Well.

And is learning acquired only from books?

Wondering, from Cowdray's slightly alarmed look, if the wild scent of her was around me like a swirling mist.

'…of God,' he was saying.

'Mercy?'

'A storm like this is seldom seen this time of year. People are saying it was the rage of God against the mire of sin and heathenism in this town.'

'Who's saying that?'

He smiled grimly, made no answer.

'Master Roberts is asking for you.'

'He's about?'

'He's been about over an hour,' Cowdray said. 'He bids you join him in the abbey. In the outhouse behind the abbot's kitchen, where the… where the body lies. Your man's cadaver.'

Always a dark shadow in front of the light.

'Now?'

'I'll prepare your breakfast, meanwhile. Not a patient man, is he, Master Roberts?'

☩

The hut seemed to have been a relic of the abbey's occupation by the Flemish weavers in Edward's reign. Its shutters had been nailed tight, its roof patched with straw. I approached it lightly enough through the fresh, chilled morn. But when I reached its open door my euphoria was broken by the foul, piercing stench of corrupting flesh.

And it was this that brought back all that had come before the excursion. Those candlelit revelations.

What happened to your servant... terrible almost beyond belief... but all this talk of devil magic, sacrifice...

'Where the *hell* have you been?'

Dudley, in the doorway, in his drab clerk's apparel, more gaunt than ever I'd seen him.

'I slept late,' I told him. 'The storm...'

'Kept all of us awake. Except for this poor bastard.'

His eyes were burning dully, not now with the fever but with a driven rage, as if some cold engine worked within him. He stepped outside, wiping the back of his hand across his mouth and moustache, grains of sweat still agleam on his forehead.

'Go in. Go and look.'

'Robbie, I've seen all I can bear to see. What's the use?'

'No!' His features sharpening, jaw tensed. It was like he'd come out of a long sleep, was smitten with urgency, real life flung in his face. 'Look again, I pray you. Closely. You know about these things, you've studied anatomy.'

'I've studied *books* on anatomy—'

Books, books, books...

'John, listen to me. You were quick to deny this was ritual sacrifice. Well, if not that, then what? What's his body have to tell us?'

'Robbie, I doubt you're even well enough to be—'

'The hell with me. Go the fuck *in*.'

I nodded. Stepping unwillingly inside the hut, breathing through my mouth.

☩

It was, in truth, no bloodier than a butcher's shop, but the sight of remains such as these will always bring me to the brink of despair. Hard not to feel that the spirit itself has not been forever extinguished and, after all I'd seen this past night, what a grievous loss that would be.

The body of Martin Lythgoe lay upon a board made from two mangers. It was dull and did not glisten. The candle had been knocked away from the mouth and lay beside the body, no longer spectral and nothing of the tor about it now. Merely a squalid insult to life and humanity.

'What can I…?' I was near to tears, shaking my head in despair at my uselessness. 'What can I tell you, Robbie… more than you can see for yourself?'

The right arm bridged the yawning chasm of the chest, and inside its elbow was lodged the crushed and shrivelled orb of Martin's heart. I remembered the phantasm of him I'd seen through the dust, trying to hold it all in, and he hadn't spoken then, and he wasn't speaking now.

The left arm dangled over the side of the board, and Dudley lifted it, supporting the hand, free by now from rigor mortis.

'What do you make of this?'

I bent over, with some reluctance, holding my breath.

'Oh.'

Wouldn't normally have noticed it. You'd see the invaded chest, the ripped-out heart, and would turn away sickened before you'd mark the small but meaningful smitterings of dried blood on the fingertips, the blackened, broken nails.

'The middle finger, John. The way the nail's been all but torn away. See?'

'Done as he fought back?' I squatted down on the greasy straw on the floor, took up the cold, marbling hand at eye-level. 'Or maybe it suggests the body was moved after death?'

'Either of those is possible,' Dudley said. 'But I think it's something worse. Look again. Closer.'

'What's this…?'

Brown flakes which had fallen into my palm. Seemed unlikely to be dried blood.

'Rust.' Dudley knelt beside me. 'It's from an old iron nail. See it?'

'Where… *Oh, Jesu*—'

The length of it was wedged hard under the split and blackened fingernail, all the way to its root, where the point stuck out. I let the hand fall, in horror, wincing.

'Hammered in,' Dudley said. 'Under his nail, until the head of it broke off.'

'Then this is…?'

'Torture,' Dudley said. 'Before he died, this poor bloody man was tortured.'

I came weakly to my feet, trying to think of another explanation and could not.

'*Why?*'

'Why are men usually tortured?'

'To make them confess to.…'

'Uh huh.' Dudley shaking his head. 'To make them talk.'

'About what? What would *he* know? He was a stranger here. He only came because of…'

'Us. He came with us. He knew who we were and why we were here.'

'And is that to kill for?'

Dudley looked at me as if I were a child, while the eyes of Martin Lythgoe, cold as pebbles, gazed forever into the cobwebbed dark.

'We need a witness to this,' Dudley said. 'Is Carew here yet? Or where's… that other fellow?'

'Fyche.'

Shows this picture of himself as a Godly man in combat with the forces of Satan, and at the core, I'll swear… that's where you'll find the real evil.

'We don't talk to Fyche,' I said. 'I'm not sure we even talk to Carew.'

Dudley looked at me with narrowed eyes.

'Take my word,' I said.

'All right. Fetch Cowdray, then.'

'No… That is… there's someone more qualified.'

Clawing aside cobwebs hanging thick as ship's rigging and stumbling to the doorway for air.

XXXIII

A Man's Path

AN ELEMENT OF self-interest. I'll admit that. Matthew Borrow, a medical man and surgeon, would be the best witness to confirm what had been done to Martin Lythgoe. But he might also know where his daughter was to be found.

I ran.

Nel: my body still shivering with soft and slippery memories of hers. And anxiety.

The sky was brightening, near cloudless, as I moved fast and hard away from the abbey, splashing through streets still pooled and roiled with red mud from the storm. Part of me wanting to go on running, between the two church towers at either end of the town, out into the wettened fields towards the sun.

Until I became aware that something was wrong, and slowed.

The air was colder and refreshed from the storm yet, past eight, no-one save me appeared to be out in it.

I stopped and looked around: stone houses, wattle houses, the smoke of awakened fires. It was as if I saw the town for the first time, how sporadic and ill-structured it was now the abbey lay in ruins. A dead planet with no sun, all the energy gone to the tor.

Gone *back* to the tor. And the tor, while it could be serene and hazed with a kind of holiness… that holiness, that *magic*, had not the formality and discipline of the abbey. It was the magic of chaos.

Of a sudden, a cold vision was upon me. For a moment, it was as though I were seeing Glastonbury as it were seen by Sir Edmund Fyche. Feeling what *he* felt. A sense of loss. A vacuum filled now with a sense of rage.

It came to me that I was watched, and I spun. Began to mark dull faces in doorways and windows and the furtive parting of shutters.

A mute fear.

News travels apace in a small town, as does sound. As if by instinct, I fled into the back streets and the alleys. By the time I reached the street under the solid new church of St Benignus, I could hear the voices unravelling like shrill ribbons. And then—

'Stop them!'

The woman's scream bringing me up sharp, flattened against a flimsy wall of bared wattle, peering with caution around its corner. The air down here was murked with smoke from morning fires. Figures dancing in it, agitated like puppets, under the new church tower.

'Stay back!' A voice like a scourge. 'Next one moves goes with us.'

Edging to the end of the wall, choking back a cough, I saw a score of people: goodwives and children and old men lining the street, as if for a parade.

In the road, I saw two men holding a third, an older man struggling vainly against them. As I watched, a man in a leather jerkin arose from behind, on the steps of a house, and appeared to strike him several times with a short stick, and he crumpled to the cobbles, as if his strings were cut.

'Jes— Stop!'

The beaten man, once down, tried to roll away. It was Dr Borrow. A foot seemed aimed at his exposed head. Me screaming, starting forward.

'Stop this! Stop it now, you bastards, in the Queen's name!'

A silence. The boot frozen in the air.

'Stay out of it.' Broken teeth framed in greying beard. 'Whoever the fuck you are.'

A glimpse of blade half pulled from the leather jerkin. Much attention on me now, squirmings in the smoke, and I saw that there were five of them, and I was in deepest shit for the townsfolk knew me not and would make no move to save me.

'We're the law, fellow,' the leather man said. 'You don't even *think* to fool with us.'

Found myself standing alone in the road and shrugging.

'And I'm Dr John, of the Queen's Commission. Rode here with Sir Peter Carew. If this man's sorely hurt, I'll see it comes back on you. All of you. You understand?'

Watching out of the side of an eye as Matthew Borrow dragged himself away.

'No,' I said. 'Let him go.'

My voice low, but it seemed to carry. I felt an unaccustomed calm in me. I stared at the man in the leather, able, somehow, to hold the silence for long moments before I spoke again.

'You'll walk away now, all of you. Or you'll be back before you know it, to your old life of stale crusts and petty thieving.'

Maybe it was the tone – a tone I hardly knew – but he very nearly did step back, his eyes swivelling, as if I'd made a move on him. Then he shook his head.

''Tis your word, friend. Your word against mine – and *his* –' thumb jerked toward his companions. 'And *his*.'

'You count for nothing,' I said quietly. 'Any of you. You're no more than a hired mob. Expendable.'

I doubt he understood the word, and although my face was unshaven, my apparel in disarray, he'd marked an element of threat and a confidence that even I could not explain. He sneered, but his eyes would no longer meet mine. At length, he sniffed, pushing the blade back into his jerkin, while I stood and waited and felt… felt apart from me. The dust rising. It was as if I stood in the air, looking down on this scene and all the poor houses and rubbish-strewn yards.

'Piss off,' I said. 'Before I think to remember your faces.'

The man in leathers signalled briefly to his companions and made to push roughly past me, and I didn't move and caught his shoulder hard with mine, which was painful, but I felt a curious elation as he stumbled.

Resisting the urge to rub my shoulder, I watched his hands as he straightened up, but the dagger didn't reappear. Looking straight ahead, oblivious of him, I saw a young man watching me, as if puzzled and, for a moment, I was also puzzled for I'd seen him before, though not in jerkin and hose.

Two women, one of them Joan Tyrre, were helping Matthew Borrow up the steps to his house, but he clearly had no wish to go in. He was looking up the street past the church, his right arm hanging like an empty scabbard.

I went to him.

'Dr Borrow, what in God's name was this about?'

He began to cough. The woman with Joan Tyrre turned to me.

'They was outside at dawn, sir, banging on the door, demanding to search the premises.'

'Bazzards,' Joan said.

'Take him inside, Joan,' the woman said. 'Do what you can, I'll be with you now, Matthew.' Her accent was of Wales, the south. She turned to me. 'I live across, by there. Vicar's wife. I saw them go in. Had him up against the wall they did, before the door was full open.'

'But they *know* him. He probably healed their—'

'No,' the vicar's wife said. 'They don't know him. These are not men of Glaston. The people here don't know any of them.'

No surprise. Some men would travel miles to join a hue and cry, just for the chase and the violence of it and what they might steal, who they might rape.

'The town's overrun with them, it is,' the vicar's wife said. 'They was in the taverns last night through the storm. Dozens of them.'

'Bazzards,' Joan said.

'*Dozens?*' I followed the vicar's wife down into the street. 'What did they want here?'

She looked at me, with uncertainty. A stout woman, fawn-coloured hair under the coif.

'It weren't no normal night, Master. My husband, the vicar, he's been at the altar since first light, praying for forgiveness. The weight of sin lies heavy on us all.'

'Joe Monger,' I said, 'will vouch for me. What did they want here, Mistress?'

'They *got* what they wanted,' she said. 'But 'twasn't enough. Well, they knowed he wouldn't take it quietly, and when he come running out after her, they laid about him. 'Twasn't his fault she was bred from his loins.'

'Beg—'

'Why she came back I'll never know.'

'Who?' It was as if cracks were forming in the sky; I almost seized her by the shoulders. '*Tell me.*'

'They must've been watching the house, all night, all I can think.'

The sky began to fall.

She said, 'You didn't see them take her?'

'Christ...'

She stared at me, appalled at my profanity and I wanted to shake her, shake out all the false piety which had replaced thought and reason.

'*Tell me!*'

My whole head felt to be alight, and I think she saw the madness in my eyes and backed away. I saw the young man again, watching us, and realised it was Brother Stephen, the younger of the two monks who'd been with Fyche when first I'd met him, on the tor.

The vicar's wife pushed straying hair back under her coif.

'Said she— Well, we heard her, we all did. Shouting down the stairs as how she'd go quietly if they left her father alone. 'Course, soon as they had her out of sight...'

I turned to look up the street, the gathering of people dispersing now. Felt my mouth moving but it could shape no words.

'En't fair for a man to get beaten for the sins of his daughter,' the vicar's wife said. 'Is it?'

I stared at her.

'Sins?'

'She never said they was wrong when they read out the charge to her face. When they said she was a witch and a murderer, she never said they was wrong. Folks here, they've seen this coming – a young woman who thinks she can walk a man's path when she should be married and keeping a man's home.'

'Mistress,' I said, 'for God's sake, if a woman has skills...'

But her face had fallen into an expression of blankness, a self-preserving forced indifference I'd seen too many times in this divided land.

From the heart of the town, I heard whoops and jeering.

XXXIV

Venus Glove

'You could be a dead man.'

Thickbuilt, uncompromising, beard like strings of peat. Sir Peter Carew, senior knight, seeking to wither me with his contempt.

'You could be lying like offal in the mud. You realise that?'

I made no reply.

'And all for an old cunning man and a witch,' Carew said. 'Tales of your learning would appear to be exaggerated. Your brains are soft as shit.'

He and his company had ridden in, mid-morning, from Taunton where they'd passed the night. He and Dudley and I were alone in the dimness of the panelled room at the George, flagons of rough cider before us. I hadn't touched mine. Carew spat out a mouthful of his onto the stone flags.

'You think this shithole's like London. *Do* you?'

'Observing its present condition,' Dudley murmured, 'I doubt that's a mistake anyone would make.'

'The law here comes with rough edges, Lord Dudley, that's all I'm saying. Rough edges.'

The sweat was cooling on me. Clothed in what remained of the fraying fabric of delusionary vision, I'd run blindly through the streets, from the foot of the town to its summit, past the Church of the Baptist, until the tor was swelling up ahead of me. Half convinced that if only I could catch them I could stop them. Bring her back.

But they were gone. *She* was gone, and now I wanted to throw myself at Carew, rip out his beard, strand by strand.

Felt Dudley's warning gaze upon me. Dudley thinking, no doubt with some reason, that Carew would welcome any opportunity to batter me into the flags.

I effected a calmness.

'Before the dissolution of the abbey, Sir Peter, I understand justice was administered by the abbot. How many witches did *he* arrest?'

Dudley frowned at me.

'This is not the answer,' I said. 'Fyche sees himself as appointed by God to control the practice of religion in this town, and that's a dangerous—'

'Control the spread of *sorcery*,' Carew said. 'Surely?'

I could not this day face another futile argument on what constituted sorcery.

'Look, *Doctor*,' Carew said. 'In my experience, nobody tried for witch-craft is ever entirely innocent.'

'That's—'

'Hear me out. They ask for it. Can't keep their fingers out of God's pot.' He eased back, hands on his thighs. 'From where *I* sit, *Doctor*, life and religion, since we ditched the Bishop of Rome, are simple and equitable. You go to church on the Sabbath, spend an hour or so on your knees thinking about your next night's jelly-jousting and – unless you're a vicar or a bishop – that's *it*. I've no time for any man or woman for whom this world, so long as they're yet in it, is not enough. And in the case of *this* bitch…'

He turned away in disgust. Dudley's expression, eyelids lowered, said, Do *not* rise to this. He shifted in his chair as a roar went up from the street, glanced up at the window but didn't move.

'All *I'd* say, Carew,' he said mildly enough, 'is that if it were demons this woman employed to chase away my fever, it beats leeches any day of the week.'

He meant well, but talk of demons was no help. Voices were still raised in the street and I rose to peer out of the window, but the glass was poor and milked. Neither of the other two moved.

'Wasn't thinking of you so much as this fellow,' Carew said. 'Truly, how helpful would it be for a man with a conjurer's reputation to be seen attempting to intervene on behalf of a proven necromancer?'

I sat down, hard.

'No-one here knows who John is,' Dudley said with menace. 'And if his true name were to become common knowledge, I'll know that it would've come from only one—'

'Why necromancer?' I said.

Carew faced me at last, a gap-toothed smile blooming in the murk of his beard.

'You know nothing of this, *Doctor*?'

'Neither of us knows of it,' Dudley said quickly.

'Even though it centres on the slaughter of your servant? Ah, but… you've been unwell, haven't you, my lord?'

'Well enough now, Carew.'

'*Necromancy*,' I said.

Carew sat up, folded his arms.

'I'm not such an expert as you, *Doctor*, but if the use of a newly murdered corpse to procure spirits—'

'What proof is there that this woman was in any way concerned with that?'

'They have the fucking murder weapons, man! The *blood* still on them!'

'Yes, but *whose* blood? These were her father's tools, were they not? And he'd done surgery that night.'

Carew looked at me with curiosity.

'Tell me, why does it concern you so, Doctor?'

This was dangerous ground, but I didn't care any more.

'I'll *tell* you why—' I began, but Dudley broke in.

'No, *I'll* tell you why, Carew. Because this is a *new age*. Because both the Queen and Cecil are wary of religious persecution.'

'The Queen,' Carew said heavily, 'is yet a young woman. Who one day will learn that what *you* call persecution and I might call an element of *discipline* is the only way to keep the lid on the kind of insurgency that could yet unthrone her. Added to which, this is an investigation of *murder*.'

'A murder used to instigate a witch hunt. Witchcraft being such an *easy* charge, much exploited in past times, as we all know. But these are enlightened times, and the broadening of human study makes what once would have been dismissed as devilry…'

Dudley broke off to drink some cider, winced at its bitterness, wiped his mouth.

'Two days ago,' he said, 'I thought I'd die, and I was healed through this woman's knowing of herbs. So you may say it's *me*. Me who finds concern about her arrest.'

I looked to Dudley in gratitude, but he didn't meet my eyes.

'Then what if I were to tell you there's more?' Carew said. 'What if I were to talk of other corpses – dug from graves?'

'Where?'

'Behind St Benignus, so I'm told. Corpses dug up by night.'

I remembered that Fyche had spoken of this. Also using the word necromancy. I liked not the sound of this, but must not show it.

'And how is *this* linked with the woman?'

'You'd need to talk to Fyche.'

Dudley said, 'The abbey's in *your* charge, Carew.'

'And the law's in his,' Carew said. 'You'll pardon me – I believe I have a cadaver to inspect, in my abbey.'

+

We went with him to the outhouse. I didn't go in. Carew had appeared to treat his inspection of the corpse as a formality, and Dudley told me later he'd decided to say nothing about the suspected marks of torture. He was now agreeing with me that we should not make simple assumptions about this man's allegiances. I couldn't help recalling poor Lythgoe's own comments as we rode through the bitter weather to Glastonbury and Carew had belittled me as a man who'd never borne arms for his country. *Yon bugger's fought for too many countries, you ask me, Dr John.*

Later we went upstairs to my bedchamber to talk, Dudley having demanded of Cowdray that his own be stripped and purged of all that remained of his sickness. It lingered still, though, in the glaze of sweat that shone on his face in the window light.

'All right, tell me,' Dudley said. 'Leave nothing out.'

I shut the door, stood with my back to it.

'The surgeon's tools *are* her father's, used that same night to deliver twin babes the Caesarean way. That accounts for the blood.'

'And that can be shown?'

'He'll tell you.'

'He's her *father*.'

'She's no witch.'

Who was I seeking to convince? Witchcraft: what was it? Where were its boundaries?

Dudley crooked an arm around one of the bedposts, the loose one which, just a few hours ago, the dust of vision had turned into an apple tree.

'John, if this Fyche is determined to show she deals with demons, he'll do it. He's a JP. He knows the courts, he knows the judges. He'll get what he seeks. She'll hang.'

'Unless someone—'

I broke off, feeling almost nauseous as I recalled my own words to Nel last night: *We live in enlightened times – relatively. What happened to your mother, that's not going to happen again.*

'People hang for less every week,' Dudley said. '*She* must know that. Why the hell did she walk into their hands? Why didn't she just move to another town? She has skills which would surely—'

'Because of her father.' I moved, in agitation, to the window. 'It's why she went home last night. She fears for her father. Her mother was hanged by Fyche, for reasons no more solid than...'

But we'd dealt with that. I stood gripping the window sill, looking down into the high street, where people had gathered around the bakery where fresh mutton pies were sold on market days and the baker studied old magic and dreamed of making gold from lead.

'Carew's a crude bastard,' Dudley said, 'but he knows how the world works. His warning to you... there's clearly some substance in that. If you're seen to be pleading for a witch's life and your true identity should ever be disclosed, then you're in the shit, John.' He shrugged. 'Both of us, for that matter.'

It was true. May have been because of his known association with me, but his own name had been placed more than once, in gossip and the pamphlets, on the threshold of sorcery. Something which men at Cecil's level made light of.

Had made light of. It came back to me what Dudley had said last night about Sir William Cecil, who was his friend yet deplored his intimacy with the Queen. How far would Cecil risk his own position by protecting Dudley if he were seen to be implicated in a scandal involving witchcraft and the murder of his groom?

Traps everywhere. I sank into the chair by the window. In the space of a few hours, my life had been lifted up higher than I could have dreamed and then brought down and smashed before my eyes.

My life – that scholar's dim-lit, book-lined existence. I lowered my head into my hands, and green eyes stared up at me through the fingers. Dudley was my friend, the best I had at court, through whose support and influence I'd won the Queen's approval. Should I now further complicate his life by reporting what Nel Borrow had told me last night about her suspicions that Fyche had obtained wealth and position through the betrayal of his abbot?

Of which there was no evidence beyond circumstance. But then, how often in a court of law was evidence any stronger than that?

'What's this?'

I'd scarce heard Dudley sliding down from the bed. When I looked up, he was on his knees, scrabbling under the board. Came to his feet, holding something between finger and thumb, his face at first just curious and then tipped into a crooked smile.

'Well, well…'

'What've you found?'

He held out his open hand, displaying a damp, shrivelled, yellowish thing in his palm. Tubular. Appeared to be a piece of animal intestine, ewe's bladder maybe. Meant nothing to me.

'John, you bastard.'

Dudley's features displaying a mischievous delight such as I hadn't seen upon them since he was a boy intent upon disrupting my lessons. I rose from the chair.

'What *is* it?'

'*What is it?*' His eyes rolling. 'Jesu, John, how long have we known one another?'

I failed to understand. Dudley dangled the fragment of organ between finger and thumb.

'Certainly, I've seen them in Paris. Indeed, used one there, on a certain occasion – unwise to take chances in France, but that's another tale.' He stared at me. 'God's bollocks, look at your face! You don't remember, do you? Were you drunk?'

'I've scarce been drunk in fifteen years, as you....'

'Not that I'm not delighted, even in such adverse times, to find you've had need of a Venus glove?'

I sank back.

'What?'

Dudley placed the remains of it upon the board, pulling out a snot-cloth to wipe his hand. The smile remained, as if a weight hung from one side of his mouth. I said nothing. The thing was surely from some previous occupant of the chamber, either that or...

'Who was it, then, John?' Dudley said. '*May* I ask? One of the kitchen maids seduced by your timid good looks and courtly reticence?'

'I...'

I think there may have been tears in my eyes.

I think maybe he saw them. A hand went to his mouth, and then he snatched it away and returned to the bed, crooking an arm around the apple-tree post and swinging lightly to and fro.

'Oh, bugger,' he said. 'How – even with the fever – could I have missed the obvious?'

XXXV

Black Energy

IT MUST HAVE taken more than an hour to enlighten him, as the sky shifted into a grey afternoon and dulled the chamber.

I doubt I left out much, from that first meeting with Fyche atop the tor and all that I'd learned from Monger about Nel's mother, to what had been spoken of between us last night. He interrupted not once. It was like when he was a boy and I a very young man: when the subject was of interest, like astronomy, he would sit calmly, all the facts digested slowly, savoured like a platter of sweetmeats.

Not much here that was sweet. Least of all the tale of a monk who was said to have stood by while his abbot, a man most fondly remembered in and out of the abbey, was tortured and killed and dismembered. Because of what he would not disclose? I posed the question and Dudley posed another.

'Who knows of this, John?'

'Nobody *knows* of it. Nobody left alive anyway. Quite a few *suspect*. But who dares speak of it?'

'The death of Mistress Borrow's mother was contrived because she had evidence against Fyche?'

'Monger the farrier thinks it was to do with the dust of vision, but that's what Nel believes, yes.'

'But it was twenty years ago. Bad things happened then. And anyway, what would Whiting not disclose to Cromwell's heavies?'

'He was said to have hidden a chalice. That's all I know.'

'Not the Grail?'

'Hardly likely. The chalice is supposed to have been found anyway. Had it been the Grail, I think King Harry would've made something of that, don't you? To be known as the custodian of the most sacred of all vessels... the field of the cloth of gold doesn't begin to compete. But it could be there was something... something Cate Borrow knew, from her friendship with the abbot, that he determined to conceal. Perhaps something *Fyche* wanted, rather than Cromwell.'

'Was there mention of Arthur's bones?'

'No, but...'

'We know for a fact that the bones disappeared during the Dissolution,' Dudley said. 'Possibly removed on instruction of the abbot to a place of safety. If he suspected the King himself wanted them either removed or destroyed, to improve their mythic status... support the legend that Arthur lives on in the Tudors...'

'Then he would certainly have hidden them. The presence of the bones of Arthur being central to the status of Glastonbury Abbey since the twelfth century.'

'And if Whiting *knew* where they were, he didn't reveal the hiding place, even under... torture.'

Torture. As soon as that word was out, I knew what he was thinking. I saw in my head that rusting point under Martin Lythgoe's blackened fingernail.

'Even facing the worst of deaths, Whiting kept quiet.' Dudley looked hard at me. 'Are you listening, John?'

'Of course.'

'You seem... not here.'

I shook my head to try and clear it. It must needs be recorded in any future notes on this experience that the effects of the dust of vision do not depart from the body and mind as swiftly as the imbiber might assume. Several times I'd returned to an otherworldly condition, losing my hold on circumstance.

This scared me – would it go on happening for the rest of my life? Maybe Fyche was right in wanting to suppress its use.

And now I must needs tell Dudley of this experience. What would his reaction be? I recalled him on the barge: *is not John Dee the greatest adventurer of them all? A man prepared... to venture beyond this world.*

'There's an air here,' I said. 'Unlike anywhere I've ever been. An air of both a dark trepidation and... an expectancy of wonders. It's what some people here cling to and what Fyche fears may ultimately undermine his control.'

'Could say that of the whole country, John. Hopes and fears.'

'It's stronger here.'

'But then you're a mystic.'

'And not the only one. Magi travel here from distant places. *Here.* Not to England, to Glastonbury. Avalon. There's something. I know it. I've... felt it.'

'Felt it how?'

I sighed.

+

The final act... I said nothing of that. Some things are too intense and personal to be shared even with a trusted friend.

But the circumstances leading to it, even though they whispered hoarsely of witchcraft, needed to be related, and in doing this I began to see the pattern of a rite which would have made sense to thrice-great Hermes himself: an initiatory journey from darkness into light.

The palms of my hands grew damp.

Daring to think that something here had cast out the demon of all my midnights – that fear of an ashy death, the final explosion of gases in the head. The memory of something which had never happened to me yet had tormented my nights for years. Gone. Burned out of me, and then...

A heat sped up my spine.

...out of fire into water. The sun finding the moon, with all its female qualities. I was aware now of all the cabalistic parallels here, as well as those less esoteric, like the journey out of books and into life.

And earthly love. No avoiding that.

By the time I finished, I was pacing circles. Dudley had barely moved.

'This is the dust that causes St Anthony's Fire?'

'I believe it is, yes.'

'God's bollocks, John, What the hell were you *about*?'

'I believed it might also open passageways to the soul. And that... may well have been right.'

Or had I been possessed by the black energy of the storm in unholy union with my own base urges? Were the places I'd been, in truth, closer to the devil than to God? Was I, in fact, bewitched? The borderline was so close and so fine.

Shutting my eyes in uncertainty and anguish, until Dudley spoke. Something in his voice that was close to compassion.

'First time, John?'

Little point in throwing up a curtain.

'As good as.'

He nodded.

'And I'm guessing that now you believe yourself… in love?'

A poet's phrase.

'I…' Shifting uncomfortably. 'From the moment we first spoke. I… didn't know at the time… how certain sensations might translate.'

Dudley laughed.

'Well,' he said, 'a woman who'll cook your meat and yet take it upon herself to see you won't have to lay a third place at the board… is a rare find indeed. How do you prefer to play this?'

'Play?'

'A bad word. Still…'

'I didn't think,' I said, 'that you'd want to play at all.'

'After what happened to Martin Lythgoe? After what we saw this morning?'

'You think Fyche is behind it?'

'If he is, he's a dead man.'

'After due process of the law,' I said carefully.

'Or not.'

'You're Lord Dudley.'

'And might soon be an earl. Indeed, Cecil gave strong intimation that on my return from this…mission… the possibility of appointment to the Privy Council might become… more than a possibility.'

'On your return…'

I think that neither of us wanted to approach the possibility that Dudley's return to London – and the Queen's bedchamber – might be seen, in certain quarters, as less than desirable, let alone the thought that…

That he was not meant *to return from here.*

'Some matters can't easily be resolved here,' Dudley said. 'But others can. And, as things stand, Dudley was never here and can't be held accountable for whatever... act of primitive justice... is carried out by Master Roberts.'

For a moment, all before my eyes was drained of colour, and I'd swear that I could see around Dudley a living blackness.

'Your witch, your... enchantress...' Dudley said. 'She'll be in some rat-infested dungeon now.'

'Yes.'

'Awaiting an assize judge.'

'Who'll be corrupt.'

'Inevitably,' Dudley said. 'So, I ask again: what will you do?'

The idea that I might simply turn away from this... did not arise. When I first thought that something of this place had begun to live inside me, I knew not the depth of it, the ways in which the structure of my being was altered.

'My mother and father,' I said tonelessly, 'were overjoyed when I came home with a doctorate in law. Thinking I'd left other matters behind. Come to my senses at last. Found a solid trade.'

'Solid enough,' Dudley said, 'when you were accused of trying to damage Mary. Displaying, it's said, a rare eloquence before the hardest judges in the land.'

'And Bonner. Himself a lawyer, once.'

'What a cunt that man is,' Dudley said.

'Sometimes.'

'Yet, by some means, you outfoxed the bastard.' He sat back against the wonky bedpost. 'You're saying you want to be her advocate?'

'If she'll have me in that... capacity.'

'I take it she knows who you are.'

'Mmm.'

'Fyche?'

'Unlikely.'

'You're still on a blade's edge, John.'

'Maybe always will be.'

The chamber was grown dim, even though it was not long past three. Neither of us had eaten this day, and I recalled what Dudley had said that Candlemas afternoon in the barge about every great quest beginning with prayer and fasting.

He arose and stood with his back to the window, and I was aware that something had caused change in him, also. He'd combed his hair and beard, but the old arrogance was gone. His arms, in drab dark green, hung limply by his sides.

'When you'd left to find the doctor,' he said, 'I couldn't stay with Martin, knowing what had been done to him while I lay there, useless. I went out to the abbey gates to wait for you. That was when I heard a commotion and had to stand and watch it. Saw them bringing her up, through the town.'

'Nel?'

My fists clenching of their own volition.

'Must've been nine of them,' Dudley said. 'They had her in chains. It was like a... festive occasion. A mob arisen from nowhere. Men jeering. Rotten apples thrown at her by women. Screams. *Murderer, witch.* Well... if you say to a crowd of uneducated peasants, if you say, this is a murderer, this is a witch... Even if it's their own sister, nobody challenges it. I've seen it before.'

I shut my eyes and saw it. Made myself watch the procession he described.

'Her head was bare. Her dress was torn at one shoulder, pulled down toward her breast. She moved with... with dignity, I suppose – as dignified as you can, in chains. Her head held up, not looking to either side. Yet they... behaved as though she might be ready to escape at any moment, and they'd keep touching her—'

'No...'

'Men are men,' Dudley said. 'Particularly out of London.'

It felt like all the muscles in my body were contracting, making me cramped and knotted inside. When I opened my eyes, Dudley was looking down at the boards.

'Tell me, John.... did I talk about Amy?'

'You oft-times talk of Amy.'

Not true.

'I mean in my fever.' Dudley looked up, no sign of fever in his eyes now. 'I think I may have spoken of Amy, and I know not if it was a sick man's dream… or if I spoke some things to you.'

There was a silence, even in the street, but it was a silence that howled like a hound at the moon.

'Must have been a dream,' I said. 'I've no memory of it.'

☩

Enough had been said. Dudley and I went down to the alehouse to be served bread and Mendip cheese by the kitchen wench. There was no sign of Cowdray, and the farmers were not yet in from the fields.

All the same, we ate without conversation, and then walked out into the dusk to find that a man was newly dead.

XXXVI

What's Coming

THE HIGH STREET was gloomed in its own shadows. No shops were open; two, I noticed, had been boarded and probably not against the elements.

Three people remained outside the baker's shop under the dusken sky. I made out Joan Tyrre and Woolly, the little dowser, but at first failed to recognise Monger, for his body movements, once languid and gliding, were now taut and rigid like some engine worked by ropes and pulleys.

It soon becoming apparent that this was a stricture caused by inner rage. The first time I'd seen it in him and this, together with the absence of both light and laughter, made the whole evening tense as drumskin.

Monger held a book I recognised at once: the *Steganographia* of Trithemius. Or what remained or it – little more, in truth, than the hide in which it had been bound. Monger's hands shook. He rammed the book under an arm and led us into a small yard behind the shop.

'Tell them,' he said to Woolly. 'Tell them everything.'

Woolly's wild, white beard was shining like the moon in the blue-grey dusk.

'They come for bread,' he said. 'Bangin' on the door, demandin' bread. Hungry men ridden from Taunton to swell the ranks.'

'I would never have thought Taunton had so many constables and bailiffs to spare,' Monger said. 'But what do I know of the recruitment of a mob? I'm but a farrier.'

'Baker had to let the bastards in, look. While they was waitin' for bread, pokin' all around the shop, in comes Master Stephen Fyche.'

'Fyche's son,' Monger said.

'Beg mercy,' I said. '*Brother* Stephen?'

'An occasional conceit. Monastic apparel's favoured at Meadwell to convey the impression that all men there are men of prayer and learning

286

in the great tradition of the abbey. The boy's brutish violence makes mockery of the robe. I think you saw him kicking Joan Tyrre.'

'Damn – thought I knew the face, but it was dark in there.'

'Typical JP's son. Drink inside him, he's prowling the streets like a rabid mastiff,' Woolly said. One of his eyes was half-closed, the skin around it turning black. 'I'd followed the buggers in, not liking the looks of this, then they had the door shut, and one's going, *Hoo! What we got here? En't no Holy Bible.* Another's fingerin' the pictures and all the symbols, and Fyche goes, *'Tis a grimoire, boys!* 'Twas all they needed.'

'All they'd come for,' Monger said.

'They've got the baker up against a wall, screamin' at him as he's a fuckin' wizard, and Fyche is rippin' pages out the book, one by one, wavin' 'em in his face and then casting 'em into his oven. Two of 'em holding him back, and he's a sobbin' and a howlin' like they're slaughterin' his babes.'

'They *were* his babes, those books,' Monger said. 'It was even his hope one day to learn to read them.'

I stared at him.

'Too late now,' he said.

'He couldn't read?'

'His old feller had the books off the abbey,' Woolly said. 'Worthy, he was brought up to think there was some'ing mirac'lous about 'em. If he kept 'em warm in his bakery, kind o' thing, their secrets'd be yielded to him… and he'd one day find gold, I s'pose.'

'Had them nigh on twenty years,' Monger said, 'and all he knew was that the title was an extremely long word and therefore extremely magical and…' His jaw wrenched away. '*God's bones,* Dr John, what are we come to?'

Woolly tapped his eye.

'When they starts knockin' him around him, look, I couldn't hold back no longer. Makes a rush for the book, thinkin' I'd snatch it and run like soft shit – wouldn't've took me long to lose 'em. But Fyche grabs me, bangs my face, side of the oven, and likely they'd've done more, if… if Worthy…'

'If he hadn't thrown a fit,' Monger said to me. 'As if his heart were held in seizure.'

'Poor ole boy collapses on 'em, all droolin' from the mouth, eyes up in his head, and one of em's goin', *A demon face, a demon face! Divil's into him, look,* and I reckon they got scared then, and they was off. Worthy breathin' like an ole sheep, well out of it. I figured best thing be to get Dr Borrow. But he weren't there.'

'*Bazzards.*'

Joan Tyrre standing there like a ragged blackbird, shifting from one foot to the other. The first frail candlelight flickering in a stone house across the yard.

'Time I got back, he was stone dead, poor ole bugger,' Woolly said. 'Could be he was already sick, but you'd never know it, would you? Picture of health, all that fat on him, and in truth he weren't n'more'n… what would you reckon, thirty-nine?'

Monger, calmer now, nodded at Dudley.

'This is your companion, Dr John, from the… ah… Queen's Commission on Antiquities?'

'Much recovered now. Master Roberts… knows all that I know.'

'Then you both should also know this is only the start of it. As JP, Fyche has the power to deal with all civil disturbance and affray and will use it to the full.'

'*Is* there affray?'

'Anything can be an affray, even a gathering to bemoan the baker's death. I keep telling people to stay off the streets, they don't listen to me. They don't see what's coming.'

'Forgive my London innocence,' Dudley said, 'but what *is* coming?'

Monger went to the yard gate, peered into the high street, then returned. It had grown cold.

'The storm's been proclaimed as an omen. The word planted that God's sorely annoyed with Glastonbury, a town ready to throw away its sanctity as Jesu's own domain in England. If homes are raided, people beaten, then it's clearly the will of God that all false belief be driven out.'

'Only through scourging,' I suggested, 'will the town find redemption?'

'For a clerk of antiquities, your grasp of provincial theology is admirably acute, Dr John. Anything that looks like an assembly, they'll pounce. Anyone named as a witch or a wizard, whether named freely or under duress... Neighbour will betray neighbour.'

'Does no-one cry out against this? The vicar – where's *he* stand?'

'Stands were he's told. There are two vicars, and one at least is an ignorant placeman who needs his fingers to read the lessons.'

Like so many. If ever a town needed a clergyman of wisdom and intellect, it was Glastonbury in this time of disarray.

'Mistress Borrow,' I said. 'Where is she?'

'Wells. Special assize on Monday.'

'What's the charge?'

'Unspoken, as yet, but nothing that doesn't carry the death penalty or t'would be dealt with by Fyche himself.'

'And the judge?'

'Does it matter? They're all tight together on this circuit.'

It was near to night now, the last lucent clouds retreating beyond the tower of the Baptist's Church. Woolly looked up at the bakery wall.

'We needs get Worthy's poor ole body out of there. Been in the oven heat the whole day.'

'Wait until full dark then we'll move him.' Monger put a hand on Woolly's shoulder. 'Not the best time for Glastonbury to be permeated by the sweet stench of decay.'

I thought of what Nel Borrow had said about the town becoming like to a wound left open... gangrene and rot, mortifying of the flesh. Turned to Monger but could not tell his expression in the gloom.

✣

Later, Dudley and I went down to the alehouse of the George to learn what we could, but it was not a good place to be. The air was greasy with tallow and rendered fraught by a trailing taper of violence which, periodically, would flare like last night's lightning.

Cowdray was serving the drink himself, no women around, and the usual farmers and wool-merchants were pushed to the periphery by the constables – must have been twenty of them, some I was beginning to recognise.

They were a rabble, thrusting others aside like pigs at a trough when their drinking vessels were empty, and anyone who dared challenge them would wish he'd stayed by his own fireside. I saw one man leaving on hands and knees, bleeding from an ear, after a kicking. Later, a vicious fight broke out between two rival constables from Wells and Taunton. By nine of the clock, the benches were agleam with blood and cider.

It was then that the man with ragged grey hair and cracked teeth, who'd led the assault on Matthew Borrow, sought to calm the situation, raising a king-size flagon and holding forth to his fellows.

Calming *me*, however, not at all.

'Longest I ever seen, look, was near to two hours.'

'Go to!'

'I'm fuckin' tellin' you! Little short, stubby feller, neck like a pig's. Hardly moved the whole time, just saggin' like a sack o' flour.'

'How'd they know he en't gone, then?'

'Ah, well, they's all *thinkin'* he's gone... goes over to cut 'im down, look, and then, of a sudden, he gives 'em a big grin. Like this... *bleaaaaargh!* Scares the livin' shit of 'em, and, oh, he d' love that, he do. He just grins and grins, and when he don't stop grinnin, they d' swing on his legs, three of 'em.'

'Then what?'

'Well, he went. Obviously, he went *then*.'

'Still grinnin'?'

'Musc'lar neck, look. They can hold out. Women, though, a poor show, most of 'em...'

'Time to leave, I think, ' Dudley murmured.

But some self-wounding impulse in me made me say and have it inflicted upon me. I stood by the door to the stairs, looking down at my boots.

'Women, it's too quick,' some man yelped. 'No fight in 'em.'

'Ah now,' cracked-teeth said. 'Not always, look. If her's scrawny, bones like a sparrer, her can hold out a good while. Not the weight there, see, to tighten the ole rope.'

'John—'

Dudley gripping my shoulder. I marked Benlow, the bone-man, slumped over his mug. He was drunk.

'They dances real pretty, mind, some of 'em does,' a small man said wistfully. 'Legs goin' this way an' that.'

'All *you* wants, Simeon, is a peek up their fuckin' skirts!'

'Surprisin' what you sees up the skirts of a woman when her's hangin',' Simeon said in the trail of the laughter.

We left then, but I slept not well that night.

XXXVII

The Heresy

THOUGH I'D DRUNK only small beer, I stumbled down next morning with a head bidding to equal my aching heart. Last night's dreams had been lit with a dark vision, reminding me of some madman's paintings I'd seen in the low countries in which tiny men and women roiled and squittered like demonic insects.

Or the maggots Fyche claimed to see on the side of the tor, writhing around my feet and ankles as I walked endlessly amid the dream hills around Glastonbury, lured by the distant chinging of church bells.

Always unreachable; when I reached the first dream-church, all that would remain would be an echo, mixed with the cawking of crows, and the insect people would still be squirming and chittering around my boots, some hacking at them with tiny axes, my feet all pricked and sore, and I'd hear the bells picked up from another far-off tower or steeple and set off in that direction only for the same to happen.

And so till dawn, and the discovery of Sir Peter Carew hefting a flagon of cider in the alehouse, still foul with last night's sweat and vomit. When I took the opportunity to tell him what I wanted, he said he hoped he'd live to see me crawling up the walls of the Bedlam from the inside.

'This would be your way of saying *no,* Sir Peter?'

Carew stroked the back of one roughened hand with the palm of another, fingers curling into a fist, indicating he could think of a more emphatic way. We were never likely to be friends. Maybe he'd glimpsed the writing on the wall which suggested that all those centuries of supremacy by the fighting man were at last yielding to the wiles of the thinking man. But not in *his* lifetime. Oh no. To Carew, a man without relish for violence was a Bessie.

I'd not walk away this time.

'You need do nothing,' I said, 'except arrange for me to ride to Wells and speak with the accused.'

'*Jesu,* you're a fucking—' Carew had turned to the doorway where Dudley now stood, rubbing his eyes. '*You* tell him. Tell him of the madness of taking on Fyche on behalf of a witch.'

'He serves the Queen, Carew,' Dudley said. 'Not Fyche. Nor even you.'

'He's a fucking *conjurer!*'

'But, even if that were true, he'd be *the Queen's* fucking conjurer. So if I were you – God forbid – I'd be tempted to go along with his proposal.'

'Tell Fyche my *friend* from the *Commission on Antiquities* deems it his role to represent the woman accused of murdering his colleague's servant?'

Dudley smiled tiredly.

'Fix it. Why not?'

Carew stood shaking his head.

'All right. I'll help you. I'll help you see the weakness of your judgement. Show you and the conjurer the truth of what you think to defend.'

☩

In his efforts to sell me a new cloak, Benlow the bone-man had suggested the deepest of winter might be yet to come, but this morning appeared to dispute his forecast. The sun shone stronger than on any day this year, and the Poet's Narcissus was budding at the roadsides. It was as if the thunderstorm, far from being an expression of God's ire, had been the herald of an early spring, the gay ghost of some long-dead Mayday dancing in the wasteland of February.

Did I feel Eleanor Borrow with me as we approached her herb garden? Did I sense her presence on this hillside? In truth, I sensed it everywhere, now, as if she were become the spirit of this curious town and all that it had brought to me.

It had taken us no more than ten minutes to walk here from the George. Across the street, to the edge of the town, then over a stile to follow a muddied path on the flank of the long hill which sheltered the town like an arm. Now I stood by a wooden gate, looking up at the strip of land hedged all around, with a fast-flowing stream down one side. Its mainly empty furrows were neat and drawn as if aligned to the tor, the battlements of whose tower crested the highest horizon. The air was shimmering with bright alchemical dew. And I felt...

What I felt was *naked*. Naked in my emotions. Close to breaking down and had to turn away from Carew and Dudley. Standing there facing the lower skyline, where the sun lit up the channels of water and pale pools all the way to the sea, until I found composure.

'What does she grow here?' Dudley asked.

'Her mother had two hundred kinds of herbs,' I mumbled, and Carew's head swivelled.

'Who told you that?'

'I... forget. Could've been Fyche.'

'There aren't two hundred kinds of herbs in the world,' Carew said.

'There are far more than that.'

And they'd grow well here... a well-sheltered place, in its way, with good soil and an abundance of water. It moved me to think of what I'd read of the herb garden of the visionary Hildegard of Bingen, a woman well ahead of her time in the relating of science to creation and the use of plants to treat the melancholic condition.

'You really want to know what she grew here?' Carew wore a slanting smile. 'I'll show you what she fucking grew. Stay *there*.'

He moved off across the land, but I ignored him, walking up the slow slope. Sensing her walking beside me, the swish of her dress in the wet grass, following the winter-brown hedge toward the top of the field, where I'd seen a wooden cross.

✠

There was no name on it, but I knew by its siting.

Felt so safe in her garden. Open to the land all the way to the sea, and the tor rising on the other side and the soaring golden pinnacles of the abbey.

I turned slowly, and it was there below me, its highest arches making gilded loops like dusty sunbeams. *A paradise. Avalon.*

This had been the abbey's ground. Most everything here, for miles around, had belonged to the abbey. And the abbot had given over this land to Cate Borrow to continue her experiments with plants and herbs. This particular place, so perfect for its views of abbey and tor and the watery lands below... as if it might absorb the influences given off by these holy sites.

And more. A crossing place for all the energies of the earth. A Christian holiness, a pagan sanctity. I felt I'd been here when my mind was given up to the dust of vision. What would have happened had I imbibed the potion here, on such a morning?

It mattered not. The dust of vision had only been the grease to unrust the lock, free the door. There was no need for more; the door was open now... or at least ajar.

Time was suspended for some moments, and I existed in a state of profound yearning, the kind I'd once experienced only when gazing into the infinite vastness of a starlit sky. And I thought of what we were told by the church: that all life is lived for the glory of God, and that any rewards for us would come not in this world but the next.

But people here, in this town where the Saviour walked, and Merlin, did not accept this. Under this canopy of ancient magic, who could blame them for coming to the belief that they could have here – now, in *this* life – a kind of heaven. As if being here could, through prayer and knowledge, endow them with more than what God, according to the Church, allows.

No book, no dogma, *just being here.*

This was the Avalon Heresy.

What Fyche hated most.

'The witch's grave, eh?'

I turned, and there was Carew, swinging back on his heels, hands behind his back, eyes lit with bright malice. Dudley with him, sombre-faced.

'Couldn't have the cow planted in consecrated ground, obviously,' Carew said.

'Or maybe,' I told him, 'this place is more consecrated, in its way, than either of the churchyards.'

Carew scowled. *This* was heresy. Well, fuck him. Hard to believe that the Queen had put the abbey into this man's horny hands.

Which now were no longer behind his back, and he was leering through the hole in his black beard, as if in foul imitation of what they held.

Two earth-brown skulls, jawless and broken-toothed.

'*This* is what she grew, *Doctor*,' Carew said. 'She grew death.'

XXXVIII

Old Bones, New Bones

DUDLEY SAID, 'THIS looks not good, John.'

As if it needed saying. We'd watched Carew walking away into the sunlight, with a lightness of step that belied his weight. Spring was in his walk and in the air, but it was a spring smirched now, like his smile, with a cold malevolence.

I moved further up the path, up the hillside, putting more distance 'twixt us and Carew… and also the herb garden, sullied now. I did not want to go back to it.

Carew had assiduously reburied the skulls where he'd uncovered them. Promising, as he walked away, that he'd send word to Wells to arrange a meeting for me with the prisoner – that I might ask her, he said, about all the other body parts which could be unearthed in her garden.

'I know how it looks,' I said to Dudley, 'and I know how it'll sound to a jury in court, but that doesn't make it any less of a contrivance. The bones were brought here *not* by Nel Borrow.'

But I was sickened to see that Dudley's patrician face was marked now with doubt.

'How do you know that, John? You don't. You can't. And didn't you tell me of evidence brought before her mother's trial that she fertilised her soil by spreading graveyard earth?'

'It's no more true than any of this.'

'You don't *know*, though, John.' Speading his hands in defeat. 'Do you? And what did this supposed necromancy create but the potion that causes St Anthony's Fire, which reduces men to tormented, gibbering madness?'

'No.' Shaking my head. 'The dust of vision's from a mould found on cereal crops. Not grown here.'

'But still produced by this woman. I know, I know… if taken by a man such as yourself, it may bring forth redemption and cleansing. But, at the end of the day, her mother was hanged as a witch and, instead of renouncing it, your… first love… chose to follow her mother's path. *That's* what they'll say – what a judge will say. And even you can't deny that.'

'Healing's an honourable path.'

We'd come some distance now, were close to the top of the hill which overlooked the town and the abbey. We stopped by a lone thorn tree, where I subsided on to the grass.

'You think Carew's part of this?'

Dudley considered, positioning himself 'twixt the roots of the thorn tree.

'He has a certain blunt integrity. He'll support Fyche because Fyche is the law. If Fyche put the abbot in the frame on false evidence… well, difficult times, and the abbot *was* a wealthy papist.'

'But do you see him *involved*?'

'In the stitching up of the abbot?'

'I'm thinking more of Cate Borrow.'

'He's not a schemer. He'll always prefer action. Though I do see him choosing, when it's deemed strategic, to look the other way. He's a soldier. A practical man. It's all means to an end.'

'I even know where the bones are from,' I said.

'Presumably dug from the graves which Carew told us had been descrated?'

'More likely procured from Benlow, the bone-seller. I'll find out.'

'Beat the truth out of him?'

'Reason with him.'

'In that case –' Dudley stood up, dusting down his doublet – 'I shall ride to Butleigh, find with the woman who was delivered of twins.'

He'd brushed out his beard, and his moustache was starting to lengthen and curl again, as if this were a sign of regained health.

I said, 'There may be another problem.'

Telling him of Monger's fear that the woman, through pressure upon her family, might well refuse to confirm Matthew Borrow's story.

'My dear John...' Dudley ran fingers through his shining hair. 'I'll swear that the woman is not yet born who'll say no to Robert Dudley.'

☩

We returned, me in slightly better heart, to the George. Dudley went to the stables to have his horse prepared and saddled, while I sought out Cowdray, who'd first directed me to the man who bought and collected bones.

Found him cleaning up the alehouse, windows flung wide, mopping vomit from the flags.

'Woman's work.'

He smiled ruefully, wiping his hands on his sackcloth apron. I pulled out a stool and sat down.

'You've known times like this before?'

'Some of them expected free ale,' Cowdray said. 'I've not known that before.'

'And did they get it?'

He made no reply.

'They've found bones on Nel Borrow's ground,' I said.

'What do you want me to say to that, Dr John? Bones everywhere.'

'Is it true what they say about graves being raided?'

Cowdray shoved his mop into the pail.

'Big Jamey Hawkes. He was dug up. Coffin broken into. Bones defiled.'

'An old grave?'

'Fifteen years. Twenty.'

'The bone—' I broke off, hesitated. 'Benlow...'

'Ah.' An impatient shake of the head. 'Who can say? Might've needed a new thighbone for St Dunstan. Sold that a hundred times over. See, I would've made certain things about him clearer when I first mentioned him to you, but I—'

'Knew me not well enough, then, to brand the man a shyster?'

'More or less,' Cowdray said.

'It's a risky trade he's in.'

'Aye. Could be.'

'You might think him lucky to have evaded arrest for so long. In many places, the church courts would take a hard view of it. And even here, in such times as these...'

'Oh, now, he's a respectable vendor of sheepskins, Dr John.'

'But everyone knows what's in his cellar.'

'I think what you're asking me,' Cowdray said, 'is... might certain people in authority choose to disregard aspects of Master Benlow's other trade?'

'In return for... favours?'

'Some may think that.'

'Where's he get the bones? In general?'

'Dr John—'

'It won't come back on you, Cowdray, I swear it.'

'Ah...' He sniffed, wiped the back of a hand across his nose and mouth. 'Man can spend all his days watching his words.'

I waited. The fresh sunlight falling through the open window turned even Cowdray's stubble into gold dust.

'Benlow buys *most* of his bones,' he said. 'Usually from wretched folk whose very poverty presses them to go out at night and dig up graves and break into mouldy tombs. That's the ones he don't do himself. For the pleasure of it.'

'Pleasure?'

'Old bones, new bones... he loves them like jewels.'

'He took me into his private charnel house.'

'I've been down there but once,' Cowdray said. ''Twas enough. That's a man not well in his mind. He loves... what should not be loved.'

'Men?'

'If that was the worst of it we'd all know where we were. He loves the dead. Poor family, son or daughter's died... if it en't some contagion, he'll make an offer for the body. To be cut up by medical students in Bristol is what he'll tell them. Truth is... oft-times the corpse won't leave his premises. Not for a long time.'

'God.'

'Keep out of his bedroom, my advice.'

I recalled the heavy smell of incense around the foot of the loft ladder.

Cowdray went back to the mop, slopping it around in the pail.

'He was in here, Dr John. Asking for you.'

'When?'

'Couple of times yesterday. Said he thought you'd've been back to see him.'

'What did you tell him?'

'Told him if you wanted him you'd know where to find him and to keep out of my inn.'

Cowdray raised his mop, stabbed it down, water pooling on the flags.

☩

I didn't go to find Benlow. If he'd provided the bones to be planted in Nel's herb garden, the last man he'd admit that to was me. For what remained of the morning, I walked the streets of Glastonbury, mostly alone with my drab thoughts.

What might I take to Sir Edmund Fyche to induce him to withdraw his factored evidence against Nel Borrow? Only the secret he'd tried to get from Whiting. *Somebody* had to know the nature of it.

But if it was too late to withdraw whatever charges had been laid against her, then I must needs go to court – a strange court in a strange city – to present my case to a hostile assize judge already primed by Fyche.

I leaned against the sun-dappled wall of the abbey, thinking back to my last time in court, when I'd faced charges of attempting to kill Mary by sorcery. Charges built upon spurious evidence and my own reputation as an astrologer, at a time when astrology itself was deemed by many to be a heresy. Realising now, with a barren dismay, that the case against Eleanor Borrow was, by comparison, as solid as the wall against which I rested.

Unless *she* knew otherwise.

☩

Around noon, a clatter of horsemen had me scurrying back to the George, where Carew and three attendants were dismounting by the stables entrance, Carew tossing the reins of his horse to a groom as I hurried across the street.

'How now, Dr John?'

He seemed happy. Not a good sign.

'You've ridden from Wells?'

'Have indeed,' he said. 'It was most pleasant. On such a day, the idea that this is Jesu's chosen bit of England seems credible indeed.' He didn't look at me. 'Suppose you'll want to know about your meeting with the witch.'

'When?'

'Tell Cowdray to bring up meat,' he said to one of the attendants. 'And best cider, none of his dog piss.' Then addressing me over a shoulder. 'I regret... not today.'

'When, then?'

'Nor tomorrow.'

'Carew, for—'

'Nor, come to that, the day after.' He turned, leaning toward me, teeth agleam through his tarry beard. 'In fact, *not ever*.'

It felt like my heart was afloat in an icy well.

'What are you saying?'

'She doesn't wish it,' Carew said gaily. 'The witch has no desire to speak with you. Or even to see your white scholar's face.'

'You're lying.'

I was numbed. One of the attendants drew a sharp breath and took a step back as a horse voided its bowels and Carew's face went blank, as if wiped like a slate.

'What did you say, then?'

I walked right up to him.

'You're such a bastard, Carew. How do I know you've even seen her?'

Carew hardly seemed to have moved, and I was unaware of what had happened until I was in the dirt by his feet, watching him rubbing a fist and feeling that my face had been smashed by a side of beef. Realising through the pain that he'd finally found cause to do what he'd been wanting to do for days.

'How do you *know*?' Carew said, 'Because, *Doctor*, you hear it from a man of honour.'

With a small prod of his boot, he put me on my back in a tump of steaming horseshit, and walked past me into the inn.

XXXIX

Nothing to Hide

DR BORROW WAS in his surgery unbinding a goodwife's broken arm. I sat and waited and watched, questions tumbling one over the other in my crowded mind.

'Best not to lift the child with this one for a while,' Borrow told the goodwife. 'I don't want to see you back here... except with the money, of course. Or, if you don't have the money, a week's milk will suffice.'

He smiled. I knew not how he could be so calm. There was a scar to one side of his mouth, a swollen lip, but I noticed that he never touched either of the wounds with fingers or tongue.

After the woman had left, he put the stopper into a jar of comfrey, the tangled plant swimming in its own dark brown oil, sunbeams from the mean windows making it look alive. He placed the jar on a shelf in a row of apothecary's vessels.

'You've come to me for balm, Dr John?'

'Um... no.' I could not but put a hand to the side of my jaw. It hurt to speak now. 'I lost my footing, and... but that's not why I'm here. I'll come directly to the point, Dr Borrow. I'd thought to defend your daughter at the assize.'

'I see.'

'I'm schooled in law. Hate injustice. I asked Sir Peter Carew to fix a meeting between us, that we might plan the case. Half an hour ago, he came back from Wells, telling me she'd refused to see me.'

Borrow nodded, or I thought he did. He seemed to me the very opposite of Carew, a deft and placid man in whom the balance of humours was held secure, although a strong mix of the melancholic and the phlegmatic was apparent in his movements and his speech, neither of which were expansive.

I said, 'Do you know why?'

'She hasn't much money.'

'God's bones, she healed my friend! I'm not asking for *money*—'

'I see.' Borrow rolled up a yard of bandage with long, slender fingers. 'You must not think this reflects on your abilities, Dr John. Which I'm sure are considerable.'

He put the bandage on the shelf and then to turned me and sighed – the first sign in him of human frailty.

'She won't see me either. Won't see anyone.'

He looked at me, still-eyed. Here was a man dealing, day to day, with death and mortal sickness, accustomed to setting aside all human response in the cause of cool diagnosis.

'It makes no sense, Dr Borrow. No more than her mother's refusal to fight for her own life.'

'Ah... Joe Monger told you.'

I nodded. He waved me to the patient's stool. I sat down, and he sat on the other side of his trestle board of scrubbed pine.

'He implied that she sought to defend your reputation,' I said. 'To keep you out of it.'

'Cate... always made little of her own abilities and too much of mine. It's true that I'd planned to give evidence on her behalf and question their facile assumptions. But never got the chance.'

'In what way – can I ask?'

'By questioning the primitive nonsense of alleged witchery.' Borrow was speaking softly, with no sign of animosity. 'I... don't know of your own views on this, but reason tells me such nonsense will be consigned to history by the time this century's out.'

'*What* will?'

'The question of a deity – *that* may take longer to depart, but it's surely already on its horse. The Pope's had his arse kicked, and the Church of England's governed by a lay person – and a woman. *A woman?* Would anyone, even thirty years ago, have believed that would ever happen? Would you?'

'I suppose not.'

''Tis all coming apart, Dr John. Mankind coming to its senses.'

'You're an atheist.'

'Can I be the only man alive who's observed that man's greatest achievements have arisen out of the will of an individual? When the expulsion from this country of the papacy itself, the strongest religious fortress the world has known, comes through a rising not of the spirit… but a man's *cock*?'

He smiled at the nonsense of it. Of course, I'd listened to such talk in darkened rooms in Cambridge and Louvain, but that was usually from young and excitable men.

'Let me understand this,' I said. 'You would've stood up in that court-room and told them there could be no witchcraft because there is no God, therefore no Satan, and so…?'

'I prefer a quiet life, but –' he shrugged – 'I'd've done it.'

'Did your wife know this?'

'She knew of my principles.'

'But you go to church…'

'It's the law.'

'How can you… I mean, this town…'

'How can I live and work in a town like Glaston? Easily. I was born here. A community where few people appear to share a creed only underlines the folly of it all.'

'But your wife…'

'Was, I'm afraid, a perfect example of one who rarely held the same beliefs two days together. I'd tease her, I'm afraid. Always going to find a new cure for this and that – and oft-times did, mind, let's not forget that. Yet would have made more of her undoubted skills had she not been so easily diverted by dreams of… of a golden age we'll never have again because it's an age that never was.' He stopped, looked at me, sorrow in his eyes. 'But you'd surely not expect me to speak ill of her.'

There was a silence, during which Borrow took down a couple of jars from the shelf and held them to the light, and I thought of Nel and wondered what it had been like growing up amid such extremes of opinion.

'To answer your unspoken question,' he said at last, 'harmony would always, in the end, prevail, thanks to a shared belief in healing.'

'And how do you feel now?'

He took in a slow breath, let it out. Was there an element of the shudder in its expulsion? Was there something inside Borrow which roiled and spat? I couldn't say. I'd met countless men and women, not least Dudley and the Queen, whose spouses or parents had died by execution, and several had exhibited this same calm, but whether it was a sign of acceptance…

He'd retired again behind his healer's screen, taking the top off one of the small jars and stirring the contents with a taper of wood. There was something about him… something I'd seen in Monger, only more so. The quality of a priest. In an atheist. As if his atheism had brought him an inner certainty he could draw on, as men drew on their trust in God and the Church.

'You know she's innocent of this.' I stood up. 'And if you don't believe she can be saved by prayer or faith in a just God… then what's to be done?'

He put down the jar and pushed it toward me.

'Contains yarrow and camomile. Make a solution of it with cold water, soak a cloth and hold it where it hurts.'

'I—?'

'Your face,' he said. 'Take it. Pay me if it works.'

'Thank you.'

He waved it away.

'And, in the future,' he said, almost kindly, 'take care where you tread.'

✠

But there was no balm for my spirit. Walking down the five steps to the surgery door, I felt more troubled than when I'd gone in

There was nothing to be read from Matthew Borrow's face – not yet an old man's face but possessed of a mature self-knowing. I'd never encountered his like. Here was a man who would never strip back the layers of his dreams in search of meaning nor aspire to measure the dimensions of the universe. A man for whom matters of the hidden were of no consequence, for there was nothing to hide.

If he had no fear of God, then he feared nothing. His inner calm was remarkable.

Of course, his anger *must* have overflowed when Fyche's mercenaries had taken his daughter. He'd fought them with no regard for himself and been badly beaten for it. Yet had he given up trying to see Nel? I thought not. But whatever he had in mind he didn't want me involved.

Did he perchance know who I was? *What* I was?

A man who sought to know the mind of God… no-one more worthy of an atheist's contempt. I was sunk into confusion and despair as I walked down past the Church of St Benignus – how ironic that Matthew Borrow should be living almost directly opposite a church. A man who loved not God and feared not Satan. In this bubbling cauldron of creeds was there a kind of purity to that?

The thought was so shocking that I broke into a run and, rounding the corner, almost collided with a lean man striding down the slope from the George.

'John… where the hell've you been? What's—?'

'Dudley, God…You found her?'

I fell back, panting against the church wall, two ragged children springing up on the other side and running away, laughing, a smell of fresh shit upon the air.

'What happened to your face?' Dudley said.

'It's of no import.' I held up the jar of balm. 'From the doctor.'

'Her father?'

'She won't talk with me,' I said. 'She won't even see me. Or anyone. The woman in Butleigh – have you talked to *her*? Will she go to the assize?'

'John…'

'You did *find* her?'

'Let's go back,' Dudley said.

'What?'

'To the doctor's. I have questions for him.'

'For Christ's sake –' throwing back my head to the sky, greenish clouds sailing in from the coast with a skreeting of gulls, my voice hurled against them – '*did you find her?*'

A goodwife with a basket of eggs crossed the road, scuttling away from us. Dudley continued down the hill, and I caught up with him.

'*Tell* me.'

'I spoke there to several people… Notably the smith, to whom I gave money in return for his honesty. And from whom I learned that there's been no twins born in Butleigh this past year. No twins. Nor, come to that, these past ten years.'

I moved ahead of him, halting his progress, a flood of bad bile entering my gut.

'You took one man's word for that?'

'*Listen* to me. No births at all in more than a month. *Including* bastards. Confirmed by the minister of the church, who also maintains that no child in recent memory has been delivered there from the belly.'

Dudley's eyes were lit with fury.

'*Now* will you go back and talk to the bloody doctor?'

XL

A Different Canon

DON'T MISUNDERSTAND ME. Robert Dudley was not like Carew. Behind the arrogance, my friend was an educated man with a questing mind. But he was yet a young man, with a young man's impulse and a soldier's spine, and there were times when all thought and reason would be kicked aside. And then you'd feel his hand quivering over the hilt of his sword, the air grown thin around him.

'These knives....'

Standing now in Borrow's doorway, shouldering out the sunlight, crisp winter in his voice.

'See me later, please.' Borrow buckling his leather bag, throwing it over a shoulder. 'I have sick people to minister to.'

'I'll see you in hell, Dr Borrow. Where goeth all fucking liars.'

The space betwixt them throbbing like the hush before a beheading.

'*Who* are you, again?' Matthew Borrow said.

'You know who I am.'

'I know who you *claim* to be.' Borrow's voice was but one notch above disinterest. 'However, a mere clerk of antiquities would be unlikely, in my experience, to employ a groom. My instinct tells me you're clad below your status, so if we're speaking of *liars...*'

No movement in his grey eyes; he'd marked Dudley's mood, yet had no fear of it. Found it, if anything, a sign of weakness.

And, in some way, this gave me small hope, for the very last thing I wanted was for Borrow to have lied about the bloodied knives. I wanted there to be some reason for them that we'd all missed. Some reason not involving Nel.

There was a tacit suspension of hostility. Borrow unslung his medical bag, and the tension went out of Dudley, who came into the surgery and closed the door behind him.

'Dr Borrow, tomorrow is Sunday. The day after that, your daughter goes on trial for her life, accused of witchcraft and the murder of my groom. Did she kill him?'

'I'm her father.'

Borrow opened out his hands, two rings of dull metal on one, the kind employed to dispel cramp.

Dudley said, 'Will you plead for her in court?'

'If I'm allowed, I'll give evidence as to her good character and appeal for her to be cleared of all accusations.'

'And tell the judge and jury the truth about the bloodied surgical tools?'

Silence.

'What *is* the truth, Dr Borrow?'

No reply.

'For God's sake, Dr Borrow,' I said. 'We're on your side. Your daughter's side.'

The look Dudley gave me implied this was not necessarily the case, but my own feelings could never be so easily discarded.

'I swear to you,' I said with a passion I could not quell, 'that I'll move all heaven to have her released.'

Borrow raised an eyebrow. I breathed in hard against a blush.

'Listen,' I said. 'Looked at with dispassion, it seems hardly credible that such a big man was killed and butchered by a woman. Nor can credible motive be shown. But the fact remains that, with no Caesarean birth in Butleigh – no birth at all – your explanation for the blood on the knives—'

'Is shown to be a lie.' Borrow's hands falling to his sides. 'Yes. Had I been given notice, I'd've come up with a better one.'

Oh Christ.

✛

Some of it was true, apparently.

What he'd said about coming home late, very tired, throwing his tools under the stairs, where both his and his daughter's were stored.

His tools which, that night, seemed to have been unused. Borrow threw open a door to show us where they were kept. It was a cramped space, with narrow wooden stairs.

I said, 'You had no cause to bring them out next day until—?'

'Why would I? They needed no cleaning. No-one came to my door in need of surgery.'

'So the bloodstained tools…?'

'One of Fyche's men pulled out the bag and passed it to him and he said, "What are these? Whose is this blood?" And held them up, and I could see that there *was* blood, and I told him… the first likely explanation that came into my head. But Fyche wasn't listening anyway. As I told you, he had his evidence. He was satisfied.'

'How do you know the bloodied tools were Nel's?'

'Mine are still here. Unbloodied.'

'Did you see Nel's tools there before Fyche took them?'

'No. They were quickly passed hand to hand and out of the door.'

'Then how do you know they *were* hers? And not some others brought here by Fyche as… as ready-made evidence?'

Knowing, even before the words were out, that I was grasping at dust-motes in the air.

'In which case… where *are* Eleanor's tools?' Borrow said. 'Dr John, I appreciate what you're trying to do, but I fear your friend is right. I lied… not well enough.'

Dudley said, 'Did she kill my servant?'

Borrow met his eyes at once.

'Of course not. A woman?'

'Then *what*?'

'I don't know…'

'Could she have lent her tools to someone who brought them back in this condition?'

'I don't *know*.'

'To whom *might* she lend her tools, Dr Borrow?'

'Master Roberts, if I knew that, I would not hesitate to name them. It must needs be someone she trusted. And maybe that's why… why she won't talk to me. Or to anyone.'

'She's protecting someone?'

Borrow shrugged. This was my last hope for her innocence, but I could see that it was not much better. She was supposed to have lent out her tools and then taken them home, still smirched with a dead man's blood?

'Who, having done this, would not clean them afterwards to remove the evidence?' Dudley said. 'Taken them to the river... or any one of these local springs.'

The Blood Well, I thought bitterly. Borrow looked at Dudley, shook his head.

'Who would she wish to protect?' Dudley said. 'Who would she *die* to protect? Does she have a lover?'

Not looking at me.

'A father,' Borrow said, 'is ever the last to know. Especially a father who seldom has time for chit-chat.'

Dudley glanced at me. His eyes said that we'd learned all we could and should be away, but I could not.

'Have you told us everything?' I said. 'Everything that might help?'

'Dr John...' A first sign of impatience in Borrow. 'How would I *know* what might help?

I thought back to the stormy night in my chamber, enclosed in what seemed to me now like a golden orb.

'All right... think on this. Nel remains convinced that her mother's death was engineered because she was believed to possess evidence against Sir Edmund Fyche... maybe evidence that he was responsible for the betrayal of Abbot Whiting.'

'You must have come to know my daughter very well indeed, in a very short time, Dr John.'

'Do *you* believe that?'

He was silent for a moment.

'No... I don't. Whiting's death, and the manner of it, would have been ordered by Thomas Cromwell. Fyche was irrelevant. Nor do I think Cate was in possession of any so-called evidence. In the papers she left behind, there was nothing... worthwhile. And she certainly never spoke to me of anything of that—'

'But you are, as you say, a man who works day and night. A man with little time for chit—'

'Don't insult me,' he said mildly. 'She would have told me. I might not have shared much with Whiting in the way of religious belief, but I respected the abbey as a centre of learning.'

'Your wife and the abbey...'

'She owed a debt to them, Dr John, and it was a simple one. She had no education as a child. The monks... taught her to read and write.'

'When was this?'

'When she was a young woman. She sought to repay them by growing herbs for them. Whiting had an interest in healing, Cate had a rare ability... for making things grow. I'm talking about herbs and fruits which had never been grown here before. Seeds would be brought to the abbey, oft-times from abroad, and she'd sow them and nurture the plants. She seemed to know, by instinct, what conditions would suit them.'

'So the ground.. the herb garden.'

'Given to her by the abbot. The abbot was impressed by her abilities. Thought them –' Borrow's lips turned down – '*God*-given.'

Dudley said, 'You say she left some papers behind?'

'They're gone.'

'What *was* in them?'

'If she'd wanted me to see them, she'd have shown them to me.'

'You weren't curious?'

'There are matters,' Borrow said, 'about which I have no curiosity whatsoever. For I know it to be a mess of myth to keep the vulgar people in their place. There was a middle ground on which we'd talk all night, Cate and I – the curative properties of plants, the quantities in which they...' He slapped a hand at the air. '*Tchah!* The idea that these curative properties were instilled into each plant by some *god*... as part of some divine plan for the great cathedral universe...'

I saw Dudley blink. Saw what Monger had meant when he'd said that Dr Borrow's science was of a different canon to mine.

'Yours is a lonely voice,' I said, 'in this town.'

'Which is why I stay silent much of the time. I seek no conversions. I wouldn't wish, Dr John, to start a *religion*.'

'But you must know… that the legends here have a power. And if it were felt that your wife was party to some secret knowledge—'

Like the rope tethering a boat to a storm-battered harbour, his restraint snapped at last.

'Knowledge? You call this superstition *knowledge?* The belief that there's a great secret here, preserved by the monks… that while the abbey might be left in ruins, the secret yet remains…? As if Cromwell and King Harry were not the winners because they never learned the *secret?* You truly think that's any more than balm for the dispossessed? It's like the foolish resentment of Wells because Wells has its cathedral and all the wealth *that* brings, and Glastonbury has only ruins.'

It was my turn to hold the calm. One way or another, I'd pursue this matter to an end.

'What do you know of this so-called secret?'

He took a steadying breath and then let it out.

'Dr John, how can I best convey my contempt for such talk? Except to say that if she hadn't been drawn into this nonsense, Cate would be alive today.'

'Drawn into it how?'

'The abbot… all these people. They led her into areas of madness and then abandoned her.'

'Which people?'

'*All* of them. Everyone who ever trod these hills in a robe. She was an expert grower of herbs, like no-one else, but she had to let herself be led down blindingly foolish pathways. And then people died.'

'The dust of vision? That's what you're—'

'You think she wasn't encouraged in that venture? As if every damned, deluded monk who ever lived didn't aspire to some visionary experience… whether it's from whipping his own flesh raw or fasting to the point of starvation. All the years she spent trying to gratify their impractical urges… it sickened me.'

He half rose, both hands on his board, his breathing harsh. Dudley was silent, intent.

After she was hanged,' Borrow said, 'Fyche came with his men – as I knew he would – to turn over the house, take possession of all her potions.'

'In search of the dust?' I said.

'So that all the ingredients of the mixture that caused the burning might be destroyed, was how he put it.'

'And what do you think he was most scared of – the burning or the vision?'

'He didn't see it as vision. He saw it as opening people to possession by demons. So he took everything away, everything he could find in her workshop, the flasks, the weights, potions, papers, recipes – once she'd learned to write, Cate took great pleasure in committing everything she could think of to paper. I like to think of Fyche and his scholars spending many fruitless weeks poring over them in search of... secrets.'

'Secrets...' I looked hard at Borrow. 'The secrets she'd learned from the monks?'

'This is what you're here for, is it?' he said. 'These antiquities. The Queen, or someone close to her, has heard of secrets here and must, therefore, possess them.'

I said nothing.

'My own belief, for what it's worth, is that any secret ever supposed to have been held by the monks of Glastonbury was a secret invented for the creation of wealth.'

I was in no mood to dispute it.

'So Fyche took everything?'

'Everything he could find. Some documents I removed from the house. I had no interest in them, but they were close to her heart and head. All that, in my opinion, reduced her. I had no wish to see any of it again, but I wasn't about to hand them to Fyche.'

'And what was this?'

'Something I neither understood nor would wish to. Too many lives wasted.'

I stared at the shelf of apothecary's jars. The sun gone now, the jars did not shine. I listened to Nel's voice in my head.

All the treasure was long gone.

But treasure did not simply *go*, transformed to vapour like the dew. It merely changed hands.

I said, 'Whatever it was... did you not think to give it to Nel?'

'Why would I...?' He looked at me as if I were mad. 'Put the source of my wife's downfall into the hands of my daughter?'

'Someone did.'

'The dust?' he said. 'Are we talking of the dust?'

'She knows how to make it. I'd guess not many people do. The various outbreaks of St Anthony's Fire seem to have been caused by accidental ingestion of the mould. Someone who knows what amounts may be used and mixed with whatever other ingredients, to produce the visions without the bodily harm... that would be valuable knowledge, would it not?'

'She worked it out for herself,' Dr Borrow said. 'But it's dangerous knowledge.'

'Then, is this one of the secrets? Is this something which may have been known here for many years, passed down? But perchance the factoring of it... the practical details... had been forgotten. Did she help the monks rediscover what had been lost?'

'Proving that the legendary magic of the place is no more than a form of intoxication? An appealing idea, Dr John.'

It wasn't at all what I'd meant to imply; I would never have wished to see the spirit of this place so diminished. But I'd give him no argument, being afraid that we'd lose him... that he would see us as no more than vulgar treasure-seekers.

'So this was not the formula for the dust?'

No reply.

'Dr Borrow,' I said, 'I'm looking for something – anything – to give me leverage on Fyche.'

'Fyche has ambition. Understand that about him and you have the measure of the man.'

I said nothing.

'I've tried to hate him,' Borrow said, 'but I'm not sure I have the right. Fyche looks around and sees the same madness that I see. The difference in us being that I see all religions conspiring to destroy any hope of mankind's progress in this world... while Fyche believes that if all men were bent to a *single* religion and all knowledge guarded by men of his own class—'

'His own class?'

'That is, not the—'

'Maggots?'

'He's an intelligent man, in his way, the abbey bursar once, who would probably have become abbot had Reform not come.'

'I didn't know that.'

'He sought it. As I say, he's ever had ambition.'

I tried again.

'So if not for the dust of vision…?'

'Nothing so useful,' Borrow said. 'She was a friend of John Leland's, you know, the…'

'Yes. Of course.'

'When he died, he left some of his papers to her. Of course, he died insane, leaving a mess behind him, and it was years before someone thought to send them.'

'And what… what *were* they?'

'Shit. Worthless. *Occultism*. The man was a slave to all that drivel. Astrology, alchemy… I'm afraid she seemed to set great store by them. Poring over them for hours in her last… few weeks.'

A tingling in me.

'You know what they're about?'

'I'm afraid I have better things…'

'Could I see them?'

'Hardly.'

Borrow laughed bleakly. Dudley leaned forward.

'Dr Borrow… this is what's thought to be the treasure… is it?'

'It's shit.'

'If neither Fyche nor your daughter possesses this… treasure… then who does?'

Borrow shook his head sadly, then sat down again, clasping his long hands together as if in parody of prayer.

'Cate,' he said, 'Cate has it yet.'

XLI

Who Fears For His Immortal Soul…

THE THIRD TIME I awoke, I lay staring at the ceiling until its oaken beams were full manifest in the moonlight, like the bars of a prison.

The prison of this world.

I lay thinking for long minutes, until the weight of it was all so intense upon my chest that I thought a seizure were come upon me and almost cried out, throwing myself from the bed into the merciless cold.

Wide awake, now. Standing at the window, looking out over the empty street and the night-grey ghost of the abbey just barely outlined under a misted moon. Then I was sinking to my knees and praying that, if only this once, I might know the mind of God. Asking, in essence, if I should take it that this third awakening was a dark summons into a deeper dark.

The idea of it filling me with such dread that it could only be countered by thoughts of Nel Borrow lying sleepless in some stinking, half-flooded dungeon, with the damp and the cold, the scurrying and the despair.

Having been, just once, consigned to such a place, I could not bear this and felt that I'd do anything. Wept over my praying hands before the abbey's shell, the tears pouring out of me like lifeblood.

Blood.

What are these? Whose is this blood?

Fyche, gleefully, to Borrow, holding aloft his bag of clanking evidence.

All bloodied. Could be pig's blood, chicken's blood. *Dear God.*

Stood up, moving slowly at first and then in a frenzy, pulling on my old brown robe.

Going at once to Dudley's chamber.

✠

Not even thinking, in my haste, that he might have his sword at the ready again.

Not this time, though. This time he slept.

'Robbie...'

If not deeply.

'Well, well.' No movement in him. 'John Dee. What took you so long?'

'Listen,' I said. 'The surgical knives. They didn't bring the knives with them.'

'Knives?'

'Fyche. He didn't bring them. The knives *were* Nel's knives, and the blood... the blood might even have been Martin Lythgoe's, but they—'

'Where's the point of this?'

'They didn't bring the knives... they brought the *blood*. They brought the blood that it might be spread on something... anything... during their search. Clothing – who can say? A bottle of blood. And the discovery of the knives... that must've seemed like a Godsend.'

'John—'

It's what he *does*. Stitches people up – the abbot and the chalice, Cate Borrow and the false witness and the grave dirt... *Fyche contrives evidence.*'

'When did this come to you?'

'Just now. I couldn't sleep.'

'So you thought to share the burden of it. So generous.'

'In case I... should forget.'

'Oh, go to,' Dudley said wearily. 'You know you'll never prove it, and we both know why you're here.'

Heaving himself up in the bed, the cover falling away, and I saw by the thin moonlight that he was full-dressed in his day apparel.

'Get your coat, you mad bastard,' he said. 'If it must be done, best t'were finished before sunrise.'

✠

Not asking you to go out with a spade and a muffled lantern, Cecil had said.

It took us a while to find a spade. Cowdray must have locked up all the best tools. The only one we could lay hand on was old and rusted, with a split in the shaft. Short of breaking into one of the outbuildings,

319

it was the best we were going to get, and it made a certain poetic sense that this should not, in any way, be easy.

But there could be no more poetry in this.

'You could at least have made preparation,' Dudley said.

'I didn't know.'

'Yes you bloody did. We both did. We just dared not speak of the unspeakable.'

And spoke not again until the houses were behind us, the sweet scent of apple-smoke gone from the air. I'd found an oil-lantern and lit it from the alehouse fire before we left. Kept it muffled until we'd left the town for higher ground, with the waxing moon all wrapped in mist and the air alive with moisture.

We found the stile without difficulty.

Dudley set foot on it and then came down again. Laughter on his breath.

'Know you what hour this is?'

'It's a long way from dawn, that's all that matters, but if you press me...' I looked up at where the moon stood. Few stars were visible, but I made out Jupiter in the south. 'I'd say approaching midnight.'

Thinking that if this was London the Watch would be out, with his staff and his dog.

Twelve of the clock, look well to your locks
Your fire and your light and God give you goodnight.

Goodnight. A comfort. In Glastonbury, there was only the owls and us, and I drew no comfort from anywhere. I was a city man, particularly after dark, when even Mortlake...

'Tis said that no man who fears for his immortal soul oughta go past your place beyond sunset, nor walk in Mortlake churchyard lest graves be open.

My God, if Jack Simm could but see me now, all ready to embrace the taint of necromancy.

'We're upon the cusp of Sunday, is what I meant,' Dudley said. 'We're doing this on the sabbath.'

'Yes.'

'I'd ask for God's blessing, but I rather fear that would be a blasphemy in itself.'

✠

The wooden cross was not quite where I'd remembered it, but the eyes cannot be trusted at night. I looked down upon it and wondered how often Nel had knelt here and the horror and revulsion she might feel if she knew what we were about to do.

The high-born gentleman and the low conjurer. *God forgive me.*

Knowing that I should be the one to begin this, I set the lantern upon the grass, reached down the bars of the cross and pulled. It was not deeply embedded and came away easily, with a small squelch.

'Water down there?' Dudley said.

'Water everywhere, here.'

I laid the cross beside the grave. Looked around. The woods round the herb garden were like the shadow of an army in the hushed moments before a battle. I could hear stirrings. Animals hunting, or the restless spirits of the people whose bones had recently been scattered over this land like horseshit? I lifted the spade and stood looking down at the grass in the greasy lamplight.

'What if he's lying?' I said. 'He's lied before.'

'Oh, he lies well,' Dudley said. 'One of the skills of his profession. *Of course I'll make you better...* The important question is, what kind of man buries his dead wife's most private documents without even finding out what they contain?'

'A man who knows what's inside. Or thinks he does. An embittered non-believer. A man who's both stricken with loss and cold with anger. A man blaming his dead wife for her own misfortune.'

'And what do *we* think we might find in them?'

'We might find nothing of consequence,' I said. 'Or we just might find the true reason for Fyche's persecution of Cate Borrow and Eleanor Borrow.'

From a neighbouring field came the barking cough of an old ewe. Might be interpeted as encouragement or outrage.

'Do it,' Dudley said.

I stabbed the spade into Cate's grave.

XLII

Twin Souls

IN MY QUESTIONING of mortality, I've watched the sexton who digs the graves at Mortlake; this was not the same. Churchyard earth is oft-times dry, tired soil, gritty with fragments of brown bone: burial upon burial, death upon death, the ground cleared, start again… But this was rich growing land, ripe with humus, warm down there and hungry.

Unused to this kind of work, a couple of feet down we stopped to rest. My throat was dry as tinder, but we hadn't thought to bring ale or cider, neither of us being exactly a labouring man.

Dudley said, 'If Martin Lythgoe were here…'

'Then we would not be.'

'True.'

A movement, and both of us were looking down the herb garden, where a rabbit bobbed. No… a night hare. It hopped away, disappeared under the hedgerow and into the mist of its own mythology.

This night of all nights, I would not look for omens.

'How should his heart be taken to London?' Dudley said. 'I've never done anything like this before.'

'You need a wooden casket. Something like a reliquary. I'd suggest going to Benlow the bone-man, but whatever *he* provided…well, you wouldn't know what had been in it before. Best to talk to the vicar at St John's or St Benignus. They'll charge you dear, but that's the way of it.'

'Normal life, I'd just give an instruction, a wave of the hand and it would be done.' Dudley pushed both fists into his spine, rocking back. 'Jesu, look at me… out at midnight with grave dirt all over my hands. The great quest. Tell me where in Malory are Arthur's knights reduced to unearthing the dead.'

He pulled down his hat as a white owl passed overhead in graceful silence.

'You know she gave me an abbey? A monastery, anyway.'

'Another one?'

'*I'm giving you a monastery*, she says. *William will see to the paper-work.*'

'When was this?'

'Ten days ago, a fortnight? Worst of it is, I can't even remember the name of the damned place. It's just a monastery, a few hundred acres. It's only when I come here and walk for a couple of hours amongst people for whom an extra loaf of gritty, grey bread...'

'You're talking of the village of Butleigh?'

'They had no fear of me. An old woman watered my horse, gave me cider and a piece of pie. An old woman who'd be hiding behind her shutters if she'd known who...' He looked at me across the hole. 'It was strange... I didn't think they had *lives*. I thought they only lived to serve. Of a sudden, I was envying them. All my life ruled by circumstance and the need for position. A monastery or a piece of pie – which is the most—?'

'*Shush.*'

Dudley spinning round. No-one there, but even mumblings would be carried away on this still night.

'Mercy,' he said softly.

'It won't last, of course.'

'Oh, no. It won't last. A couple of days in that village, I'd be off my head with the workaday boredom of it. But for just a few hours... maybe it was through the release from the fever...' Dudley's teeth flashed in the lamplight. 'I did used to envy *you*... for the freedom to travel abroad and study and kick at God's own boundaries.'

'Now a lodger at my mother's house by the river. And all I can aspire to is one day to inherit it and fill it full of books.'

'More than that, John, and you know it. You certainly taught me... well, nothing *useful*...'

'Taught you mathematics. Arithmetic to enable you to calcule how many thousand acres your family had managed to appropriate over the years, and… we're wasting time, aren't we? We're delaying the moment.'

'Of course we are.' He grinned, tossed the spade at me. 'Your turn.'

He held the lamp against the tump of earth, which we'd at least had the wit to raise on the town side, to shield our light.

And I dug down with a fury, my bookman's hands already raw. The deeper we went, the easier the soil and stones were to move, or so it seemed. As if we were beckoned deeper into the sin of what we did. Digging ourselves into hell.

Dudley said, from above, '*Do* they come back? The dead?'

'I think it can happen.'

'But you haven't yet seen… I mean, with your own eyes…'

'And you… in the abbey?'

'Fever. We make our own ghosts.'

'And maybe also, through magic, make the ghosts that others see.' I stepped back as dank water splashed up. 'Who else saw the shade of Anne Boleyn at the Queen's bedside? Anyone?'

'She needs a man at her side,' Dudley said. 'And not just Cecil.'

No, no, *no.* Not now.

I kept on shovelling, hard and steady. I'd stripped off my doublet and my shirt was already soaked with sweat and there was slippery mud down my boots. Yet, knowing there was more dangerous ground than this, I threw myself at it until I was panting and there was a roaring in my ears. And I could swear we were being watched, that the night movements in the trees and hedgerows were not the movements of rabbits but the scufflings of men.

Take him.

'Say it, John. Just say whatever you think should be said.'

I raised the spade out of the pit.

'You know there can be no future in it.' Plunged the spade in again. 'You're wed.'

'For now.'

'No… whatever you're thinking to say— *Oh Christ.*'

The spade had skidded on something hard.

'She's not well,' Dudley said.

I pulled the spade out of the hole. Wanting to throw it in the bushes and run. Didn't move. On the edge of the herb garden a shadow bulged and I jerked upright.

'People think I hide her away in the country,' Dudley said. 'The truth is, there's something amiss with her… She's ill.'

Amy. His wife.

'In what way?'

'Varies. Pains. Weakness.'

'In her head, maybe?'

'I think not. We've talked about it. She said to me, she actually said… *I think I may die soon.* As if she'd had notice of it, from God.'

'What about from a doctor?'

'She's seen them. Several. They're clowns, John. They don't know where to start.'

Nor I. With the lamp lowered, I couldn't see his face, but in my mind's eyes it was smirched again with sweat and fever.

Found myself half wishing that she were… gone from my life… No such thing as a half-wish, is there?

'You love her,' I said desperately. 'You love Amy.'

'Always. It was a marriage for love. How often does that happen to a man in my position?'

Dudley sat down on the tump of grave dirt, his legs overhanging the hole and me.

'Broke me up, the way she looked at me, saying that. Almost as if she thought it was ordained. For the greater good of the country.'

'She's been talking to… who?'

'I know not. Daren't think on it. I kneel in my own chapel, all twisted up with hatred of myself, and I'm crying aloud to God to—' He leaned down in the shuddery lamplight. 'John, I don't know what I'm praying for. I can't say it's not self-serving ambition, but I feel it's *more*…'

A tawny owl answered another's call across the valley. Owls. Spirits of the dead.

Please God, no omens.

Dudley said, 'I ask God that I might… know his will. Know what's right… or what's *meant*.'

'Help me,' I said.

I was standing on a flat stone.

'Bess and me… we're twin souls. Born in the same hour of the same day.'

This was a legend much put about by Dudley himself. I knew not if it were true. He'd once asked me to do a joint horoscope for the Queen and himself but I'd avoided it.

'We lie and talk and laugh all night, and put the world to rights. Talking of all we might do, and it's more… Oh, for Christ's sake, *it's more than love.*'

'Just *help* me.' Putting my hands down and finding water. The stone lay in water. 'Give me more light.'

'This is wrong,' Dudley said. 'This is sacrilege.'

'Yes.'

Not knowing if he meant what we were doing or what he'd been saying. *All* was wrong.

He was lying on his stomach now on the rim of the hole, holding the lamp low, and I saw something under the stone and thought it was a bony hand. Looked quickly away began to dig all around, making a channel for the water.

'All right, come out,' Dudley said. 'I'll do this. My soul's a lost cause.'

☩

There were three flat stones covering the body, either to protect it against digging animals or to show where it lay so that another might one day lie on top. Dudley managed to lift each in turn, handing them up to me.

Underneath, a thin layer of earth amongst which ragged flaps of fabric were visible.

The remains of her winding sheet.

Dudley was hacking with the spade at the side of the trench, bringing down shards of clay to widen the hole inside. A narrow space for him to stand there now, next to the body, as if it were on an earthen catafalque. A moat of dark water around it. Stagnant grave water.

It was worse doing nothing, no longer finding refuge in the oblivion of toil. With no doublet on, my arms and chest were chilled, my hands numbed, and the feeling that we were watched grew near-impossible to bear. I sensed figures creeping across the field of bones behind me, rising up as they reached—

A pulse ran through me. The lamplight wavered behind its milky glass. 'Uuuuh!'

Dudley rearing back as if two arms reached out for him. Then the smell came to me, too.

'Oh God...'

'It's all right. I've smelled worse, John. It was just... sudden.'

'Listen... please... better it were me, who... It's probably going to be ruined, anyway. Rotted away long ago. We're likely wasting our time.'

After a few moments, Dudley clambered out.

'Yes.' The relief in his voice all too evident. 'Better it were you.'

☩

I saw her face just once.

The smell.... musty rather than putrid after all this time. Still, I tried to breathe through my mouth. The lantern glass was fogged with vapour, its glow like to a small and clouded moon. Or a nightlight, by a bedside.

She lay there before me in her rotted winding sheet: small, bent.

What now?

Hadn't asked Borrow, how could I? *Where is it? Is it clasped to her breast?*

This was the most likely place, and I hoped for that, bringing the lamp close to what I judged to be the middle of her, but the hands were fallen away, rotted skin and dull bone, nothing between them but sodden linen, and a glistening slime like the pulp of some putrefying windfall fruit.

What did I expect? Guinevere? All slender bones and a twist of golden hair, which would go to dust at first touch?

The eyes, which might once have been green, were gone and the jaw had fallen and the teeth were full of black gaps, and then all was black, Dudley calling out.

'Did you see it?'

'Lamp's out. Lamp's drowned.'

'*I* saw something. I think it's under her… I think her head lies on it, like a pillow.'

'You're sure?'

'No, but… you're going to have to lift her head to find out.'

'I can't even see it.'

'Better, maybe… that way. *I'll* do it if you—'

'No… no…'

I took steadying breaths. Recalling the gasps when I'd lifted a waxen effigy from its small coffin near the bank of the Thames.

Dr Dee, the authority on matters of the hidden. *Jesu…*

Shutting my eyes, as if that might make it easier. But what it brought up, in an instant of glorious anguish, was an image of the unremembered. Moments lost to me since the night of the storm, moments following the river of blinding white light. The moments of the sunrise in the heart, Nel Borrow in my arms, the conjurer and the witch, twin souls.

More than love. I felt that my heart bled.

'John, are you—?'

'Yes,' I cried out. 'Yes, I'm doing it.'

Letting both hands fall into hair which went not to dust but only curled greasily around them, the wet and rotted skin from which it had grown coming away in slimed flakes, and then my fingers were sunk into the holes where her eyes had been. Eyes which had last seen daylight bulging against the constriction of a rope.

If her's scrawny, her can hold out a good while.

With a sickening little bonecrack, I was raising her head. Heavier than you'd think. All the weight of mortality.

For this spoke not of afterlife.

XLIII

Drawings for Children

IN THE SMALL, panelled room at the George, we closed the shutters over the fogged and dripping glass, urgently refreshed the old red fire with applewood, piling on log after log, then finding more candles and lighting them all, until we sat within a nest of light and heat.

Yet still shivered. I tell you, this is what it means to be cold to the soul.

'If it's all destroyed...' Dudley eased off his sodden boots in the ingle. 'I may find it hard to laugh.'

My hands were reddened and chapped and scored all over with cuts and scratches. I was trying to flex them over the fire when we heard footsteps on the stairs, and then Cowdray was with us. He stood in the doorway, hands linked over his ale-belly, blue bags under his eyes.

'We're not thieves, innkeeper,' Dudley said. 'Unless you count an armful of logs.'

Cowdray glanced at the board and then looked away, for the gravedirt was yet all over it. And us. We stank of the grave.

'I seen you go out. Wondered if there was anything I could do for you.'

'Do you never sleep?'

'Not unless I'm sure I'm gonner wake up, Master Roberts.'

'Who can ever be sure of that?' Dudley said. 'What hour is it, Master Cowdray?'

'Gone three. I'd be up and about in a couple of hours, anyway. I get you anything?'

'Small... small beer would be... most acceptable.' No way to keep the tremor from my voice. 'And some peace. If you please.'

'I think he means that if you see anything of Carew, you should keep the bastard away from us,' Dudley said.

'I'll leave the beer out for you. And Sir Peter lies at Meadwell.'

'*Does* he?'

'Word is, he and Sir Edmund'll leave here after church, for Wells.'

'For the assizes.'

'On the morrow,' Cowdray said. 'Monday.'

'Cowdray...'

He turned to me. Flakes of drying soil crumbled from my sleeve.

I said, 'If you saw us leave, did you see if we were followed?'

Dudley frowned at me. I cared not a toss. The state of us, what was Cowdray supposed to think?

'No, Doctor,' he said. 'Nobody.'

Tipping just one glance at what lay on the board before he left.

It was about a foot long, maybe nine inches wide, but no thicker than my wrist, and stinking, still smirched with the unspeakable.

✠

'He knows who we are,' I said. 'He bloody *knows*—'

'No,' Dudley said. 'He only knows who we are not. Now open it.'

We pulled the board closer to the fire, and I turned over the pouch. It was made of leather and appeared to have been sealed all around with wax.

Dudley kept his distance.

'This is what you expected?'

'I know not what I was expecting.'

Bringing out my dagger and prising up the edging of wax. We'd replaced the stones one by one, filling in the grave, stamping down the earth to make it as level as we could, banging the cross back in place with the handle of the spade. After which, despite the cold, the fear that we were watched, the aching need to run, I'd bent for long minutes in the stream that bordered the herb garden, scrubbing my hands in the freezing water, washing my face of all mud-spatter.

Dudley said. 'If it turns out to be a damned Bible...'

Lifting the flaps now, one by one, until it was all opened out.

'It's a notebook,' I said. 'Bound in hide.'

Sat and looked at it, not touching. Nothing was scribed on the front.

Its pages were browned and damp, some stuck together.

'Undamaged, John? Readable?'

I slid the blade between two pages. Saw inked diagrams, scribbled notes.

'Readable... *is* it?'

'Give me a chance...'

Peering closer, I saw that some of it had been slashed out and scarred and ink-spattered, as if in rage. Turned over more pages – there were no more than twenty of them, a few blank.

'Over half of it seems to be filled with fragments of charts. There are some across two pages. And some –' I upended the book – 'to a different scale.'

'But what does it all *show*?'

'I have...' Looked up. 'Absolutely no idea.'

'So the cleverest man in the world...'

'Sometimes it takes months... years.'

'Which, of course, you *have*.'

'Wait...'

The unmistakable word *Tor* had appeared.

Not in the middle of the page, but in its top right-hand corner. And then, further in, *Abbey*.

I gathered more candles, arranging them around the notebook, as if their very symmetry could translate to what was writ in these pages.

'It's a plan of the land around here... some of it, anyway.'

'A treasure chart?'

I shrugged. Gradually, I made out place names: Glastonbury, of course. Also Meare and an arrow pointing to Wells. Hills were marked, and roads and the river and wavy lines to suggest wetland. Across the centre pages a circle was scribed in ink and inside the circle were shapes, some crudely drawn, others more complete. Symbols – a cross, a bell, a small skull. An arrow signifying north.

I sat back and thought about it. Dudley was staring at me, as if waiting for the exposition to begin, the unravelling.

My hands hurt. My brain was cold.

'Drawn by Leland?' Dudley said.

'Looks like his writing. I've several of his manuscripts in my library. And seen many more. Copied them, even, when I was younger and studying the arts of geography and chorography. And we know he was working with Cate Borrow.'

'On a plan of the area? Something to do with his itinerary?'

'It's what he did.'

I turned the pages slowly, twice more. Words were few and all of them place names or topographical features – *hedge, stream, stone, boundary*. And the shapes of things.

'It's incomplete. Something in its early stages. The bones of a chart.'

'Then why would she keep studying it?'

'Maybe she was also still working on it. Maybe she thought he'd return some day.'

'And then he went mad?'

'Overwork. So it's said. The magnitude of the task he'd set himself in charting all England and writing down its topography. He'd vowed to chronicle details of every hill and vale and river in the country… everything that could be marked. Not having realised the size of the task. And the limitations of one lifetime.'

I could sympathise. All the times I'd awoken in the night, panicked by realisation of the brevity of life and the impossibility of learning all that was to be learned. No wonder that Leland, like me, had been drawn toward alchemy and astrology, the hope that we might call down celestial influences to guide us toward some elixir.

'Maybe he was on his way into madness when he did this,' Dudley said. 'Defacing his own charts with drawings for children.'

'What?'

'Animals.'

I looked up at him.

'Are you pissing up my leg?'

'Well, what do *you* see them as? Look.' He leaned over, tracing the shape with a finger. 'There's a hound… and a bird, with tail fanned?'

'Robbie,' I said. 'Just fetch the beer.'

✠

Leland. A driven man. Who knew the magic of charts. Vast areas of land and sea reduced to small shapes upon a page, so that our eyes can see it as if from on high. As above, so below, Leland, like me, having studied Plato, Pythagoras and, beyond them, thrice-great Hermes of ancient Egypt.

A driven man. Driven into insanity.

Dudley went out of the room and padded across the passage to the alehouse, leaving me turning over pages, time and time again, in a quiet frenzy. Tilting the notebook on end, almost scorching the thin paper in the candle flames.

Found a second drawing on which the tor was marked. This time, one flank of it, as if seen from above, was picked out in heavy ink and became part of a far bigger shape which resembled what Dudley had thought to be a bird with tail fanned. Within its shape, the outlines of fields were thinly scribed.

Maybe if I was at home in my library, with all that I possessed of Leland's works, I might make something of this.

Or maybe I'd understand it enough to know that it was of no relevance. The meaningless scribblings of a broken man, blaming himself for all that Cromwell had stolen from Glastonbury.

Dudley set down an ale jug and two mugs – good pewter mugs, I noticed, the first time we'd been given them.

'Might it be clearer, if you tore out all the pages,' Dudley said, 'and put them together? I'm clutching at straws.'

'If he'd wanted that, he'd've done it.' In truth, I hated to destroy a book. 'I need time, Robbie.'

'You don't *have* time.' Dudley drained his mug, then stretched out his arms, yawning. 'Defeats me. I don't think myself an idiot, but it defeats me how a man can stand on the ground and chart the land as if he were a bird flying over it.'

'It's a long and complicated process involving much walking. Robbie... You've been ill. You need rest. Why not go to your bed till dawn?'

He looked down at me, his smile askew.

'That means you want to be on your own with this, doesn't it?'

'Who said I taught you nothing of use?'

I laughed, I suppose a little sadly.

The disappointment over what we'd found must have been etched on my face.

+

When I awoke, two hours later, head on an arm on the boardtop, three tallow candles had burned to a foul mush, and I was sickened at myself. The logs were all red and ashy in the hearth and I thought of Nel in the dungeon in Wells, another day of it before being hauled before a hanging judge and a jury of self-satisfied, pious minnows.

My apparel was stiff with dried mud. With the first light palely aflare in the northeast, I stood up and went out back for a piss. Listening to the chittering of the early birds and Cowdray calling orders to the maids. In the yard, the ass was watching me benignly from the entrance to his stable.

The moon was yet visible and there was a scatter of stars, the remains of my night garden.

My garden.

John Dee... the greatest adventurer of them all... a man of deepest learning and erudition... her Merlin.

What a deluded fool I was. Nothing, going nowhere. Just a failed bone-collector.

XLIV

Harlot

CLEANED UP AS best I could, clad in the spare doublet over an old, tattered shirt, I dragged myself to church. Dudley had not emerged from his chamber, and so I went alone: Dr Dee, specialist in *matters of the hidden*, throwing himself at the mercy of the God whose mind, with unspeakable arrogance, he'd determined to know. Dr Dee, lovesick, bent with sorrow, smirched with sin, in vain hope of absolution.

The morning sky had become very quickly ominous: a fine line of salmon putting a sandy cast upon the long hill before the sun rose but briefly into a mantle of dense cloud which smothered Glastonbury from horizon to horizon.

The beginning of the end of the world, the vicar said. Dear God, what had I expected: calm, fortitude and the sure hope of redemption?

St Benignus, this was, the lesser church. Fyche and Carew, I'd guessed, would be at the more impressive St John's, and I'd no wish to encounter either of them.

The farmers and their families had come down from the hills and the modern church was packed to the doors, me standing at the very back, where it was darkest.

Hell, in truth, all of it was dark. No candles on the altar, and there'd be no communion, nothing approaching the Mass, no enfolding element of the mystic. And, in this plump Welsh vicar, I heard the voice of an Abel Meadows.

'At the end of days, it is foretold that the angels of light and the angels of darkness will engage in a great battle, and the field of that battle is the soul of mankind – your souls, my soul. Within every one of us... *every one of us* – that final battle will be fought. Will you give yourself, body and soul, to God?'

The vicar panting, as he leaned over his pulpit, passing his eyes across all the congregation. I watched men go pale, a woman wring her hands, felt the air go cold with menace.

'Or will you give your soul away? As some already have done, though they knew it not, by putting their faith in charms and talismans. By opening their mouths to receive potions from a witch's cauldron. By... *sucking the syrup of Satan...*'

I pressed myself against the wall in anger, felt that the cultured Abbot Bere, who built this place, would abhor this man.

'Isaiah saeth, *Now is the faithful city become a harlot! It was full of judgment; righteousness lodged in it, but now murderers!*'

The vicar bulging from his pulpit, wagging a flaccid forefinger.

'We have not long, I tell you, to purge ourselves and this once-holy town of all sin, unbelief and *wrong belief...* before that which is foretold at the Bible's end shalt indeed come to pass. And then shalt them – them as repents not – be embraced by a final darkness!'

A skittering of feet on the flags as a woman collapsed into a faint. I marked Matthew Borrow – doubtless here only to avoid a twelve pence fine – squeezing through the congregation to aid her, his face without expression. I felt a profound guilt at what we'd done to his poor, dead wife, and all for nothing. I would avoid him afterwards.

'The voice of God is heard in the thunder!' the vicar roared, bumptious little twat. 'Yeah, God hath split the night with his mighty voice, commanding us to root out and destroy the evil, before the end of days. And we must not turn our backs from what must be done, or the Lord God...'

The finger scribing a steady line from face to face.

'The Lord God will *know*. I say to you, reclaim your souls while there's yet time!'

I was the first out of there.

✝

Monger came to me at the church gate, still clad in his workaday cut-off monk's robe. Coming at once to the guts of it.

'Man's reading from Fyche's gospel. Fyche wants a crowd to see Nel hang, and he wants that crowd hungry for it. Only a death—'

'How can they turn against her? People who've been *healed* by her?'

'People who thought themselves to have been healed by *God*? People who'll now be in terror, having been touched by *Satan*? A witch amongst them all this time, the spawn of another. You can hear them – *Oh, how could we not see what she was? How could we be deceived by her merry manner?* Those who were healed are now in fear that they were healed by the foul touch of the deceiver.'

While, in truth, they were deceived by a man who, to my mind, was barely a priest.

'The woman who collapsed in there?' Monger said. 'You know *why* she fainted? I'll tell you. Treated of a sore throat by Nel and is now convinced her voice has changed, and deepened, as if a demon speaks through her. You see? *Ah…* enough of this shit. The word is that Nel won't see you.'

When I confirmed it, Monger sucked in his lips and led me to the bottom of the street where the green land fell away to the grey and limpid river.

'Makes no clear sense to me, Dr John. I thought that you and she had… common ground.'

'Me, also,' I said. 'Joe…'

He'd turned away. It was beginning to rain.

''Tis happening again,' he said. 'Some perversion of fate. As if she's inherited some curse.'

'Yes.'

'Maybe 'twould help if *I* rode to Wells. But if she'd see neither her father nor you, what hope for a tired old farrier? *Can* you still plead her innocence at the assize without her agreement?'

'Would hardly look well, but I hope to try.'

'Under your own name?'

'There,' I said, 'you have the principal problem.' But there was another now. 'Joe… help me. What was Cate Borrow working on before she was arrested?'

'I don't know, many things. She lived for her work.'

'Like?'

'Long-standing things – she and Matthew were trying for years to find a treatment for wool-sorters', or the cause of it.'

'I'm thinking of something related to topography. She worked with Leland, didn't she, way back?'

Monger began to walk toward the river through the spitting rain, his head half turned – I thought at first to avoid the rain, then realising that the rain was now full in his face. He was turning away from *me*. I caught up with him.

'This is important. There was something Cate Borrow had – or knew – that Fyche wanted. Something she'd been working on with Leland.'

'You should ask Matthew.'

'I've asked him. Leland left her a— some papers. He'd buried them with her because she'd've hated them to fall into Fyche's hands.'

'Sounds like a private matter. I know nothing about it.'

'What would an antiquarian want with a gardener?'

He began to stride toward the riverbank so rapidly that I thought he'd walk off the bank.

'Something to do with charts,' I said.

Monger stopped, inches from the water, staring into it, as if he might see the shadow of Arthur's sword, Excalibur, cast away by Sir Bedivere.

'Leland came after all of us. All who'd been at the abbey and were still in the town. He wanted to know what secret the abbot had failed to disclose under torture that he should be so brutally put to death.'

'And you told him… what?'

'We told him nothing. We knew nothing. The ones who might've known were long gone.'

'Gone where?'

'Everywhere. Some to Bristol, London… France even, the more devout of them. Where they might practise their faith unmolested. However, someone must've told Leland about all the time the abbot spent with Cate.'

'So that was how Leland met Cate?'

'No, they… they'd met before. When he was here to chronicle the antiquities. I believe he'd gone lame in one foot, and she or Matthew attended him. When he returned in forty-five, though, he was a different man. A man possessed. Made a nuisance of himself, I'd guess.'

Can still see his beardless face, all bony like a Roman statue. I remember him shouting, 'You don't understand, I'm my own man now.'

Of a sudden, this made sense to me: Leland seeking to assure Cate that he was no longer working for the Crown, that whatever she told him would go no further.

'When you say possessed…'

'Only that he was in thrall to this town and its peculiarities.'

I remembered what Nel had told me her father had thought: that Leland's first visit was to collect treasure, and his second was *to collect the place itself.* This might simply refer to the notation of its features. Yet knowing of Leland's interest in the hidden…

'This secret that Leland believed the monks kept, *do* you think Cate knew what it was?'

'I can't say. She was certainly closer to the abbot than anyone outside the abbey – and closer than most of us *inside.*' He wiped rain and maybe sweat from his forehead with the sleeve of his dark brown robe. 'I must needs go back, Dr John. I go to my old mother's on a Sunday.'

'Joe… what are you're not telling me?'

'Nothing that can help you. Nothing I *know.*'

He began to walk away, and although I'd known him only a short time I knew this was not like him. I didn't move. After about ten paces, he turned back to me. Hesitated for a moment and then cried out quickly, 'Talk to Joan. Last hovel on the left, top of town, past the alehouse.'

Then turned, stumbling, dragging his cowl over his head and almost running back to the town through the rain, all his old composure gone.

Why?

✠

Joan Tyrre's house might once – and not too long ago – have been a stable or a winter sheepshed, built of mismatched timbers and rubblestone, with two open doorways and chickens pecking around in the straw. Inside, another door was patched with wads of grey wool, probably plucked from hedgerows and brambles. It opened into the place where Joan lived.

'Shillin'?' she said. 'Seein' it be Sunday and I don't work, normal way of it. Howzat zound, Master Lunnonman?'

Bringing down from a niche in the wall above the fire, with some reverance, her skrying crystal. I knew not how a woman of her limited means might have come by it. It was small but of good quality, near as clear as my own. I tried to convey to her that I would not be troubling her for a reading today.

'Sixpence, then?'

'Mistress Tyrre…'

I took from my pocket a new shilling, placing it on the boards which made an old manger into a table. The place was cleaner than I might have expected and the strongest smell was from the iron stewpot hanging over a grizzling fire which fugged the air with smoke.

'*Ahaaaah.*' Joan broke out a toothless smile. Then she was putting down the crystal to unwrap her shawl and loosen the faded garment that covered her bosom. '*This* be what you—'

'*No!* I … I just… I just want to *talk* to you.'

'Talk?'

'Talk.'

Joan settled back into the sheepskins lining her bench. Light came through cracks in the shutters and the smoke-hole 'twixt the rafters.

'You en't easy with a woman, is you? I feels… a real *moylin'* in you. You'ze shook up real bad. *Real* bad. En't that right?'

'Yes.'

''Tis a woman, no doubt 'bout that. A woman in there, sure as I be alive.'

'Mistress Tyrre, I don't know what you've heard…'

Joan pulled her shawl back around her bony shoulders, adjusted her eyepatch, peered at me through the smoke.

'Joe Monger, he d'say you'ze a gonner plead for Nel.'

'I'll do anything that might…'

I swallowed.

'You'ze a good man,' Joan said. 'I feels that. An honest man, if only enough folk knowed it, and a kind, zad face on you. But the *zaddest* thing…' She looked up into the smoke, nodding slightly. 'The zaddest thing of all… they en't *never* gonner know, most of 'em. Now.' She picked up the shilling, sat back in satisfaction, arms folded. 'You ass me what you wants, boy.'

'Tell me about the faerie,' I said, of a sudden.

Not knowing where the question came from. Sometimes there's an instinct of what will open a door.

XLV

Eye

THE FAERIE WERE real. As real as the people in the street. As real as her own family. And closer. She'd heard them since... oh, a long time back, maybe since around her first monthly bleeding.

The voices of the faerie.

I said, 'What kind of voices?'

Joan was hunched like a winter bird on a fence.

'Man's voices, woman's voices. Tellin' me to do things... things as got me in bother with my mam. 'Tis what they does, the faerie, tests you out, look, puts you on your mettle. And round about then it started. I knowed things...'

She leaned forward, a smell of mint around here.

'Things as I shouldn't know. Things what folks done.'

She was enjoying telling of it. It struck me – although I was wrong in this – that nobody had ever asked her these things before. She went and stirred the stew in the pot with a long wooden spoon and tasted some and came back and beamed at me in the meagre firelight, a brown dribble on her chin.

'My mam, her throwed me out!' she said proudly. 'Her said I knowed too much, look.'

'Because you told her things? Things the faerie had told to you?'

'Things I *knowed*.' Joan put her face close to mine, the one eye boring into me until I flinched. 'Only, I *said* it were the faerie. You gettin' me? It was what I learned was best, look. Allus tell 'em 'twas the faerie, then you don't get no blame.'

'But you knew...'

'*Pah*. I was young. I tells *meself* it were the faerie. Made it easier. Only it don't, Master Lunnonman. In the end it surely don't. You put the blame

342

on the faerie, the faerie an't gonner like it… then you're deep in the shitty.'

It had been bad when they took her to the church court in Taunton. All of it thrown at her. What the faerie could do to you if you fell into their thrall. How they could take away your sight. When she confessed all before God and they let her go, folk feared her. Pointing at her in the street. Piles of turds left outside her door. Dead rats.

And the only ones who came to her now were bad folk, who wanted the faerie to harm other folk, exact revenge for some slight. Once or twice, she was so hard up that she took their money. And then whenever folk died and it wasn't obvious why, they were pointing at *her.*

And all this time, the voices were at her, chittering in her head, waking her up in the night… and, just like they'd warned her in the church court, her sight growing dim, and then one eye… the faerie took it.

Joan lifted away the eyepatch. There was only a pit of skwidged and puckered skin.

'Wouldn't give me no rest, look. Screechin' *do it! Do it!* Sendin' me out in the woods to the faerie tump, and there on the top… nice sharp stick, and I done it there and then! *Aaaagh!'*

Joan grasping a bony fist with her other hand, slamming it at the ruined eye.

'Jesu!'

'Hadda get away, Mr Lunnonman. Went in the night with all I could pack into an ole shawl.'

✝

So this was what came before the flight to what Joe Monger had called *the more openly mystical humours of Glastonbury.* A town where friendship with the faerie might win you a welcome in some homes.

Of course, even in Glastonbury, she was still thought a little mad, this bird-boned woman building her rude shelter on the tor. The difference being that these people, who had grown up with divers kinds of madness, at least found her harmless. Notably Cate Borrow, who'd taken her in and then found her work with an old woman of some means, who'd died not long afterwards, leaving Joan a little money, enough to get by for a while without recourse to a misuse of her abilities.

But when it ran out, Joan, encouraged as ever by the voices in her head, had turned again to the faerie. And to the tor, where lived the king of the Faerie. And, having heard at the market about the dust of vision, she'd gone, as Joe Monger had told me, back to Cate Borrow.

'Why else was I come here, look, if not summoned by the Lord Gwyn?'

Joan cackling, then springing up for another taste of her stew. When she sat down again, I made no attempt to hurry her. Oft-times, unusual talents are to be found among those cast out by society. When I was at Cambridge, one of my bolder tutors took me to a hovel in the fens, there to consult with a wild-eyed old man said to be possessed of the ability to summon the spirit of Hereward the Wake and speak with his voice in the old Saxon. The hovel stank to heaven, and the man was clearly deranged in his mind... yet I heard him speak in a younger man's voice and knew enough of Anglo-Saxon to translate his words of glee at ever evading the Normans by becoming near invisible in the marshes.

And so to the tor at All Hallows.

'What happened?' I said softly. 'Can you tell me?'

'Dunno.' Her eye glancing away at a strange angle. 'Dunno.'

I said, 'Joe Monger spoke of me, did he?'

You'ze a good man. I feels that.

'Nothin' happened, Master,' Joan said. 'You gettin' it? Nothin'.'

I tried again.

'The farmer... Moulder? He told the court at Cate's trial that you'd been howling to the moon. Something like that. This was before Cate said she was alone, and Moulder told the court that the others must therefore have been spirits.'

''Twas me and her, was all,' Joan said. 'We never done no howlin'. We was quiet. Quiet as the dead. Her showed me how to sit, look.'

'What about the potion?'

'Potion, Master?'

'The potion of the dust of vision.'

'Never gived it me. You gettin' this?' Joan's eye all over the place now. 'Her never fuckin' gived it me.'

'Then what...?'

'Us sat an' talked, look. Sat an' talked till dawn. Like I en't never talked before and never since.'

'What about?'

'The faerie. The voices. Her says to me the voices wasn't the faerie. Her says the voices was just voices. Her says the Lord Gwyn and his kind wasn't for tellin' nothin' to the likes o' me. Her says if I needed someone to talk to I oughter talk to the Lord Merlin, who dealed with the faerie all his life.'

'What did you think to that?'

'Din't know whadda think. Up there by the ole tower, 'twas real quiet, it being All Hallows. Her showed me how to sit. Her said all the stars was out, but I couldn't see none of 'em. My eye... real bad by then. Only made it to the top holdin' on to Mistress Cate's arm, couldn't even see the path. But we's sittin' there, and her's tellin' me 'bout what the Lord Merlin seen – all the folks and the creatures in the stars.'

'The creatures...? Oh, the constellations.'

'What?'

'Doesn't matter. Go on.'

'Her just talked, and I seen 'em in my head. The ole voices... I could still hear the voices, but they was a long way away. I felt real peaceful, look, and all I remember after that was the dawn a-comin' up, and the mist, look, a big white mist, thick as you like, all round the hill, and when we looks down we can't see nothin' but white, and it's like we're on...'

'An island? The way it used to be.'

I was with her, dear God, I was there.

'But the sky's all bright like gold over us, what I could see of it through the weepin'. Oh, I wept 'an wept, Master Lunnonman. All the tears that come out o' my one eye, 'twas like the Blood Well in full flow. Never wept like that, not even when I was a babby, and Mistress Cate, she got her arms round me, and I'm broke up, broke into bits. And then her says, "Look... look, Joan".'

Joan half risen from her chair, looking down at the fire.

'All the mist was a driftin' away, and her's goin', "See, Joan, see the fishes, see the eagle. *See the stars*".'

'Looking down?'

I felt the building turning about me like a great millwheel, a grinding of the mind.

'And did you? Did you, Joan?'

Joan Tyrre gazed up at the smoke spiralling up the hole in the ceiling.

'No, Master,' she said. 'But I d'zee most everythin' else.'

✛

I could scarce restrain myself from running out, down the street, back to the George, to seize Leland's notebook.

Out of the mouths of mad women and children.

There's a hound... and a bird, with tail fanned?

Yes, and even noblemen. My God!

'Wazzat?' Joan had sprung up again, scuttling across to the door and flinging it open. 'Come out! Come outer there, you evil bazzard!'

I was up and at the door. Benlow stood there in the middle of the outer stable, the chickens flying up, Benlow's hands up to protect his face as Joan threw something at him.

'Spyin' again!' Joan screamed. 'You fuckin' shitlicker. Out!'

Benlow had retreated to the doorway, straw sticking to his green and yellow slashed doublet.

'I been waiting for you to come back to me, my Lord. I can help you, see, I can help you find what you want.'

'He's a lyin' bazzard,' Joan said. 'You don't want nothin' to do with him.'

'I can help you.' Benlow's voice was hoarse. 'I know who you are, and I can help you.'

'Out! Get your sorry arse out of my house!'

There was a wafting in the air, and I saw that Joan Tyrre gripped a rusting sickle. Took another slash at Benlow and he ducked out of the door.

'I mean it, my lord. You come see me.'

When he was gone, Joan turned back to me, in the doorway, the sickle held to her chest.

'You stay away of him, Master. Snitchin' bazzard, he is. Anybody lower in this town than me, then surely 'tis he. Stay away.'

'Yes,' I said, 'I probably will.'

A mistake. Though how could I have known it, all alight as I was then, with vision?

Quelling my excitement for a while, for I'd come here for information.

'Cate Borrow,' I said.

'Gived me my eye back, look.'

I nodded.

'Her and the Lord Merlin. Sees all now, this eye. Him's better'n *two* eyes.' Joan's good eye glittering in the gloom. 'A holy saint, that woman. Gived me my eye back, lost her own life. A holy martyr!'

'And never gave you the dust.'

'No need for it. Had her own magic.'

'What did Matthew Borrow say?'

'The doctor? Her said not to tell him.'

'But he'd know anyway, if he was there. Would he not?'

'Doctor weren't there.'

'But Joe Monger said— did not the three of you go up?'

'Doctor weren't there. Just us two and the Lord Merlin.'

'Mistress Tyrre,' I said. 'What did Nel know of this? Does she know you were not given the dust of vision? Has she known from the beginning?'

'Mistress Cate, her said to tell nobody. So I never did. Not till the storm come, and I knew 'twas all changed.'

'The storm? The storm of last week?'

'Her come to me.'

'Nel... she came?'

Joan Tyrre will take me in. It's no more than a hovel, but better than a dungeon.

I'd thought, the way things had turned out, that she'd gone at once to her father's house, but Joan told me now that she hadn't left here till close to dawn.

'How was she? How was her mood?'

'Mood? Oh, happy. For all they was lookin' for her, her was happy as

I've seen her since her was a young 'un. We sat and we talked for two hour or more...'

'And you told her about the tor.'

'Her said why wasn't I out a trailin' ole Gwyn, and I telled her 'bout Merlin and Mistress Cate.' Joan laughed. 'Her thought when I said Merlin I muster meant the doctor.'

'And did you tell her... about Merlin's secret?'

She looked at me, her head cocked on one side.

'Merlin's treasure,' I said. 'The vision of heaven.'

But she had no understanding of what I meant.

I patted her arm.

'Thank you,' I said. 'Thank you, Joan.'

She beamed.

''Twill come, Master! Never fear.'

'Um...?'

'You be a late starter, but you'll make up for that, look. You'll marry...' She began counting on her fingers. 'Once... twice... *thrice*? Holy Lord, thrice it is! And the third – listen to me now – the third will be *the finest match of all,* and you know some'ing?' She leaned forward, her exposed eye seeming to gather all the light in the place. 'Her en't barely born yetawhile. En't barely born! Fine young flesh! Think on that, Master Lunnonman.'

XLVI

The Vision of Heaven

THE DISTANT SEA was lit the dull metallic grey of a discarded breastplate upon a battlefield, and all the land… was it changed forever?

And me?

I'd not slept for over a day, eaten not even communion bread. And now something was set out before me that I was not sure I could believe. Either I was at the heart of a great delusion or at my life's turning point.

Dudley and I standing atop the tor. I was in no doubt that Fyche could see us, and cared not a toss if he did.

'I see the fishes,' Dudley said. '*Do* I see the fishes? Whereas the eagle… made more sense in the notebook.'

'It's also described as a Phoenix, in some way representing Aquarius the water-carrier. Follow the lines of the hills, how they curve. Not so much the carrier as the vessel.'

He couldn't see it. Neither, in truth, could I, though already it burned in my soul. To know the truth we'd have to be higher, far higher. Flying like…eagles.

I'm flying.

Come, she'd said. *This may be too much too soon.*

The vision of heaven. Glimpsed when I was made of air and walked in my night garden, tending the stars with my hands. In the moments when I felt I almost knew His mind. Had I? Had that happened, or was it a false memory?

'*John?*'

'Mercy,' I said.

There were few men of his status likely to be more receptive than Dudley to this intelligence, yet I wished to heaven that it were *she* who was with me now. She who, on hearing that stormy night what Joan

349

Tyrre had to say, would surely have understood, forged the links. And then, heedless of the dangers, would have gone to her father, slipping through the dawn streets to ask what *he* knew of the great secret… Matthew Borrow, atheist, practical man who, if he knew at all, had thought so little of it that he'd buried it with his wife, considering it more trouble that it was worth. Merlin's secret. Buried.

Not any more.

✛

We sat down on the edge of the tor's small plateau, maybe where Joan Tyrre had sat with Cate Borrow, and I could scarce keep a limb still. If I truly had been a conjurer, then I might have summoned the spirit of mad John Leland to join us. But at least I had his notebook. At least I knew *his* mind.

And so began to talk of Arthur, said by some to be descended from Brutus the Trojan, first King of Britain. Arthur had been Leland's passion. Everywhere he went on his itinerary he'd discover more of his hero's footprints, memorably proclaiming that the earthworks around the hill at Cadbury – not a long ride from here – made it, unquestionably, the site of Arthur's Camelot.

'So we can see why he spent so much time in Somersetshire,' I said, 'and why he returned here after the fall of the abbey. It was all about *Arthur*.'

'Arthur's bones, perchance?'

'Nothing so prosaic. This town stands for the magic side of Arthur. Here's the place to which he was carried by barge, by fey women, either to die or to lie until his country hath need of him. And *this* – where we're sitting – was where lived his magician. Merlin. Who came before Arthur and gave to him, in particular, the round table. Do you begin to see now?'

'In truth,' Dudley said, 'no.'

'Nel Borrow said her mother knew nothing of the Holy Grail but had once said that some of Arthur's round table was still to be found here. Clearly, this must have become part of local legend, because Benlow the bone-man offered to sell me a piece of it.'

I reached into a bare patch of earth and scratched up some soil, holding it out on the palm of my hand.

'In truth, *this* is a piece of it.'

Bringing out the hide-bound notebook, then, opening it up and turning it on end, so that a drawing of what had appeared to be a serpent now looked more like a swan with open beak.

'These are the creatures of the stars... the signs of the Zodiac – Pisces, Aquarius, Libra... I could draw them all in my sleep. Yes, they look different here – the shapes are not as recent astronomers have drawn them. Which is why it took me so long to work it out. These may be much older versions.'

'On the... *ground?*'

'The signs of the Zodiac created upon the land... giant signs, in a circle which appears to be ten miles or more across. Marked out in physical features of the landscape – in the shape of hills and the paths of rivers and roads, fields, hedgerows. This... is the great secret of Glastonbury, passed on by Merlin the Druid, guarded by the monks.'

'But who—?'

'*I* don't know. The ancient people. The old Britons. Maybe the people who were here when Pythagorus was alive. Or earlier... when Hermes Trismegistus walked the earth. The very builders of the landscape... perchance with the help of the cosmos itself—'

'Calm yourself, John, you'll have a seizure.'

'Mercy.' I swallowed, leaning over with hands on knees, could barely breathe. 'A... a *celestial mirror*. The earth here – the holiest earth. Dear God, it's wondrous.'

'If it's right, my friend,' Dudley said. 'If it's *there*. It's just I don't see how they could have done it. If it's not possible for anyone to see it fully, even from the highest ground...'

'You also,' I reminded him, 'found it impossible to see how one man might chart the land, the shapes of hills, the shape of the coastline. The point *is*... if it were possible to stand in one place and see the whole circle, it would be no secret. Its power lies in the *knowledge* of its existence... how it lives in the mind. *As above, so below.*'

Of course, it would not be so obvious now as it might have been in centuries past. Hills would be eroded, rivers grown wider, some dried up.

'But if it would've meant altering the paths made by roads,' Dudley said, 'and maybe changing the direction of rivers and streams… then too many people would have to know the secret, and it wouldn't *be* a secret and we'd all know of it.'

I shook my head.

'Not so. Who owned all this land, or most of it? The abbey. Who decreed how it should be maintained? Who decided where roads might go, how the flat lands might best be drained… The abbot. The farmers and builders would do as the abbot decreed.'

'So you're saying this was the secret Abbot Whiting would not reveal?'

I shrugged.

'*Jesu,*' Dudley said.

'It was also, I'd guess, the secret that drove Leland out of his mind. Did it not bring together the two most important things in this man's life – the charting of the country…?'

'And Arthur.' Dudley came to his feet. 'By the Lord God, John, what have we stumbled upon?'

'We didn't stumble upon it. We had to dig for it.'

I looked down at the notebook, these rough sketches: the design of insanity? For all I knew I was on the same path as Leland, destined for the Bedlam.

'Let's look at this chronologically. We don't know when it was made, but we must assume it was before the time of Christ.'

'So no abbey…'

'Hell, Robbie, it explains the *reason* for the abbey. If this was a wonder of the ancient world, an island of the stars, then surely it justifies the story of the Saviour being brought here as a child. There would've been a college here, where the knowledge was held and passed on by the Druids.'

'Merlin?'

'Merlin indeed, whoever he was. In all probability, a Druid. Someone best qualified to reveal to Arthur, when he came of age, the great celestial secret… in other words, *presenting to him the round table.*'

'But did Arthur come before or after Christ? I mean, in Malory—'

'Malory wrote stories, not history. It matters not a toss which came first, the Zodiac fits either version. Arthur comes to die in the most sacred place in all England, Christ is brought here to learn the mysteries of astrology. Joseph of Arimathea founds the abbey to guard and maintain the great Zodiac.'

'But then the abbey falls...'

'Which is where the darkness comes down. If we assume that the secret of the Zodiac was held only by the abbot and maybe one or two of his most trusted monks... were these the two executed with him?'

'Here.' Dudley glancing over a shoulder. 'Here where we sit.'

I could not but sense the agony of Abbot Whiting. Dragged up here upon a hurdle. Hanged. Cut down when not yet dead to be gutted and quartered. I looked at Dudley, saw the tightening of the muscles of his face, knew he was thinking not only of Whiting but of Martin Lythgoe.

Neither of whom were at peace.

'I think we can assume,' I said, 'that Fyche was not one of the monks trusted with the secret. Yet, having aspirations to become the next abbot, would be close enough to know that there *was* a secret. Which he'd do anything to discover.'

'For himself?'

'For himself.'

☩

Dudley stood looking across the town on the purple-grey edge of evening. You could, at least, see all of that, from the crow-picked skeleton that had been an abbey to the fish hill on whose flank Cate Borrow lay.

'You believe Fyche tortured Whiting?'

'Or had it done.' I arose, went to stand beside him, looking down. 'I'd give anything to prove it.'

'But even if you could... it was more than twenty years ago. Hard times. Atrocities happening daily. And the Papists were worse. I won't shed too many tears over a Papist. And anyway, who'll charge Fyche now? And with what?'

'It wouldn't help his reputation,' I said.

'He'd still be a monk, then, right?'

'So? He's from a moneyed family. Not too difficult to get the ear of Thomas Cromwell.'

'Luring him with this talk of a secret?'

'May not have been necessary,' I said. 'Cromwell only sought evidence of the abbot's treachery. Who better to plant it than a monk at the abbey?'

Thinking back to the night of Nel Borrow, her conviction that Fyche had betrayed his abbot, and then...

It was more than betrayal.

'It seems likely,' I said, 'that Cromwell was satisfied enough with evidence of Whiting concealing a chalice and possessing documents critical of the King.'

'Fyche thinking to learn the greater secret and keep it for himself?'

'Wouldn't you?'

'I'm not sure I'd torture an old monk to get it.'

'He hanged an innocent woman,' I said, 'and he wants to hang another.'

'And Lythgoe? Was Lythgoe...?'

'I think I've said enough.'

The twisting of a knife in a new wound. And if a charge against Fyche were needed...

A few moments of silence. Even the crows had fled the tower. Then Dudley's shoulders relaxed and he turned and gazed over to where the sun, if there'd been one, would be setting.

'Is this the centre of the wheel of stars?'

'No. I've not yet worked that out. But I will.'

'How do you think Leland heard of it?'

'Don't know.' I sighed. 'Unlikely we'll ever know. But he, more than any man of his time, had an eye for the patterns in the land. He travelled constantly. He spoke with divers people – noblemen and yeomen and peasants. He also had access to every book in the abbey's library.'

Awe and stupor, I remembered. Awe and stupor, indeed.

'Both Nel and Monger the farrier attest that Leland approached various monks who'd been at the abbey. According to Monger, the only ones who might've known are long gone from here... but Leland *may* have found one. He moved around.'

But betwixt times he'd been to talk to Cate Borrow, close friend of

Abbot Whiting. Prompting the thought that Whiting, knowing he might otherwise be taking the intelligence of the Zodiac to his grave, had imparted at least some of it to Cate.

It seemed not improbable.

But Cate to Leland? From what I knew of her, she'd never have betrayed the abbot's trust.

'John…'

'Mmm?'

'Someone coming.'

Voices. Laughter.

'If this is Fyche, I've' – Dudley wore no sword, but I saw his hand moving to where it usually hung – 'not yet met the man.'

'Nor should you. Not now.' I looked around for the best way down. 'He'll ask why we're here. We don't want to give him any inkling of what we know. Until we're ready.'

It was clear the voices were coming from the Meadwell side so I motioned Dudley towards the common path. If we continued down that way, we'd be seen, so we must needs cut across the flank of the tor. Best, then, to wait a while, just out of sight of the summit. In the thickening dusk, we crouched on a shelf of turf which once had been part of the tor's maze-like ramparts, and I listened out for Fyche's voice.

Sounds of stress and effort. Men labouring to the top of the tor, hauling something behind them? Put me in fresh mind of Abbot Whiting on his hurdle. No wonder the old man was said to haunt this town still. Should be haunting it forever.

Men were calling to one another as they worked. Shards of it reaching me.

'…there, is it?'

'Bit too… out of… shadow… tower.'

'…be no shadow then.'

'…be seen, mind.'

Footsteps in the turf, coming towards us. Me pressing myself into the slope, head in the grass. Dudley, too, but with obvious reluctance; Lord Dudley bent before no man and only one woman. Looked up, saw a pair of shiny leather boots not five yards away, tried not to breathe.

'Hold it.' The voice on top of me. 'Hold it there!'

When the boots moved away, I risked lifting my head to peer through the longer grass, saw Brother Stephen, Fyche's son.

'Further left,' he shouted. 'I said *left*, you fucking idiot.'

On the flat land in front of the broken tower of St Michael, two men were supporting the two stocks of a wooden gibbet.

XLVII

Little Bear

I FINALLY SLEPT, full-dressed, my head on an arm across the board in my chamber and, at some stage, the dream began again, where I was walking the hills to follow the tolling from distant steeples. But this time my steps transcribed a careful pattern on the land which I knew to be a magical glyph that would open doors to the soul, and when I reached the summit of the tor all the bells were clanging from the empty tower.

But these bells rang in painful discord, so loud that I flung myself on the ground, covering my ears and rolling in the grass with the agony of it. Rolling over and over and coming to rest – coming to *un*rest – in the black, T-shaped shadow of the gibbet and awakening into the birth-tunnel of my darkest dawn, the fleshy stench of tallow, and Robert Dudley in the doorway with a candle on a tray.

'Christ, John, you look like a week-old dog turd.'

Said with pity as he walked over to the window and opened the casement.

'How long have you slept?'

'Five… six?'

Dudley sighed.

'You mean minutes, don't you?'

I shifted, finding Leland's notebook still under my hand, greasy with tallow.

'I meant to get everything from this that anyone could.'

'And if anyone could, it would be you.' Dudley wrinkling his patrician nose at the stink from the dead candles. 'Come on, old friend… Wells?'

The thought of it made this day harder to face than any I'd known. Harder than those long days when I was held at Hampton Court awaiting trial for sorcery. I wondered how Dudley had felt on the morning of his father's trial, knowing how it would end. We'd never discussed it.

'There's bread and cheese on the board downstairs,' Dudley said.

'Couldn't eat.'

Last night, I'd asked Cowdray if there'd been a hanging on the tor in recent years... any hanging.

Not since the abbot, Cowdray had said. All others, including Cate Borrow, had been hanged at Wells. He'd looked at me sorrowfully, saying nothing more. But it was clear that, even though it must have been dark before it was raised, the erection of the gibbet upon the tor had not gone unnoticed.

How *could* I have slept?

'And the horses... are made ready,' Dudley said.

'Yes.'

'You *are* still committed to...?'

'Yes. Dear God, yes.'

I arose, aching, the weight of Wells a cannonball in the gut. Picked up Leland's notebook. All through the night, I'd examined the notes in the smallest detail, drawing my own charts, throwing all my attention into the unravelling of it. Shaking my fuddled head, remembering what now seemed such a mean triumph.

'Um, Robbie...' Pulling hair from my tired eyes. 'For what it's worth, I think I can point you to the bones of Arthur.'

✝

We rode out into mild rain and a silvery sky which roiled like eels in a tub, as if a dark energy were already abroad. Hardly alone on the road this day. Apart from goods carts, there were clusters of horsemen dressed as for a fair. I knew them not. Wool-merchants and minor squires, I guessed, making the assize an excuse for a day in the taverns.

Glastonbury, in the pre-dawn, had been subdued. Waiting for Cowdray's boy to bring out the horses, I'd marked Benlow, crossing from Magdalene Street and about to approach me until he'd seen Dudley and thought better of it. I'd run after him, catching him, seizing him by the shoulders, pushing him against a house wall.

You think you can help me?

Oh I can help you, my lord, count on it…

Benlow giggling, but his voice had been hoarse, and he'd looked not well. Sweating. Maybe he'd been drinking too much, though there was no smell of it. I let him go, backed away to reason with him.

Please… come with us to Wells. Tell the assize how you provided the bones to be scattered on Eleanor Borrow's herb garden.

In court? In front of Sir Edmund? I may be a sick man, my lord, but I'm not a madman. What's the matter with you?

He'd shaken his head and I'd said, *We can protect you.*

My lord, I wouldn't even get out of Wells alive.

Then… you can't help me.

I can tell you where to find more relics of Arthur. I can tell you where to find his bones.

I doubt that, Master Benlow.

I swear to you.

You can swear all you like.

Me turning away, frustrated, and Benlow fading back into his own darkness.

✝

When the other travellers were ahead of us and we were able to ride side by side, Dudley slowed his horse.

'What's your plan?'

I'd thought of little else this past hour, and there was no light in my head.

'Can only see who they produce as witnesses. See how they might be examined. Who, for example, will they have to testify about the bones found in the herb garden? Who, in the absence of Matthew Borrow, will be the doctor who'll describe the injuries inflicted on Martin Lythgoe?'

'If you'd officially been her lawyer you'd know all this,' Dudley said. 'What if she publicly refuses to have you represent her? Have you thought of that? Tells the court she doesn't want you?'

'Conducts her own defence? Not allowed. She can only call witnesses.'

'And if no witnesses are come forward… I mean, even if she does accept you, how could you turn it around? '

'I may know enough now to discredit the lies of the witnesses *they* have.'

'Discredit before whom? For that to work, you'd need a sympathetic judge. An unbiased judge. An unbiased jury.'

'It would help.'

Dudley pulled down his hat.

'I think it was Carew who said, *this is not London.*'

✝

Half a dozen miles to Wells. So *not* like Glastonbury, they said, with its fine and functioning cathedral and its moated bishop's house. It was full light when we at last came in sight of it.

Or as full as it would ever be this drab day. Dudley reined in his horse on the edge of watery ground, maybe half a mile from the city.

'The assize court, according to Carew, is one half of a building overlooking the market place. The other half's apparently a wool store.'

'At least they have their priorities right.'

'Yes. Um… John… assuming we'll have little time or opportunity to talk… I…'

'You want to know about the bones of Arthur.'

'It's why we're here.'

'Yes.'

All flat land here, the colours of mould and enchannelled with dank water. We dismounted at the roadside and I laid upon Dudley the results of three, maybe four hours' work.

'It's about the centre of the earthly Zodiac. You asked last night if it was the tor. I thought it wasn't, and that's true. And then realised the possible significance of finding the centre. Set myself the task of working it out, with the help of the existing charts.'

'And?'

'As far as I can judge, the centre is in or close to the village of Butleigh. Where you… seem to be a popular figure. A wood's been marked on Leland's chart. A skull drawn, looks like.'

'Go on.'

'The centre of the *celestial* Zodiac is the northern star. The axis on which the great wheel turns. A place of considerable cosmic significance. Lying in the star group of Ursa Minor.'

I look up at the sound of hooves. A couple of riders coming towards us, more of them behind. Outriders, it looked like, for a company of horsemen and a cart.

'The Little Bear,' Dudley said.

'Exactly.'

'And?'

The outriders slowing as they marked us. I saw that one of them was the grey-haired fellow with cracked teeth who'd supervised the arrest of Nel Borrow and the battery of her father before holding forth in the alehouse on the subject of hanging. He rode across to us, and I turned quickly back to Dudley.

'What's the Welsh for bear?'

'How would I know that?

'*Arthur*,' I said. 'The Welsh for bear is Arthur.'

'*Jesu.*'

'See?'

'At the centre of his own round table?'

'Maybe.'

'*Holy shit...*'

'Clear the way, you fellows,' the cracked-teeth man said.

Dudley strode out.

'I can't see that we're *in* the way. *Fellow.*'

Cracked-teeth leaned down from his horse as if he would slap Dudley across the face.

'Well, don't *get* in the way.'

I marked the tightening of Dudley's gut, his right arm making that familiar diagonal across his body toward where the hilt of the sword might have been. But cracked-teeth turned his horse away, and we stood at the side of the road as the main body of men drew level. About a dozen of them before, behind and alongside the cart.

On the cart, a broken statue.

In my chest, a feeling like to a collapsing mountain.

The cart kept on moving, and I started towards it, and then a black energy possessed my legs and I was running alongside it, with a fury, through the slanting rain. Arms reaching for me, and I elbowed them away with the pulsing strength of desperation.

Some man demanding, 'Who are you, fellow?'

'A clerk from London.' Cracked-teeth from his horse. 'Thinks himself—'

I howled at the cart, 'Where are you *going?*'

Panting now, as the company increased its pace.

Seeing that she was in chains, with a fat woman beside her. Grey-faced, still as stone. No cloak, hair in draggles. Bare arms. Freckles and goosebumps.

'Stop!'

'For whom?'

'I'm her advocate.'

A rattle of laughter in the rain.

'Bit late now, fellow. We're taking her home.'

For one uncertain moment, I thought there might be hope of her release and then saw the weight of those chains and that the horseman looking down on me was Brother Stephen, son of Fyche. Clad not in monkish robes this day but a wine-coloured doublet, a short cape, a wide-brimmed black hat.

I clutched at the wooden side of the cart, meeting, just for an instant, the widening eyes of Nel Borrow, the only movement I'd seen in her, before my hands were dragged behind my back and a swordpoint was at my throat, just tickling, and Stephen Fyche was dismounting.

'No, no.' Waving the sword away. 'He's but a harmless clerk. You'll frighten him to death.'

I was thrust back, panting, and the cart lurched away, leaving Stephen Fyche standing before me, his eyes without expression.

I said, 'I don't understand. The trial can't be over.'

'What trial?'

A thin face made more vulpine by a new beard, and his eyes and voice were lazy with power. He was all of eighteen years old.

'Obviously, I'm aware, Dr John, that you have a certain interest in this woman, in relation to the ailment of your colleague. But I see he's fully recovered now. For which I'm sure you're grateful.'

I said nothing.

'There's no issue to be made of this,' he said. 'The woman decided yesterday to save us all the inconvenience of a trial and made a confession. Appeared before the judge for sentence at first light.'

Stephen Fyche cast a glance at the cart rumbling away behind him.

'As you can imagine, it took not long.'

XLVIII

Black Hearts

My laughter, if laughter it was, must have sounded half crazed. Half in this world, half in purgatory, that same purgatory the Protestant reformers told us no longer existed. They could rearrange the structure of the universe on a whim, the reformers, demolish a cathedral at a stroke.

Back at the George, a letter had awaited me, evidently from Blanche Parry, and I'd torn it open at once, in front of Dudley and Cowdray, in the alehouse.

It began, *Anwyl Sion…*

The look on my face making Dudley sigh.

'What's wrong now?'

Pushed the letter in his face. My father, as you know, was Welsh to the bone; far more useful, he'd say, *far* more useful, boy, the Welsh tongue, than Latin or Greek, with all the living people speaking it, that wealth of oral, bardic tradition…

'You mean you don't speak this language?' Dudley said.

'Blanche evidently assumes I do.'

Anwyl Sion. My dear John. I knew that much.

'God's bollocks, John, there must be someone here who reads it.'

'Like the bastard vicar at St Benignus?' I might have screamed it. 'Not exactly a man who I'd have know the content. Which I'd guess to be of singular significance, else why send it in this… old British cipher?' I turned on Cowdray – could we trust him? I hardly cared. 'Is there anyone here who speaks Welsh and is not shackled to Fyche?'

'I'll think on it,' Cowdray said.

'Think not too long, Master Cowdray.'

Shutting my eyes, flinging back my head, squeezing my fists. When I straightened, Cowdray was staring bleakly at me, his eyes tired, his skin the colour of lead. God knows how I looked to him.

'I should tell you,' Cowdray said hesitantly, 'what they were saying here last night. Fyche's hirelings. About a… hanging.'

'I'm assuming they don't plan to delay it,' Dudley said.

'Next dawn.'

Choked on my own breath.

'Not leaving much time for the royal pardon,' Dudley said sourly.

Bent over, coughing, I struggled to think what time it was now, how much we had left, Dudley not looking at me as I struggled for some semblance of emotional restraint.

'Town's divided,' Cowdray said. 'Times of crisis, there'd always be leadership from the abbey. Taken as the word of God without a thought. But now the vicars…'

Looking worriedly at Dudley, doubtless the most confirmed Protestant in the room.

'Go on, man,' Dudley said.

'All the people cured by Nel, her father, mother. Now they're told she stands for all that needs purging. Two minds, Master Roberts, is the answer. The one thing that's sure is they en't gonner band together and raid the Meadwell. Word is there's more weaponry in there than the royal armoury.'

'I can't believe,' Dudley said, 'that they intend an execution on the tor, rather than with… discretion.'

'*Jesu!*' I cried. 'She's to be an *example.* Just as Whiting's killing was for the papists. An example to all who dare to think outside of the Bible, whichever version of it's favoured these days, and *we*… we have the rest of a day and one night to get it stopped.'

'Only Carew can get it stopped, John. Well, not stopped, but maybe he can have it delayed long enough for us to organise intervention… at a higher level. If he feels moved to it.'

'But Carew—'

Cowdray was glancing beyond my shoulder; I turned and saw Monger was at the doorway, nodded, bidding him enter.

'—Carew knows the trial was a travesty.'

'Of course he does, but where witches are concerned he'll accept rude justice. It's the seaman in him. Hang them from the high mast, throw them in the sea. To sway him at all, we must needs challenge the very foundation of it. If... *if*... we can show who really killed Martin Lythgoe, then that...'

'And tortured him,' I said. 'Forget not *that*.'

'You think I fucking *could*? You think I'm *ever* going to forget that?'

Dudley's eyes were inflamed, the humour in this place choleric and inside me lay the cold black bile of autumn.

'In the first instance,' I said, 'if Carew can be shown, beyond doubt that the bones were planted in the herb garden...'

'Beat the truth out of this bloody bone-man, you think?'

Monger cleared his throat. Dudley looked at him.

'The bone-man's sick,' Monger said.

'How sick?'

'Maybe mortally.'

'Spit it out.'

'We think wool-sorters.'

Cowdray drew breath. Monger shrugged.

'Truly, there's not much doubt. Matthew's seen him. He has the lumps with the black hearts.'

'God-damned fleeces, this is,' Cowdray said. 'Likely some farmer sold him some cheap skins from a flock rotten with it. You'd think he'd know better by now. Hell, we don't want that in town again.'

'Anyway, if you want to speak with him,' Monger said, 'I'd not delay. Just keep your distance.'

There was a silence. Benlow had looked unwell this morning, and I'd thought it was the drink.

'I'll go,' I said. 'He wanted to talk to me earlier. Said he could point me to the location of the bones of Arthur. Which I thought was a try-on, not least because—'

I looked at Dudley, who opened out a hand to convey that it was a little late for circumspection. I turned to Monger.

'We have reason to think Arthur's bones could be reburied at Butleigh. A wood? Near a church?'

'There *is* a wood near Butleigh church,' Monger said. 'But 'tis not an old wood.'

'Wouldn't need to be. We're only talking twenty or so years ago, if the bones were removed before Whiting's arrest. Maybe they planted the wood around the grave?'

'Can you help with this, Farrier?' Dudley asked.

'No, but I know people in Butleigh who might, if they thought there was good reason. 'Tis not a big place.'

'You could persuade them? Come with us?'

'Us?' I said.

'If they're there, we should find them quickly,' Dudley said. 'Deal with this now, I say. Waste no more time. For tomorrow…'

He looked at me and then looked away, as if far from certain that tomorrow I would not do something foolish enough to render our mission an abort.

'Let's have a dozen men,' he said to Cowdray. 'Don't bother Carew with this. I'll see him later.'

A dozen? I stared at him and then at Cowdray. Cowdray nodded.

'Oh, for God's sake, John…' Dudley slumping down into a chair, looking pained. 'You don't think I'd bring us here without shielding our spines?'

'*What?*'

'Why do you think Carew displays such antagonism? Because he resents having to spare so many trained soldiers, working under cover to guard the arses of men he—' Dudley blew out his cheeks. 'Well, me he merely dislikes, it's you he despises.'

'How many?'

'Men? I don't know. Twenty at the most. I mean… not an *army*.'

Whatever had made me think this man and I inhabited the same world?

'Let me get this right… You're saying there's been armed men watching our backs since we arrived?' Whirling on Cowdray. '*You* knew of this?'

'The guard… it got doubled after your man's murder,' Cowdray said. 'Even Sir Peter was alarmed. Hadn't expected that.'

'But he was expecting trouble?'

'He didn't know,' Dudley said. 'None of us knew. A few men had come here ahead of us, orders of Cecil. It appears I am, after all... considered of some value to England. And maybe even you, in your peculiar way.'

'Half a dozen sleeping in my cellars,' Cowdray said. 'Come out to watch the entrances at night. Nobody noticed the extra, with all the lowlife in town for the hue and cry.'

'And, um, when Carew went to Exeter,' Dudley said, 'in fact he went no further than Wells. Now you know.'

'Good of you.'

'John, *look*... if ever a man spends his days looking over his shoulder, it's you. You must know how you are.'

'Unstable in my mind?'

'It was simply considered unwise to... trouble you with this.'

'*Who* considered it unwise? You? Carew? Cecil? You going to tell me *Fyche* knows?'

'Fyche knows *nothing* of this,' Dudley snapped. 'You see? There you go again. *That's* why you weren't told. Would you have dug up a grave knowing you were being watched? Not that we—' Dudley raising both hands. 'No more than two of them, on that occasion. Instructed to come no closer than the bottom of the hill. They were *not* to see what we were doing.'

For me, the humiliation was as solid as an another person in this cider-stinking cell. I thought to leave. Then, at the door, recalled what Dudley had said that afternoon in his barge on the Thames, turned and threw it in his face.

'*A rare freedom to move around as a common man, unencumbered by the trappings of high office...?*'

'Figure of speech,' Dudley said. 'You're right. You're my friend, and I should've told you. Blame the fever.'

'Go and look for your damned bones.'

Turning away, walking out of the alehouse, into the grey afternoon. Still hadn't eaten, but there was no time. At least I'd fulfilled my purpose, decoding Leland's notebook. If Arthur's bones lay not at Butleigh then the monks of Glastonbury had not the wit I'd credited to them.

At least I was free now to apply what remained of my energies to that which was most important to me. The rain had stopped and, though the sky was cold, the day was unseasonably warm.

Wild lights were blazing in my head as I walked down the high street.

Half in purgatory, half in the Bedlam.

PART FIVE

'Oh Glastonbury, Glastonbury... the Threasory of the carcasses of so famous and so many rare persons... how Lamentable is thy case now?'

John Dee.

XLIX

His Diversion

CANDLES EVERYWHERE.

A cathedral's worth of candles albaze in Benlow's ossuary. Cheap tallow candles, fine beeswax candles, many of them hot-waxed to the craniums of the anonymous dead who posed as kings and saints.

'Burning them all,' Benlow said. 'Go out in light.'

The whole cellar was flickering white-gold. Somewhere, a forbidden incense burned, and the air was all sickly-sweet as if the bones themselves, as was sometimes said of saintly relics, were become fragrant.

'I wanted you to take me to London,' Benlow said. 'I was going to ask you. Before you set that old bitch on me.'

Sitting on his bench in a fine gold-hued doublet and his soft velvet hat. Cradling what he said was the skull of King Edgar, the good Saxon. Light and shadows shivering all around him, and it was as if we were taken into the astral sphere where nothing was solid.

'How could I trust you,' I said. 'Knowing that your trade was founded on lies.'

'No lies no more, my lord. Silence, maybe, but no lies.'

'Silence helps no-one.'

'No-one helps me.'

'Do some good.'

'What is good?' He leaned out from the bench. 'You tell me what is good. You can't! No-one knows no more! To which God do I commend my soul? Do I cry to His mother? Am I allowed? Is He allowed a mother?'

Benlow began to laugh, and it turned to coughing. He covered his mouth and then looked down at his hand.

'How soon before the blood comes?' He moved to the end of the bench. 'Sit with me. Are you afraid? Afraid I'll give you the black lumps?'

Tentatively, I crossed the cellar, a brittle bone ground to fragments under my boot. Sat down at the opposite end of the bench. Even so, straining to hear what Benlow said next, for it was said in not much above a whisper, borne on poor breath.

'Who are you?'

'I'm John Dee.'

He sighed.

'The royal conjurer.'

'The royal astrologer and consultant.'

'Conjurer. Admit it.'

'No. It would be a lie.'

'It's all lies. All life's a lie. Tell me – which God's a lie? Or are *they* all lies? Even no God's a lie. Everybody lies in this town. *You're* a wise man. Tell me that. Tell me that and I'll tell *you* something. Bargain. Folks bargains with me all the time.'

'Oh, there *is* a truth,' I said. 'At the core of it, Master Benlow, there's a truth.'

'How do you know?'

'Because I'm a mathematician and I can see the geometry of it. I can chart the geometry of heaven and earth.'

'Good, good… good so far. You're a clever man. No more clever man in the whole of Europe, I've heard.'

'That's a lie also. But… clever enough.' I felt a sweat in my hands. 'Your turn, Master Benlow.'

'I do resurrect the dead,' he said. 'To order.'

'Tell me something I *don't* know.'

'What do you know?'

'I know you provided the bones to be buried in the herb garden. I know that you dug up certain graves at the Church of St Benignus. As you say, to order.'

'Good so far.'

'I know that you perform these tasks for Sir Edmund Fyche and, in return, he's permitted you to continue your business. Undisturbed.'

Benlow leaned back, his breath a thin wheezing. He brought out a small bottle, resting it on King Edgar's cranium.

'Dr Borrow give me this.'

'For your… illness?'

'Can't be cured. He says this will give me sleep when I need sleep.'

'You'll rest easier,' I said, 'with a clear conscience.'

'So they say. What's all this to you, Dr Dee?'

'Dr Borrow's daughter's to be hanged. For no good reason.'

He turned his face to me. It was creamed with sweat.

'Like her, do you, my lord?'

'Yes.'

'She never judged me. I'll say that for her.' He closed his eyes. 'Tell me something else.'

'You've told me nothing yet. Not much of a bargain.'

'Your servant… he was a fine, big man.'

'And a good man.'

'I followed him.' Benlow said. 'I follow people a lot. Especially men. I had nothing better to do, and following a fine big man…'

'When was this?'

'He was following *you* at the time. When you walked off with the fair Eleanor, up to the tor and the Blood Well, he followed you, and I followed him.'

'Thinking you might learn something. Something you could pass on to Fyche.'

'The business of relics is not what it was.'

'Where did he go?'

'What a funny voice he had. Could hardly understand a word.'

'You heard him talking? Where was that?'

'By the Blood Well. Are you *testing* me, Dr Dee? You sent him away, to find Joe Monger. Only he never went where he was bid. He kept on following you, keeping back a good way behind when you went up the tor, the two of you. I stayed even further back, for all's visible from the tor. But I saw you talking to Fyche, and the old monk was there and Fyche's cruel son, and when you left, your man followed *them*.'

'He followed Fyche?'

'All the way back to Meadwell. He went over the wall to have a look and came back through the gate, two of them twisting his arm behind his back.'

'Who?'

'Two of the retainers. One of them had a hammer, I think they'd been putting a fence up. I kept my distance. I don't go there. Then Stephen Fyche comes back – and he… Tell me' – Benlow slapped his hands on the sides of the skull – '*secrets.*'

I started to tell him how I'd made the owls which seemed to fly, but that seemed not to satisfy him, probably because it could be explained by mechanics, so I talked about the spheres, the earthly, the celestial and the supercelestial, and he looked at me, his eyes filling up.

'Where will *I* go when I die?'

'Where would you wish to go?'

'Nowhere,' he said. 'I'd wish to live on here. Free of the body and all its sickness.' He lifted the skull. 'An empty vessel, see? Is the skull not like a cup, from which the liquid of life has been poured out?'

'Maybe. Liquid… evaporates. Goes to air.'

'Yes.'

A silence, then he told me.

'Stephen Fyche… is a cruel boy. Likes to cause hurt. He had three men with him. They took your big fellow into the wood. Couldn't hear too well, but they knew who he was and how he'd come here with you. They were demanding he should tell them who you were and what your business was here. He refused, of course. Not knowing whom he refused. For a long time, he refused. Too long. I'd've told them what they wanted without a thought. But then I know what Stephen Fyche is like. What he did to animals in the fields as a boy. Horses. For his diversion.'

Benlow said that once they'd starting trying to make Lythgoe talk, they wouldn't stop till he did. It went too far. Too far, too quick.

'Stephen was in a frenzy. *Do this to him, let's try this… move away, I'll do it.* By the time he'd given them your name, he was so cut about, *real cut about* – I couldn't stand to watch no more. And Master Stephen said it was best to finish him. I didn't stay for that, but his screams, before they were stifled, were pitiful.'

'How close were you?'

'Hidden in some brambles, which was torture enough for me. Yet I can be still for long periods. Still as the dead.' He smiled. 'I'm real tidy, my lord. I can dig up a grave and put it all back and no-one knows I've been. Except when they want me to, like Big Jamey Hawkes.'

I remembered Big Jamey Hawkes.

'By the church of St Benignus? Benlow... How can I persuade you to tell all of this to Sir Peter Carew? What they did to Lythgoe. What happened to the bones of Jamey Hawkes.'

He tried to laugh. It would not come, He clutched at his throat, distressed.

'You're ill,' I said.

'So quick... In full health, not a week ago I was in full health. God help me...'

'Come with me.'

'That man's a pig.'

'Do you want to see Nel Borrow hang?'

'I won't see it.'

He leaned forward, and some small breath came into him, strained through the wheezing.

He put a hand on my knee. I tried not to cringe away.

'Never thought I'd meet a man as famous as you, my lord. I would've asked you to take me to London. That's what I planned. A bargain. Would've told you anything if you'd take me to London.'

'You could have gone to London anytime.'

'But not with... with *introductions*. You don't just *go to London*. You go as *someone*. Or you go *with* someone. Too late now.' He peered at me, closer, as if I were going faint in his sight. 'Will I see King Edgar when I die? If I die holding him, will he be waiting for me?'

He'd seem to have forgotten this was not King Edgar, that none of the bones were likely to be the remains of anyone of note.

'In the celestial sphere,' I told him, 'all is... possible.'

'Do you truly believe that? Do you know these things, with all your science and your magic?'

'Some believe,' I said, 'that living here helps. I didn't quite see how that were possible, but… today I've seen evidence that this place is blessed by the heavens like no other. But you know this. When I was here before, you said death came easier here.'

Where the fabric between the spheres is finer than muslin. The most memorable thing he'd said.

'Do you know why this is?' I said. 'I can tell you.'

And told him – why not? Time was running away from me – the secret which the monks had guarded and John Leland had tried to chart. Bringing the notebook from out of my doublet. Showing him the drawings. Explaining about the Zodiac. The mirror of heaven.

'Ah.' Benlow smiled at me. 'So that's what it is. Where did you find this, my lord?'

'I can't tell you.'

'Where did you *unearth* it?'

His fingernails clawing my hose as I sprang up, my head bumping painfully against the boarded ceiling, and I could see the lumps now, on his neck. The lumps all black at the centre of them.

'Someone had to bury it,' Benlow said. 'Pity they wouldn't let me take the bones. I could've cleaned her up real nice. Made her look pretty again.'

Within minutes, I was out of that temple of death and running back to the George as though pursued by all the demons of hell.

L

Emanation

Found Cowdray in the dimness of the panelled room, replacing burned-out stubs with new candles.

'Where's Monger?'

'Gone with Master Roberts. To Butleigh. I thought you knew.'

'Of course I did.' Sinking into a chair, head in my hands. '*Shit.*'

Cowdray put down the candles.

'Let me get you some meat, Dr John.'

'No.... no time. But some small beer...?'

'Look, I should say...' Cowdray brushed at his apron. 'I didn't realise there were things you hadn't been told... by Carew and your friend. I'm not a man who... That is, I must needs keep these walls from falling down, you know?'

'Cowdray, I'm not blaming you for my friend's deceit. The money you'd make for accommodating Carew's men, that was hardly to be turned down. It's just... there's something wrong here. Something very wrong.'

Wanting to tell him what Stephen Fyche had done to Lythgoe. Wanting to cry it in the streets.

'Dr John...'

Cowdray's gaze was in the gloom behind me. I turned quickly.

The woman sitting in the most shadowed corner, to the left of the window, had long, silver hair, uncoifed, unbound. I'd never seen her before. In front of her on the board were pen and ink and paper.

'Mistress Cadwaladr,' Cowdray said. 'A speaker of Welsh.'

I inclined my head to her. Yet cautious.

'My brother was a monk at the abbey of Strata Florida,' Mistress Cadwaladr said. 'I came here with him some years ago, and stayed. I was a cook at the abbey.'

'After which,' Cowdray said, 'she worked with Cate Borrow in her herb garden. If that helps.'

If ever a man spends his days looking over his shoulder, it's you. You must know how you are.

'Thank you,' I whispered. 'Thank you, Cowdray.'

✠

My dear John

I am writing in our own tongue in case this letter should be intercepted, which I fear it might. I am aware that you do not speak the Cymraeg, but I think you might be able to read it.

I believe the prophecies to have been conveyed to our sister through the good offices of her correspondent in France. The source would seem to be the French family's own consultant. I know not the circumstances of this, except that they appear to have been secretly obtained.

Here is the latest prophecy in full. The translation from French to English to Welsh will not, I hope, present too much fuddle in the meaning of it.

Our sister is no better.

I looked up.

'I'm sorry all's not well with your family,' Mistress Cadwaladr said. 'But what I've read, I shall forget.'

'Thank you.'

I stared at the translation.

Two names had at once presented themselves.

Her correspondent in France: Sir Nicholas Thockmorton, the Queen's ambassador. I'd met him once, only briefly, but knew he'd been close to the Dudley family. That he came from an old Catholic family, yet was now unquestionably Protestant. Knew also that he was considered a trusted adviser to the Queen and would keep her well informed about plans by the power-hungry Guise family to ensure that the daughter of Mary of Guise, the Queen of Scots, now Queen of France, would also one day be Queen of England.

As for *the French family's own consultant,* this could only be Nostradamus. Christ above, I could scarce believe it.

Michele de Nostradame. This man had thrown a long and faintly sinister shadow over my career from the start. Some twenty-five years older than I, beloved by the French court and held in reverence over half Europe... for doing what I would *not* do. I'd never met him, nor sought to. If pressed, I'd say I was suspicious of his prophecies, so pretentiously laid out in four lines of verse... whilst wondering privately if the bastard possessed some faculty with which I'd not been endowed.

He was known to be an astrologer but, if these prophecies were drawn from the heavens, then oft-times he and I saw different stars.

I read the verse, as neatly transcribed by Mistress Cadwaladr.

> *In the land of the great religious divide*
> *The dead witch shall haunt her daughter*
> *Till she shall kiss the bones of the King of all Britons*
> *And have them entombed again in glory*

Explicit. *The dead witch,* not Morgan le Fay.

What was the sequence here? When had the forecast been received? Had the Queen believed herself haunted before or after its receipt? Either way, Nostradamus, if it *was* he, would know precisely what he was doing, the alleged bond of witchcraft between the Queen and her late mother having long been common gossip in France.

Was it, then, an invented prophecy designed to unbalance the Queen in her mind? How much of this was going on? *Think...* the waxen effigy, all talk of which Walsingham had suppressed before it could reach court... the pamphlet prediction of the Queen's death which had somehow found its way through the security. How organised was it, this mixture of sorcery and Machiavellian mind-play?

And why had the Queen not been advised of what appeared to be a subtle, many-pronged assault on her senses, the higher mind and the lower mind, in wakefulness and sleep?

Unless she was given *false* advice, whether knowingly or in ignorance.

Did the answer to this lie in the line, *they appear to have been secretly obtained?*

Obviously, we had spies in France at all levels of society. Had one of them got his hands on unpublished Nostradamus quatrains relating to the Queen of England? If this verse, for example, had been received *as intelligence*, then its credibility would obviously be enhanced.

The Queen was superstitious, and there was no denying the eminence of Nostradamus, the respect afforded to him in France. I'd heard him credited many times with that terrifying prophecy of the killing of King Henri in the jousting, even though it came out of Italy. If Nostradamus said there was a bad air, people in France stayed indoors, farmers delayed the harvest. Our own archbishop, Parker, was once said – though he'd denied it – to have been deterred from accepting the Canterbury post by a prophecy of Nostradamus.

And the man's published predictions relating to the Queen had been so full of spleen as to be considered French Catholic filth. *Never in the kingdom has arrived one so bad,* he'd written when her path to the throne had been clear. Making reference also to her *poor parentage.* Anne.

Intelligence from France would be passed to the Queen in person by Sir Nicholas Throckmorton. Did Cecil know of this?

'You look perturbed, Dr John,' Mistress Cadwaladr said. 'And, if I may say so, very tired.'

Cowdray had left us alone, with a jug of small beer.

'I'm well,' I said.

No use in further conjecture. This should be discussed with Dudley, who knew Throckmorton far better than I did.

'Master Cowdray,' Mistress Cadwaladr said, 'in asking for my help… told me you'd become quite intimate with Eleanor.'

I looked up, startled. This was, it must be said, a woman of mature beauty, and the level of translation had said much for her intellect.

'We'd known one another only days,' I said. 'But there was… much we had in common. I was intent on becoming her advocate at the assize. Distressed when she wouldn't see me.'

'I also find that hard to accept. Do you think you were lied to?'

'It occurred to me. But… no. I think she was in some way persuaded to…'

'Confess? How could she be *persuaded* to confess away her life?'

'I don't know.'

Mistress Cadwaladr placed her hands together, palm to palm, touching her fingers to her lips.

'Anything relating to witchery seems yet to be outside all normal rules. Her mother's confession was the same. I worked with Cate in her garden. I'd grown herbs for the abbey kitchens, and later we'd both studied the works of St Hildegard of Bingen, regarding the curative properties of plants.'

'Does that mean you were her first link with the abbey?'

'In a way. Before her marriage, she worked alongside me there, as a kitchen maid. But when, much later, she became the abbot's friend, I was never party to their discussions.'

'I wish I'd known of you earlier,' I said.

'Oh….' She looked not comfortable. 'It's some years since I left the garden. Not everyone would remember.'

Disappointing. I'd been about to ask her if she knew what Cate Borrow had been engaged in before her arrest. I can only think my next question came out of an instinct.

'Mistress Cadwaladr, why did you stop working with her? If that's not an intrusive question.'

'It's something I'd normally consider *quite* intrusive. I've never spoken of it. I'm a private person and would not, in usual circumstances, even have come here today. But then… these circumstances are far from normal, aren't they?'

Kissing her fingertips again, as if this helped her reach a decision. I heard the clatter of hooves outide the window.

She said, 'Dr Matthew Borrow… is a good doctor. Studied at the famous Montpellier College. A great finesse in bone-setting, extraction of teeth. Able to conduct clever surgery to drain fluids from the brain, remove stones from the bladder. His hands… so deft and sensitive. Skills of a kind seldom – or so I'm told – found even in London. Glastonbury has been fortunate to keep him.'

'He can't have made much money here.'

'No. I...' She closed her eyes for a moment, bit her lip. 'Friendship with Cate led me to assist Matthew in his work. Which, after a time, became... difficult. He has a strong... presence. A powerfully attractive emanation.'

'Oh.'

I'm not sure what explanation I might have been expecting, but it hadn't been this.

'I had a respect for Cate,' she said, 'and she was devoted to Matthew and all that he'd done for her. I didn't want to... It became that I could not be near him.'

'And did *he*...?'

'No. He is a good man. A man of steadfast purpose. A Godly man.'

'But—'

'So I went back to Wales, to my brother's house. Only returning last year, after his death. That was when I learned what had happened to Cate. What she'd become, that was tragic.'

There was a silence. I heard the inn doors opening and voices in the passage.

'What are you saying, Mistress?'

'The herbs she used to grow were good herbs. I can only think she'd been mixing with the wrong folk, and it all went bad. He must have been sorely disappointed in her.'

'Matthew Borrow?'

She looked, for a moment, shocked at what Pandora's Box she might have opened. Yet, in my fatigue, I could not see what was in it.

'And now her daughter gone the same way... I should have seen it in her. She became my physician when I returned, and I thought she displayed the best qualities of her father. Not realising...'

'You've.... seen Matthew since your return? I mean—'

'Most certainly not. Please.' She stood up. 'Forgive me. I'm glad I was able to assist with your translation.'

The fatigue in me put subtlety beyond reach.

'You think Cate—? You're saying you believe both of them truly were *witches?*'

'I…. know not quite what I'm saying. And, indeed, would not be saying it at all if Eleanor were not facing the same fate. I can't help thinking it beyond a coincidence. I beg mercy. Must go.'

I should have persisted. Should not have let her leave so easily. Should have insisted on asking her more, but I'd heard Joe Monger's voice in the passageway and was impatient to hear the news from Butleigh.

'Thank you,' I said. 'Thank you for your help.'

I held open the door was for her – yet a small and slender woman, not made shapeless by childbearing.

'Yes, indeed,' Monger was saying outside. 'Master Roberts found exactly what we were looking for.'

LI

Reward

THE TASK HAD not, it seemed, presented any great difficulty. Not with Lord Dudley in his finery and a posse of armed men. And, in the background, Monger, the farrier, who was known and trusted by the vicar, the blacksmith, the miller.

One wood which was spreading so that the circle of oak trees was no longer at its centre. Oh, yes, it had been known there was a grave here, a burial by night many years ago, and no-one talked of it and no-one went near for fear of ghosts.

'Thick with brambles,' Monger said, 'except for one bare patch.'

'Where nothing will grow,' I said. 'I've heard of such places. Oft-times it's the grave of a murderer, as if the ground itself were poisoned.'

'Lord Dudley set the men to dig,' Monger said. 'First, about four feet down, a stone cross was unearthed. A fine thing – a crucifix, bearing a figure of Christ. Old but not *that* old. As if it were from a church. And then, a couple more feet down… not a full length casket, more like a household chest.'

Monger had suggested it should be brought back to Glastonbury, but Dudley had thought for a few moments and then said no, it should be broken open in case it was not what it seemed.

'In truth,' Monger said, 'I think it *was* a household chest, rudimentary and not very old.'

As there'd been some superstition among the men, Dudley himself had prised it open up with a spade. There, inside, was a far more ornate container of oak, with a glass top.

'A leaded window, in effect,' Monger said. 'With six square panes. Through which we could see the bones. It was, in its way, a very solemn moment.'

They'd found lettering indented in the oak. A simple legend:

Rex Arturus.

Legend, indeed. Some of the men had been sorely afraid, one even instinctively crossing himself in the old way, trying at once to hide the gesture.

'So you didn't try to open the inner box?' I said.

'Why would we? As Lord Dudley said, and I was inclined to agree, the opening should be done with full ceremony, before a high altar. Relics last entombed before Edward I, he said, should not be exposed to the air of another time except before its monarch.'

Even though all my instincts had said this was where Arthur's bones would be found, it was yet strange to think it had all happened so quickly, as if destiny were at work.

Would have been strange. And glorious and mystical. Had I not known what I knew.

Monger opened out hands still browned with earth.

'Lord Dudley said we should give thanks to God for this and at once fell upon his knees, and the rest of us followed. Then he bade me say some suitable prayer. Which I did. And we then we knelt in silence for two minutes or more before Lord Dudley arose and commanded that the box be placed upon the cart.'

Dudley taking off his own cloak to cover the box. Then more prayers had been said before it was driven into the village.

What had happened then was that the cart, with the bones upon it, had been driven to the church where, to pre-empt gossip, an announcement was made that the remains of King Arthur had this day been discovered by Lord Dudley, the Queen's Master of the Horse, and were to be taken at once to London. Riders then being dispatched to the sheriff at Bristol to arrange for a company of men to ride out to join them.

'No undue ceremony, then,' I said.

Monger looked at me and smiled.

'Such a pity that you aren't with Lord Dudley, to share the glory of such a famous discovery. It being, after all, the result of your scholarship.'

'Lord Dudley said that?'

'He said you'd understand.'

'Oh yes. Perfectly.'

A man who brings to his Queen such an irrefutable symbol of her royal heritage... something which bestows upon her monarchy's most mystical aura. That man... he may expect his reward.

'Scholarship is its own reward,' I said. 'Um... Joe. Before the box was covered over, did you get a good look into it? Did you see the bones... clearly?'

'Well enough. The box was, I suppose, more like a reliquary than a coffin and, having been boarded up inside the chest, was largely free of dust. The glass was a little milked but, on the whole, it could not have been better for its purpose.'

'Large bones? Is it possible to say?'

'Certainly, the leg bones were of such a size that some were laid diagonally. The skull placed at the centre.'

'Large skull.'

'I'd say so.'

'Any marks upon it?'

'Damaged, certainly. Several dents, and a clear hole in the cranium, as if made by a heavy blow from a sword or mace.'

Thus matching the description set down by Giraldus Cambrensis all those years ago, and committed by me to memory for just such an eventuality.

...in the skull there were ten or more wounds which had all healed into scars, with the exception of one which had made a great cleft...

'Arthur, then,' I said. 'Or, at least, the Arthur the monks claimed to have uncovered back in the twelfth century?'

'Brown with age, certainly,' Monger said. 'But, truly, how could it ever be proved? It must have been quite hastily done by my brother monks, but accomplished with all reverence, the bones placed on...'

He looked at me. I felt for a moment that we were actors in a play, intoning old lines.

'On what?'

'On a soft bed,' Monger said. 'To ensure they should not suffer any more damage. In fact... a sheep's fleece.'

An intelligent man. Maybe he'd thought of the further implications before I had. Maybe he'd picked up on my sceptic's tone. Either way, the eyes which met mine were fogged with suspicion. And then a kind of fear.

Fully justified.

'Help me,' I said.

✛

So we both went, and his state was pitiful.

Crouching on the floor, in a nest of bone. He'd pulled down shelves, and the unjawed skulls and bones lay in piles like the site of some old massacre. Fresh blood on some of them now. There was a broken bottle in his bunched hands, pointed at his throat, all quivering. I think he'd already tried to cut his wrists with it, leaving bracelets of blood to the elbows.

Still the candles burned, but the scent of incense was sharpened with piss. A brown fluid was dripping from the smashed neck of the bottle. I thought it was the bottle of potion Matthew Borrow had given to Benlow.

'Too weak.' Monger prised his fingers away from it, tossing it into a corner of the cellar. 'Too weak to do it.'

Tears in Benlow's eyes.

'We must needs bring Matthew here,' Monger said.

'Yes.'

I, too, thought I should like to talk again to Dr Borrow.

'I'll get him now. Could you stay with Benlow.' He paused. 'One moment.'

From his robe he pulled a metal cross on a chain, dropping the chain over Benlow's head.

'God be with you,' he murmured. 'Now and always.'

'Take it *off*...' Benlow rolling onto his side, gasping, clawing at his throat, his fine doublet all ripped open. Making a strangled kind of bleating only approximate to laughter. 'I've given up God.'

'Then talk to this man.' Monger moved away. 'Make your peace. Don't take it all with you.' Grasping the ladder, he said to me, 'Ask what you need. You may not have long.'

✛

I knelt on the floor, rolling away the skull of King Edgar or some other king.

'Master Benlow...'

He grinned up at me. I think it was a grin. There was blood between his sharp little teeth. I think he must have been tearing at his wrists with them before he lost the will and the very breath to do it.

'They've finished me,' he whispered. 'Is that not so?'

'The doctor's coming.'

'Wrap me in fleece, my lord. Put me in my grave... wrapped in good fleece, so my bones...'

'May lie like Arthur's bones?'

There was no time no waste. Not a minute. I waited, holding his eyes, which were become still and watchful.

'What do you know?'

'I know what you buried at Butleigh.'

He opened his mouth wide, as if he might take in more air, then shut it, and his words came feebly.

'Not worth a piece of fleece, am I?'

'A better fleece than Arthur's.'

'*Offered* them a fleece. A *good fleece*. One of mine.'

'They didn't want a good fleece, though, did they?' I said softly. 'It was supposed to look twenty years old.'

He tried to sniff, his eyes wide with distress.

'Dis...gusting old thing. Left for me.'

'Where?'

'Abbey grounds, behind... behind the abbot's kitchen. Dis*gusting* old thing. I was ashamed...'

'They brought you the box, first? When was this?'

'Yesterday? Day before? Day before that? What's today?'

'Monday.'

'A week ago? Who knows? Time passes quick when you're dying.'

'Who brought the fleece, Master Benlow?'

'Dunno. Just lying there. They told me to collect it.'

'Who?'

'Tell me some secrets.'

'You know all my secrets.'

I could imagine the fleece being brought from some farm where wool-sorters' disease had been found amongst the sheep. Brought from there at night. On the end of a very long pitchfork.

Till she shall kiss the bones of the King of all Britons...

'Whose bones?' I whispered. 'Whose bones did you put into the fleece. Whose bones did you bury at Butleigh?'

Thought I knew. Just couldn't recall the name.

Benlow made no reply. I asked him again, close enough now to see the lumps on his neck, one of them an inch across, the black at its centre like a hole.

'A big man,' I said. 'The biggest man in the graveyard.'

'Arthur,' Benlow croaked. 'A hundred saints in the wall, and all they ever want is Arthur.'

He tried to take a breath, and it wouldn't come, a terrible panic flaring his eyes before he subsided against a wall of crumbling death.

'Help me, Benlow. Do some good.'

'What's good?' His eyelids fluttered like moths. 'What's evil? What's in between? They all lie. Even God lies.'

'And *no* God?'

'Uh?'

'You said... When I was here before, you said even no God was a lie. Who were you talking about? Perchance Dr Borrow?'

Thinking now of what Mistress Cadwaladr had said. Thinking of my own feelings on leaving Borrow's surgery the first time, when my thoughts had not been swamped by Leland's dreams.

'He filled me with an awe, my lord. I was drawn to him.'

'Followed him?'

'Like the Messiah.'

'You said you followed people all the time.'

'Folk goes to unexpected... places.'

'Like? Where does Dr Borrow go?'

'Church, once, at night when it was quiet. The doctor went to the Church of St Benignus, and he lit a candle, and I—'

Benlow reached out and gripped my arms, fighting for his breath.

'What else did you see?'

'Heard. He cried out. He was alone in the darkness at the altar, and he cried out, like Christ on on the cross. Angry.'

'*Father, why have you forsaken me*?'

'Uh?'

'What Christ said on the cross.'

'I… don't know.'

'Where else does he go? Where else did you follow Dr Borrow?'

'Walking to the sea, once, but I… got tired. Too far. Came back. And he'd go at night to the Meadwell.'

'When?'

Feet on the ladder.

'When, Benlow?'

'Two times, three times…' His eyes grew sly. 'I'm tired of doing good. This en't good, my lord. 'Tis all a lie.'

'Gone,' Monger said, stepping down. 'He's gone.'

His face was aglow with sweat, eyes wide and bright with a bewilderment I'd never seen in him.

'Matthew… he's not there. Must be out on his rounds, can't find him. We have no doctor.'

Benlow moved. A noise from his throat like the thinnest, distant birdsong.

'As you thought?' Monger said, and I nodded.

'You go and do whatever you must do,' he said. 'I'll clean him up, make him comfortable. Can't see a man die like this.'

'Better in your hands.' I stood up carefully, head bent under the ceiling. 'Better a doctor of horses, than… Joe, he must be stopped.'

Benlow's mouth was agape, like one of his skulls, a thin finger crooked, beckoning me.

'Dudley,' I said. 'We have to bring him back. And the bones. Bury the bones again. Somewhere no-one ever digs.'

'Then somebody has to ride like hell,' Monger said. 'Tell Cowdray. If he sends all his boys out… With a cart, they can't travel too hard.'

'And will have to stop somewhere tonight.'

'Pray God.'

Benlow was trying to raise himself up, and Monger went to him.

Benlow kept on looking for me, looking at where I'd been a moment ago, his eyes unseeing.

'They didn't...' His throat creaking, no laughter left in him. 'They didn't... call him Big Jamey Hawkes for nothing, my lord.'

☩

We watched the riders leave, Cowdray and I. The sky was like lead, the daylight dying without having had much of a life.

Three of them were gone after Dudley: the stable boy, the kitchen boy and another who may have been Cowdray's son. One had taken my horse. Each of them carrying my own copies of a brief letter for Dudley, scribed, in the absence of a fitting seal, with the symbol of the eyes I'd once made for the Queen as my signature, for a jest. Each letter inked and sand-dried and bound, conveying the message that if Dudley did not return at once, with the box of bones unopened, his only reward would be death. The worst of deaths. Hard to think how best to convey this. *The grave of love*, I'd written finally. Underlining it twice.

'Whatever you were thinking to charge,' I said now to Cowdray, 'you should double it.'

He was silent for a moment, and then he shook his head.

'I'll take nothing for this.'

He didn't know. Couldn't know. But he was a good man.

I nodded in the direction of the tor, tried to speak evenly.

'Where will Nel pass the night?'

'Meadwell, I reckon. Used to be an old gaol up town, but they wouldn't rely on that now. There are cells at Meadwell. 'Tis almost fortified, that house. Well... so they say. I've never been.'

'Never?'

'Not since it was rebuilt.'

'Will Carew be there?'

'Most likely, aye.' He cast eyes on me and winced. 'Dr John, man... you're in sorest need of sleep. You're like the walking bloody dead. You en't eaten... In truth I don't know how you're still on your feet.'

'I'm well. And must needs talk to Carew, without delay.'

Better it were Dudley, but who could say when, or if, we'd see Dudley again this night. I told Cowdray what Benlow had said about Stephen Fyche and the murder of Martin Lythgoe.

'Let this come out, Master Cowdray. Let it be spread far and wide. Too late now to rebound on poor Benlow.'

A weary disbelief on Cowdray's face.

'You think it en't known? What that boy *is*. Folks might've chose to forget the tales about Fyche, in view of his charity, but they've seen what his boy's like, loose in the town of a summer night, well into his cups.'

'Where's the mother?'

'Long gone. Fyche and the boy, 'tis said they goes whoring together in Wells.'

'Carew knows of this?'

'It would alarm Carew?'

'No. I suppose not. Look, what's the quickest way to Meadwell? I only know it's the other side of the tor.'

'No, Doctor.' Cowdray sighed. ''Tis only the other side of the tor when you're *on* the tor. The Meadwell's a mile or so out of town. If you follows the track *after* the one to the tor, keep heading east, you'll come to the gates.'

I nodded. I was thinking of Borrow, where he might be. Where he'd been educated thirty years ago or more.

'You're thinking to go there on your own?'

'No-one else. No, no...' I held up a hand. 'Thank you. Look to your inn.'

Cowdray shook his head. I wanted to say, *Cowdray, they want to kill the Queen. They've poisoned her heritage.* Yet, if he'd asked who, I could not have told him with any degree of certainty.

'I assume... there's no-one left to watch for me, is there?' I said. 'Carew's guard?'

'You never was the one they was guarding, you must know that.' Cowdray laid a hand on my shoulder. 'You just watch out for yourself, hear me?'

'Yes. Thank you.'

So much now to watch out for. The sky was all the colours of mould, but wild lights were blazing in my head as I walked into the street. I'd go to Meadwell, but not yet.

The darkening town was silent, streets deserted, the air laden with comforting smoke as I walked down towards the church of St Benignus. The doctor's surgery was sinking into the gloom of early dusk, and I was just another shadow at the top of the steps as I took out my dagger.

I'm no expert at this, but it was an old lock and the wood splintered around the blade.

Inside, the fire in the grate was near dead, but I managed to light a couple of candles from it, setting them on the trestle board. Not yet sure what I was looking for but I'd know when I found it.

LII

Abominations

WHAT HAD I expected? Maybe not the severity of it.

For those of a certain wealth, as I've said, this is the first age of light. Big houses have big windows.

Not like the mean mullions at Meadwell. I stood in the gateway. No-one in attendance, the house rearing before me, like a cliff face in the dusk.

The gates were open. I'd not expected that either, imagining myself accosted by some surly jobsworth and having a message sent to Carew who, in his own good time, would emerge before me, angry or sneering. But he'd be forced to listen. By Christ, I'd make him listen. And an execution would, by God's good offices, be halted pending an inquiry which might take many weeks and end with different necks in nooses elsewhere.

I wanted Carew, not Fyche. Out here.

But only the owls were out. Fluting across the valley behind me, in a sky which, perversely after such a day, was clearing.

No stars yet, though. I was on my own. Kept on walking.

It had not entered my mind that Carew himself might be party to any of this. He was not, in essence, that complicated. True, he'd served different kings in Europe, fought at different times with opposing armies. But since returning to England he seemed solely committed to England's interests, Protestant to his spine, an adventurer, not a conspirator.

Not that I could ever like the oaf. But he'd been given the abbey by the Queen or Cecil, and the owner of the abbey was yet the owner of this sorry town.

I thought to call out for Carew but, in the end, simply walked up to the house, until I came to a door of green oak, set into the stone wall without porch or overhang. Hardly the main entrance, but it would do. I banged upon it with a fist, twice.

No response. No echo within.

Standing there, unsure, for some moments before twisting the iron ring above the keyhole, somehow knowing that it would not be locked.

✝

I'd gone back to Cowdray. Nobody knew more about a town than its principal innkeeper, observing who came and who went, listening to all the careless words which fell nightly from lips loosened by drink.

First, I'd taken the letters I'd found in Borrow's surgery and hid them under a beam high in the ass's stable. Asses could keep secrets.

Then I'd beckoned Cowdray from the alehouse – filling up now, much talk of the execution on the morrow.

You couldn't find Meadwell, Dr John?

Not even tried yet. We don't have much time. Dr Borrow – when did he leave the town, as a boy?

Which was how I'd learned about Borrow's father, a wealthy wool-merchant and prominent Catholic, who'd done much of his trade in France and found the humours there more to his liking.

In the '20s, this was, when there was no inkling of Reformation and King Harry was safely wed to his brother Arthur's widow, Catherine.

The only one who came back was Matthew, as a qualified doctor. A fine doctor, as he soon proved. Glastonbury had been grateful to have him. And many of the wealthier merchants and landowners in the area, Cowdray said, would have been grateful to have him wed their daughters.

But, to the dismay of the merchants and their daughters, Borrow took up with an orphan who'd become a kitchen maid at the abbey.

She was beautiful, mind, Cowdray said. *But, obviously, she had no money. Nobody could understand it.*

✝

Some houses, whatever the season, are colder inside than the open air. Without coat or cloak and or even food that day, I stiffened at the chill of Meadwell.

397

No candles or lamps, no flicker of fire or scent of woodsmoke.

Only a passage. I stood, quiet and without obvious direction, while the foolish lower mind was conjuring its own steps down to the dungeons, which would, of course, be unguarded, a bunch of keys hanging, in full view, from a nail.

And then what? Run away from here with Nel Borrow, hand in hand? Flee the country together?

Life would never be that simple any more, not for anyone. I turned to the left, there being more light that way, from high slit windows. I surely could not be alone in here and thought to call out. But what if it were Fyche? What I needed was a servant whom I could bid fetch me Carew.

The passage ended in a T and a door was facing me, so I simply opened it. As far as it would go, which was not far. I thought at first that the resistance was someone pushing from the other side and sprang back, and there was a toppling sound which I recognised at once.

Books. A long room full of books. A smell of old leather and damp.

Not a library, though. All the books, none of the shelves. Books in squalid piles on the floor. Good books, well bound, in incredible quantity. At the far end, a window gave into a high-walled yard, and almost the first title I was able to discern through its meagre light was at once familiar.

Euclidis Elementa Geometrica

My God.

Within a few minutes, I'd happened upon *Alberti Magni Minerarium* and then Aquinas's *Quaestionum Disputartarum* and divers other scientific and philosophical volumes, copies of which were in my own humble collection at Mortlake.

All of these leaving me in little doubt that I'd found a large part of the library which had aroused such awe and stupor in Leland at Glastonbury Abbey in the days of Abbot Richard Whiting.

Yet unshelved, uncatalogued. Haphazardly stored, mainly uncared for, some thick with dust and eroded with damp. A veritable charnel house of knowledge.

With all the books, I'd failed to notice that the room also contained divers items of furniture: chairs and screens and chests, all of an ecclesiastical appearance. I opened the nearest chest and found there, wrapped in cloths, two silver platters and a cup with handles.

Books and furniture and altar goods.

This was not goods being stolen and accommodated into the fabric and furnishings of someone's house. This was the abbey in storage.

Did Carew know of this?

His abbey, his property.

Unlikely. While I myself might have spent the next five years here, books of any kind would have little appeal for a notorious truant who legend said had threatened to jump from Exeter city wall rather than be hauled back to school.

✠

I neither knew nor cared which way I went after that. Stumbled through walkways and doorways, under arches where the mortar seemed barely dry. If this place would ever be a college, it was unlike any I'd known.

Came at last to a dead-end. A door to either side of it. The one on the left had a window with bars. The cells? The armoury, more like.

The door on the right opened into a short passage, with almost no light. I edged my way slowly along the left-hand wall.

Steps. Narrow steps leading down. From the stairwell, the faintest of glows.

Was this the way to the dungeons? Was my phantasy to be realised? I held down the brief flaring of excitement. It could never be so easy.

And then, as I descended slowly, there was a voice, yet some distance away. A single voice, a low and rhythmic mumble. One voice, no exchange, just one man addressing not another man but… his God?

In Latin, I thought then, which is my own second language and the language in which God was habitually addressed.

Sometimes, we find ourselves in situations which seem to have been fore-planned by some greater agency. I may have written earlier of the feeling of becoming a chess piece upon a board, moved by a player in some bigger game whose rules I could not yet comprehend, and I had

399

the sense of it again – that sense of the predestined – as I walked softly towards the sound of the voice.

And also the only light. Reaching an archway of stone, beyond which candles glimmed piercingly upon what looked to be an altar.

In a niche above the altar was a statue of Mary, the Virgin. The kind of statue which, all too recently, was torn from the walls of churches throughout the land. A man was kneeling before it, arms at his sides, head bent, and the litany he was chanting came not from our Book of Common Prayer but from something older that lived in his head.

Its language proving not to be Latin after all, but French. My third language, or possibly fourth.

I stood and watched and listened for what must have been over a minute. And then, for some reason, I felt obliged to cough.

At which the man arose, quite slowly, and turned in the stone space, the prayer continuing to issue from his lips.

Not a prayer, nor a voice I'd heard before.

Nor expected to, from a deaf mute.

LIII

In the Night Garden

I MADE NO move.

'*Frère Michel,*' I said softly.

'*Qu'est-ce qui se passe?*'

Peering at me. After staring into the altar candles, he'd see me only as a shadow, while I saw his full face: eyes bulging slightly under heavy lids, a jutting lower lip, that grey beard like a pointed shovel.

Seizing this momentary advantage, I told him, in French, how delighted I was at the miraculous restoration of his speech, trusting this would not affect his renowned visionary powers.

Fyche in my head from that first afternoon on the tor.

…with no men's talk to distract him, he hears only the voices of angels. Thus, as you may imagine, his moral and spiritual judgement is… much valued.

Brother Michael blinked and, without ceremony, snatched up one of the candlesticks from the altar and held it aloft, to the right of me.

Then nodded solemnly.

'Forgive me,' I said. 'When we met upon the tor, your host seemed to think he had no duty to introduce us.'

He made no reply.

His age? Yes, that would be about right. Around my mother's age, nearing sixty. The way his felt hat was pulled down suggestive of baldness.

'I should have realised,' I said, 'that you'd be here. Obviously, much to interest you. Not least in the remains of the finest library outside London. Or even Paris.'

Continuing to speak in French, for I wasn't aware that he knew English. As good a reason as any for someone in his position to be introduced as deaf and dumb.

'And more than this,' I said. 'Far more. I've read of your interest in old monuments and Druidical remains. Which here are, I'd guess, more numerous and more impressive than in France. One of the advantages of being an island.'

He still held his candlestick... and his peace.

'One of the disadvantages, of course,' I said, 'is that more people here are superstitious and less open to progressive learning. One good reason for your presence to be concealed – although some of us would welcome it. All the hours we might spend in discussion of astrology, alchemical texts, the Cabala...'

It occurred to me then that he thought my questions speculative, posed to draw him out, establish final proof of his identity, and he was holding out. In truth, I was burning up. Time to lay down my cards.

'I didn't, at first, think that you'd have been at Montpellier College at the same time at Matthew Borrow – you being most of a decade older than him. And then I remembered, from my documents, that you were there as a *mature* student of medicine – in your thirtieth year?'

I'd watched his eyes move for the first time at the mention of Matthew Borrow.

'I've been reading some of the letters you'd sent him. Not easy. How the hell did the apothecaries decipher your instructions? You could've poisoned someone.'

Neither of the two letters I'd stolen from Borrow's surgery had been signed, but handwriting's been one of my more recreational studies. I've ever enjoyed the analysis of styles and the development of divers approaches to lettering.

'Your writing's even worse now than in the early manuscripts on my shelves,' I said.

He might have smiled. I don't know, for that was the moment when he chose at last to lower the candlestick.

'I heard you were building a library,' he said.

'Early days.'

Absurdly flattered that he'd heard of my library. Or even of me. Gratified that he'd spoken at last.

'The day we were on the tor,' I said. 'Were you aware then... of who I was?'

I watched him pondering the question, as if it might contain some hidden snare. As indeed it might.

'Not then,' he said, 'no.'

'Maybe later, though?' What was to be lost? 'Maybe after Fyche's crazed son had extracted the information from my colleague's groom? Before finding it necessary to kill him?'

No reply, and I could no longer see his eyes, but I kept on, the wild lights back inside me, and now they were dancing.

'Whose idea was it to have the dead man taken to the abbey and then dress up this murder of expediency as a ritual killing? I only ask because – as the assize court would have been told, had the trial of Eleanor Borrow ever taken place – the mutilation of the body seemed to call for a certain surgical skill. The kind of skill for which a younger Michel de Nostradame was, I believe, quite well known.'

With that first use of his full name, a mystifying lightness was grown within me. As if I were thrown back into the night of the storm when the dust of vision had me and I floated like an angel in the night garden. I gripped a stone ledge behind me, as if it would hold me down.

At length, there came a reply.

'I was – and am – a physician. A physician, he does not kill. Well...' He shrugged. 'Not with intent.'

'Not invariably true,' I said.

He replaced the candlestick upon the stone altar.

✠

I looked around. On the wall nearest the entrance where I stood, there was a crucifix and, in niches where stones had been removed either side of it, small statues, presumably of saints.

There was a tabernacle on the altar. In the air a vagueness of incense.

'You look cold, my friend.'

Still wearing his monk's robe. A quite practical form of apparel in this house. I was yet angry with myself that I'd made no link betwixt Nostradamus and the deaf mute Brother Michael until I'd heard him speak. One of the letters in Borrow's surgery had confirmed that he was to arrive in February and would be lodging with *our mutual friend of the judiciary*. The rest of the letter had made little sense and I'd guessed it to be coded.

'I left my lodgings in rather a hurry,' I said. 'Having not long before read your latest prophetic quatrain. Relating to the Queen of England and the bones of King Arthur? I was wondering how it had found its way to Throckmorton.'

I'd gone too far. His tolerant smile said that this time he knew I was on the wing.

'Dr Dee, there are questions I cannot answer.' He touched an ear. 'Questions I cannot even hear.'

'Do you get many… messages… about the Queen of England?'

'I receive what I receive.'

'But you obviously put each one before your masters at court. There must needs be scrutiny of them prior to publication… surely?'

He took a patient breath.

'Dr Dee,' he said. 'I know not how you came to be here this evening, but I'm happy to greet you as a fellow man of science… and would positively *relish* a discussion with you on our common ground – astrology, alchemical texts, meditation, all matters scientific. The first rule, however, must be that… the matters of state, they are not for us.'

I found this sentiment disingenuous in the extreme but said nothing.

'Come.' He extended an arm. 'Rest awhile. We'll not be disturbed, I promise. No-one comes down here at night but me.'

There was a stone seat projecting from the wall to the side of the altar. I lowered myself into it. Just taking the weight off my feet brought on a quivering drowsiness which made me glad of the cold. Nostradamus fitted himself into a wooden chair with arms and pulled it up opposite me. He placed his hands in his lap.

'It offends me, you know, that – from what I hear – your talents are regarded less well in your native country than are mine in France. As you suggested… a sad indictment of England's values.'

'I'm not sure,' I said, 'that our talents are identical.'

He shrugged, opened out his hands, and I reminded myself that his apparel was misleading, maybe deliberately so. This was not, nor had ever been, a man in holy office.

'Why are you *really* here?' I said.

'A question most reasonable. Which you answered yourself. A fascination with these islands. The portals to the past, they are open here in ways which are not so apparent in most of Europe. This place in particular... has a sense of continuity denied to us. And, it appears, a relationship with the cosmos which elsewhere... is long-lost.'

'Ah.' Now I was no longer on the wing. 'You mean the Zodiac.'

'My God...' He spread his arms wide. 'When I heard of *that*...'

'How long *since* you heard of it?'

'Not long.'

'And how came you by the knowledge?'

'A*ha!*' The smiling Nostradamus wagging an admonitory forefinger. 'How came *you* by the knowledge of it, Dr Dee?'

So he knew. I must have shown my discomfort, for he laughed.

'But what's to be *done* with the thing, that's the biggest question. I am perfectly ready to accept that the celestial Zodiac is refashioned, by whatever means, on the ground, but what are we to *make* of it?'

He didn't know either, then. Or was he testing me?

I said slowly, 'If it were designed by God, it's miraculous. If by man, then it shows that civilisations far more advanced than ours once lived – as you've suggested – in these islands.'

'*Excellent* thinking.' Nostradamus leaned forward, alarmingly squeezing my arm, the way an uncle would. 'You're a man of perception, Dr Dee. *Was* this Merlin's secret? What are your thoughts?'

I sensed, at last, a curiosity. I must not lose this advantage. It was clear now that neither Cate Borrow nor John Leland had discovered the final secret – how the terrestrial Zodiac might be employed – which Abbot Whiting may well have died without passing on. If there was no-one alive who knew the key, it would tax all our skills for years to come.

'My thoughts,' I said carefully, 'are, as yet, incomplete. Being more concerned, at this time, with the matter of Arthur.'

'Oh. Does he not yet live, as the Britons believe?' Nostradamus folded his arms, looking down at them for a moment, considering, then raising his head with a sly smile. 'Does he not live as the spirit of the Tudor line? *Tut!*' Lightly smacking his own hand. 'I break my own rule about avoiding matters of state.'

'I'd guess in your position they'd be near impossible to avoid.'

No reply.

'The matter of Arthur,' I said, 'and of Avalon. In seeking to... understand the Tudor line's ancient right to the throne of England and Wales, certain elements within the French court must surely have realised that the role of Glastonbury must needs be considered.'

'You flatter your country, Dr Dee.'

'I don't think so, Dr de Nostradame. Consider your own country. Until such time as the boy François is deemed fit to rule, France is protected by the Guise family, whose deepest desire is to see its daughter Mary, the Scot, become Queen of England.'

'As is her right. As the Pope himself—'

'Ah.... the Pope. There lies the crux of the problem. England being once again free of Rome. Indeed... almost *happily* free.'

'You delude yourself.'

'You don't live here. Consider the blood-letting which followed King Harry's division from Rome. And consider the even worse blood-letting... the *fire* and blood of Mary Tudor's reign, when the Pope was invited back. When Mary was gone, England was sick to its heart of religious persecution and the new Queen saw that. Had the vision to realise that Protestants and Catholics could live together, if not in harmony, at least in relative peace...'

'In *chaos*, my friend! This sorrowful town, with all its witches and quackery, it is England in microcosm. London not much better. Do they not say Parker had virtually to be blackmailed into accepting Canterbury?'

'The fact remains that in the year or so since Elizabeth became Queen, not one man or woman has been executed for religious belief.' I opened my hand to the altar. 'Look at us. Here we are, sitting in a Catholic chapel, with everything to hand for a Mass. There are chapels like it in houses throughout the country. Are they raided? Are they sacked and ruined?'

'My good friend—'

'And that's the problem for the Pope, isn't it? And for France… France is never sated. And with Elizabeth as Queen, its acquisition of England begins to look highy unlikely. The longed-for Catholic rebellion to remove Elizabeth and put Mary of Guise on the throne – where will that come from now? People *enjoy* the peace, even most Catholics. Why have most of the bishops sworn the Oath of Supremacy?'

'Only the corrupt ones.'

'And, of course, the Queen's only twenty-six years old. She could be Queen for another half century. France… the Guises… the Pope… you're all damned. Unless…'

His face was without expression.

Unless…

✝

Slowly, it was coming together.

A Catholic chapel in the cellars of Meadwell gave the lie to Fyche's assertion that *every man here has put papacy well behind him and is ready to swear allegiance to the Queen.*

Quite the reverse. Fyche had been playing a double game from the beginning. Appearing to change sides at the Reformation, having betrayed his abbot to Cromwell in return for land and money, a knighthood and the status of Justice of the Peace. A betrayal viewed, maybe, as a necessary sacrifice, in the best long-term interests of the Roman Church.

Not that Catholicism was likely to be closest to the heart of Fyche, from what I knew of him. He'd been a bursar, an administrator of accounts, had expected to become the next abbot… in effect, the supreme lord of Glastonbury and all points west, with limitless riches.

Had he been led to believe that this, or something similar, could still happen? I thought of the long room full of books, furniture, minor treasures – the abbey in storage. Thought of how Cowdray, on our first night here, had told us of the severe penalties now imposed by Fyche on anyone caught stealing stone from the ruins.

The abbey had not, as expected, been restored by Mary Tudor. *But it*

407

might be under the sovereignty of Mary Queen of Scots, with all the wealth of France behind her.

What had Fyche been promised in return for his assistance in the early removal of the Queen of England?

How extensive was the part in this of Nostradamus?

And why – in sudden discomfort, I glanced over my shoulder – was he still looking disturbingly at peace with himself?

LIV

A Cold Inversion

OF COURSE, HE had no cause to explain anything to me. Unlike poor Benlow, he wasn't even dying.

I'd need to tempt him, and there was, as far as I could see, only one jewel I could offer him: the key to the mysteries of the round table, the Glastonbury Zodiac. And I didn't have it.

Not that he knew that.

'Who comes here for the Mass?' I asked him.

'If you wish me to name anyone, I shall... decline.'

'Not the rabble, I imagine. Only men of influence. Who might also attend... meetings. Maybe with guests from Europe? Leading theologians? Men of state? Not forgetting renowned prophets and forecasters of world affairs.'

Nostradamus smiled

'You journeyed to Glastonbury yourself,' I said, 'in the hope of deciphering the secret at the heart of Leland's notes?'

He toyed with the girdle of his robe, but I could feel the heat of his mind's engine. There was only one way he could have got hold of Leland's notes, so recently reburied.

'Presumably, Matthew Borrow sent you the notebook. Having, despite his many skills, been unable to extract any sense from it.'

'No more than could Leland,' Nostradamus said.

Probably true. He'd left his notes to Cate in the hope that she might one day make something meaningful of them.

How had Leland himself found out about it originally? Maybe from one of the monks – just a whisper of it, on one of his first visits to Somersetshire, in the '30s, in search of antiquities and Arthur. When at last he'd found time to investigate it, he'd returned. Most of the monks having gone by then, but Cate Borrow had still been around and he'd gone to her. *I'm my own man now.*

Had Cate found out more? Had she ever got close to the real meaning and intentions of the Zodiac? We would probably never know. She hadn't had much time, anyway, between receiving the notebook long after Leland's death and her own arrest for witchcraft and murder.

After which the book had fallen, inevitably, into Borrow's hands. Borrow would have seen the possible significance and alerted either his masters or Nostradamus himself. How long had it taken Michel de Nostradame, with the help of a translator, to decipher Leland's notes? Had *he* discovered the whereabouts of the bones of Arthur buried by the last faithful monks of Glastonbury? *Had* the bones of Arthur been buried in Ursa Minor? If so, where were they now? On their way to France?

It was clear that Nostradamus, with his fascination for ancient remains, *had* come to Glastonbury to investigate the Zodiac. Returning the notebook to Borrow? *Worthless,* Borrow had said to Dudley and me. *Occultism.* Knowing how rapidly the last of these words might persuade *me* to approach the unspeakable – taking the bait, waking into the snare. If the journey to Arthur's grave had been less of a perilous and harrowing quest we'd be far more likely to question what we'd found.

Matthew Borrow was a cunning man.

✠

'When were you at Montpellier?' I said. 'May I ask?'

Nostradamus shrugged.

'Around 1529. I was twenty-six.'

'Would've taken him under your wing then. The young Matthew Borrow.'

'He was quite capable of looking after himself, Dr Dee. A Jesuit education does that for one.'

I gripped the stone seat hard.

Hell.

A Jesuit. The steel in the blade of the Catholic Church.

Tried not even to blink, only nodded, as if I'd known of this already.

It at once rang true. The town thought him an unbeliever, a man who went to church only to avoid the fines. Well, safer to be assumed an atheist than a cutting-edge Catholic. The target of Matthew Borrow's quiet venom would, in his own mind, be the Protestant Church. *When the expulsion from this country of the papacy itself comes through a rising not of the spirit... but a man's cock...*

It also explained his cruelty. The callousness of the zealot with a Jesuit's cold intelligence and almost mystical intuition.

I don't think I smiled.

'Was it you who suggested at the French court that he'd make a perfect secret agent in the town of his birth?'

No reaction. But I could see the reason for it. Fyche had established Meadwell, as a possible hub of Catholic rebellion. But how far could the French trust him? François of Guise, and Charles, Cardinal of Lorraine, would have wanted their own man in Avalon.

'I wondered what he receives for his services to France – maybe an income and the promise of land and a title when the Queen of Scots and Queen of France is also Queen of England.'

'Dr Dee...' Nostradamus scowled. 'I've been tolerant of your unceasing—'

'One more question... before I offer you, in the interests of science, my theory of at least one use for the Glastonbury Zodiac. What do you know of wool-sorters' disease?'

☩

It could have been Borrow himself who'd thought of using wool-sorters', the disease on which he was now an expert. Or maybe some spy-master close to the French court or the Guise family, some ambitious young Walsingham, had seen that notebook and thought how it might be used.

But had Nostradamus really known nothing of this?

'As a doctor, you tended plague victims?'

I was thinking of Aix-en-Provence, fifteen or so years ago. So ravaged by the plague that scores of houses were abandoned, churches closed, graveyards overflowing. Into this hell, Nostradamus, according to an account I'd received, had entered as a physician. A brave thing.

'An experience most harrowing,' he said. 'There was, in truth, little I or anyone could do, except to aid the healthy in their efforts to remain free of contagion. Still... good for one's immortal soul, is it not, to risk death in such a cause? Forgive me, but whether the disease of the wool-sorters can be compared...'

'There's a man dying of it in the town. Maybe dead by now.'

'It happens. Especially in areas such as this.'

'Do you know how it's spread?'

'I believe through the meat and skins of animals dead of it.'

'Oft-times long after their deaths?'

'It is as well to bury them deep.'

'Yes.'

'What is your interest, Dr Dee?'

I took a breath and repeated to him the third and now most chilling line in his Elizabeth quatrain.

'Jusqu'ele beisera les os du roi des Isles Britanniques.'

Sat back against the stone. He appeared unmoved.

I said, 'Does that mean *physically* to kiss the bones?'

'I have no idea.'

'You composed it.'

'No, my friend, *God* composed it.'

''God composes in rhyme and metre?'

One of the altar candles went out. A draught from somewhere.

'See?' Nostradamus said. 'See how He responds to your impudence?'

He picked up the smoking candle and relit it from its neighbour.

However...' Placing his hands on his knees and levering his back straight. 'I repeat to you... a physician only heals.'

'Yet you know which road I'm on.'

'No, Dr Dee, I confess to bewilderment.'

'And I admit to fury, because someone seeks to make me part of a plot to destroy my Queen.'

I tried to tell him. He made the hand-behind-the-ear motions, shook his head violently.

'You leave me far behind again, Dr Dee.'

I leaned toward him.

'The bones which it's intended should be kissed… are laid upon the fleece of a ewe dead of wool-sorters' disease. The man charged with laying the bones on the fleece is become its first victim. A plot, of cold complexity, to kill the Queen.'

It was the first time I'd spoken aloud of this: a journey to enlightenment contrived as a difficult and perilous quest, involving even a journey to the underworld – grave dirt and distress.

But why had the arcane knowledge of the Zodiac been made attainable… Been given away? Maybe the answer was supplied by Nostradamus himself when he'd demanded, *But what's to be done with the thing?* Nobody knew. It was a wonder, but an enigma and maybe always would remain so.

And, as such, had been found expendable in what was considered to be a greater cause: the death of Queen Elizabeth just over a year after her coronation.

Would the Queen have kissed the bones?

Oh, indeed.

Without a doubt.

Before a breathless crowd of onlookers, smiling with a gracious pride as she bent her noble head to the recently shattered brainbox of Big Jamey Hawkes.

☩

'You truly think,' Michel de Nostradame said, 'that I journeyed here to supervise the murder of your Queen?'

'You think that it wouldn't cause considerable rejoicing amongst your patrons at the French court? In France, is not Queen Elizabeth seen as satanic? How many of your forecasts have named Elizabeth as the worst of women? Flawed parentage.'

'I lose count. It comes from God. I spend long hours alone, in vigils deep and silent, opening my heart to the divine spirit and, at some point… am granted entry into what you would call *the mist of perceiving.*'

I snatched a candlestick from the altar and held the light close to his face and stared into his deep-lidded eyes. He was calmness itself, as if he might drift at any moment into his prophetic mist. I leaned into his face.

I was beyond fatigue, my body felt weightless and my hand shook, and the candle went out.

'Where is he?' I said. 'Where's Borrow?'

His eyes remained benign, untroubled.

'Matthew? Not here.'

I looked around me. The quietness of Meadwell had seemed an advantage when I was first here. Now the wrongness of it hit me like a blow to the heart.

'Why is it nobody's here but you?'

'Because they're all out on the hill,' Nostradamus said. 'Me – I've seen too much death.'

'Hill?'

'But not Matthew, of course,' he said. 'Surely no-one, even in England, would compel a man to attend the hanging of his daughter.'

LV

Tainted

I'VE SEEN HANGINGS, we all have. Hangings and beheadings and burnings, mostly undeserved. The one which had most affected me was the burning of Barthlet Green. Just a man with whom I'd shared a prison cell. A mild good-natured man.

Who'd burned.

A harder death than hanging. Or so it was said.

But who knew? Who'd ever come back from the flames or the noose?

✝

An unearthly last glare in the west. Amber and white streaks, a dawn sky at night.

Half in this sick world, half in hell, the bookman went scrambling up the flank of the conical hill, legs numbed, hands torn on barbs and briars, print-weakened eyes straining at the glow which fanned around the summit as if the whole hill were opened into the golden court of the King of Faerie.

When, close to the top, I was sinking to my knees in exhaustion, heaving my guts into the mud, her voice came to me, soft and light.

Be not alarmed, Dr John, you're hardly the first to lose his balance up here.

Tears blinded me.

Why was it not to be done with discretion? Robert Dudley had asked, and now it was. Dawn was become dusk. Misinformation to forestall any outcry from the town, deal with it in darkness then leave the body hanging until it were ripped clean of all womanly beauty and the place where it was done tainted again.

A place which was tainted and tainted and tainted again. A hill persecuted for being different. I scrambled up into a ground mist which seemed to come from within, as if the tor sought to hide itself from man and what he did.

'May God have mercy on this sinful town! May the light of God shine upon this poisoned place.'

The twisted indignity of it.

The fat vicar of St Benignus with his unwashed robe and his Book of Common Prayer.

I dragged myself to the top, bleeding from both hands, as muted male voices were descending in lumpen *amen*.

Stood trembling.

A ground mist was rising on the summit, where two blazing torches were lofted on poles bringing the ruined tower of St Michael to an unreal life. There were men with staffs and pikes, but not more than a dozen. One of them the man with grey hair and cracked teeth and a knowledge of death by hanging and why women made not much of a show of it.

The gibbet, maybe ten feet tall, was firmly staked before the tower, like a open doorway, its feet swathed in mist but the top of its frame hard against the lingering light, pink now, like bloodied milk.

Grunts and mutters. The bottom of an orchard ladder could be seen propped against the stock of the gibbet, rising from the brown mist.

Carew stood a few yards away, in leather hat and jerkin, hands linked behind him, rocking back and forth, impatient, and when I ran to him he didn't look at me, his voice a murmur.

'God's spleen, Dee, will I never get you from under my fucking boots?'

'Sir Peter, I need you to listen to me.'

Was what I meant to say, but the smoke from the torches caught at my throat.

'Damn mist,' Carew said. 'Would've had three of 'em brought up if I'd thought.'

'I must needs tell you—'

'Never been up for learning, *Doctor*. Not your kind anyway.' He turned, a firelit flash of teeth in the beard. 'If you have any magic to spare to give the poor bitch a swift death, she'd doubtless appreciate it.' Sniffed the air. 'Quite a beauty. Hadn't realised.'

Nodding at the gibbet, a small group of men round it now, the vicar of St Benignus telling us we should not suffer a witch to live, as they brought her out, in her blue overdress, smirched and muddied, though her hair looked combed and drifted behind her shoulders.

'Stop them… please… for Christ's sake!'

I think she looked towards me as if she recognised a voice and then turned away as I threw at Carew the only words that might wake him from his mental slumber.

'It's part of a papist plot.'

He laughed.

'You see any papists here?'

'*Yes!*'

He looked at me, his curiosity at last alive, but it was too late then.

✛

You forgot how quick it could be.

The torchlight had gone pale with vapour, and of a sudden she was there on the ladder, hands bound behind her, the vicar's voice floating over her in the dusk.

'*May the death of this sinner bring atonement and cleanse this town forever of all filth and wickedness, idolatry and the worship of all false gods.*'

'That arsehole annoys me nearly as much as you,' Carew said.

A movement on the ladder, a crisp slap.

'I swear to God if you touch me there again, I'll die cursing you to perdition.'

Laughter and coughing in the mist, and someone asked her if she had anything to say before sentence was carried out, and I heard her say with contempt, 'To *you?*'

The bookman throwing his gasping, sorry self through flickering air as the short ladder was tipped to the ground and the group of men parted before him to reveal the body of Nel Borrow swaying slowly against the flesh-coloured sky.

The vicar, with his Bible and his back to the hanging woman, singing out.

'*The witch is gone to Satan. May the light of God come to us all.*'

LVI

Brown Blanket

A HALF CIRCLE of men were around us, the two torch-carriers standing either side of the gibbet frame, and in the fuzzy light I saw Fyche and his son, Stephen, and Sir Peter Carew, pale-eyed in the thick air. A jabbering amongst them, and then Carew's voice was lifted above it.

'Hellfire, let him alone. If he wishes to pull her neck like a chicken, so be it, the end's the same.'

Still I held her up, arms wrapped about her covered legs, my cheek against a thigh. Could feel the rope that bound her hands. Gripped one of the hands, and it was cold. Prayed, as I'd never prayed before, to God and all the angels, the noise in my head like the bells crashing in the tower from which all the bells were long gone.

'In fact, give a hand, Simmons,' Carew said.

The man with cracked teeth moving forward, pushing aside the vicar, who was still bent and retching from my blow to his throat…

…and then stopping.

'Well, go on, man!' Carew roared. 'Before his feeble fucking spine snaps.'

I looked up and saw what the man with cracked teeth saw.

'Angels!' he screamed.

But what I saw was a white-gold bird rising from the fire of two torches meeting in the mist with a burst of gases.

Then the rope gave, and she felt into my arms, her body slumped against my head and shoulders. Dead weight but I would not let go, would never let go.

The mist gathering around us, wrapping us in its brown blanket.

✝

'Say it!' Dudley snarled. 'Say what you did.'

Stephen Fyche was backed up against a leg of the gibbet. He stumbled, swore. I had the impression he'd been drinking. His father turned and walked away.

'You had a nail hammered under his fingernails,' Dudley said. 'Then, when he yielded nothing, you started to slit his gut.'

The pikemen's hands were tensed around their weapons for they knew not this man who'd strode through the mist, his sword out to cut through the hangman's rope.

'No...' Stephen glancing around, maybe looking for his father. He wore his monk's robe and his new beard looked to have been cut fine and sharp for the occasion. 'That's horseshit. Who *is* this fucking bladder?'

I kept quiet, sitting in the mud under the still-swinging rope, my arms around Nel, listening to her breath coming in harsh snorts. Celestial music.

Fyche was back. Somebody must have told him who Dudley was, most likely Carew.

'My Lord, before you accuse my son—'

'Who took out his guts?' Dudley said to Stephen Fyche. 'Who took out his heart with the doctor's tools?'

'The fucking *witch!*'

'Why not the doctor himself?'

A small sound came out of Nel's half-strangled throat. Dudley edged closer to Stephen Fyche.

'Tell us, boy.'

'Aye,' Carew said. 'Maybe you better had.'

'How...' Stephen Fyche rose to his full height, swaying. Even I could smell the wine on his breath. 'How dare you accuse a man of God, sirrah?'

And turned slightly, and I saw that he held a dagger close to his side and that Dudley saw it, too, and his hand was making a familiar short journey to his belt.

'No trial needed here, then,' Dudley said.

'Uh... no.' Carew gripping his wrist, twisting his sword out of his grasp. 'Not your place.'

I'd seen something akin to this before.

Carew half turning this time, holding Dudley's side-sword in both hands, and then the sword was a tongue of flame in the light of the torches and there was a look of faint puzzlement on the youthful face of Stephen Fyche as his body sagged below it.

Carew moved twice more, short hacks, and Stephen's head seemed, for an instant, to be quite still in the air before it dropped to earth and rolled once into the grass where the body already lay, spouting its blood into the soil.

'*My* place, I think,' Carew said.

The silence on the tor seemed eternal. It was as if it were done by the hill itself. As if, deprived of one life, it had taken another.

LVII

The Void

THE FISH HILL was where Joseph of Arimathea had disembarked, stabbing his staff into the good soil of Avalon.

Soil so good, in fact, that the staff sprouted buds and grew into a thorn bush which yet survived, or descendants of it, and came into flower each Christmas Day.

Joe Monger had told me that. A pretty tale with many echoes, this hill being one of the fishes in the starsign of Pisces, whose age began with the coming of Christianity. I'd sat by this thorn bush before, not knowing of the legend, and sat there again in the chill breeze as the year approached the day when St David died, aged one hundred, a thousand or so years ago.

St David? Oh, yes, he was here too, how could he not have been?

Sitting here, you could see both the abbey and the tor. Maybe this was the medium between the two worlds, Christian and pagan, natural and celestial. He'd known what he did, the abbot, in giving this land to Cate Borrow, for the purpose of healing.

'The abbot's thought,' Nel said, 'was that if the medical herbs traditionally related to certain starsigns in the sky were to be grown inside the corresponding formations upon the *ground...* then the healing properties of them would be quite marvellously increased.'

'She told you this?'

'Of course not. It came to me when I awoke this morning. I remembered that when a particular herb did well here – yarrow or camomile, I forget which – then she'd say, Aha, this plant is responsive to the sign of the fishes. And I remembered how she'd go off with the abbot to plant herbs in other fields belonging to the abbey and... that's my guess.'

The logic of it was beyond assail. Cate taken into the confidence of the monks at the abbey who held the secret of the Zodiac. Working with them on a new kind of astrological healing. The implications were fascinating.

'I suppose 'tis not the only secret of the Zodiac, and far from the most important, but...'

She smiled and squeezed my hand, and I looked at her with longing but no real hope. Though we'd lain together four nights now, I was sensing, in the sweetness of it, a parting rather than a beginning.

☩

It had been nearly a week before she was able to speak without pain. She said this was only because of the burns and the weals yet apparent on her throat despite all the balms and ointments applied to it by Joan Tyrre. But I thought there was more. My feeling was that she'd foresworn all speech until she had an understanding.

She wore the blue overdress and a worn muslin scarf to keep the breeze from her throat. Below us, we could see the tip of the cross marking Cate's grave, beyond it the abbey laid out like some broken golden coronet.

'You're sure you didn't see him?' she said. 'He was standing next to you for several moments.'

I shook my head. I think she meant the abbot. Cowdray had said there were more people seen on the top of the tor that night than had come down from it.

'I saw only the phoenix made by the torches,' I said. 'I'm just a dull and bookish man who has not the sight.'

The laughter came from deep in her throat, which must have hurt.

And I was still wondering what was real, what was dream or the runaway imagination of a man starved of food for a day, and sleep for longer. I'd mentioned to no-one my meeting with Nostradamus, who was gone by the time Carew's men went into Meadwell. As were all the statues and the tabernacle in the chapel.

Little firm evidence against Fyche himself, Carew claimed, though it was Dudley's suspicion that Fyche knew too much about Carew for him to be brought before an assize. But his status as Justice of the Peace seemed likely to be short-lived.

His son would be buried without ceremony. *Raising a dagger to the Queen's Master of the Horse?* Carew had said mildly. *What choice did I have?*

I couldn't help dwelling on the possible reasons for Fyche trying to pass off the malignant Stephen as a monk. Had he actually thought that when Mary was Queen of England, the Pope back as head of the Church and the abbey rebuilt, it might be placed under *Stephen's* control?

Madness. But then, many abbots and many bishops had been closer to the devil...

Had Brother Michael returned to France in the company of his old friend, Matthew Borrow? If I were looking for cause to believe that Michel de Nostradame was guilty of epic deceit, I could think of no better evidence than his friendship with Borrow.

What *was* this man?

Why had neither his wife nor his daughter, even in the shadow of the noose, been prepared to raise voice against him?

✝

In the week since Dudley's departure, I'd attended Benlow's burial, along with the re-burial, in the goose field behind the Church of the Baptist, of all the bones in his cellar, and also revisited Mistress Cadwaladr. Now that Borrow was gone from the town and Fyche's status was in question, many more truths were emerging.

Monger had recalled how, in the early '30s, not long after the King had proclaimed himself head of the Church, *someone* had suggested to the abbot that the abbey's treasures should be sent to France, where they might remain in the care of the Catholic Church. Fyche, the bursar? Almost certainly. But Richard Whiting, an Englishman to his soul, had been unconvinced – still, apparently, believing that the dark hand of Cromwell would never descend upon the fount of English Christianity. And, indeed, it would be five years or more before it did.

From Mistress Cadwaladr, I'd learned of Cate's first meeting with the man who was to become her husband, when he'd come to the abbey to spear a boil on the abbot's neck. An unlikely match for the doctor, this recently illiterate kitchenmaid.

For while she was undoubtedly beautiful, Cate was also with child.

Was ever a woman more grateful to a man? Mistress Cadwaladr said. *I swear she would have died for him.*

And had.

The way I saw it, Borrow had known his mission might take years. He needed a wife to keep the other women and their ambitious fathers from his door. If he turned down too many he'd arouse suspicions. Or be thought a Bessie. He'd be looking for a woman of...

'Little education,' Mistress Cadwaladr had said. 'Knowing her place. No inclination to question his movements. A housemaid with a ring.'

And that, for a number of years, was what he had. I suppose it was learning to read which had begun the change in her, but it was a slow change and a long time before she became a threat to him and his clandestine work for the French. Maybe Cate, working ever closer to her husband, had begun to suspect that he was not all he seemed. Perchance when he'd gone out to see some sick person whom she'd met in the market next day, perfectly fit, not having seen the doctor in months. She was no longer the woman he thought he'd married. One way or another she'd have found him out. And from then on she'd be marked for death.

The inhumanity of the religious zealot. What were two women's lives against the delivery of a country back to Rome and the one true Church?

Fyche's hatred of witches and the dust of vision must have seemed opportune. And I'd bet my library that the theft from the surgery, leading to the death of the boy in Somerton, had somehow been contrived by Borrow.

✠

The wind rattled the thorn tree born of Joseph's staff. It was grown colder now, in keeping with Benlow's warning that winter was not yet gone.

Nel said, 'I was brought up to revere him for his skills and saintly generosity. And not to bother him with childish matters.'

Staring out across the town, her voice even, without heat or bitterness. The voice of a woman who was back from the dead but not entirely. A Persephone who'd left some part of herself in the underworld. I knew then that there were elements of her which would also be beyond the understanding even of a man of science and a student of the hidden.

'She never told you you were not his child?'

'She told no-one.'

'When did you learn?'

'Not from my mother. Not till after her death.'

'When Mistress Cadwaladr returned to Glastonbury?'

'She was only one who knew. The only one who *cared* to know.'

Nel said nothing for a few moments, then she turned to look at me, hot pain in her eyes.

'John, it only made me want to be closer to him. I've been *proud* to be the daughter of Matthew Borrow, the finest physician in all Somerset.'

She looked across to the abbey ruins.

'One day,' she said, 'I'll find him. So many questions.'

It was my hope she'd never find him.

'Your mother…Could she not see the void in him where the heart should be?'

'She owed him her life. Don't you see? Whatever the reason for it, all the good that had ever come of her life… she owed to *him*.'

'She wouldn't look at him in the court. She turned her eyes away.'

'Maybe she had no wish to see the…' She looked down the field to where stood the wooden cross. ''twas not something to take to your grave.'

She began to weep and I held her to me, and time passed, and I tried to understand and could not. Both of us knowing the question I must needs ask or be forever tormented.

At last, she said, 'She must have felt the wind of it. I was home from medical school, and my mother said – not a week before her arrest – that when I was qualified I should go far from here. London… anywhere. As soon as I left the college. I couldn't bear the thought of not seeing her again. But she made me promise.'

'And you promised?'

She stiffened.

'I would not. I laughed. And it haunts me. It haunts me that she thought her own death might make me realise. Maybe she thought me cleverer than I turned out to be. Something always drew me to him. This… this *saintly man* who…' She seized my hand hard enough to stop the blood. 'When I was held at Wells… they told me he'd confessed to save me.'

'*Who?* Who told you?'

'The gaoler. The woman gaoler. She said he'd told them— Said they were *his* knives with all the blood over them.'

'They were…. God damn it, they *were* his knives.'

'I'd watched him fighting them when they came to take me. They knocked him down. He lay in the street, they dragged him up…'

I saw some of that too, as I and everybody in that street was meant to. A play. A masquerade. He was good at that. The next time I'd seen him, in his surgery, he'd been working through the pain, and I – and doubtless the whole town – had thought him brave and selfless, like the women who'd thought they'd loved him… if not for himself, then for what he was.

Thought they *should* love him.

A man so cold and remorseless that he'd betray his country and then, to conceal his treachery, dispose of his wife of convenience. And then, a year later, seize an opportunity to do away with the young woman who was not his daughter.

'It was made clear to me in the prison in Wells,' Nel said. 'Made clear that it would be either me… or him.' She was staring right through me. 'What had I done that he wanted me dead?'

I said nothing. He'd seen his chance, that was all. He'd been called in to get Stephen Fyche out of trouble, to make a disposal after torture look like a ritual killing, and the cold bastard had seen his chance.

'At least,' I said, 'you now know who your father was.'

She plucked grass from her dress.

'He dined at the abbey, with the abbot. The abbot had fine meals prepared. Salmon and trout. He was, it seems, charmed by the maid who'd served it.'

'And he didn't know… about you? I mean, when he returned after the sacking of the abbey…?'

'My mother was a respectable married woman by then, with a child and an education. Their relations were good… but of a different kind.'

I looked into her green eyes. She tossed back her hair against the wind. She'd lived nearly all her life under a lie and very nearly died under one.

'Poor Leland,' she said.

ENDWORD

September 1560

I do not understand the efforts
of certain people who rise up against me.

John Dee
Monas Hieroglyphica.

ANOTHER DAWN. I sit at my mother's board in the window of our parlour with the letter from my stricken friend.

God help me, John, but I had no part in it. I say this to you, who have least cause to believe me. I place my hand upon my Bible and I swear it over her poor dead body, through my tears...

Could sleep hardly at all last night after reading this five times, six times... more... The wind was up and the river was high and I'm lying open-eyed and cursing fate.

If fate it was. All London talks of black sorcery. The steeple of St Paul's is gone to ashes these past two months, struck by summer lightning. An earth trembling was recently felt in London, causing panic in the streets.

Two days ago, I was summoned to Cecil's house in the Strand where he received me in a private garden with high hedges. An afternoon of sultry heat but little sunshine.

'The end of days,' he said. 'There's been much talk of it.'

'Except in the night sky,' I assured him. 'The stars have *nothing* to say about the end of days.'

'And the Second Coming. The Queen makes light of it but is nonetheless perturbed.'

'Nor do the stars herald another Christ.'

'Who speaks of Christ?' The Queen's chief minister handed me a pamphlet. 'This comes to us from Paris.'

It was in French. I was permitted to sit down at the garden table to read it. At first, I was inclined to laugh, but a sight of Cecil's face warned against.

ENGLAND AWAITS THE CHILD OF SATAN

The pamphlet said that the magicians in England were now claiming London, the fastest-growing city in the world, to be the New Jerusalem.

In fact, London's growth was as a centre of evil, its cold and smoky streets filled with murder, robbery, whoring and all the disfiguring diseases known to man. All this having begun with the rejection of the Church of Rome, the plunder of God's holy houses throughout the kingdom, the slaying of priests and the occupation of the throne by the repellant daughter of the union of a wife-murderer and a witch.

No wonder, the pamphlet went on, that the stars foretold that London expected soon to welcome a *dark messiah,* whose birth was to be kept secret until such time as the child was grown.

The coming of Satan incarnate. And if London was the satanic Jerusalem then the black Bethlehem, where the child would be born, was the town of Glastonbury, celebrated as the birthplace of Christianity in England until its abbey, founded by St Joseph, uncle of Christ, was torn down and its streets filled not with pilgrims but witches and sorcerers.

Just as the first Tudor to usurp the throne had ensured that his first son was born in Winchester, claimed for the court of the great King Arthur, so this child would be born in the town of Arthur's death.

Born to Elizabeth, the witch queen.

The pamphlet reported that England's most notorious black sorcerer, 'Dr' John Dee was himself just returned from a visit to Glastonbury to meet the circle of witches there and make preparation for the birth of the child. The sorcerer having journeyed to Glastonbury with the child's…

'*Father?*'

I let the paper fall.

Cecil said, 'It's not been the only pamphlet to suggest that the Queen's already pregnant by Dudley.'

Described here as *a known wizard, trained in the black arts from boyhood by the evil Dee.*

'We found signs of a similar campaign being planned for London,' Cecil said. 'While you were away, Walsingham raided the premises of a disreputable lawyer called Ferrers. Took away a printing press. Copies of pamphlets purporting to contain your astrological forecasts. Usual end-of-the-world drivel. Ferrers, naturally, denies any connection with France. Even Walsingham sees him as just another lunatic.'

'I've… had dealings with this man,' I said.

'Yes.'

'Probably quite annoyed that he failed to get me burned.'

But there was surely more than an old hatred behind this.

Cecil took the French pamphlet out of my hands and crumpled it.

'We're not too worried as yet, but a word or two from you to the Queen about the absence of sinister signs in the sky would do no harm. I'll make you an appointment.'

I said, 'How is she now?'

'Well,' Cecil said. 'Quite well.'

Despite my full written report, he hadn't once mentioned the bones of Arthur or the attempt to afflict the Queen with wool-sorters' disease. She would have had the full story at length from Dudley, but I wanted to discuss it with Cecil. I wanted to know exactly how the Queen had received those Nostradamus predictions and who had suggested she might act on them. But he wasn't giving me an opening.

Cowdray's boys had caught up with Dudley in the Mendip Hills, turned him round, and thank God for that. Twice I'd awoken in a sweat after dreaming that he was putting the poisoned bones before the Queen. And once I'd dreamed Nel Borrow had not been cut down, and my arms had given way through exhaustion and I'd looked up to see the whites of her eyes and her lolling tongue.

Big Jamey Hawkes had gone back to his old grave at the church of St Benignus, with a weight of rocks piled on top of his box so that his toxic remains might never be disturbed.

Cecil smiled. 'You see, we kept your mother and her housekeeper quite safe in your absence.'

'Did you?'

With Catherine Meadows back and no evident threat from her puritan father, I'd not asked for protection.

'More safe than when you were in the house,' Cecil said. 'Turning out to be a good man, Walsingham.' He paused. 'Makes one think, John… are they more secure when you're away?'

'You have more work for me, don't you, Sir William?'

'For the Queen,' Cecil said.

✟

I'd left angry, swearing that on the morrow I'd make plans to go back to Glastonbury to undertake full and detailed research into the Zodiac formed on the ground. A garden of stars upon the earth. What could be more important than finding the key to that?

And also finding Nel. Not an hour passed when I didn't think of her.

A month ago, I had a letter from Monger, telling me she'd successfully taken over the medical practice opposite the church of St Benignus while continuing her work in the herb garden with the help of himself and Joan Tyrre.

She seems happy. I tried to find some small solace in Joan's prediction of my future marriages. Until shortly before dusk yesterday, when Blanche Parry arrived in Mortlake with the letter from Dudley and word of what it contained and the hellish and piteous scandal with my friend at its heart.

✟

I think I've said that his ailing wife, Amy, lived in the country.

This was true, but not in any great style. Even after ten years, Dudley had kept postponing plans to set his wife up in a grand house, and she seemed to spend her time at the homes of friends or relatives, journeying from one to another.

With Dudley at Windsor with the Queen, Amy has been found dead at the bottom of a flight of stairs in Oxfordshire. Her neck is broken.

Dudley maintains she'd been unwell for some time. What he's never spoken of are the rumours that she was being poisoned, with at least one doctor refusing to attend her because he feared for his own life whether she was cured or dead.

The staircase down which Amy is said to have fallen apparently is quite short. Dudley tells me in his letter that her bones were made thin and fragile by some malady in her breast.

God help me, John, but I had no part in it. I swear she was ill. I swear I loved her and always will…

The Queen, meanwhile, is said to be recovered from her nightmares.

'What happens now?' I said to Blanche, when we were alone.

'She's ordered full mourning at court while in a constant state of barely concealed merriment. She thinks they'll marry. I have my doubts.'

There's to be an inquest. No danger that Dudley will be implicated… except in the minds of everyone in Europe.

The inquest is also unlikely to hear of a story I heard not from Blanche but from my mother, who had it from a relative of Goodwife Faldo whose sister is maid to a minor lady-in-waiting.

The crux of it is that, only days ago, the Queen told the Spanish ambassador that Dudley would soon be free to marry her as his wife was close to death.

Nostradamus again?

Given the alternative explanations of the Queen's foresight, just for once I'd dearly like to think this was something from Michel's mist of perceiving.

Strange to think that under different circumstances, we might even have worked together to uncover the secrets of Arthur's round table. Such matters are beyond religion and matters of state. I'll make a point, now, of acquiring all the manuscripts of Leland I can afford.

One day, if the boundaries of science are pushed that far, I may even be equipped to talk to Abbot Whiting.

He was standing next to you for several moments.

Not much use to a dull and bookish man who has not the sight.

I fold Dudley's letter and walk out of my mother's house and into the orchard, where a hare lopes across my path.

Notes and Credits

Many elements in this story are part of recorded history – Dee's background, his relations with Bonner and Dudley. Carew, Cowdray and Joan Tyrre all existed.

And the Queen did visit Dee at Mortlake, several times, although she didn't go into the house. Dee would often bring out items to demonstrate to her what he was working on.

Three major biographies should be mentioned: *John Dee, The World of an Elizabethan Magus,* by Peter J. French, *John Dee, Scientist, Geographer, Astrologer and Secret Agent to Elizabeth I* by Richard Deacon and, most recent and best, *The Queen's Conjurer* by Benjamin Woolley.

The surviving diaries of John Dee don't really begin until many years after the events recorded in this book, but do offer many clues about his character, particularly his paranoia, often turning to anger, at other people's attitudes to his work. Dee's distaste for spectator bloodsport is more than hinted at (along with his fondness for cats) when he doesn't exactly shed tears over the collapse of a stand at Paris Gardens, causing the death of a number of bear-baiting fans on a Sunday. *'The godly expowned it as a due plage of God for the wickedness there usid and the Sabath day so profanely spent.'*

Some of Dee's eccentric spelling has been modernised, as has some of his terminology.

The incident of the wax doll, with Dee called in, is mentioned by some biographers, although they suggest it happened some years later than Dee's account here. Given Walsingham's talent for the clandestine, either it was covered up for years or there was an earlier case.

The story of Joan Tyrre and the faerie folk is recorded in several volumes on the history of witchcraft, including Christina Hole's authoritative *Witchcraft in England* and Keith Thomas's magisterial *Religion and the Decline of Magic.* Joan lived in Taunton but Dee's experience of her later activities in Glastonbury is hardly surprising.

The full story of Lord Neville and the hiring of a psychic contract killer is wonderfully told in Alec Ryrie's *The Sorcerer's Tale,* perhaps the best book yet about magic and criminality in Tudor times.

There's little evidence that the concept of the Glastonbury Zodiac was floated by anybody before Kathryn Maltwood in the 1930s. However, the Dee connection is widely mentioned and given as fact in the late Richard Deacon's 1968 biography, which quotes Dee's observation that *'the starres which agree with their reproductions on the ground do lye onlie on the celestial path of the Sonne, moon and planets, with notable exception of Orion and Hercules.... this is astrologie and astronomie carefullie and exactly married and measured in a scientific reconstruction of the heavens which shews that the ancients understoode all which today the lerned know to be factes.'*

It has to be said that this is seriously questioned by other biographers, including Benjamin Woolley, author of the excellent *The Queen's Conjuror* , some even suggesting that Deacon made it up. But why would he? The great Glastonbury historian, Geoffrey Ashe, who remains unconvinced about the existence of the Zodiac, seems nevertheless to have been the first – in his book *Avalonian Quest* – to link the line in a Nostradamus quatrain:

'In the land of the great heavenly temple'

to the idea of a terrestrial Zodiac. The Nostradamian scholar John Hogue's suggestion that this refers to a temple of Apollo which once stood on the site of Westminster Abbey is a bit lame, especially as the phrasing suggests a location away from London. And, as Geoffrey Ashe notes, even Stonehenge was not known at the time as an astronomical temple or observatory.

The best book I found on Nostradamus himself was Ian Wilson's *Nostradamus: the Evidence.*

John Leland: the facts, as given by Dee, are largely provable. Leland did provide information for Thomas Cromwell. He did return to Glastonbury after the Dissolution, with an over-ambitious project in mind. And he did go mad, almost certainly regretting the way his information had been used. It's suggested he might have been overwhelmed by the enormity of the topographical task he'd taken on.

Leland was also well into the hidden.

Wool-sorters' disease would later be called anthrax.

Ignis sacer, the holy fire, is a recorded phenomenon, caused by the grain fungus later known as ergot, a natural hallucinogen used in the twentieth century during the development of LSD. It was known as St Anthony's Fire after an eleventh-century religious order was founded, in the name of St Anthony, to help the large number of people in the south of France afflicted by convulsions, madness and that awful burning sensation.

You can find much about this in Andy Roberts's history of LSD, *Albion Dreaming.*

Nicholas Culpeper, born in 1616, was the first in 'modern' England to write of the links between astrology and herbalism, though such beliefs were obviously common in Dee's time. *Culpeper's Herbal* is still available.

For help with Elizabethan speech, my thanks to the master linguists, David Crystal and Ben Crystal, author of the fascinating *Shakespeare on Toast.* Also Jo Fletcher and Kathy McMullen. Sadly, I had to ignore much of the advice to help Dee meet the new level of clarity to which he aspired in telling this story. Because we're unable to hear Elizabethan speech – which was unlikely to follow Shakespeare's iambic pentameter – a strict adherence to Elizabethan written structures and terminology would only have made it sound stilted in ways it never would have been at the time.

Thanks also to:

From the British Society of Dowsers: Graham Gardner, Helen Lamb, Ced Jackson, John Moss, Richard Bartholomew.

In Glastonbury: Geoffrey Ashe, Jackie Edwards, Sig Lonegren, John Mason, Simon Small, Francis Thyer.

The tireless Mairéad Reidy supplied me with more background information and commentary on Dee than I even knew existed.

Prof. Bernard Knight on matters of decomposition and crucial forensic details.

Caitlin Sagan, curiously, on the Bible.

Sir Richard Heygate, co-author with Philip Carr-Gomm of *The Book of English Magic* and his, um, friend from Mortlake for personal information not available in the biographies.

Grant Privett for astronomical lore.

Geraldine Richards for early French.

The Tudor oracle David Starkey directed me to the fascinating work of James P. Carley, author of *Glastonbury Abbey, the Holy House at the Head of the Moors Adventurous*. Starkey's own works on Elizabeth and Henry VIII were hugely valuable, even if he doesn't seem to have much regard for Dee – but, then, he wouldn't, would he?

Tracy Thursfield's informed esoteric advice was as perceptive and valuable as ever.

Adrian Vine and Brian Morgan at Nant-y-groes (both of them) showed us the Dee family's Welsh roots.

Frances Yates's book *The Occult Philosophy in the Elizabethan Age* still stands alone. From it comes the explanation of John Dee as a Christian cabalist. Ruth Elizabeth Richardson's *Mistress Blanche, the Queen's Confidante,* collects virtually all that's known about Dee's cousin, Blanche Parry. And *The Ends of Life* by Keith Thomas is a wonderful guide to the psychology of the sixteenth century.

Thanks to my paranormally laid-back editor, Nic Cheetham, who's been pushing me at Dee for well over two years. To my agents Andrew Hewson and Ed Wilson for encouraging noises throughout. As for my brilliant wife Carol, devious plot-doctor, assiduous researcher, ruthless editor... words like *chestnuts... fire... yet again...* come to mind.

For the record, John Dee was never a sorcerer and there's no evidence that he was psychic (much as he would have loved to be).

The *Monas Hieroglyphica*, Dee's first significant book, was finally published in 1564, four years after the events related here. It's JD at his most impenetrable, a meditation on a symbol which connects astrology with the creation theories in the Cabala and a supporting element of Christianity. The circle is the sun, the semi-circle the moon, below which we have the cross and, at the foot, the symbol of Aries, the first sign of the zodiac, the very base of creation.

The dot in the middle says,
You are here.